"M"
IS FOR MALICE

SUE GRAFTON

"M"

IS FOR MALICE

MACMILLAN

First published in the United States of America 1996 by
Henry Holt and Co. Inc., New York

First published in the United Kingdom 1997 by Macmillan
an imprint of Macmillan Publishers Ltd
25 Eccleston Place, London SW1W 9NF
and Basingstoke

Associated companies throughout the world

ISBN 0 333 66981 9

1 3 5 7 9 8 6 4 2

A CIP catalogue record for this book is available
from the British Library

Printed and bound in Great Britain by
Mackays of Chatham PLC, Chatham, Kent

For my good friends . . .
Barbara Brightman Jones and Joe Jones
and
Joanna Barnes and Jack Warner

The author wishes to acknowledge the invaluable assistance of the following people: Steven Humphrey; John Mackall, attorney-at-law, Seed, Mackall & Cole; Sam Eaton, attorney-at-law; B. J. Seebol, J.D.; William Tanner, Tanner Investigations; Dan Deveraux, plant manager, Granite Construction; Marcia and David Karpeles, The Karpeles Manuscript Library; Captain Ed Aasted, Detective Sergeant Don F. Knapp, Detective Jill Johnson, Detective Roger Aceves, Detective Lieutenant Nicholas Katzenstein, and Lieutenant Richard Glaus, Santa Barbara Police Department; Dana Motley; Melinda Johnson, Santa Barbara Newspress; and Lucy Thomas, Reeves Medical Library, Cottage Hospital.

"M"
IS FOR MALICE

1
———————

Robert Dietz came back into my life on Wednesday, January 8. I remember the date because it was Elvis Presley's birthday and one of the local radio stations had announced it would spend the next twenty-four hours playing every song he'd ever sung. At six A.M. my clock radio blared on, playing "Heartbreak Hotel" at top volume. I smacked the Off button with the flat of my hand and rolled out of bed as usual. I pulled on my sweats in preparation for my morning run. I brushed my teeth, splashed water on my face, and trotted down the spiral stairs. I locked my front door behind me, moved out to the street where I did an obligatory stretch, leaning against the gatepost in front of my apartment. The day was destined to be a strange one, involving as it did a dreaded lunch date with Tasha Howard, one of my recently discovered first cousins. Running was the only way I could think of to quell my uneasiness. I headed for the bike path that parallels the beach.

Ah, January. The holidays had left me feeling restless and the advent of the new year generated one of those lengthy internal discussions about the meaning of life. I usually don't pay much attention to the passing of time, but this year, for some reason, I was taking a good hard look at myself. Who was I, really, in the scheme of things, and what did it all add up to? For the record, I'm Kinsey Millhone, female, single, thirty-five years old, sole proprietor of Kinsey Millhone Investigations in the southern California town of Santa Teresa. I was trained as a police officer and served a two-year stint with the Santa Teresa Police Department before life intervened, which is another tale altogether and one I don't intend to tell (yet). For the last ten years, I've made a living as a private investigator. Some days I see myself (nobly, I'll admit) battling against evil in the struggle for law and order. Other days, I concede that the dark forces are gaining ground.

Not all of this was conscious. Much of the rumination was simmering at a level I could scarcely discern. It's not as if I spent every day in a state of unremitting angst, wringing my hands and rending my clothes. I suppose what I was experiencing was a mild form of depression, triggered (perhaps) by nothing more complicated than the fact it was winter and the California sunlight was in short supply.

I started my career investigating arson and wrongful-death claims for California Fidelity Insurance. A year ago, my relationship with CFI came to an abrupt and ignominious halt and I'm currently sharing space with the law firm of Kingman and Ives, taking on just about anything to make ends meet. I'm licensed, bonded, and fully insured. I have twenty-five thousand dollars in a savings account, which affords me the luxury of turning down any client who doesn't suit. I haven't refused a case yet, but I was strongly considering it.

Tasha Howard, the aforementioned first cousin, had called to offer me work, though the details of the job hadn't yet been specified. Tasha is an attorney who handles wills and estates, working for a law firm with offices in both San Francisco and Lompoc, which is an hour north of Santa Teresa. I gathered she divided her time just about equally between the two. I'm normally interested in employment, but Tasha and I aren't exactly close and I suspected she was using the lure of business to insinuate herself into my life.

As it happened, her first call came on the day after New Year's, which allowed me to sidestep by claiming I was still on vacation. When she called again on January 7, she caught me off guard. I was at the office in the middle of a serious round of solitaire when the telephone rang.

"Hi, Kinsey. This is Tasha. I thought I'd try you again. Did I catch you at a bad time?"

"This is fine," I said. I crossed my eyes and pretended I was gagging myself with a finger pointed down my throat. Of course, she couldn't see that. I put a red eight on a black nine and turned up the last three cards. No play that I could see. "How are you?" I asked, perhaps a millisecond late.

"Doing well, thanks. How about you?"

"I'm good," I said. "Gee, your timing's uncanny. I was just picking up the phone. I've been making calls all morning and you were next on my list." I often use the word *gee* when I'm lying through my teeth.

"I'm glad to hear that," she said. "I thought you were avoiding me."

I laughed. Ha.Ha.Ha. "Not at all," said I. I was about to elaborate on the denial, but she plowed right on. Having run out of moves, I pushed the cards aside and began to tag my blotter with a little desktop graffiti. I block-printed the word *BARF* and gave each of the letters a three-dimensional cast.

She said, "What's your schedule like tomorrow? Can we get together for an hour? I have to be in Santa Teresa anyway and we could meet for lunch."

"I can probably do that," I said with caution. In this world, lies can only take you so far before the truth catches up. "What sort of work are we talking about?"

"I'd rather discuss it in person. Is twelve o'clock good for you?"

"That sounds fine," I said.

3

"Perfect. I'll make reservations. Emile's-at-the-Beach. I'll see you there," she said, and with a click she was gone.

I put the phone down, set the ballpoint pen aside, and laid my little head down on my desk. What an idiot I was. Tasha *must* have known I didn't want to see her, but I hadn't had the nerve to say so. She'd come to my rescue a couple of months before and though I'd repaid the money, I still felt I owed her. Maybe I'd listen to her politely before I turned her down. I did have another quick job in the works. I'd been hired to serve two deposition subpoenas in a civil case for an attorney on the second floor of our building.

I went out in the afternoon and spent thirty-five bucks (plus tip) on a legitimate salon haircut. I tend to take a pair of nail scissors to my own unruly mop about every six weeks, my technique being to snip off any tuft of hair that sticks out. I guess I must have been feeling insecure because it wouldn't ordinarily occur to me to pay real bucks for something I can do so handily myself. Of course, I've been told my hairstyle looks exactly like a puppy dog's backside, but what's wrong with that?

The morning of January 8 inevitably arrived and I pounded along the bike path as if pursued by wild dogs. Typically, I use my jog as a way to check in with myself, noting the day and the ongoing nature of life at the water's edge. That morning, I had been all business, nearly punitive in the energy I threw into the exercise. Having finished my run and my morning routine, I skipped the office altogether and hung around my place. I paid some bills, tidied up my desk, did a load of laundry, and chatted briefly with my landlord, Henry Pitts, while I ate three of his freshly baked sticky buns. Not that I was nervous.

As usual, when you're waiting for something unpleasant, the clock seems to leap forward in ten-minute increments. Next thing I knew I was standing at my bathroom mirror applying cut-rate cosmetics, for God's sake, while I emoted along with Elvis, who was singing "It's Now Or Never." The sing-along was taking me back to my high school days, not a terrific association, but amusing nonetheless. I hadn't known any more about makeup in those days than I do now.

I debated about a new outfit, but that's where I drew the line, pulling on my usual blue jeans, turtleneck, tweed blazer, and boots. I own one dress and I didn't want to waste it on an occasion like this. I glanced at the clock. It was 11:55. Emile's wasn't far, all of five minutes on foot. With luck, I'd be hit by a truck as I was crossing the street.

Almost all of the tables at Emile's were occupied by the time I arrived. In Santa Teresa, the beach restaurants do the bulk of their business during the summer tourist season when the motels and bed-and-breakfast establishments near the ocean are fully booked. After Labor Day, the crowds diminish until the town belongs to the residents again. But Emile's-at-the-Beach is a local favorite and doesn't seem to suffer the waxing and waning of the out-of-town trade.

Tasha must have driven down from Lompoc because a sassy red Trans Am bearing a vanity license plate that read TASHA H was parked at the curb. In the detective trade, this is what is known as a clue. Besides, flying down from Lompoc is more trouble than it's worth. I moved into the restaurant and scanned the tables. I had little appetite for the encounter, but I was trying to stay open to the possibilities. Of what, I couldn't say.

I spotted Tasha through one of the interior archways before she spotted me. She was seated in a small area off the main dining room. Emile had placed her by the front window at a table for two. She was staring out at the children's play equipment in the little beach park across the street. The wading pool was closed, emptied for the winter, a circle of blue-painted plaster that looked now like a landing pad for a UFO. Two preschool-age children were clambering backward up a nearby sliding board anchored in the sand. Their mother sat on the low concrete retaining wall with a cigarette in hand. Beyond her were the bare masts of boats slipped in the harbor. The day was sunny and cool, the blue sky scudding with clouds left behind by a storm that was passing to the south of us.

A waiter approached Tasha and they conferred briefly. She took a menu from him. I could see her indicate that she was waiting for someone else. He withdrew and she began to peruse the lunch choices. I'd never actually laid eyes on Tasha until now, but I'd met her sister Liza the summer before last. I'd been startled because Liza and I looked so much alike. Tasha was cut from the same genetic cloth, though she was three years older and more substantial in her presentation. She wore a gray wool suit with a white silk shell showing in the deep V of the jacket. Her dark hair was streaked with blond, pulled back with a sophisticated black chiffon bow sitting at the nape of her neck. The only jewelry she wore was a pair of oversized gold earrings that glinted when she moved. Since she did estate planning, she probably didn't have much occasion for impassioned courtroom speeches, but she'd look properly intimidating in a skirmish nonetheless. Already I'd decided to get my affairs in order.

She caught sight of me and I saw her expression quicken as she registered the similarities between us. Maybe all the Kinsey girl cousins shared the same features. I raised a hand in greeting and moved through the lunch crowd to her table. I took the seat across from hers, tucking my bag on the floor beneath my chair. "Hello, Tasha."

For a moment, we did a mutual assessment. In high school biology, I'd studied Mendel's purple and white flowering peas; the crossbreeding of colors and the resultant pattern of "offspring." This was the very principle at work. Up close, I could see that her eyes were dark where mine were hazel, and her nose looked like mine had before it was broken twice. Seeing her was like catching a glimpse of myself unexpectedly in a mirror, the image both strange and familiar. Me and not me.

Tasha broke the silence. "This is creepy. Liza told me we looked alike, but I had no idea."

"I guess there's no doubt we're related. What about the other cousins? Do they look like us?"

"Variations on a theme. When Pam and I were growing up, we

6

were often mistaken for each other." Pam was the sister between Tasha and Liza.

"Did Pam have her baby?"

"Months ago. A girl. Big surprise," she said dryly. Her tone was ironic, but I didn't get the joke. She sensed the unspoken question and smiled fleetingly in reply. "All the Kinsey women have girl babies. I thought you knew."

I shook my head.

"Pam named her Cornelia as a way of sucking up to Grand. I'm afraid most of us are guilty of trying to score points with her from time to time."

Cornelia LaGrand was my grandmother Burton Kinsey's maiden name. "Grand" had been her nickname since babyhood. From what I'd been told, she ruled the family like a despot. She was generous with money, but only if you danced to her tune—the reason the family had so pointedly ignored me and my aunt Gin for twenty-nine years. My upbringing had been blue collar, strictly lower middle-class. Aunt Gin, who raised me from the age of five, had worked as a clerk/typist for California Fidelity Insurance, the company that eventually hired (and fired) me. She'd managed on a modest salary, and we'd never had much. We'd always lived in mobile homes—trailers, as they were known then—bastions of tiny space, which I still tend to prefer. At the same time, I recognized even then that other people thought trailers were tacky. Why, I can't say.

Aunt Gin had taught me never to suck up to anyone. What she'd neglected to tell me was there were relatives worth sucking up to.

Tasha, likely aware of the thicket her remarks were leading to, shifted over to the task at hand. "Let's get lunch out of the way and then I can fill you in on the situation."

We dealt with the niceties of ordering and eating lunch, chatting about only the most inconsequential subjects. Once our plates had been removed, she got down to business with an efficient change of tone. "We have some clients here in Santa Teresa caught up in a

7

circumstance I thought might interest you. Do you know the Maleks? They own Malek Construction."

"I don't know them personally, but the name's familiar." I'd seen the company logo on job sites around town, a white octagon, like a stop sign, with the outline of a red cement mixer planted in the middle. All of the company trucks and job-site Porta Potti's were fire engine red and the effect was eye-catching.

Tasha went on. "It's a sand and gravel company. Mr. Malek just died and our firm is representing the estate." The waiter approached and filled our coffee cups. Tasha picked up a sugar pack, pressing in the edges of the paper rim on all sides before she tore the corner off. "Bader Malek bought a gravel pit in 1943. I'm not sure what he paid at the time, but it's worth a fortune today. Do you know much about gravel?"

"Not a thing," I said.

"I didn't either until this came up. A gravel pit doesn't tend to produce much income from year to year, but it turns out that over the last thirty years environmental regulations and land-use regulations make it very hard to start up a new gravel pit. In this part of California, there simply aren't that many. If you own the gravel pit for your region and construction is booming—which it is at the moment—it goes from being a dog in the forties to a real treasure in the 1980s, depending, of course, on how deep the gravel reserves are and the quality of those reserves. It turns out this one is on a perfect gravel zone, probably good for another hundred and fifty years. Since nobody else is now able to get approvals . . . well, you get the point I'm sure."

"Who'd have thunk?"

"Exactly," she said and then went on. "With gravel, you want to be close to communities where construction is going on because the prime cost is transportation. It's one of those backwater areas of wealth that you don't really know about even if it's yours. Anyway, Bader Malek was a dynamo and managed to maximize his profits by branching out in other directions, all building-related. Malek Construction is now the third-largest construction company in the state. And it's still family owned; one of the few, I might add."

"So what's the problem?"

"I'll get to that in a moment, but I need to back up a bit first. Bader and his wife, Rona, had four boys—like a series of stepping-stones, all of them two years apart. Donovan, Guy, Bennet, and Jack. Donovan's currently in his mid-forties and Jack's probably thirty-nine. Donovan's the best of the lot; typical first child, steady, respon-sible, the big achiever in the bunch. His wife, Christie, and I were college roommates, which is how I got involved in the first place. The second son, Guy, turned out to be the clunker among the boys. The other two are okay. Nothing to write home about, at least from what Christie's said."

"Do they work for the company?"

"No, but Donovan pays all of their bills nonetheless. Bennet fan-cies himself an 'entrepreneur,' which is to say he loses great whacks of money annually in bad business deals. He's currently venturing into the restaurant business. He and a couple of partners are opening a place down on Granita. Talk about a way to lose money. The man has to be nuts. Jack's busy playing golf. I gather he's got sufficient talent to hit the pro circuit, but probably not enough to earn a living at it.

"At any rate, back in the sixties, Guy was the one who smoked dope and raised hell. He thought his father was a materialistic, capi-talistic son of a bitch and told him so every chance he could. I guess Guy got caught in some pretty bad scrapes—we're talking criminal behavior—and Bader finally cut him off. According to Donovan, his father gave Guy a lump sum, ten grand in cash, his portion of the then-modest family fortune. Bader told the kid to hit the road and not come back. Guy Malek disappeared and he hasn't been seen since. This was March 1968. He was twenty-six then, which would make him forty-three now. I guess no one really cared much when he left. It was probably a relief after what he'd put the family through. Rona had died two months before, in January that same year, and Bader went to his attorney with the intention of rewriting his will. You know how that goes: 'The reason I have made no provision for my son Guy in this will is not due to any lack of love or affection on my part, but simply because I have provided for him during my lifetime and feel that those provisions are more than adequate—blah, blah, blah.' The truth was, Guy had cost him plenty and he was sick of it.

"So. Fade out, fade in. In 1981, Bader's attorney died of a heart attack and all of his legal files were returned to him."

I interrupted. "Excuse me. Is that common practice? I'd assume all the files would be kept by the attorney's estate."

"Depends on the attorney. Maybe Bader insisted. I'm not really sure. I gather he was a force to be reckoned with. He was already ill by then with the cancer that finally claimed him. He'd also suffered a debilitating stroke brought on by all the chemo. Sick as he was, he probably didn't want to go through the hassle of finding a new attorney. Apparently, from his perspective, his affairs were in order and what he did with his money was nobody else's business."

I said, "Oh, boy." I didn't know what was coming, but it didn't sound good.

" 'Oh, boy' is right. When Bader died two weeks ago, Donovan went through his papers. The only will he found was the one Bader and Rona signed back in 1965."

"What happened to the later will?"

"Nobody knows. Maybe the attorney drew it up and Bader took it home for review. He might have changed his mind. Or maybe he signed the will as written and decided to destroy it later. The fact is, it's gone."

"So he died intestate?"

"No, no. We still have the earlier will—the one drawn up in 1965, before Guy was flung into the Outer Darkness. It's properly signed and fully executed, which means that, barring an objection, Guy Malek is a devisee, entitled to a quarter of his father's estate."

"Will Donovan object?"

"He's not the one I'm concerned about. The 1965 will gives him voting control of the family business so he winds up sitting in the catbird seat regardless. Bennet's the one making noises about filing an objection, but he really has no proof the later will exists. This could all be for naught in any case. If Guy Malek was hit by a truck or died of an overdose years ago, then there's no problem—as long as he doesn't have any kids of his own."

"Gets complicated," I said. "How much money are we talking about?"

"We're still working on that. The estate is currently assessed at about forty million bucks. The government's entitled to a big chunk, of course. The estate tax rate is fifty to fifty-five percent. Fortunately, thanks to Bader, the company has very little debt, so Donovan will have some ability to borrow. Also, the estate can defer payment of estate taxes under Internal Revenue Service code section 6166, since Malek Construction, as a closely held company, represents more than thirty-five percent of the adjusted gross estate. We'll probably look for appraisers who'll come up with a low value and then hope the IRS doesn't argue too hard for a higher value on audit. To answer your question, the boys will probably take home five million bucks apiece. Guy's a very lucky fellow."

"Only nobody knows where he is," I said.

Tasha pointed at me. "That's correct."

I thought about it briefly. "It must have come as a shock to the brothers to find out Guy stands to inherit an equal share of the estate."

Tasha shrugged. "I've only had occasion to chat with Donovan and he seems sanguine at this point. He'll be acting as administrator. On Friday, I'm submitting the will to the probate court. In essence, all that does is place the will on record. Donovan's asked me not to file the petition for another week or so in deference to Bennet, who's still convinced the later will will surface. In the meantime, it makes sense to see if we can determine Guy Malek's whereabouts. I thought we'd hire you to do the search, if you're interested."

"Sure," I said promptly. So much for playing hard to get. The truth is, I love missing-persons' cases, and the circumstances were intriguing. Often when I'm on the trail of a skip, I hold out the prospect of sudden riches from some recently deceased relative. Given the greediness of human nature, it often produces results. In this case, the reality of five million dollars should make my job easier. "What information do you have about Guy?" I asked.

"You'll have to talk to the Maleks. They'll fill you in." She scribbled something on the back of a business card, which she held out to me. "This is Donovan's number at work. I wrote the home address and home phone number on the back. Except for Guy, of course, the 'boys' are all still living together on the Malek estate."

I studied the back of the card, not recognizing the address. "Is this city or county? I never heard of this."

"It's in the city limits. In the foothills above town."

"I'll call them this afternoon."

2

I walked home along Cabana Boulevard. The skies had cleared and the air temperature hovered in the mid-fifties. This was technically the dead of winter and the brazen California sunshine was not as warm as it seemed. Sunbathers littered the sand like the flotsam left behind by the high tide. Their striped umbrellas spoke of summer, yet the new year was just a week old. The sun was brittle along the water's edge, fragmenting where the swells broke against the pilings under the wharf. The surf must have been dead cold, the salt water eye-stinging where children splashed through the waves and submerged themselves in the churning depths. I could hear their thin screams rising above the thunder of the surf, like thrill seekers on a roller-coaster, plunging into icy terror. On the beach, a wet dog barked at them and shook the water from his coat. Even from a distance I could see where his rough hair had separated into layers.

I turned left onto Bay Street. Against the backdrop of evergreens, the profusion of bright pink and orange geraniums clashed with the magenta bougainvillea that tumbled across the fences in my neighborhood. Idly, I wondered where to begin the search for Guy Malek. He'd been gone for eighteen years and the prospects of running him to ground didn't seem that rosy. A job of this kind requires ingenuity, patience, and systematic routine, but success sometimes hinges on pure luck and a touch of magic. Try billing a client on the basis of *that*.

As soon as I got home, I washed off my makeup, I changed into Reeboks, and traded my blazer for a red sweatshirt. Downstairs in the kitchenette, I turned on the radio and tuned the station to the Elvis marathon, which was moving right along. I lip-synched the lyrics to "Jailhouse Rock," doing a bump and grind around the living room. I pulled out a city map and spread it on my kitchen counter. I leaned on my elbows, backside still dancing while I located the street where the Maleks lived. Verdugo was a narrow lane tucked between two parallel roads descending from the mountains. This was not an area I knew well. I laid Donovan's business card on the counter beside the map, reached for the wall phone, and dialed the number printed on the front.

I was routed through the company receptionist to a secretary who told me Malek was out in the field but due back at the office momentarily. I gave my name and phone number, along with a brief explanation of my business with him. She said she'd have him return the call. I'd just hung up when I heard a knock at the door. I opened the porthole and found myself face-to-face with Robert Dietz.

I opened the front door. "Well, look who's here," I said. "It's only been two years, four months, and ten days."

"Has it really been that long?" he asked mildly. "I just drove up from Los Angeles. Mind if I come in?"

I stepped back and he moved past me. Elvis had launched into "Always On My Mind," which, frankly, I didn't need to hear just then. I reached over and turned off the radio. Dietz wore the same blue jeans, same cowboy boots, the same tweed sportscoat. I'd first seen him in this outfit, leaning against the wall in a hospital room where I was under observation after a hit man ran me off the road. He was two years older now, which probably put him at an even fifty, not a bad age for a man. His birthday was in November, a triple Scorpio for those who set any store by these things. We'd spent the last three months of our relationship in bed together when we weren't up at the firing range doing Mozambique pistol drills. Romance between private eyes is a strange and wondrous thing. He looked slightly heavier, but that was because he'd quit smoking—assuming he was still off cigarettes.

"You want some coffee?" I asked.

"I'd love some. How are you? You look good. I like the haircut."

"Forty bucks. What a waste. I should have done it myself." I put a pot of coffee together, using the homey activity to assess my emotional state. By and large, I didn't feel much. I was happy to see him in the same way I'd be happy to see any friend of long standing, but aside from mild curiosity, there was no great rush of sexual chemistry. I felt no strong joy at his arrival or rage that he'd shown up unannounced. He was a man of impulse: impatient, restless, abrupt, reticent. He looked tired and his hair seemed much grayer, nearly ashen along his ears. He perched on one of my kitchen stools and leaned his forearms on the counter.

I flipped on the coffeepot and put the bag of ground coffee back in the freezer. "How was Germany?"

Dietz was a private eye from Carson City, Nevada, who'd developed an expertise in personal security. He left to go to Germany to run antiterrorist training exercises for overseas military bases. He said, "Good while it lasted. Then the funding dried up. These days, Uncle Sam doesn't want to spend the bucks that way. I was bored with it anyway; middle-aged man crawling through the underbrush. I didn't have to get out there with 'em, but I couldn't resist."

"So what brings you back? Are you working a case?"

"I'm on my way up the coast to see the boys in Santa Cruz." Dietz had two sons with a common-law wife, a woman named Naomi who had steadfastly refused to marry him. His older son, Nick, was probably twenty by now. I wasn't sure how old the younger boy was.

"Ah. And how are they?"

"Terrific. They've got papers due this week so I said I'd hold off until Saturday and then drive up. If they can get a few days off, I thought we'd take a little trip somewhere."

"I notice you're limping. What's that about?"

He gave a pat to his left thigh. "Got a bum knee," he said. "Tore the meniscus during night maneuvers, stumbling on a pothole. That's the second time I've injured it and the docs say I need to have a knee replacement. I'm not interested in surgery, but I agreed to give the knee a rest. Besides, I'm in burnout. I need a change of scene."

"You were burned out before you left."

"Not burnout. I was bored. I guess neither one is cured by doing more of the same." Dietz's gray eyes were clear. He was a good-looking man in a very nonstandard way. "I thought I might stay on your couch for four days if you don't object. I'm supposed to stay off my feet and put ice on my knee."

"Oh, really. That's nice. You drop out of my life for two years and then you show up because you need a nurse? Forget that."

"I'm not asking you to make a fuss," he said. "I figure you're busy so you'll be off at work all day. I'll sit here and read or watch TV, minding my own business. I even brought my own ice bags to stick in the freezer. I don't want anyone hovering. You won't have to lift a finger."

"Don't you think this is a tiny bit *manipulative,* springing it on me like this?"

"It's not manipulative as long as you have the option of saying no."

"Oh, right. And feel guilty? I don't think so," I said.

"Why would you feel guilty? Turn me down if it doesn't suit. What's the matter with you? If we can't tell the truth then what's the point in a relationship? Do as you please. I can find a motel or I can drive on up the coast tonight. I thought it'd be nice to spend a little time together, but it's not compulsory."

I regarded him warily. "I'll think about it." There was no point in telling him—since I was barely willing to admit it to myself—how flat the light had seemed in the days after he left, how anxiety had stirred every time I came home to the empty apartment, how music had seemed to whisper secret messages to me. Dance or decline. It didn't seem to make any difference. I'd imagined his return a hundred times, but never this way. Now the flatness of it was inside and all of my past feelings for him had shifted from passionate involvement to mild interest, if that.

Dietz had been watching me and his squint showed he was perplexed. "Are you *mad* about something?"

"Not at all," I said.

"Yes, you are."

"No, I'm not."

"What are you so mad about?"

"Would you *stop* that? I'm not mad."

He studied me for a moment and then his expression cleared. He said, "Ohhh, I get it. You're mad because I left."

I could feel my cheeks brighten and I broke off eye contact. I lined up the salt and pepper shakers so their bases just touched. "I'm not mad because you *left*. I'm mad because you came back. I finally got used to being by myself and here you are again. So where does that put me?"

"You said you *liked* to be alone."

"That's right. What I don't like is being taken up and then abandoned. I'm not a pet you can put in a kennel and retrieve at your convenience."

His smile faded. " 'Abandoned'? You weren't *abandoned*. What's that supposed to mean?"

Just then the telephone rang, saving us from any further debate. Donovan Malek's secretary said, "Miss Millhone? I have Mr. Malek on the line for you. Can you hold?"

I said, "Sure."

Dietz mouthed *Did not.*

I stuck my tongue out at him. I'm very mature that way.

Donovan Malek came on the line and introduced himself. "Good afternoon, Miss Millhone . . ."

"Call me Kinsey if you would."

"Thanks. It's Donovan Malek here. I just spoke to Tasha Howard and she said she talked to you at lunch. I take it she filled you in on the situation."

"For the most part," I said. "Is there some way we can get together? Tasha wants to get moving as soon as possible."

"My attitude exactly. Listen, I've got about an hour before I have to be somewhere else. I can give you some basic information—Guy's date of birth, his Social Security number, and a photograph if that would help," he said. "You want to pop on out here?"

"Sure, I can do that," I said. "What about your brothers? Is there some way I can talk to them, too?"

"Of course. Bennet said he'd be home around four this afternoon. I'll call Myrna—she's the housekeeper—and leave word you want to talk to him. I'm not sure about Jack. He's a little harder to catch, but we can work something out. What you don't get from me, you can pick up from them. You know where I am? On Dolores out in Colgate. You take the Peterson off-ramp and turn back across the freeway. Second street on the right."

"Sounds good. I'll see you shortly."

When I hung up the phone, Dietz was checking his watch. "You're off and running. I've got to touch base with an old friend so I'll be out for a while. Are you free later on?"

"Not until six or so. Depends on my appointment. I'm trying to track down a guy who's been gone eighteen years and I'm hoping to pick up some background from his family."

"I'll buy you dinner if you haven't eaten, or we can go out and have a drink. I really don't want to be a burden."

"We can talk about it later. In the meantime, you'll need a key."

"That'd be great. I can grab a shower before I take off and lock up when I leave."

I opened the kitchen junk drawer and found the extra house key on a ring of its own. I passed it across the counter.

"Are you okay with this? I know you don't like to feel crowded. I can find a little place on Cabana if you'd prefer peace and quiet."

"This is fine for now. If it's too much, I'll say so. Let's just play it by ear," I said. "I hope you like your coffee black. There's no milk and no sugar. Cups are up there."

He put the key in his pocket. "I know where the cups are. I'll see you later."

Malek Construction consisted of a series of linked trailers, arranged like dominoes, located in the cul-de-sac of an industrial park. Behind the offices, a vast asphalt yard was filled with red trucks: pickups, concrete mixers, skip loaders, and pavers, all bearing the white-and-red company logo. A two-story corrugated metal garage stretched across the backside of the property, apparently filled with maintenance and service equipment for the countless company vehicles. Gas pumps stood at the ready. To one side, against a tangle of shrubs, I could see six bright yellow Caterpillars and a couple of John Deere crawler dozers. Men in hard hats and red coveralls went about their business. The quiet was undercut by the rumble of approaching trucks, an occasional shrill whistle, and the steady *peep-peep-peep* signal as a vehicle backed up.

I parked in the side lot in a space marked VISITOR beside a line of Jeeps, Cherokee Rangers, and battered pickups. On the short walk to the entrance, I could hear the nearby freeway traffic and the high hum of a small plane heading for the airport to the west. The interior of the office suggested a sensible combination of good taste and practicality: glossy walnut paneling, steel blue wall-to-wall carpet, dark blue file cabinets, and a lot of matching dark red tweed furniture. Among the male employees, the standard attire seemed to be ties, dress shirts, and slacks without suit coats or sports jackets. Shoes looked suitable for hiking across sand and gravel. The dress code for the women seemed less codified. The atmosphere was one of genial productivity. Police stations have the same air about them; everyone committed to the work at hand.

In the reception area where I waited, all the magazines were work-related, copies of *Pit & Quarry, Rock Products, Concrete Journal,* and the *Asphalt Contractor.* A quick glance was sufficient to convince me that there were issues at stake here I never dreamed about. I read briefly about oval-hole void forms and multiproperty admixtures, powered telescopic concrete chutes, and portable concrete recycling systems. My, my, my. Sometimes I marveled at the depths of my ignorance.

"Kinsey? Donovan Malek," he said.

I looked up, setting the magazine aside as I rose to shake hands with him. "Is it Don or Donovan?"

"I prefer Donovan, if you don't mind. My wife shortens it to Don sometimes, but I make a rare exception for her. Thanks for being so prompt. Come on back to my office and we can chat." Malek was fair-haired and clean shaven, with a square, creased face and chocolate brown eyes behind tortoiseshell glasses. I judged him to be six feet tall, maybe two hundred twenty pounds. He wore chinos and his short-sleeved dress shirt was the color of café au lait. He had loosened his tie and opened his collar button in the manner of a man who disliked restrictions and was subject to chronic overheating. I followed him out a rear door and across a wooden deck that connected a grid of double-wide trailers. The air conditioner in his office was humming steadily when we walked in.

The trailer he occupied had been subdivided into three offices of equal size, extending shotgun style from the front of the structure to the back. Long fluorescent bulbs cast a cold light across the white Formica surfaces of desks and drafting tables. Wide counters were littered with technical manuals, project reports, specs, and blueprints. Sturdy metal bookshelves lined the walls in most places, crammed with binders. Donovan didn't seem to have a private secretary within range of him and I had to guess that one of several women up front fielded his calls and helped him out with paperwork.

He motioned me into a seat and then settled into the high-back leather chair behind his desk. He leaned sideways toward a bookshelf and removed a Santa Teresa high school annual, which he opened at a page marked by a paper clip. He held out the annual, passing it across the desk. "Guy, age sixteen. Who knows what he looks like these days." He leaned back and watched for my reaction.

The kid looking out of the photograph could have been one of my high school classmates, though he preceded me by some years. The two-by-two-inch black-and-white head shot showed light curly hair worn long. Braces on his teeth gleaming through partly opened lips. He had a bumpy complexion, unruly eyebrows, and long, fair sideburns. His shirt fabric was a wild floral pattern. I would have bet money on bell-bottom trousers and a wide leather belt, though neither were visible in the photograph. In my opinion, all high school annuals should be taken out and burned. No wonder we all suffered from insecurity and low self-esteem. What a bunch of weirdos we were. I said, "He looks about like I did at his age. What year did he graduate?"

"He didn't. He got suspended six times and finally dropped out. As far as I know, he never even picked up his GED. He spent more time in Juvie than he did at home."

"Tasha mentioned criminal behavior. Can you tell me about that?"

"Sure, if I can think where to start. Remember the rumor that you could get high off aspirin and Coca-Cola? He went straight out and tried it. Kid was disappointed when it had no effect. He was in the eighth grade at that point. Discounting all the so-called 'harmless pranks' he pulled back then, I'd say his first serious transgressions dated back to high school when he was busted twice for possession of marijuana. He was into dope big time—grass, speed, uppers, downers. What did they call 'em back then? Reds and yellow jackets and something called soapers. LSD and hallucinogens came in about the same time. Teenagers didn't do heroin or cocaine in those days, and nobody'd ever heard of crack. I guess that's been a more recent development. For a while he sniffed glue, but said he didn't like the effect. Kid's a connoisseur of good highs," he said derisively. "To pay for the stuff, he'd rip off anything that wasn't nailed down. He stole cars. He stole heavy equipment from Dad's construction sites. You get the picture, I'm sure."

"This may sound like an odd question, but was he popular?"

"Actually, he was. You can't tell much from the photograph, but he was a good-looking kid. He was incorrigible, but he had a sort of goofy sweetness that people seemed to find appealing, especially the girls."

"Why? Because he was dangerous?"

"I really can't explain. He was this shy, tragic figure, like he couldn't help himself. He only had one buddy, fellow named Paul Trasatti."

"Is he still around somewhere?"

"Sure. He and Jack are golfing buddies. Bennet pals around with him, too. You can ask when you talk to him. I don't remember any other friends offhand."

"You didn't hang out with Guy yourself?"

"Not if I could help it," he said. "I was busy keeping as much distance between us as possible. It got so I had to lock the door to my room so he wouldn't walk off with everything. You name it, he'd boost it. Stereos and jewelry. Some stuff he did for profit and some was just plain raising hell. After he turned eighteen, he got kind of crafty because the stakes went up. Dad finally flat told him he'd hang him out to dry if he fucked up again. Excuse my bad language, but I still get hot when I think about this stuff."

"Is that when he took off?"

"That was when he shifted gears. On the surface, he cleaned up and got a job out here, working in the maintenance shed. He was clever, I must say. Good with his hands and he had a good head on his shoulders. He must have seen this place as the answer to his prayers. He forged checks on Dad's accounts. He used the company credit card to charge stuff and then sold the goods. Dad, God bless him, was still covering. I begged him to blow the whistle, but he just couldn't bring himself to do it. Guy strung him along, telling lie after lie.

"What can I tell you? Dad wanted to believe him. He'd talk tough. I mean, he'd act like he was really cracking down this time, but when it came right down to it, he always gave in and offered him 'one more chance.' Jesus, I got sick of his saying that. I did what I could to close the loopholes, but I could only do so much." Donovan tapped his temple. "Kid had a screw loose. He was really missing some essential sprocket in the morals department. Anyway, the last stunt he pulled—and this didn't come out until he'd been gone a couple months—was a scam where he cheated some 'poor old widder woman' of her nest egg. That was the last straw. Dad had already kicked his ass out, but we were still stuck with the mess."

"Where were you at that time? I take it you were working for your father."

"Oh, yeah. I'd graduated by then. I'd been in and out of Vietnam, and I was working here as a mining engineer. I got my degree at Colorado School of Mines. My dad's degree was civil engineering. He started Malek Construction back in 1940, the year I was born, and bought his first gravel pit in forty-three. We were a construction outfit first and ended up owning all our aggregate sources. In fact, we built the business around that because it gives us a competitive edge. There's a lot of companies around here that do construction that don't own their aggregate sources and they end up buying from us. I'm the only one of the kids who went into the family business. I didn't get married till I was thirty-five."

"I understand your mother died the year Guy left," I said.

"That's right. She'd been diagnosed with lung cancer maybe ten years before. Fought like an alley cat, but she finally went under. I'm sure the uproar didn't help. Dad never remarried. He didn't seem to have the heart for it. All he cared about was the company, which is why I was so surprised about the will. Even in 1965, I can't believe he wanted Guy getting so much as a nickel from his estate."

"Maybe someone will come across the second will."

"I'd like to think so, but so far I've turned the house upside down. There was nothing like it in the safe deposit box. I hate to consider what's going to happen if Guy shows up again."

"Meaning what?"

"He'll cause trouble of some kind. I can guarantee it."

I shrugged. "He might have changed. People sometimes straighten out."

Donovan gestured impatiently. "Sure, and sometimes you win the lottery, but the odds are against. That's how it is and I guess we'll have to live with it."

"You have any idea where he might be?"

"No. And I don't lie awake at night trying to figure it out either. Frankly, it makes me crazy to think of him coming home to roost. I understand that by law he's entitled to his fair share of the estate, but I think he ought to be a brick about it and keep his hands to himself." He picked up a piece of paper and slid it in my direction. "Date of birth and his Social Security number. His middle name is David. What else can I tell you?"

"What about your mother's maiden name?"

"Patton. Is that for ID purposes?"

"Right. If I find him, I'd like to have a way to confirm it's really Guy we're dealing with."

"You're picturing an impostor? That's hard to imagine," he said. "Who'd want to be a stand-in for a loser like him?"

I smiled. "It's not that far-fetched. The chances are remote, but it's been done before. You don't want to end up turning money over to a stranger."

"You got that right. I'm not all that thrilled to give the money to *him*. Unfortunately, it's not up to me. The law's the law," he said. "At any rate, I leave this to you. He was a hard-livin', hard-drinkin' kid before the age of twenty-one. As to his current whereabouts, your guess is as good as mine. You need anything else?"

"This should do for the time being. I'll talk to your brothers and

24

then we'll see where we stand." I got to my feet and we shook hands across the desk. "I appreciate your time."

Donovan came around the desk, walking me to the door.

I said, "I'm sure Tasha will have the proper notices published in the local paper. Guy may get wind of it, if he hasn't already."

"How so?"

"He might still be in touch with someone living here."

"Well. That is possible, I suppose. I don't know how much more we're obliged to do. If he never turns up, I guess his share of the estate gets placed in an escrow account for some period of time. After that, who knows? The point is, Tasha insists we get it settled and you don't want to mess with *her*."

"I should think not," I said. "Besides, closure is always nice."

"Depends on what kind you're discussing."

3

I stopped by the office and opened a file on the case, recording the data Donovan had given me. It didn't look like much, the merest scrap of information, but the date of birth and Social Security number would be invaluable as personal identifiers. If pressed, I could always check with Guy Malek's former high school classmates to see if anybody'd heard from him in the years since he left. Given his history of bad behavior, he didn't seem like a kid others would have known well or perhaps cared to have known at all, but he might have had confederates. I made a note of the name Donovan had given me. Paul Trasatti might provide a lead. It was possible Guy had turned respectable in the last decade and a half and might well have come back to his reunions from time to time. Often the biggest "losers" in high school are the most eager to flaunt their later successes.

If I had to make an educated guess about his original destination on the road to exile, I'd have to say San Francisco, which was only six hours north by car, or an hour by plane. Guy left Santa Teresa when the Haight-Ashbury was at its peak. Any flower child who wasn't already brain-dead from drugs had gravitated to the Haight in those days. It was the party to end all parties, and with ten grand in his pocket his invitation would have been engraved.

At three-thirty, I locked up my office and went down to the second floor to pick up instructions for service on the two deposition subpoenas. I retrieved my car and headed to the Maleks' place. The house was at the end of a narrow lane, the fifteen-acre property surrounded by an eight-foot wall intersected by an occasional wooden gate. I'd grown up in this town and I thought I knew every corner of it, but this was new to me, prime Santa Teresa real estate dating back to the thirties. The Maleks must lay claim to the last section of flat land for miles. The rear portions of the property must have tilted straight uphill because the face of the Santa Ynez Mountains loomed above me, looking close enough to touch. From the road, I could pick out individual patches of purple sage and coyote brush.

The iron gates at the entrance to the property stood open. I followed the long, curved driveway past a cracked and neglected tennis court into a cobblestone turnaround tucked into the L of the main residence. Both the house and the wall that encompassed the grounds were faced with dusky terra-cotta stucco, an odd shade of red halfway between brick and dusty rose. Massive evergreens towered above the grounds and a forest of live oaks stretched out to the right of the house as far as the eye could see. Sunlight scarcely penetrated the canopy of branches. Near the front of the house, the pine trees had dropped a blanket of needles that must have turned the soil to acid. There was little if any grass and the damp smell of bare earth was pervasive. Here and there, a shaggy palm tree asserted its spare presence. I could see several outbuildings to the right—a bungalow, a gardener's shed, a greenhouse—and on the left, a long line of garages. The driveway apparently continued on around the rear of the house. A Harley-Davidson was parked on a gravel pad to one side. There were flowerbeds, but even the occasional suggestion of color failed to soften the somber gloom of the mansion and the deep shade surrounding it.

The architectural style of the house was Mediterranean. All of the windows were flanked with shutters. A series of balustrades punctuated the stark lines of the facade and a lovers' stairway curved up along the left to a second-story veranda. All the trim was done in dark green, the paint color chalky with age. The roof was composed of old red tile, mottled with soft green algae. The poured concrete urns on either side of the front door were planted with perennials that had died back to sticks. The door itself looked like something that had been lifted from one of the early California missions. When I pressed the bell, I could hear a single resonating note strike within, tolling my presence to the occupants.

In due course, the door was opened by a white woman of indeterminant age in a gray cotton uniform. She was of medium height, thick through the middle, her shoulders and breasts slumping toward a waist that had expanded to accommodate the gradual accumulation of weight. I pegged her in her early forties, but I couldn't be sure.

"Yes?" Her eyebrows needed plucking and her blond hair showed dark roots mixed with gray. This was a woman who apparently whacked at her own hair with some kind of dull instrument, a not-unfamiliar concept. Her bangs had been cut slightly too short, curling across her forehead unbecomingly. Maybe forty dollars for a haircut wasn't too much to pay.

I handed her my business card. "Are you Myrna?"

"That's right."

"I'm Kinsey Millhone," I said. "I believe Donovan called to say I'd be stopping by this afternoon. Is Bennet at home?"

Her expression didn't change, but she seemed to know what I was talking about. She was plain, her nose maybe half a size too big for her face. Her lips were antiqued with the remnants of dark lipstick, probably eaten off at lunch or imprinted on the edge of her coffee cup. Now that I'd become an aficionada of drugstore cosmetics, I was acting like an expert. What a laugh, I thought.

"He just got in. He said to put you in the library if you arrived before he came down. Would you like to follow me?"

I said, "Sure." I loved the idea of being "put" in the library, like a potted plant.

I followed her across the foyer, toward a room on the right. I took in my surroundings surreptitiously, trying not to look like a mouth breather in the process. In the homes of the rich, it doesn't do to gape. The floor was dark parquet, a complicated herringbone pattern with the polished wooden chevrons blending together seamlessly. The entrance hall was two stories high, but little if any light filtered down from above. Tapestries were hung along the walls at intervals, faded depictions of women with high waists and faces shaped like hard-boiled eggs. Gents in cloaks rode on horseback, trailed by hunting dogs on chains. Behind them, a merry band of woodcutters toted a dead stag that had spears sticking out of its torso like Saint Sebastian. I could tell right away that theirs was a world devoid of animal-rights activists.

The library had the look of a private men's club, or what I imagine such a place would look like if women were allowed in. Several large red Oriental carpets had been laid side by side to form a continuous floor covering. One wall was paneled in dark walnut and there were floor-to-ceiling bookshelves on the other three. The windows were tall and narrow, diamonds of leaded glass admitting more chill air than afternoon light. There were three groupings of ripped red-leather club chairs and an enormous gray stone fireplace with a gas starter, its inner hearth blackened by countless fires. The room smelled of charred oak and book mold and suggested the kind of dampness associated with poorly laid foundations. For a family that had amassed a fortune in the construction business, they really ought to think about pumping money into the place. Failing major home improvements, a quick trip to Pier I would have done wonders.

For once, left to my own devices, I didn't bother to snoop. Guy Malek had been gone for eighteen years. I wasn't going to find a copy of his outbound bus schedule or a drawer filled with personal diaries he'd kept as a lad. I heard someone walking on the second floor, the ceiling creaking as the steps passed from one side to the other of the room above. I circled the library, glancing out of every window I passed. The room was a good thirty feet long. At the far end, a solarium looked out on the rear lawn, a large expanse of dormant grass with a murky-looking koi pond in the center. The surface of the water was choked with lily pads.

I moved back toward the door and heard someone come down the stairs and traverse the hall. The door opened and Bennet Malek came in. He was four years younger than Donovan with the same fair hair. Where Donovan's was glossy, Bennet's was coarse, and he kept it cut short to discourage a visible tendency to curl. He'd apparently given up his battle to stay clean shaven and a blond beard and mustache now defined the lower portion of his face. He was heavyset, looking beefy across the shoulders and thick through the chest. He wore jeans and a navy sweatshirt with the sleeves pushed up along forearms densely matted with hair. Tasha had tagged him as a man who invested and lost sums of money on various faulty commercial ventures. I wondered how I might have responded to him if I hadn't been told in advance of his poor business sense. As it was, I found myself disregarding the hearty confidence he was at pains to project. Belatedly, I noticed that he carried the last half inch of a drink in his right hand, gin or vodka over ice with a twist. He set the drink on the end table closest to him.

He held out his hand and shook mine with unnecessary strength. We weren't about to arm wrestle so what was the point? His fingertips were icy and faintly moist to the touch. "Bennet Malek, Miss Millhone. Nice to meet you. Don said you'd be coming. Can I offer you a drink?" He had a big booming voice and made solid eye contact. Very manly, I thought.

"Thanks, but I'm fine. I don't want to take any more time than I have to. I know you're busy."

"Fair enough. Why don't you have a seat?" he said. His attentiveness seemed feigned, a salesman's maneuver for putting the customer at ease. I'd been in this man's company thirty seconds or less and I'd already developed an aversion to him.

I perched on the edge of a club chair with a wide, sunken seat. The leather surface was slippery and I had to fight a tendency to skid backward into the depths. As a child, I used to polish the trailer park sliding board to lightning-fast speeds by vigorous rubbings with sheets of Cut-Rite waxed paper. The glossy leather cushion had the same slick feel to it. To avoid losing traction, I had to keep my weight pitched forward, feet together and flat on the floor.

Bennet settled into the chair to my left with a series of creakings. "I understand you're a private investigator," he said.

"That's right. I've been licensed for ten years. I was a police officer before that. What about you? What sort of work do you do?"

"I'm into venture capital. I look for promising little companies with cash-flow problems."

And drain them dry, no doubt. "Sounds like fun," I remarked.

"It's gratifying. Let's put it that way." His voice had dropped into a confidential tone. "I take it you met with Don?"

"That's right. I talked to him earlier this afternoon."

He shook his head almost imperceptibly. "Did he mention the missing will?"

"Tasha told me about that when she was briefing me at lunch," I said. Vaguely, I wondered why he was raising the subject. The existence of a second will was really not my concern. "I guess your brother lucked out," I said.

He snorted. "I'll tell you what bugs me. I remember when Dad signed the second will. I can picture the day just as clear as I'm sitting here. Dad's attorney and two witnesses came out to the house."

"Well, that's interesting. Do you remember who they were?"

"The witnesses? Two women. I remember that much. I assumed they worked for the attorney, but I may have made that up. They weren't personal friends of Dad's as far as I know. The four of them came in here and emerged maybe half an hour later."

"Have you told Tasha about this?"

"I mentioned I was here the day the second will was signed. I can't remember now if I mentioned witnesses or not."

"I'd tell her, if I were you. She may find a way to determine who they were. From what I've heard, no one disputes the fact that a second will was drawn up, but was it signed in your presence? Were you apprised of the provisions?"

"Well, I wasn't in the room with him if that's what you're getting at. Dad referred to it later, but he never spelled it out. The question is, what happened to it?"

I shrugged. "Your father could have changed his mind. He could have torn it up and tossed it out."

Bennet stirred restlessly. "So everyone says, though I'm not convinced. It's an interesting issue, if you think about it. I mean, look at the facts. The will comes up missing and the black sheep of the family makes out like a bandit. Dad signed it in March and Guy left within days."

"You're saying your brother stole it?"

"I'm saying, why not? I wouldn't put it past him. He stole everything else."

"But what good would that do? Even if he snitched a copy, the attorney probably kept the original. Once Guy was gone, he had no way of knowing your father wasn't going to turn around and make another will just like it. Or write a third will altogether. From what Donovan's told me, your father was good at talking tough and not so good when it came to follow-through."

He shook his head and his expression was patronizing. "True enough. That's why I'm going back through all of Dad's personal papers. It's not that we want to deny Guy any monies he may be entitled to, but this is bullshit in my opinion. He collected his share once. Dad had the second will drawn up with every intention of eliminating Guy's claim. That's why he gave him the cash to begin with—to pay him off in full. I heard him allude to it many times over the years. As far as he was concerned, the ten grand he gave my brother was the end of it."

"Well, I wish I could help, but this is really not my turf. Tasha's the expert. I suggest you sit down and talk to her."

"What about my father's deal with Guy?" he went on argumentatively. "It was a verbal agreement, but doesn't that count for anything?"

"Hey, you're asking the wrong person. I have no idea. No one knows where Guy is, let alone what kind of bargain he made the day he left."

His smile flickered and I could see him curb a desire to continue arguing the point. "You're right, of course," he said. "So what can I tell you about Guy?"

"Let's start with the obvious. Did he say anything to you about his plans before he left?"

"I'm afraid Guy wasn't in the habit of discussing anything with me."

I shifted the subject slightly. "Could he have headed up to San Francisco? Donovan says he was into drugs in those days and the Haight might have been a draw."

"It's always possible. If that's where he went, he never said a word to me. I should probably warn you, the two of us weren't close. I don't mean to seem uncooperative, but I don't have much to offer in the way of information."

"Did you ever hear him mention a possible career? Did he have any personal passions?"

Bennet's smile was thin. "He made a career out of doing as little as possible. His passion was getting into trouble, making life miserable for everyone else."

"What about his employment? What kind of jobs did he have?"

"None significant. When he was still in his teens, he worked in a pizza place until he got caught skimming cash. He also got a job doing telephone sales. That lasted two days. I don't remember his ever doing much else until he started working for Dad. He pumped gas for a while so I suppose he might have become a career gas station attendant."

"What kind of car did he drive?"

"He drove the family Chevy until he was involved in a hit-and-run accident and his license was suspended. After that, Dad refused to let him use any of the family vehicles."

"Do you know if his license was ever reinstated?"

"If it wasn't, he probably drove without. He never cared much about life's petty little rules and regulations."

"Did he have any hobbies?"

"Not unless you count smoking dope and getting laid."

"What about his personal interests? Did he hunt, or fish? Did he skydive?" I was floundering, casting about in an attempt to develop a sense of direction.

Bennet shook his head. "He was a vegetarian. He said nothing should ever have to die so that he could eat. He was petrified of heights so I doubt he ever jumped out of airplanes or climbed mountains or bungee-jumped."

"Well, at least we can eliminate that," I said. "Did he have medical problems?"

"Medical problems? Like what?"

"I don't know. I'm just trying to find ways to get a bead on him. Was he diabetic? Did he have allergies or any chronic illnesses?"

"Oh. I see what you're getting at. No. As far as I know, his health was good—for someone so heavily into drink and drugs."

"Donovan says he had one good friend. Somebody named Paul?"

"You're talking about Paul Trasatti. I can give you his telephone number. He hasn't gone anywhere."

"I'd appreciate that."

He recited the number off the top of his head and I made a quick note in the little spiral-bound notebook I carry.

I tried to think about the areas I hadn't covered yet. "Was he a draft dodger? Did he protest the war in Vietnam?"

"He didn't have to. The army wouldn't take him. He had bad feet. Lucky him. He never gave a shit about politics. He never even voted as far as I know."

"What about religion? Did he do Yoga? Meditate? Chant? Walk on hot coals?" This was like pulling teeth.

He shook his head again. "None of the above."

"What about bank accounts?"

"Nope. At least he didn't have any back then."

"Did he own any stocks or bonds?"

Bennet shook his head again. He was beginning to seem amused at my persistence, which I found irritating.

"He must have cared about something," I said.

"He was a fuckup, pure and simple. He never lifted a finger for anyone except himself. Typical narcissist. The girls couldn't get enough of him. You figure it out."

"Look, Bennet. I understand your hostility, but I can do without the editorializing. You must have cared about him once."

"Of course," he said blandly, averting his gaze. "But that was before he became such a pain in the ass to all of us. Besides, he's been gone for years. I suppose at some level I have some kind of family feeling, but it's hard to sustain given his long absence."

"Once he left, none of you ever heard from him?"

His eyes came back to mine. "I can only speak for myself. He never called me or wrote. If he was in touch with anyone else, I wasn't told about it. Maybe Paul knows something."

"What sort of work does he do?"

"He's a rare-book dealer. He buys and sells autographs, letters, manuscripts. Things like that." He closed his mouth and smiled faintly, volunteering nothing unless I asked point-blank.

I wasn't getting anywhere and it was probably time to move on. "What about Jack? Could Guy have confided in him?"

"You can ask him yourself. He's right out there," Bennet said. He gestured toward the windows and I followed his gaze. I caught a glimpse of Jack as he crossed the back lawn, heading away from the house toward a slope to the left. The rear of the property picked up just enough sun to foster a mix of coarse, patchy grasses, some of which were dormant at this time of year. He had a couple of golf clubs tucked carelessly under one arm and he carried a bucket and a net in a blue plastic frame.

By the time we caught up with him and Bennet had introduced us, Jack was using a sand wedge to smack golf balls at the net he'd set up twenty yards away. Bennet withdrew and left me to watch Jack practice his chipping shots. He'd swing and I could hear the thin whistle as the club cut through the air. There'd be a whack and the ball would arc toward the net, with an unerring accuracy. Occasionally, a shot would hit the grass nearby, landing with a short bounce, but most of the time he nailed the target he was aiming for.

He wore a visor with PEBBLE BEACH imprinted on the rim. His hair was light brown, a shock of it protruding from the Velcro-secured opening at the back. He wore chinos and a golf shirt with the emblem for St. Andrew's stitched on the front like a badge. He was leaner than his two brothers and his face and arms were tanned. I could see him measure the trajectory of the ball as it sailed through the air. He said, "I hope this doesn't seem rude, but I've got a tournament coming up."

I murmured politely, not wanting to break his concentration.

Whistle. Whack. "You've been hired to find Guy," he said when the ball landed. He frowned to himself and adjusted his stance. "How's it coming?"

I smiled briefly. "So far all I have are his date of birth and his Social Security number."

"Why did Donovan tell you to talk to me?"

"Why wouldn't I talk to you?"

He ignored me for the moment. I watched as he walked out to the net and leaned down, gathering the countless balls, which he tossed in his plastic bucket. He came back to the spot where I was standing and started all over again. His swing looked exactly the same—time after time, without variation. Swing, whack, in the net. He'd put the next ball down. Swing, whack, in the net. He shook his head at one shot, responding to my comment belatedly. "Donovan doesn't have much use for me. He's a Puritan at heart. It's all work, work, work with him. You have to be productive—get the job done. All that rah-rah-rah stuff. As far as he's concerned, golf isn't worthy of serious consideration unless it nets you an annual income of half a million bucks." He paused to look at me, leaning lightly on his golf club, as if it were a cane. "I don't have any idea where Guy went, if that's what you're here to ask. I was finishing my senior year at Wake Forest, so I heard about it by phone. Dad called and said he'd told Guy to hit the road. They'd had a quarrel about something and off he went."

"When was the last time you saw him?"

"When I was home for Mother's funeral in January. When I came home again for spring break, he'd been gone maybe three days. I figured the whole thing would blow over, but it never did. By the time I graduated and came home in June, the subject was never mentioned. It's not like we were forbidden to refer to him. We just didn't, I guess out of consideration for Dad."

"You never heard from Guy at all? Not a call or a postcard in all these years?"

Jack shook his head.

"Didn't that bother you?"

"Of course. I adored him. I saw him as a rebel, a true individual. I hated school and I was miserable. I did poorly in most classes. All I wanted was to play golf and I didn't see why I had to have a college education. I would have gone off with Guy in a heartbeat if he'd told me what was going on. What can I tell you? He never called. He never wrote. He never gave any indication he gave a shit about me. Such is life."

"And nobody outside the family ever reported running into him?"

"Like at a convention or something? You're really scraping the bottom of the barrel on that one."

"You think you'd have heard *something*."

"Why? I mean, what's the big deal? People probably pull this shit all the time. Go off, and nobody ever hears from them again. There's no law says you have to stay in touch with people just because you're related."

"Well, true," I said, thinking of my own avoidance of relatives. "Do you know of anyone else who might help? Did he have a girl-friend?"

Jack smiled mockingly. "Guy was the kind of fellow mothers warn their little girls about."

"Donovan told me women found him attractive, but I don't get it. What was the appeal?"

"They weren't women. They were girls. Melodrama is seductive when you're seventeen."

I thought about it briefly, but this seemed like another dead end. "Well. If you have any ideas, could you get in touch?" I took a card from my handbag and passed it over to him.

Jack glanced at my name. "How's the last name pronounced?"

"*Mill*-hone," I said. "Accent on the first syllable. The last rhymes with bone."

He nodded. "Fair enough. You won't hear from me, of course, but at least you can say you tried." He smiled. "I'm sure Don was way too cool to mention this," he said mildly, "but we're all hoping you won't find him. That way we can file a petition asking the court to declare him dead and his share can be divided among the three of us."

"That's what 'diligent search' is all about, isn't it? Tell Donovan I'll call him in a day or two," I said.

I walked back across the grass toward the house. What a bunch, I thought. Behind me, I could hear the whistle of Jack's swing and the sound of the clubhead on impact. I could have knocked at the front door again and asked the housekeeper if Donovan's wife, Christie, was at home. As an old college chum of Tasha's, she might at least be gracious. On the other hand, she wasn't married to Donovan at the point when Guy departed, and I couldn't believe she'd have anything of substance to contribute. So where did that leave me?

I got in my car and started the engine, shifting into first. I eased down the long drive toward the street beyond. At the front gate, I paused, shifting into neutral and letting the car idle while I considered the possibilities. As nearly as I could tell, Guy Malek hadn't been a property owner in Santa Teresa County, so there wasn't any point in checking the tax rolls or real property records. From what his brothers had indicated, he'd never even rented his own apartment, which meant I couldn't consult with a past landlord, or query the water, gas, electric, or phone companies for a forwarding address. Most of those records aren't kept for eighteen years anyway. What else? At the time he'd left Santa Teresa, he had no job and no significant employment history, so there wasn't any point in checking with the local labor unions or with Social Security. He didn't vote, own a car or a gun, didn't hunt or fish, which probably meant he didn't have any permits or licenses on record. He'd probably acquired a driver's license and a vehicle by now. Also, using past behavior as a future indicator, he probably had a criminal history in the system somewhere, certainly with the National Crime Information Center. Unfortunately, I didn't have access to that information and, offhand, I couldn't think of anyone who'd be willing to run a computer check. A law enforcement officer with proper authorization has all sorts of databases available that I couldn't tap into as a licensed private eye.

I put the VW in first gear, hung a left, and drove over to the Department of Motor Vehicles. It was just shy of closing time and the place was clearing out. I filled out a form, asking for a records' search. Often, DMV records will be out of date. People move, but the change of address won't show up in the DMV computers until a driver's license or a vehicle registration is renewed. In this case, if Guy Malek had left the state, all the data might well be years out of date, if it showed up at all. At the moment, however, it seemed like the quickest way to get a preliminary fix on the situation. Since I didn't have his driver's license number, I picked up an ANI Multiple Record Request Form, filling in his full name and date of birth. The

Automated Name Index file would either show no record for the criteria given, or would show a match for last name, first name, middle initial, and birthdate. As soon as I got back to the office, I'd put the form in the mail and ship it off to Sacramento. With luck, I could at least pick up his mailing address.

In the meantime, since the office was nearly empty, I asked one of the DMV clerks to check the name through her computer.

She turned and gave me her full attention. "Are you nuts? I could get fired for doing that," she said. She turned the monitor on its swivel so I couldn't peek at the screen.

"I'm a PI," I said.

"You could be the Pope for all I care. You'll have to wait to hear from Sacramento. You get nothing from me."

"It was worth a try," I said. I tried a winsome smile, but it didn't get me far.

"You got a nerve," she said. She turned away with a reproving shake of her head and began to pack away her desk.

So much for my powers of persuasion.

4

I returned to the office, typed up the envelope, wrote a check to the state, attached it to the form, affixed a stamp, and stuck the packet in the box for outgoing mail. Then I picked up the phone and called Darcy Pascoe, the secretary/receptionist at California Fidelity Insurance. We chatted briefly about the old days and I caught up on minor matters before making the same request to her that I'd made to the DMV clerk. Insurance companies are always running DMV checks. Darcy wasn't actually authorized to inquire, but she knew how to bend the rules with the best of them. I said, "All I need is a mailing address."

"What's your time frame?"

"I don't know. How about first thing tomorrow?"

"I can probably do that, but it'll cost you. What's this kid's name again?"

• • •

When I got home, lights were on in the apartment, but Dietz was still out someplace. He'd brought in a soft-sided suitcase that he'd placed beside the couch. A quick check in the closet showed a hanging garment bag. In the downstairs bathroom, his Dopp kit was sitting on the lid to the toilet tank. The room smelled of soap and there was a damp towel hung across the shower rod. I went back to the kitchen and turned on the radio. Elvis was singing the final chorus of "Can't Help Falling In Love."

"Spare me," I said crossly and turned the thing off. I went up the spiral stairs to the loft where I kicked off my Reeboks and stretched out on the bed. I stared up at the skylight. It was well after five o'clock and the dark had fallen on us like a wool blanket, a dense, leaden gray. Through the Plexiglas dome, I couldn't even see the night sky because of the overcast. I was tired and hungry and strangely out of sorts. Being single can be confusing. On the one hand, you sometimes yearn for the simple comfort of companionship; someone to discuss your day with, someone with whom you can cele- brate a raise or tax refund, someone who'll commiserate when you're down with a cold. On the other hand, once you get used to being alone (in other words, having everything your way), you have to won- der why you'd ever take on the aggravation of a relationship. Other human beings have all these hotly held *opinions*, habits, and man- nerisms, bad art and peculiar taste in music, not to mention mood disorders, food preferences, passions, hobbies, allergies, emotional fixations, and attitudes that in no way coincide with the correct ones, namely yours. Not that I was thinking seriously of Robert Dietz in this way, but I'd noticed, walking into the apartment, an unnerving awareness of the "otherness" of him. It's not that he was intrusive, obnoxious, or untidy. He was just *there*, and his presence acted on me like an irritant. I mean, where was this going? Nowhere that I could tell. I'd no more than get used to him than he'd hit the road again. So why bother to adjust when his company wasn't permanent? Personally, I don't consider flexibility that desirable a trait.

I heard a key turn in the lock and I realized, with a start, I'd drifted off to sleep. I sat up, blinking fuzzily. Below me, Dietz was turning on additional lights. I could hear the crackle of paper. I got up and moved over to the railing, looking down at him. He turned on the radio. I put my fingers in my ears so I wouldn't have to listen to Elvis sing soulfully about love. Who needs that shit? Dietz was a big country music fan and I was hoping he'd flip the station to find something more twangy and a lot less to the point. He sensed my presence and tilted his face in my direction. "Good. You're home. I didn't see your car outside," he said. "I picked up some groceries. You want to help me unload?"

"I'll be there in a minute." I made a quick detour to the bathroom, where I ran a comb through my hair, brushed my teeth, and availed myself of the facilities. I'd forgotten how domesticated Dietz could be. When I thought about the man, it was his personal-security expertise that came foremost to mind. I padded down the stairs in my sock feet. "How'd you know what we needed?"

"I checked. Surprise, surprise. The cupboards were bare." He had the refrigerator open, placing eggs, bacon, butter, lunch meats, and various other high-fat, high-cholesterol items in the bins. On the counter was a six-pack of beer, two bottles of Chardonnay, extra-crunchy peanut butter, canned goods and assorted condiments, along with a loaf of bread. He'd even remembered paper napkins, paper towels, toilet paper, and liquid detergent. I put the canned goods in the cabinet and turned off the radio. If Dietz noticed, he said nothing.

Over his shoulder, he said, "How'd the interview go?"

I said, "Fine. I haven't made a lick of progress, but you have to start someplace."

"What's the next move?"

"I'm having Darcy run a DMV check through the insurance company I used to work for. She hopes to have something early tomorrow morning. Then we'll see what's what. I have other lines of pursuit, but she's my best bet so far."

"You're not working for California Fidelity these days?"

"Actually, I'm not. I got my ass fired because I wouldn't kiss someone else's. I rent an office in a law firm. It works out better that way."

I could see him toy with other questions, but he must have decided that the less said the better.

He changed the subject. "Can I talk you into eating out?"

"What'd you have in mind?"

"Something in walking distance where we don't have to dress."

I looked at him for a moment, feeling strangely unwilling to cooperate. "How's the old friend?"

Dietz surpressed a smile. "He's fine. Is that what's bothering you?"

"No. I don't know. I think I've been depressed for weeks and just now got in touch with it. I'm also nervous about the job. I'm working for my cousin Tasha, which I probably shouldn't be doing."

"A cousin? That's a new one. Where did she come from?"

"God, you *are* out of date."

"Grab a jacket and let's go. You can talk about it over dinner and bring me up to speed."

We walked from my apartment to a restaurant on the breakwater, three long blocks during which little was said. The night was very chilly and the lights strung out along the harbor were like leftover Christmas decorations. Over the softly tumbling surf, I could hear the tinkle of a buoy, the tinny sound mixing with the gentle lapping of water against the boats in the marina. Many vessels were alight and the occasional glimpses of the live-aboards reminded me of a trailer park, a community of small spaces, looking cozy from outside. Dietz's pace was rapid. He had his head bent, his hands in his pockets, heels clicking on the pavement. I kept up with him, my mind running back over what I knew of him.

His upbringing had been a strange one. He'd told me he was born in a van on the road outside Detroit. His mother was in labor and his father was too impatient to find an emergency room. His father was a brawler and a bully who worked the oil rigs, moving his family from one town to the next as the mood struck. Dietz's granny, his mother's mother, traveled with them in the vehicle of the moment—a truck, a van, or a station wagon, all secondhand and subject to breakdown or quick sale if the money ran low. Dietz had been educated out of an assortment of old textbooks while his mother and granny drank beers and threw the cans out the window onto the highway. His dislike of formal schooling was an attribute we shared. Because he'd had so little experience with institutions, he was fiercely insubordinate. He didn't so much go against regulations as ignore them, operating on the assumption that the rules simply didn't apply to him. I liked his rebelliousness. At the same time, I was wary. I was into caution and control. He was into anarchy.

We reached the restaurant, the Tramp Steamer, a cramped and overheated gray-frame establishment located up a narrow flight of wooden stairs. A modest effort had been made to give the place a nautical feel, but its real attraction was the fare: raw oysters, fried shrimp, peppery chowder, and homemade bread. There was a full bar near the entrance, but most of the clientele preferred beer. The air was saturated with the smell of hops and cigarette smoke. Between the honky-tonk jukebox, the raucous laughter, and conversations, the noise was palpable. Dietz scanned the room for seating, then pushed through a side door and found us a table on the deck, overlooking the marina. Outside, it was quieter and the chill air was offset by the red glow of wall-mounted propane heaters. The briny scent of the ocean seemed stronger up here than it had down below. I took a deep breath, sucking it into my lungs like ether. It had the same sedative effect and I could feel myself unwind.

"You want Chardonnay?" he asked.

"I'd love it."

I sat at the table while he moved back inside to the bar. I watched him through the window in conversation with the bartender. As he waited for the order, his gaze moved restlessly across the crowd. He crossed to the jukebox and studied the selections. Dietz was the sort of man who paced and tapped his fingers, subterranean energy constantly bubbling to the surface. I seldom saw him read a book because he couldn't sit still that long. When he did read, he was out of commission, utterly absorbed until he was finished. He liked competition. He liked guns. He liked machines. He liked tools. He liked climbing rocks. His basic attitude was "What are you saving yourself for?" My basic attitude was "Let's not jump right into things."

Dietz wandered back to the bar and stood there jiggling the change in his pocket. The bartender set a mug of beer and a glass of wine on the counter. Dietz peeled off some bills and returned to the deck, trailing the smell of cigarette smoke like a strange aftershave. He said, "Service is slow. I hope the food's good." We touched glasses before we drank, though I wasn't sure what we were drinking to.

I opened a menu and let my eyes trace the choices. I wasn't really that hungry. Maybe a salad or soup. I usually don't eat much at night.

"I called the boys," he remarked.

"And how are they?" I asked. I'd never met his two sons, but he spoke of them with affection.

"They're fine. The boys are great," he said. "Nick turns twenty-one on the fourteenth. He's a senior at Santa Cruz, but he just changed his major so he'll probably be there another year. Graham's nineteen and a sophomore. They're sharing an apartment with a bunch of guys this year. They're smart kids. They like school and seem to be motivated. More than I ever was. Naomi's done a good job, without a lot of help from me. I support 'em, but I can't say I ever spent much time on the scene. I feel bad about that, but you know how I am. I'm a rolling stone. I can't help it. I could never settle down and buy a house and work nine to five. I can't behave myself in a situation like that."

"Where's Naomi?"

"San Francisco. She got a law degree. I paid her tuition—I'm good about that end—but all the hard work was hers. The boys say she's getting married to some attorney up there."

"Good for her."

"How about you? What have you been up to?"

"Not a lot. Mostly work. I don't take vacations so I haven't been anywhere that didn't somehow involve a stakeout or a background check. I'm a bundle of laughs."

"You should learn how to play."

"I should learn how to do a lot of things."

The waitress approached, moving toward us from a table in the angle of the deck. "You two ready to order?" She was probably in her late twenties, a honey blond with her hair in a boy-cut and braces on her teeth. She wore matching black shorts and tank top as if it were August instead of January 8.

"Give us a minute," Dietz said.

We ended up splitting a big bowl of steamed mussels, nestled in a spicy tomato broth. For entrées, Dietz had a rare steak and I had a Caesar salad. We both ate as though we were racing against the clock. We used to make love the same way, like some contest to see who could get there first.

"Tell me about the depression," he said when he had pushed his plate aside.

I gestured dismissively. "Forget it. I don't like to sit around feeling sorry for myself."

"Go ahead. You're allowed."

"I know I'm allowed, but what's the point?" I said. "I can't even tell you what it's about. Maybe my serotonin levels are off."

"No doubt, but what's the rest of it?"

"The usual, I guess. I mean, some days I don't get it, what we're doing on the planet. I read the paper and it's hopeless. Poverty and disease, all the bullshit from politicians who'd tell you anything to get elected. Then you have the hole in the ozone and the destruction of the rain forests. What am I supposed to do with this stuff? I know it's not up to me to solve the world's problems, but I'd like to believe there's a hidden order somewhere."

"Good luck."

"Yeah, good luck. Anyway, I'm struggling for answers. Most of the time, I take life for granted. I do what I do and it seems to make sense. Once in a while I lose track of where I fit. I know it sounds lame, but it's the truth."

"What makes you think there are any answers?" he said. "You do the best you can."

"Whatever that consists of," I remarked.

"Therein lies the rub." He smiled. "What about the job? What scares you about that?"

"I always get amped on the eve of a big one. One of these days I'm going to fail and I don't like the thought. It's stage fright."

"Where'd the cousin come from? I thought you didn't have any family."

"Don't I wish," I said. "Turns out I have a bunch of cousins up in Lompoc, all girls. I'd prefer not to have anything to do with them, but they keep popping up. I'm too old to cope with 'togetherness.' "

"Such a liar," he said fondly, but he let it pass.

The waitress came by. We declined dessert and coffee. Dietz asked for the check, which she produced from a sheaf tucked in the small of her back, taking a few seconds to total it out. Her yellow socks and black high-tops really gave the outfit some class. She placed the bill facedown on the table slightly closer to Dietz's side than to mine. This was probably her tactic for playing it safe in case we were a twosome whose roles were reversed.

She said, "I can take that anytime you want." She moved off to deliver ketchup to another table. She must have the metabolism of a bird. The cold wasn't even producing goose bumps.

Dietz glanced at the check briefly, recalculating the total in the blink of an eye. He leaned sideways to extract his wallet and pulled out a pair of bills that he slid under his plate. "Ready?"

"Whenever you are."

We took the long way home. It seemed easier talking in the dark without looking at each other. The conversation was superficial. I'm an expert at using words to keep other people at bay. When we got home, I made sure Dietz had everything he needed—sheets, two pillows, an extra blanket, a small alarm clock, and a fresh towel—all of life's little amenities, except me.

I left him below and headed up the spiral stairs. When I got to the top, I leaned over the rail. "With your bum knee, I take it you won't be jogging with me in the morning."

"Afraid not. I'm sorry. It's something I miss."

"I'll try not to wake you. Thanks for dinner."

"You're welcome. Sleep well."

"Use your ice pack."

"Yes ma'am."

As it turned out, I slept a lot sooner than he did. Dietz was a night owl. I'm not sure how he occupied himself. Maybe he polished his boots or cleaned his handgun. He might have watched late-night television with the sound turned down. I sure never heard him. Once in a while, in turning over, I realized the light was still on in the living room. There was something so parental about his being on the premises. One thing about being single, you don't often feel protected. You tend to sleep with your mental shoes on, ready to leap up and arm yourself at the least little noise. With Dietz on guard duty, I got to cruise through a couple of rounds of REM, dreaming right up to the split second before the alarm went off. I opened my eyes, reached out, and caught it just before it blared.

I did my morning ablutions behind closed doors so the sound of running water wouldn't carry. Shoes in hand, I crept down the stairs in my stocking feet and tiptoed out the front door without waking him. I laced up, did a quick stretch, and set off at a fast walk to get warmed up. The night had shifted from pitch black to charcoal gray and by the time I reached Cabana, the darkness was beginning to lift. Dawn painted the early-morning sky in pale watercolor hues. The ocean was silver blue, the sky washing up from a smoky mauve to soft peach. The oil derricks dotted the horizon like clusters of irides-cent sequins. I love the sound of the surf at that hour, the squawk of seagulls, the soft cooing of the pigeons already strutting along the path. A platinum blond and a black standard poodle were heading in my direction, a pair I saw most of the mornings I was out.

The run was good. Often three miles just feels like a pain in the ass, something I do because I know I must. For once, here I was feeling grateful to be physically fit. I wouldn't do well with an injury like Dietz's that prevented exercise. I'll never be any kind of champ, but for lifting a depression there's really nothing better. I did the turn at East Beach and started back, picking up my pace a bit. The sun was coming up behind me, sloshing rivulets of yellow light across the sky. Walking home again, winded and sweating, my mood was light and I was feeling good.

Dietz was in the shower when I got in. He'd brought in the paper and set it on the kitchen counter. He'd tidied the bedcovers and folded up the sofa bed, tucking the pillows out of sight somewhere. I put on a pot of coffee and then went upstairs, waiting until I heard him turn off his shower before I started mine. By 8:35, I was dressed, I'd finished breakfast, and I was gathering up my jacket and my car keys. Dietz was still sitting at the kitchen counter with his second cup of coffee and the morning paper spread out before him.

"See you later," I said.

"Have a good one," he replied.

On the way downtown, I stopped off at a nearby condominium with the two subpoenas in hand. I served both without incident, though the fellow and his girlfriend were hardly happy with me. Occasion-ally, I'll have someone who goes to absurd lengths to avoid service, but for the most part people seem resigned to their fates. If someone protests or turns ugly, my response is usually the same: "Sorry, pal, but I'm like a waitress. I don't cook up the trouble, I just serve it. Have a nice day," I say.

For a change, I parked in the public lot across from the courthouse and walked the two blocks to work. My current office is the former conference room for the law firm of Kingman and Ives, located in downtown Santa Teresa. From my apartment, the drive takes about ten minutes, given the usual traffic conditions. The Kingman building appears to be a three-story stucco structure, but the ground floor is an illusion. Behind a fieldstone facade, complete with barred and shuttered windows, there's actually a small parking lot, with twelve assigned spaces. Most of the office staff and the lesser tenants in the building are forced to scrounge parking elsewhere. The surrounding blocks aren't metered, but parking is restricted to ninety minutes max and most of us receive at least one ticket a month. Some mornings, it's comical watching us pass and repass, trying to beat one another to the available spaces.

I climbed the two flights of stairs, forgoing the pleasures of the elevator, which is small and takes forever, often giving the impression it's on the verge of getting stuck. Once in the office, I exchanged pleasantries with the receptionist, Alison, and Lonnie Kingman's secretary, Ida Ruth. I seldom see Lonnie, who's either in court or working doggedly behind closed doors. I let myself into my office, where I paused to make a note of the date, time, and a brief physical description of the couple to whom I'd served the subpoenas. I typed up a quick invoice, then picked up the telephone, leaning back in my swivel chair as I tossed the paperwork in my out box. California Fidelity didn't open until nine, but Darcy usually came in early.

"Hey, Darcy. It's me," I said when she answered on her end.

"Oh hi, Kinsey. Hang on a minute. I'm not at my desk." She put me on hold and I listened to leftover Christmas carols while I waited, feeling mildy optimistic. I figured if she hadn't found anything she'd have said so.

Half a minute passed and then she clicked back in. "Okay. Guy David Malek doesn't have a current driver's license in the state of California. His was surrendered in 1968 and apparently it's never been reissued."

"Well, shit," I said.

Darcy laughed. "Would you just *wait?* You're always jumping to conclusions. All I said was he doesn't drive. He has a California identification card, which is where I picked up the information. His mailing address is Route 1, Box 600, Marcella, California, 93456. That's probably the same as his residence. Sounds like a ranch or a farm. You want to see the picture?"

"You have a current *picture* of him? This is great. I don't believe it. You're a wizard."

"Hey, you're dealing with a pro," she said. "What's your fax number?"

I gave her Lonnie's fax number while I reached for the telephone book. "Are you sure he's in Marcella? That's less than a hundred miles away."

"According to DMV records. That should make your job easy."

"Ain't that the truth. What do I owe you?"

"Don't worry about it. I had to fake out some forms to make the request look legitimate, but nobody's going to check. Took less than a minute."

"You're a doll. Thanks so much. I'll be in touch and we'll have lunch. I'll pay."

Darcy laughed. "I'll take you up on that."

I put the phone down and paged through the telephone book, looking up the area code for Marcella, California. It was actually in the 805 area, the same as Santa Teresa. I tried directory assistance, giving the operator Guy Malek's name. There was no telephone listed at the address I'd been given. "You have any other listing for Guy Malek in the area? G. Malek? Any kind of Malek?"

"No ma'am."

"All right. Thanks."

I trotted down the hall to the fax machine just in time to see a copy of Guy Malek's photo ID slide out. The black-and-white reproduction had a splotchy quality, but it did establish Guy David Malek's SEX:

52

M; HAIR: BLND; EYES: GRN; HT: 5-08; WT: 155; DOB: 03-02-42. He looked ever so much better than he had in his high school annual. Three cheers for him. I confess I felt smug as I sat down at my desk, the little show-off in my nature patting herself on the back.

I called Tasha's office and identified myself to her secretary when she picked up. She said, "Tasha's in a meeting, but let me tell her it's you. She can probably take a quick call if it's important."

"Trust me, it is."

"Can you hold?"

"Sure." While I waited, I laid out a hand of solitaire. One card up and six cards down. In some ways, I was sorry everything had come together so fast. I didn't want Donovan to think he was paying for something he could have done himself—though in truth, he was. There's a lot of information available as a matter of public record. Most people simply don't have the time or the interest in doing the grunt work. They're all too happy to have a PI do it for them, so in the end everybody benefits. Still, this one was almost too easy, especially since I wasn't sure the family would believe their real interests had been served by my discovery. I turned the next card up on the second pile and placed another five cards down.

Tasha clicked on, sounding terse and distracted. "Hi, Kinsey. What's up? I hope this is important because I'm up to my ass in work."

"I have an address for Guy Malek. I thought I'd better let you know first thing."

There was half a second's silence while she processed the information. "That was fast. How'd you manage?"

I smiled at her tone, which was the perfect blend of surprise and respect. "I have my little ways," I said. Ah, how seductive the satisfaction when we think we've impressed others with our cleverness. It's one of the perversities of human nature that we're more interested in the admiration of our enemies than the approbation of our friends. "You have a pencil?"

"Of course. Where's he living?"

"Not far." I gave her the address. "There's no telephone listed. Either he doesn't have phone service or it's in someone else's name."

"Amazing," she said. "Let me pass this along to Donovan and see what he wants to do next. He'll be delighted, I'm sure."

"I doubt that. I got the impression they'd all be happier if Guy turned up dead."

"Nonsense. This is family. I'm sure things will work out. I'll have him give you a call."

Within fifteen minutes, my phone rang. Donovan Malek was on the line. "Nice work," he said. "I'm surprised how quick it was. I thought the search would take weeks."

"It's not always this easy. We got lucky," I said. "You need anything else?"

"Tasha and I just had a chat about that. I suggested we have you go up there in person. She could contact him by letter, but people sometimes react oddly getting mail from an attorney. You feel threatened before you even open the envelope. We don't want to set the wrong tone."

"Sure, I can talk to him," I said, feeling puzzled what the right tone would be.

"I'd like a firsthand report about Guy's current circumstances. Are you free sometime in the next two days?"

I checked my calendar. "I can go this afternoon if you like."

"The sooner the better. I want this handled with kid gloves. I have no idea if he's heard about Dad's death, but even with the estrangement, he could be upset. Besides, the money's a touchy issue. Who knows how he'll react."

"You want me to tell him about the will?"

"I don't see why not. He's bound to find out eventually."

5

I glanced at my watch. Since there was nothing on my schedule, I thought I might as well hit the road. It was just now nine-thirty. A round-trip to Marcella would take a little more than an hour each way. If I allowed myself an hour to track down Guy Malek, I'd still have plenty of time left to grab a quick lunch and be back mid-afternoon. I opened my bottom desk drawer and took out my map of California. According to the legend, Marcella was maybe eighty miles north, with a population of less than fifteen hundred souls. I didn't think it would take even an hour to locate him once I hit town, assuming he was still there. The conversation itself probably wouldn't take more than thirty minutes, which meant I might get this whole job wrapped up by the end of the day.

I put a call through to Dietz and let him know what was going on. I could hear the television in the background, one of those perpetual news broadcasts riddled with commercials. At the end of the hour, you know more about dog food than you do about world events. Dietz indicated he had no particular plans. I wasn't sure if he was angling for an invitation to accompany me, but since he didn't ask the question, I didn't answer it. I didn't want to feel responsible for his entertainment anyway. I told him I expected to be back by three and would bypass the office and come straight home. We could figure out what to do about dinner when I finally rolled in.

I gassed up my VW and headed north on 101. The sunshine was short-lived. Where the highway hugged the coastline, the fog had rolled in and the sky was now milky white with clouds turning thick at the edge. Along the road, the evergreens stood out against the horizon in a variety of dark shapes. Traffic moved steadily, mostly single-passenger cars with an occasional horse van, probably heading to the Santa Ynez valley just north of us. We hadn't had much rain and the hills looked like dull hay-colored mounds with an occasional oil rig genuflecting in a series of obsequious bows toward the earth.

The road turned inland and within the hour, the clouds had burned off again, fading back into a sky of pale blue, streaked with a residual haze as wispy as goose down. Just outside Santa Maria, I took 166 east and drove for ten miles on the two-lane road that paralleled the Cuyama River. The heat from the January sun was thin up here. Through the valleys and canyons, the earth smelled dry and a string of bald brown hills rose up in front of me. Rain had been promised, but the weather seemed to flirt, teasing us with high clouds and a hint of a breeze.

The town of Marcella was situated in the shadow of the Los Coches Mountain. Driving, I was aware of the unseen presence of the great San Andreas Fault, the 750-mile fracture that snakes up the California coastline from the Mexican border to the triple junction near Mendocino, the Pacific and North American plates grinding against each other since time began. Under the thin layers of granite and marine sediment, the crust of the earth was as cracked as a skull. In this area, the San Andreas Fault was intersected by the Santa Ynez

Fault with the White Wolf and the Garlock not far away. It's specu-
lated that the mountains in this part of the state once ran north-south
like other mountains along the coast. According to theory, the southern tip of this chain was snagged by the Pacific plate many millions
of years ago and dragged sideways as it passed, thus shifting the
range to its current east-west orientation. I'd been driving my car
once during a minor quake and it felt like the VW had suddenly
been passed by a fast-moving eighteen-wheeler. There was a lurch to
the right, as if the car had been sucked into a sudden vacuum. In
California, where the weather seems to change so little, we look to
earthquakes for the drama that tornadoes and hurricanes provide
elsewhere.

At the junction of two roads, I caught sight of a discreet sign and
turned southward into the town of Marcella. The streets were six
lanes wide and sparsely traveled. An occasional palm or juniper had
been planted near the curb. There were no buildings over two stories
high and the structures I saw consisted of a general store with iron
bars across the front windows, a hotel, three motels, a real estate
office, and a large Victorian house surrounded by scaffolding. The
only bar was located in a building that looked like it might have been
a post office once, stripped now of any official function. A Budweiser
sign was hanging in a window. What did the citizens of Marcella do
for a living, and why settle here? There wasn't another town for miles
and the businesses in this one seemed weighted toward drinking beer
and going to bed soon afterward. If you wanted fast food or auto parts,
if you needed a prescription filled, a movie, a fitness center, or a
wedding gown, you'd have to drive into Santa Maria or farther north
on 101 to Atascadero and Paso Robles. The land surrounding the
town seemed barren. I hadn't seen anything that even halfway resem-
bled a citrus orchard or a plowed field. Maybe the countryside was
devoted to ranches or mines or stock-car races. Maybe people lived
here to escape the hurly-burly of San Luis Obispo.

I found a gas station on a side street and stopped for directions.
The youth who emerged was about seventeen. He was skinny, had

pale eyes, hair shaved very close up to his ears, and a tangle of teeth, all reminiscent of someone in an early episode of *The Twilight Zone.* I said, "Hi. I'm looking for a friend of mine named Guy Malek. I think he lives on Route 1 somewhere, but he didn't give me directions." Well, okay. I was fudging, but I didn't outright *lie.* I *would* be Guy's friend when he heard the news about the five million bucks.

The youth said nothing, but he pointed a trembling finger like the Ghost of Christmas Past.

I glanced over my shoulder. "Back that way?"

"That's the house."

I turned to stare with astonishment. The property was enclosed by chain-link fencing. Beyond a rolling chicken wire gate, I could see a small house, a shed, a large barn with corrugated metal siding curling away from the seams, an old yellow school bus, a single gas pump, and a sign too faded to read at any distance. The gate was open. "Oh. Well, thanks. Do you know if he's home?"

"No."

"He's not?"

"No, I don't know. I didn't see him today."

"Ah. Well, I guess I'll go knock."

"You could do that," he said.

I pulled out of the station and drove across the road. I nosed the VW through the open gate and parked on a length of raw dirt that I took for a driveway. I got out. The surface of the yard was white sand with a rim of brown grass around the edge. The house was frame, painted once-upon-a-time white, one story with a wooden porch built across the front. A trellis that shielded the windows on the left sported only one bare vine, which twisted through the latticework like a boa constrictor. A matching trellis on the right had collapsed under its burden of dry, brown vegetation. Various wires extended from the roofline, connecting the occupants to telephone, cable, and electricity.

I climbed the wooden stairs and knocked on the dilapidated screen. The front door was shut and there were no signs of life. There

was a fine dusting of soot everywhere, as if the structure were down-
wind of a smelting plant. The porch floor began to tremble in a way
that suggested that someone was traversing the wooden floor inside of
the house. The door was opened and I found myself face-to-face with
the man I took to be Guy Malek. Aside from a three-day growth of
beard, he didn't look anywhere near his age. His hair looked darker
and straighter than it had in his high school yearbook, but his features were still boyish: khaki green eyes fringed with dark lashes; a
small, straight nose; and a generous mouth. His complexion was
clear and his color was good. Age had sketched in fine lines around
his eyes and the flesh along his jaw was beginning to sag, but I'd
have pegged him in his mid-thirties. At fifty and sixty, he'd no doubt
look just the same, the years making only moderate adjustments to
his good looks. He wore denim overalls on top of what looked like a
union suit. He was in the process of putting on a blue jeans jacket
when he answered the door, and he paused to straighten the collar in
the back before he said, "Hey."

As an adolescent, Guy Malek had been as dorky looking as
the rest of us. He was the bad kid, lawless and self-destructive,
one of life's lost souls. He must have been appealing because he
was so in need of rescue. Women can't resist a man who needs
saving. Now his good angel had apparently taken up residence,
bestowing on his countenance the look of serenity. It seemed
odd that his brothers had matured so differently. Already, I liked
this man better than his siblings. Aside from the scruffiness, he
didn't look like he was snorting, sniffing, or mainlining illegal sub-
stances.

"Are you Guy Malek?"

His smile was hesitant, as though I might be someone he had met
before whose name he wished he remembered. "Yes."

"My name is Kinsey Millhone. I'm a private investigator from
Santa Teresa." I gave him a business card. He studied the card, but
didn't offer to shake hands. His were as soiled as an auto mechanic's.
I could see a muscle work in his jaw.

His eyes came up to mine and his entire body became still. The smile faded. "My family hired you?"

"Well, yes," I said. I was about to launch into a diplomatic account of his father's death when I saw tears rise in his eyes, blurring the clear green of his gaze. He looked upward, blinking, and took a deep breath before he brought his attention back to mine. He dashed at his cheeks, laughing with embarrassment.

He said, "Whoa," pinching at his eyes with the fingers of one hand. He shook his head, trying to compose himself. "Sorry. You caught me by surprise. I never thought it would matter, but I guess it does. I always wished they'd send someone, but I'd about given up hope. How'd you find me?"

"It wasn't that hard. I ran a DMV check and came up with your California identification card. I tried directory assistance, but they didn't have you listed. I take it you don't have a phone."

"Can't afford one," he said. "You want to come in?" His manner was awkward and he seemed unsure of himself. His gaze fell away from mine and then came back again.

"I'd like that," I said.

He stepped back to allow me entrance and I passed into a room that was about what you'd expect. The interior construction was crude and featured wide, unfinished floorboards and windows that didn't quite shut. Various pieces of old furniture had been moved into the space, probably cadged from the city dump . . . if there was one in this town. Every surface was piled high with soiled clothes and books and magazines and utensils, pots and pans and canned goods and tools. There were also what looked like farm implements whose functions were unclear. There was a tower of used tires in one corner of the room and a toilet that didn't seem connected to much of anything. Guy caught my puzzlement. "I'm holding that for a fellow. I have a real bathroom in there," he said, smiling shyly.

"Glad to hear that," I said and smiled back at him.

"You want a cup of coffee? It's instant, but it's not bad."

"No, thanks. Were you on your way out?"

"What? Oh, yeah, but don't worry about that. I have to be some-place shortly. Have a seat." He pulled out a handkerchief and paused to blow his nose. I could feel anxiety stir in my chest. There was something touching about his openness. He gestured toward a frayed, lumpy couch with a spring sticking through the cushion. I perched on the edge, hoping not to do serious damage to my private parts. My discomfort was related to the fact that Guy Malek appar-ently thought his family had hired me to conduct the search out of sentiment. I knew their real attitude, which was actually hostile if the truth be known. I did a quick debate with myself and decided I'd better level with him. Whatever the outcome of our conversation, it would be too humiliating for him if I let him harbor the wrong im-pression.

He pulled up a wooden chair and sat facing me directly, occasion-ally mopping at his eyes. He didn't apologize for the tears that con-tinued to spill down his cheeks. "You don't know how hard I prayed for this," he said, mouth trembling. He looked down at his hands and began to fold the handkerchief in on itself. "The pastor of my church . . . he swore up and down it would come to pass if it was meant to be. No point in praying if it isn't God's will, he said. And I kept saying, 'Man, it seems like they'd have found me by now if they cared enough, you know?' "

I was struck by the fact that his circumstances were oddly reminis-cent of mine, both of us trying to assimilate fractured family connec-tions. At least he welcomed his, though he'd misunderstood the purpose of my visit. I felt like a dog having to set him straight. "Guy, as a matter of fact, it's more complicated. I have some bad news," I said.

"My father died?"

"Two weeks ago. I'm not sure of the date. I gather he'd had a stroke and he was also struggling with cancer. He'd been through a lot and I guess his body just gave up on him."

He was silent for a moment, staring off into space. "Well. I guess I'm not surprised," he said. "Did he . . . do you know if he was the one who asked for me?"

"I have no idea. I wasn't hired until yesterday. The probate attorney is getting the process underway. By law, you're required to be notified since you're one of the beneficiaries."

He turned to me, suddenly getting it. "Ah. You're here on official business and that's all it is, right?"

"More or less."

I watched as the color rose slowly in his cheeks. "Silly me," he said. "And here I thought you were sent by someone who actually gave a shit."

"I'm sorry."

"Not your fault," he said. "What else?"

"What else?"

"I'm wondering if you have any other news to impart."

"Not really." If he'd picked up on the fact that he was due to inherit money, he gave no indication.

"I don't suppose there's any chance my father asked for me."

"I wish I could help, but I wasn't given any details. It's possible, I'm sure, but you may never know. You can ask the attorney when you talk to her. She knows a lot more than I do about the circumstances of his death."

He smiled fleetingly. "Dad hired a woman? That doesn't sound like him."

"Donovan hired her. She went to school with his wife."

"What about Bennet and Jack? Are they married?" He said the names as if the sounds hadn't been uttered for years.

"No. Just Donovan. I don't think he and Christie have any kids as yet. He runs the company, which I understand is now the third-largest construction firm in the state."

"Good for him. Donnie was always obsessed with the business," he said. "Did you talk to the other two?"

"Briefly."

The character of his expression had completely changed as we spoke. What had started out as happiness had shifted to painful enlightenment. "Correct me if I'm wrong, but I get the impression they're not really interested in me. The attorney said they had to do this so they're doing it. Is that it? I mean, the three of them aren't burdened by a lot of warm, gooey feelings where I'm concerned."

"That's true, but it probably stems from the situation when you left. I was told you were in a lot of trouble, so their memories of you aren't that flattering."

"I suppose not. Nor mine of them if it comes right down to it."

"Besides, nobody really believed I'd find you. It's been what, eighteen years?"

"About that. Not long enough, apparently, from their perspective."

"Where'd you go when you left? Do you mind if I ask?"

"Why would I mind? It doesn't amount to much. I went out to the highway to hitch a ride. I was heading for San Francisco, zonked out of my head on acid. The fellow who picked me up was a preacher, who'd been hired by a church about a mile from here. He took me in. I was tripped out so bad I didn't even know where I was at."

"And you've been here all this time?"

"Not quite," he said. "It wasn't like I cleaned up and got straight, just like that. I screwed up more than once. I'd backslide . . . you know, get drunk and take off . . . but Pete and his wife always found me and brought me back. Finally, I realized I wasn't going to shake 'em off. Didn't matter what I did. They were sticking to me like glue. That's when I took a stand and found Jesus in my heart. It really turned my life around."

"And you never got in touch with your family?" I said.

He shook his head, his smile bitter. "They haven't exactly been clamoring for me, either."

"Maybe that will change when I talk to them. What else can I tell them? Do you work?"

"Sure, I work. I do maintenance at the church and, you know, general handyman jobs around town. Painting and repairs, plumbing, electrical. About anything you need. Mostly minimum wage, but I'm the only one does it, so I stay busy."

"Sounds like you've done all right for yourself."

He looked around him. "Well, I don't have much, but I don't need much either. Place isn't mine," he said. "The church provides my housing, but I make enough to take care of the basics. Food and utilities, that sort of thing. I don't drive, but I have a bike and that gets me most places in a town this size."

"You've changed quite a lot."

"I'd be dead otherwise." He glanced at his watch. "Listen, I don't mean to rush you, but I probably ought to get myself on over to the church."

"I won't keep you then. I appreciate your time. Can I give you a lift?"

"Sure. We can talk on the way."

Once in the car, he directed me back to the highway. We turned right onto 166, heading east again. We drove for a while in companionable silence. He slid a look in my direction. "So what's your assignment? Find me and report back?"

"That's about it," I said. "Now that we have a current address, Tasha Howard, the attorney, will be sending you notice of the probate."

"Oh, that's right. I forgot. I'm a beneficiary, you said." His tone had turned light and nearly mocking.

"That doesn't interest you?"

"Not particularly. I thought I needed something from those people, but as it turns out, I don't." He pointed at an upcoming junction and I took a right-hand turn onto a small side road. The roadbed had been downgraded from blacktop to loose gravel, and I could see the plumes of white dust swirling up in my rear window as we drove. The church was situated at the edge of a pasture about a half mile down. The sign said: JUBILEE EVANGELICAL CHURCH.

"You can pull up right here," he said. "You want to come in and see the place? If you're paid by the hour, you might as well have the full tour. I'm sure Donnie can afford it."

I hesitated slightly. "All right."

He cocked his head. "You don't have to worry. I won't try to convert you."

I parked and the two of us got out. He didn't issue a proclamation, but I could tell from his manner that he was proud of the place. He took out a ring of keys and let us in.

The church was small, a frame building, little more than one room. There was something about its plain appearance that spoke of goodness. The stained glass windows were not elaborate. Each was divided into six simple panels of pale gold with a scripture written across the bottom. There was an unadorned wood pulpit at the front, positioned to the left of a raised and carpeted platform. On the right, there was an organ and three rows of folding chairs for the choir. Last Sunday's flowers consisted of a spray of white gladiola. "Place was destroyed by fire about ten years back. Congregation rebuilt everything from the ground right on up."

I said, "How'd you get on track? That must have been hard."

He sat down in one of the front pews and I could see him look around, perhaps seeing the place as I saw it. "I give credit to the Lord, though Pete always says I did the work myself," he said. "I grew up without much guidance, without values of any kind. I'm not blaming anybody. That's just how it was. My parents were good people. They didn't drink or beat me or anything like that, but they never talked about God or faith or their religious beliefs, assuming they had any, which I don't guess they did. My brothers and I . . . even when we were little kids . . . never went to Sunday school or church.

"My parents disliked 'organized religion.' I don't know what that phrase meant to them or what their perception was, but they took pride in making sure none of us were ever exposed to it. Like a disease of some kind. I remember they had a book by this guy named

Philip Wylie. *Generation of Vipers*. He equated the church teachings with intellectual corruption, the stunting of young minds."

"Some people feel that way," I said.

"Yeah, I know. I don't get it, but it's something I run into out there in the world. It's like people think just because you go to church you're not all that bright. I mean, just because I'm born-again doesn't mean I lost IQ points."

"I'm sure you didn't."

"Thing is, I was raised without a moral compass. I couldn't get a sense of what the rules were so I just kept pushing. I kept crossing the line, waiting for somebody to tell me where the boundaries were."

"But you were getting into trouble with the law from what I heard. You must have known the rules because every time you broke one, you ended up in court. Donovan says you spent more time in Juvenile Hall than you did at home."

His smile was sheepish. "That's true, but here's what's weird. I didn't mind Juvie all that much. At least I could be with kids as screwed up as I was. Man, I was out of control. I ran wild. I was a maniac, freaked out about everything. It's hard to think about that now. I have trouble relating to myself and who I was back then. I know what happened. I mean, I know what I did, but I can't imagine doing it. I wanted to feel good. I've thought about this a lot and that's the best explanation I've been able to come up with. I felt bad and I wanted to feel better. Seemed to me dope was the quickest way to get there. I haven't touched drugs or hard liquor for more than fifteen years. I might have a beer now and then, but I don't smoke, don't play cards, don't ballroom dance. Don't take the Lord's name in vain and don't cuss . . . all that much. Stub my toe and I can turn the air blue, but most of the time, I avoid swear words."

"Well, that's good."

"For me, it is. Back then, I was always teetering on the brink. I think I was hoping my parents would finally draw the line and mean it. That they'd say, 'Here, this is it. You've finally gone and done it this time.' But you know what? My dad was too soft. He waffled on everything. Even when he kicked my ass from here to next Tuesday, even when he threw me out of the house, he was saying, 'Give this some thought, son. You can come back when you've figured it out.' But like what? Figured what out? I didn't have a clue. I was rudderless. I was like a boat going full throttle but without any real direction, roaring around in big circles. Know what I mean?"

"Sure I do. In high school, I was a screwup myself. I ended up as a cop before I did this."

He smiled. "No kidding? You drank and smoked dope?"

"Among other things," I said, modestly.

"Come on. Like what?"

"I don't know. Kids in my class were all clean-cut, but not me. I was a wild thing. I ditched school. I hung out with some low-life dudes and I liked that. I liked *them*," I said. "I was the odd one out and so were they, I guess."

"Where'd you go to high school?"

"Santa Teresa High."

He laughed. "You were a low-waller?"

"Absolutely," I said. Low-wallers were the kids who quite literally perched on a low wall that ran along the back of the school property. Much smoking of cigarettes, funky clothes, and peroxided hair.

Guy laughed. "Well, that's great."

"I don't know how great it was, but it's what I did."

"How'd *you* get on track?"

"Who says I am?"

He got to his feet as if he'd come to a decision. "Come on out to the parsonage and meet Peter and Winnie," he said. "They'll be in the kitchen at this hour setting up supper for the Thursday night Bible study."

I followed him up the center aisle and through a door at the rear. I could feel the first stirrings of resistance. I didn't want anyone pushing me to convert. Too much virtue is just as worrisome as wickedness in my book.

6

The parsonage was situated on the property adjacent to the church and consisted of a rambling white frame farmhouse, two stories tall, with green shutters and a shabby green shingled roof broken up with dormers. Across one end was a wide screened-in porch distinctly tilted, as though an earthquake had pulled the concrete foundation loose. Behind the house, I could see a big red barn with a dilapidated one-car garage attached. Both the house and the barn were in need of a fresh coat of paint, and I noticed sunlight slanting through the barn roof where it was pierced with holes. Metal lawn chairs were arranged in a semicircle in the yard under a massive live oak tree. A weathered picnic table flanked with benches was set up close by where I pictured Sunday school classes and church suppers during the summer months.

I followed Guy across the yard. We went up the back steps and into the kitchen. The air was scented with sautéed onions and celery. Peter was a man in his sixties, balding, with a wreath of white hair that grew down into sideburns and wrapped around his jaw in a closely trimmed beard linked to a matching mustache. Pale sunlight coming through the window illuminated a feathery white fuzz across his pate. He wore a red turtleneck with a ribbed green sweater over it. He was just in the process of rolling out biscuit dough. The baking sheets to his right were lined with rows of perfect disks of dough ready for the oven. He looked up with pleasure as the two of us came in. "Oh, Guy. Good, it's you. I was just wondering if you were here yet. The furnace over at the church has been acting up again. First it clicks on, then it clicks off. On then off."

"Probably the electronic ignition. I'll take a look." Guy's posture was self-conscious. He rubbed his nose and then stuck his hands in his overall pockets as if to warm them. "This is Kinsey Millhone. She's a private detective from Santa Teresa." He turned and looked at me, tilting his head at the minister and his wife as he made the introductions. "This is Peter Antle and his wife, Winnie."

Peter's complexion was ruddy. His blue eyes smiled out at me from under ragged white brows. "Nice to meet you. I'd offer to shake hands, but I don't think you'd like it. How are you at homemade biscuits? Can I put you to work?"

"Better not," I said. "My domestic skills leave something to be desired."

He was on the verge of pursuing the point when his wife said, "Now, Pete . . ." and gave him a look. Winnie Antle appeared to be in her late forties with short brown hair combed away from her face. She was brown-eyed, slightly heavy, with a wide smile and very white teeth. She wore a man's shirt over jeans with a long knit vest that covered her wide hips and ample derriere. She was chopping vegetables for soup, a mountain of carrot coins piled up on the counter next to her. I could see two bunches of celery and assorted bell peppers awaiting her flashing knife. She was simultaneously tending a stockpot filled with vegetable cuttings boiling merrily. "Hello, Kinsey. Don't mind him. He's always trying to pass the work off onto the unsuspecting," she said, sending me a quick smile. "What brings you up this way?"

Peter looked at Guy. "You're not in trouble, I hope. You have to watch this man." His smile was teasing and it was clear he had no real expectation of trouble where Guy was concerned.

Guy murmured the explanation, apparently embarrassed to be the recipient of such bad news. "My father died. Probate attorney asked her to track me down."

Peter and Winnie both turned their full attention on Guy, whose earlier emotions were well under control. Peter said, "Is that the truth. Well, I'm sorry to hear that." He glanced over at me. "We've often talked about his trying for a reconciliation. It's been years since he had any contact with his dad."

Guy shifted his weight, leaning against the counter with his arms crossed in front of him. He seemed to be directing his comments at me, his tone wistful. "I don't know how many letters I wrote, but none of them got sent. Every time I tried to explain, it just came out sounding . . . you know, wrong, or dumb. I finally let it be till I could work out what it was I wanted to say. I kept thinking I had time. Mean, he wasn't old, by any stretch."

"It must have been his time. You can't argue with that," Peter said.

Winnie spoke up. "If you don't feel like work today, you go ahead and take off. We can manage just fine."

"I'm all right," Guy responded, again with discomfort at being the center of attention.

We spent a few minutes going through an exchange of information; how I'd managed to locate Guy and what I knew of his family, which wasn't much.

Peter was shaking his head, clearly regretful at the news I was bringing. "We think of Guy as one of our own. First time I ever saw this boy, he's a sorry sight. His eyeballs were bright red, sort of rolling around in his head like hot marbles. Winnie and me, we'd been called to this church and we'd driven all the way out to California from Fort Scott, Kansas. We'd heard all sorts of things about hippies and potheads and acid freaks, I think they called 'em. Kids with their eyes burned out from staring at the sun completely stoned. And there stood Guy by the side of the road with a sign that said 'San Francisco.' He was trying to be 'cool,' but he just looked pitiful to me. Winnie didn't want me to stop. We had the two kids in the backseat and she thought sure we'd be turned into homicide statistics."

"It's been a lot of years since then," Winnie said.

Pete looked over at Guy. "What are you thinking to do now, Guy, go back to Santa Teresa? This might be time to sit down with your brothers and talk about the past, maybe clean up some old business."

"I don't know. I suppose. If they're willing to sit down with me," Guy said. "I guess I'm not quite ready to make a decision about that." He glanced at me. "I know they didn't send you up here begging me to come back, but it seems like I might have *some* say in the matter. Would it be all right if I called you in a day or two?"

"No problem. In the meantime, I need to head home," I said. "You've got my card. If I'm not in the office, try that second number and the call will be forwarded automatically." I took out a second business card and jotted down Tasha Howard's name. "This is the attorney. I don't remember her phone number offhand. She has an office in Lompoc. You can call directory assistance and get the information from them. She's not that far away. If nothing else, you might make an appointment to have a chat with her. You'll need advice from an attorney of your own. I hope everything works out."

"I do, too. I appreciate the fact you made the trip," Guy said. "It's a lot more personal."

I shook hands with him, uttered polite noises in the direction of Peter and Winnie Antle, and made my getaway. I cruised down the main street of Marcella again, trying to get a feel for the place. Small and quiet. Unpretentious. I circled the block, driving along the few residential streets. The houses were small, built from identical plans, one-story stucco structures with flat rooflines. The exteriors were painted in pastel shades, pale Easter egg colors nestled in winter grass as dry as paper shreds. Most of the houses seemed shabby and dispirited. I saw only an occasional occupant.

As I swung past the general store, heading out to the main road, I spotted a sign in the window advertising fresh sandwiches. On an impulse, I parked the car and went in and ordered a tuna salad on rye from the woman at the deli counter in the rear. We chatted idly while she busied herself with the sandwich preparations, wrapping my dill pickle in a square of waxed paper so it wouldn't make the bread all mushy, she said. Behind me, two or three other customers went about their business, guiding small grocery carts up and down the aisles. No one turned to stare at me or paid me the slightest attention.

I let her know I'd just been over at the church. She exhibited little curiosity about who I was or why I was visiting the pastor and his wife. Mention of Guy Malek produced no uneasy silences nor any unsolicited confidences about his past history or his character.

"This seems like a nice town," I said as she passed my lunch across the counter. I handed her a ten, which she rang into the cash register.

"If you like this kind of place," she remarked. "Too quiet for my taste, but my husband was born here and insisted we come back. I like to kick up my heels, but about the best we can manage is a rummage sale now and then. Whooee." She fanned herself comically as if the excitement of used clothing was almost more than she could bear. "You want a receipt?" she said, counting out seven ones and change.

"I'd appreciate it."

She tore off the register receipt and handed it to me. "You take care of yourself."

"Thanks. You, too," I said.

I ate while I drove, steering with one hand as I alternated bites of dill pickle and tuna sandwich. The price had included a bag of potato chips, and I munched on those, too, figuring I'd cover all the necessary food groups. I'd forgotten to ask Guy his mother's maiden name, but the truth was, I had no doubt he was who he said he was. He reminded me of Jack, whose coloring and features were quite similar. Donovan and Bennet must have favored one parent while Guy and Jack looked more like the other. As cynical as I was, I found myself taking at face value both the reformation of Guy Malek and his current association with Jubilee Evangelical. It was always possible, I supposed, that he and the minister were singularly crafty frauds, who'd cooked up a cover story for any stranger who came calling, but for the life of me I didn't see it and I didn't believe anything sinister was afoot. If bucolic Marcella was the headquarters for some cult of neo-Nazis, Satanists, or motorcycle outlaws, it had sure escaped my notice.

It was not until I had passed Santa Maria, heading south on 101, that I realized Guy Malek had never asked how much his share of the estate would be. I probably should have volunteered the information. I could have at least given him a ballpark figure, but the question had never come up and I'd been too busy trying to evaluate his status for my report to Donovan. His emotional focus was on his father's death and the loss of his opportunity to make amends. Any profit was apparently beside the point as far as he was concerned. Oh, well. I figured Tasha would be in touch with him and she could give him the particulars.

I arrived in Santa Teresa without incident at two P.M. Since I was home earlier than I'd thought, I went into the office, typed up my notes, and stuck them in the file. I left two phone messages, one for Tasha at her office and one on the Maleks' home machine. I calculated my hours, the mileage, and miscellaneous expenses, and typed an invoice for my services to which I affixed the receipt for the tuna

sandwich. Tomorrow, I'd include it with the typed report of my findings, send a copy to Tasha and one to Donovan. End of story, I
thought.

I retrieved my car, unticketed, from an illegal space and drove
home, feeling generally satisfied with life. Dietz fixed supper that
night, a skilletful of fried onions, fried potatoes, and fried sausages
with liberal doses of garlic and red pepper flakes, all served with a
side of drab, grainy mustard that set your tongue aflame. Only two
confirmed single people could eat a meal like that and imagine it was
somehow nutritious. I handled the cleanup process, washing plates,
flatware, and glasses, scrubbing out the frying pan while Dietz read
the evening paper. Is this what couples did any given night of the
week? In my twice-married life, it was the drama and grief I remembered most clearly, not the day-to-day stuff. This was entirely too
domestic . . . not unpleasant, but certainly unsettling to someone
unaccustomed to company.

At eight, we walked up to Rosie's and settled into a back booth
together. Rosie's restaurant is poorly lighted, a tacky neighborhood
establishment that's been there for twenty-five years, sandwiched
between a Laundromat and an appliance repair shop. The chrome-
and-Formica tables are of thrift-shop vintage and the booths lining
the walls are made of construction-grade plywood, stained dark, complete with crude hand-gouged messages and splinters. It's an act of
reckless abandon to slide across the seats unless your tetanus shots
are current. Over the years, the number of California smokers has
steadily diminished, so the air quality has improved while the clientele has not. Rosie's used to be a refuge for local drinkers who liked
to start early in the day and stay until closing time. Now the tavern
has become popular with assorted amateur sports teams, who descend en masse after every big game, filling the air with loud talk,
raucous laughter, and much stomping about. The regulars, all four
bleary-eyed imbibers, have been driven to other places. I rather
missed their slurred conversation, which was never intrusive.

Rosie was apparently gone for the night and the bartender was someone I'd never seen before. Dietz drank a couple of beers while I had a couple of glasses of Rosie's best screw-top Chardonnay, a puckering rendition of a California varietal she probably bought by the keg.

I freely confess it was the alcohol that got me into trouble that night. I was feeling mellow and relaxed, somewhat less inhibited than usual, which is to say, ready to flap my mouth. Robert Dietz was beginning to look good to me, and I wasn't really sure how I felt about that. His face was chiseled in shadow and his gaze crossed the room in restless assessment while we chatted about nothing in particular. Idly, I told him about William and Rosie's wedding and my adventures on the road, and he filled in details about his stay in Germany. Along with the attraction, I experienced a low-grade sorrow, so like a fever that I wondered if I were coming down with the flu. At one point, I shivered and he looked over at me. "You okay?" he asked.

I stretched my hand out on the table and he covered it with his, lacing his fingers through mine. "What are we doing?" I asked.

"Good question. Why don't we talk about that? You go first."

I laughed, but the issue wasn't really funny and we both knew it. "Why'd you have to come back and stir things up? I was doing fine."

"What have I stirred up? We haven't done anything. We eat dinner. We have drinks. I sleep down. You sleep up. My knee's so bad, you're in no danger of unwanted advances. I couldn't make it up those stairs if my life depended on it."

"Is that the good news or the bad?"

"I don't know. You tell me," he said.

"I don't want to get used to you."

"A lot of women can't get used to me. You're one of the few who seems remotely interested," he said, smiling slightly.

Here's a word to the wise: In the midst of a tender discussion with one woman, don't mention another one—especially in the plural. It's bad policy. The minute he said it, I had this sudden vision of a long line of females with me standing not even close to the front of the pack. I could feel my smile fade and I retreated into silence like a turtle encountering a dog.

His look became cautious. "What's wrong?"

"Nothing. I'm fine. What makes you think there's anything wrong?"

"Let's don't talk at cross-purposes," he said. "You obviously have something to say, so why don't you say it?"

"I don't want to. It doesn't matter."

"Kinsey."

"What."

"Come on. Just say it. There's no penalty for being honest."

"I don't know how to say it. You're here for four days and what am I supposed to do with that? I'm not good at being left. It's the story of my life. Why get enmeshed when all it means is I get to have my heart ripped out?"

He lifted his eyebrows, shrugging with his face. "I don't know what to tell you. I can't promise to stay. I've never stayed in one place for more than six months max. Why can't we live in the present? Why does everything have to have a guarantee attached?"

"I'm not talking about guarantees."

"I think you are," he said. "You want a lien against the future, when the fact is you don't know any more than I do about what's coming next."

"Well, that's true and I'm not arguing that. All I'm saying is I don't want to get involved in an on-again-off-again relationship, which is what this is."

Dietz's expression was pained. "I won't lie. I can't pretend I'll stay when I know I won't. What good would that do?"

I could feel my frustration rise. "I don't want you to pretend and I'm not asking you to promise. I'm just trying to be honest."

"About what?"

"About everything. People have rejected me all my life. Sometimes it's death or desertion. Infidelity, betrayal. You name it. I've experienced every form of emotional treachery there is. Well, big

deal. Everybody's suffered something in life and so what? I'm not
sitting around feeling sorry for myself, but I'd have to be a fool to lay
myself open to that shit again."

"I understand that. I hear you and believe me, I don't want to be
the one to cause you pain. This is not about you. It's about me. I'm
restless by nature. I hate to feel trapped. That's how I am. Pen me in
and I'll tear the place apart trying to get out," he said. "My people
were nomads. We were always on the move. Always on the road. We
lived out of suitcases. To me, being in one spot is oppressive. You
want to talk about death. It's the worst. When I was growing up, if we
stayed in one town for long, my old man would get busted. He'd end
up in county jail or in the hospital or the local drunk tank. Any
school I attended, I was always the new kid and I'd have to fight my
way across the school yard just to stay alive. The happiest day of my
life was the day we hit the road again."

"Free at last," I interjected.

"That's right. It's not that I might not want to stay. It's that I'm
incapable of it."

"Oh, right. 'Incapable.' Well, that explains it. You're excused," I
said.

"Don't be so touchy. You know what I mean. God almighty, I'm not
proud of myself. I don't relish the fact that I'm a rolling stone. I just
don't want to kid myself and I don't want to kid you."

"Thank you. That's great. In the meantime, I'm sure you have ways
of amusing yourself."

He squinted. "Where did that come from?"

"This is hopeless," I said. "I don't know why we even bother with
this. You're addicted to wandering and I'm rooted in place. You can't
stay and I can't leave because I love where I am. This is your bien-
nial interlude and I'm here for the duration, which means I'm probably doomed to a lifetime of guys like you."

" 'Guys like *me?*' That's nice. What does that mean?"

"Just what it says. Emotionally claustrophobic. You're a basket
case. So as long as I'm attracted to guys like you, I can bypass my

own—" I stopped short, feeling like one of those cartoon dogs, skidding on a cartoon floor.

"Your own what?"

"None of your business," I said. "Let's drop the conversation. I should have kept my mouth shut. I end up sounding like a whiner, which is not what I intend."

"You're always so worried about sounding like a whiner," he said. "Who cares if you whine? Be my guest."

"Oh, *now* you say that."

"Say what?" he said, exasperated.

I assumed an attitude of patience that I scarcely felt. "One of the first things you ever said to me was that you wanted—how did you phrase it—'obedience without whining.' You said very few women ever mastered that."

"*I* said that?"

"Yes, you did. I've tried very hard ever since not to whine in your presence."

"Don't be ridiculous. I didn't mean it that way," he said. "I don't even remember saying it, but I was probably talking about something else. Anyway, don't change the subject. I don't want to leave it on this note. As long as the issue's on the table, let's get it settled."

"What's to settle? We can't settle anything. There's no way to resolve it, so let's drop the whole business. I'm sorry I brought it up. I've already got this ongoing family nonsense. Maybe I'm upset about that."

"What nonsense? You're related to these people, so what's the problem?"

"I don't want to get into it. Aside from whining, I hate to feel like I'm repeating myself."

"How can you repeat yourself when you never told me to begin with?"

I ran a hand through my hair and stared down at the tabletop. I'd been hoping to avoid the subject, but the topic did seem safer than discussing our relationship, whatever that consisted of. I couldn't come up with any rational defense of my reluctance to engage with this newfound family of mine. I just didn't want to do it. Finally, I said, "I guess I don't like to be pressured. They're so busy trying to make up for lost time. Why can't they just mind their own business? I'm not comfortable with all this buddy-buddy stuff. You know how stubborn I get when I'm pushed."

"Why did you agree to work for that attorney then? Isn't she your cousin?"

"Well, yes, but I didn't *intend* to agree. I intended to turn her down, but then greed and curiosity got the better of me. I have a living to earn and I didn't want to refuse out of perversity. I know I'll regret it, but I'm into it now so there's no sense beating myself up."

"Sounds harmless enough on the face of it."

"It's not harmless. It's annoying. And besides, that isn't the point. The point is, I'd like for them to respect my boundaries."

"What boundaries? She hired you to do a job. As long as you get paid, that's the end of it."

"Let's hope. Besides, it's not her so much as the other two. Liza and Pam. If I give an inch, they'll invade my space."

"Oh, bullshit. That's California psychobabble. You can't live your life like a radio talk show."

"What do you know? I don't notice you all cozied up to your family."

I could see him flinch. His expression shifted abruptly to one of injury and irritation. "Low blow. What I say about my kids, I don't want you throwing back in my face."

"You're right. I'm sorry. I withdraw the remark."

"Withdraw the knife and the wound's still there," he snapped. "What's the matter with you? You're so bristly these days. You're doing everything you can to keep me at arm's length."

"I am not," I said, and then I stared at him, squinting. "Is that true?"

"Well, look at your behavior. I haven't even been here two days and we're already fighting. What's that about? I didn't travel all this way to pick a fight with you. I wanted to see you. I was excited we'd have time together. Hell. If I'd wanted to fight, I could have stayed with Naomi."

"Why didn't you? I don't mean the question in a mean-hearted way, but I'm curious. What happened?"

"Oh, who knows? I have my version, she has hers. Sometimes I think relationships have a natural lifespan. Ours ran out. That's all it was. The explanations come afterwards when you try to make sense of it. Let's get back to you. What's going on in your head?"

"I'd rather fight than feel nothing."

"Those are your only two options?"

"That's what it feels like, but I couldn't say for sure."

He reached out and gave my hair a tug. "What am I going to do with you?"

"What am I going to do with *you?*" I replied.

7

When we returned to the apartment at ten-fifteen, Henry's kitchen light was on. Dietz said his knee was killing him, so he let himself into the apartment where he intended to take a couple of pain pills, prop his feet up, and put his ice pack to work. I said I'd be along momentarily. Our conversation at Rosie's hadn't really gone anywhere. I couldn't bear to continue and I couldn't bear behaving as though the subject hadn't been broached. I didn't know what I wanted from him and I wasn't sure how to say it anyway, so I just ended up sounding needy. My general policy is this: If your mind isn't open, keep your mouth shut, too.

I knocked on Henry's backdoor, waving at him through the window when he looked up at me. He was sitting in his rocking chair with the evening paper and his glass of Jack Daniel's. He smiled and waved back, setting the paper aside so he could let me in. He had the heat turned up and the inside air was not only warm, but deliciously scented with yesterday's cinnamon rolls.

"This feels great. It's really cold out there," I said. The kitchen table was covered with old black-and-white photographs sorted into piles. I glanced at them briefly as I pulled out a kitchen chair and turned my attention to him. From my point of view, Henry Pitts is perfection—smart, good-natured, and responsible—with the cutest legs I've ever seen. He's been my landlord for five years, since the day I spotted the ad for the apartment in a Laundromat. Henry was looking for a long-term tenant who was clean and quiet; no children, loud parties, or small, yapping dogs. As a lifelong mobile-home inhabitant, I was addicted to compact spaces, but ready to limit contact with a lot of close, unruly neighbors. Trailer-park life, for all its virtues, entails an intimate acquaintance with other people's private business. Since I make a living as a snoop, I'd just as soon keep my personal affairs to myself. The converted single-car garage Henry was offering was better than my fantasies and affordable as well. Since then, the place had been bombed and rebuilt, the interior fitted out in teak and as cleverly designed as a ship's.

From the outset, Henry and I established just enough of a relationship to suit us both. Over the years, he's managed to civilize me to some extent and I'm certainly more agreeable now than I was back then. Little by little, we forged the bond between us until now I consider him the exemplary mix of friend and generic family member.

"You want a cup of tea?" he asked.

"No, thanks. I just stopped to say hi before I hit the sack. Are these family pictures?" I asked, picking one at random.

"That's the claim," he said. "Nell sent me those. She came across two boxes of old family photographs, but none are labeled. No names, no dates. She hasn't any idea who these people are and neither do the other sibs. What a mess. Take my word for it. You should mark all your photographs, even if it's just a quick note on the back. You might know who's who, but nobody else will."

"Do they look familiar to you?"

"A few." He took the print I was looking at and squinted as he held it to the light. I peered over his shoulder. The woman in the picture must have been in her twenties, with a broad, bland face and hair drawn back in a bun. She wore a white middy blouse, with a calf-length skirt, dark stockings, and flat, dark shoes with a bow across the instep. Standing beside her was a glum-faced girl of eight with a drop-waist sailor dress and ankle-high lace-up shoes. "I believe this is a picture of my mother's younger sister, Augusta, taken in Topeka, Kansas, back in 1915. The child's name was Rebecca Rose, if memory serves. She and her mother both died in the big influenza epidemic of 1918." He picked up another one. "This is my mother with my grandfather Tilmann. I'm surprised Nell didn't recognize them except her eyesight's fading. Now that I think of it, I'm not sure why it matters. None of us have children, so once we're gone, it won't make any difference who these people are."

"Well, that seems sad. Why don't you put 'em in an album and pass them on to me? I'll pretend they're mine. What was his first name?"

"Klaus. My mother's name was Gudrun." The man staring fixedly at the camera must have been in his late seventies, the daughter beside him in her fifties by the look of her. I said, "What's the name Tilmann. Is that German? I somehow imagined you were all Swedes or Finns."

"Oh no, we're not Scandinavian. They're gloomy sorts, in my opinion. The Tilmanns were good German stock. Headstrong, autocratic, vigorous, and exacting. Some would say impossible, but that's a matter of interpretation. Longevity is genetic and don't ever let anybody tell you otherwise. I read those articles about folks who live to be a hundred. They all try to take credit, claim it's because they smoke or don't smoke, eat yogurt, take vitamins, or a tablespoon of vinegar a day. What nonsense. War and accidents excepted, you live a long time because you come from other people who live a long time. You have to take responsibility. You can't subject yourself to any kind of gross mistreatment. My mother lived to be a hundred and three and I imagine the remaining five of us will live that long as well."

"You certainly seem to be in good shape. Nell's what, ninety-six? And you have your eighty-sixth birthday coming up on Valentine's Day."

Henry nodded, making a motion as if to knock on wood. "We're healthy, in the main, though we're all shrinking down to some extent. We've talked about this and it's our contention that the shrinkage is nature's way of assuring you don't take up so much space in your coffin. You lighten up, too. Feels like taking air into your bones. Makes it easy on the pallbearers. And, of course, your faculties shut down. You get blind as a bat and your hearing fades. Charlie says it sounds like he's got a pillow on his head all the time these days. Get old, you might as well not worry about your dignity. Anybody talks about dignity for old folks has never been around one as far as I can tell. You can keep your spunk, but you have to give up your vanity early on. We're all in diapers. Well, I'm not, but then I'm the baby in the family. The rest of them leak any time they cough or laugh too hard.

"Nell says one reason she misses William so much now he's moved out here is because they can't play bridge like they used to. Have to play three-handed, which isn't as much fun. Lewis was thinking about asking a cousin to move in, but Nell won't tolerate another woman in the house. She says she's had her brothers to herself now for sixty years and she's not about to change. Nell says once she 'goes' they can do anything they want, depending on whose left."

"I can't believe they're still willing to endure the winters in Michigan. Why don't they all move out here? You could play all the bridge you want."

"There's talk of that. We'll just have to see. Nell has her ladies' luncheon group and she hates to leave them." Henry put the photo down and took his seat again. "Now then, how are you? I had a nice chat with your friend Dietz. He says you picked up some work."

"Actually, I finished it. One of those quickies you remember fondly when the tough ones come along," I said. I took a few minutes to fill him in on the search for Guy Malek.

Henry shook his head. "What's going to happen? Do you think he'll get his share of the estate?"

"Who knows? I don't always hear the end of it, but Tasha thinks they'll be able to work something out."

"How long will Dietz be here? I thought I'd have the two of you over for supper one night."

"Probably not long. He's on his way up to Santa Cruz to see his sons," I said.

"Well, let me know if he's still going to be here Saturday and I'll cook something special. We'll invite William and Rosie and Moza Lowenstein, if she's free."

By the time I let myself into my place, Dietz had fallen asleep in his underwear, slouched down in his chair, snoring lightly. The television set was on, the volume low, the channel tuned to a nature show about underwater shark attacks. Dietz had his leg propped up on the edge of the sofa bed, a blanket pulled up across his chest and shoulders. The partially melted ice pack had toppled to the floor. I put that ice pack in the freezer and took out a second one, laying it carefully across his knee without waking him. His kneecap was swollen, the bare flesh looking pale and vulnerable. I left him as he was, knowing he'd wake long before morning. He sleeps in fits and starts like an animal in the wild, and I knew from past experience he seldom manages to make it through the night without getting up at least twice.

I eased off my shoes and made my way up the spiral stairs. From above, I stared down at him. His lined face looked alien in sleep, as if sculptured in clay. I seldom saw him at ease. He was restless by nature, perpetually in motion, his features animated by the sheer force of his nervous energy. Even as I watched, he stirred himself awake, jerking upright with a look of disorientation. I could see him wince, reaching for the ice pack balanced on his distended joint. I stepped away from the loft rail and went into the bathroom, where I washed my face and brushed my teeth. It was no doubt the proximity to all that testosterone, but I could feel the murmur of sexuality at the base of my spine. I grabbed an oversized T-shirt from a hook on the bathroom door. I usually sleep in the nude, but it seemed like a bad idea.

Once ready for bed, I turned out the light and slipped under the quilt. I reached out and set my alarm, watching the digital clock flip from 11:04 to 11:05. Below, I could hear Dietz get up and move into the kitchen. The refrigerator door opened and closed. He took down a glass and poured himself a drink—wine, orange juice, or milk— something liquid at any rate. I heard him pull out a kitchen stool, followed by the rustle of newspaper. I wondered what he was thinking, wondered what would happen if I heard him climbing the stairs. Maybe I should have pulled on a robe and gone down to join him, thrown caution to the wind and to hell with the consequences, but it was not in my nature. Being single for so long had made me cautious about men. I stared up at the Plexiglas skylight above my bed, thinking about the risks involved in reaching out to him. Passion never lasts, but then what does? If you could have it all, but only briefly, would the rush of love be worth the price in pain? I could feel myself sinking into sleep as though weighted down with stones. I didn't rise again until 5:59 A.M.

I pulled on my sweats, preparing for my run as usual. Dietz was in the shower when I left the house, but I noticed with a pang he was in the process of packing. He'd laid the soft-sided suitcase open on the floor near the sofa bed, which he'd folded away. The blanket had been refolded and placed across one end. He'd piled the sheets he'd used near the washer. Maybe he felt his exodus would address my issues with him, minimizing the chances of my forming an attachment. What I noticed, perversely, was that, having felt nothing on his arrival, I was now afflicted with a stinging sense of loss at his departure. He'd been with me for two days and I was already suffering, so maybe I'd been smart not to take things any further. I'd been celibate for so long, what was another year without sex? I made an involuntary sound that might have been a whimper if I allowed myself such things.

I closed the door quietly behind me, breathing deeply as though the damp morning air might ease the fire in my chest. Having passed through the front gate, I paused while I stretched, keeping my mind a blank. In the last several years as a private investigator, I've developed a neat trick for shutting off my feelings. Like others who work in the "helping" professions—doctors and nurses, police officers, social workers, paramedics—emotional disconnection is sometimes the only way to function in the face of death with all its tacky variations. Originally, my detachment took several minutes of concentrated effort, but now I make the shift in the blink of an eye. Mental-health enthusiasts are quick to assure us that our psychological well-being is best served by staying in touch with our feelings, but *surely* they're not referring to the icky, unpleasant ones.

The run itself was unsatisfactory. The dawn was overcast, the sky a brooding gray unrelieved by any visible sunrise. Gradually, daylight overtook the lowering dark, but the whole of it had the bleached look of an old black-and-white photograph. My gait felt choppy and I never really hit my stride. The air was so chilly I couldn't even generate a decent sweat. I dutifully counted off the miles, feeling gratified to be doing it in spite of myself. Some days the discipline is an end in itself, a way of asserting the will in the face of life's little setbacks. I walked the half block home, carefully brushing aside any slovenly sentiment.

Dietz was sitting at the counter when I got in. He'd put on a pot of coffee and set out my cereal bowl. His bowl was already washed, rinsed, and drying in the dish rack. His suitcase, fully zipped, was waiting by the door along with his garment bag. Through the open bathroom door, I could see he'd tidied the basin of all his personal possessions. The scent of soap mingled with his aftershave, a damp male perfume permeating everything.

"I thought it might be easier if I took off," he said.

"Sure, no problem. I hope you're not doing it on my account."

"No, no. You know me. I'm not that good at staying put," he said. "Anyway, you probably have a lot of work to do."

"Oh, tons," I said. "You're heading up to Santa Cruz?"

"Eventually, yes. I'll drive on up the coast, maybe spend a day in Cambria. With this knee, I have to break up the trip, anyway. You know, get out and stretch every hour or so. Keep it warm and loose. Otherwise, it locks up."

"What time are you taking off?"

"Whenever you leave for work."

"Well, great. I'll just grab a shower then and you can hit the road."

"Take your time. I'm in no hurry," he said.

"I can see that," I remarked, as I headed up to the loft. This time he didn't ask if I was mad. This was good because, in truth, I was furious. Under the fury was the old familiar pain. Why does everyone end up leaving me? What did I ever do to them? I went through my morning routine as efficiently as possible, flung on my clothes, and ate my cereal without pausing to read the paper. To demonstrate my indifference to his abrupt departure, I took out fresh sheets and asked him to help me remake the sofa bed. I hoped the implication was that some other guy was lined up for bed space as soon as he left. Neither of us said much and what we said was transactional. "Where's the other pillowcase?" About like that.

Once the sofa was redone, he took his suitcase to the car and came back for the garment bag. I walked him out to the curb and we exchanged one of those insincere kisses with the sound effects attached. *Mmch!* He fired up his Porsche and I dutifully waved as he roared off down the street. You little shit, I thought.

I went into the office, ignoring a faint tendency to tear up for no reason. The day yawned in front of me like a sinkhole in the street. This was just what it felt like when he left before. Now how does this happen to someone of my rare spunk and independence? I played a few rounds of solitaire, paid some bills, and balanced my checkbook. Anxiety whispered in my gut like a stomachache. When the phone finally rang just before lunch, I snatched up the receiver, absurdly grateful at the interruption.

"Kinsey. This is Donovan. How are you?"

"Gee, I'm just fine. How are you?"

"Well enough. Uh, listen, we got your message and we'd like to compliment you on a job well done. Tasha had to fly back to San Francisco this morning, but she said she didn't think you'd mind giving us the information firsthand. Could you stop by the house for a drink late this afternoon?"

"Well, sure. I could do that. I was going to type up my report and put it in the mail, but I can give you a rundown in person if you'd prefer."

"I'd appreciate that. I expect Jack and Bennet will want to be there as well. That way, if they have questions, you can fill us all in at the same time and save yourself the repetition. Would five-thirty be convenient?"

"Fine with me," I said.

"Good. We'll look forward to seeing you."

After I hung up, I could feel myself shrug. I had nothing against an informal report as long as I didn't somehow get sucked into the family drama. Aside from Guy, I wasn't crazy about the Malek brothers. I happened to believe Guy had changed his wicked ways, so maybe I could do him a service and convince the others. Not that it was any of my business how the monies were distributed, but if there were any lingering questions about his "worthiness," I certainly had an opinion. Besides, with Dietz now gone, I didn't have anything better to do.

I skipped lunch and spent the afternoon cleaning my office. Lonnie Kingman had a maintenance crew that serviced the premises weekly on Friday afternoons, but it felt therapeutic to get in there and scrub. I even spent twenty minutes dusting the artificial ficus plant someone had once mistaken for real. The space I occupied had originally been a conference room with a full "executive" bathroom attached. I found a plastic bucket, sponges, cleansers, a toilet brush, and mop and entertained myself mightily killing imaginary germs. My method of coping with depression is to take on chores so obnoxious and disgusting that reality seems pleasant by comparison. By three o'clock, I smelled of sweat and household bleach and I'd forgotten what I was so unhappy about. Well, actually, I remembered, but I didn't give a shit.

Having sanitized the suite, I locked the door, stripped off my clothes, hopped in the executive shower, and scrubbed myself. I dressed again in the same jeans, pulling on a fresh turtleneck from the ready supply I keep handy for sudden travel. What's life without a toothbrush and clean underpants? I typed up the official version of my encounter with Guy Malek, tucking one copy in my office files, another in my handbag. The third I addressed to Tasha Howard at her San Francisco office. The end. Finito. Done, done, done. This was the last job I'd ever take from her.

By 5:25, dressed in my best (and only) wool tweed blazer, I drove through the entrance to the Malek estate. It was close to dark by then, the winter-shortened days still characterized by early twilights. My headlights swept in a forlorn arc across the stucco wall surrounding the fifteen-acre property. Along the rim of the wall, three strands of rusted barbed wire had been strung years ago, broken now in places and looking singularly ineffective. Who knows what intruders were anticipated back then? A chilly wind had picked up and the darkened treetops swayed and shivered, whispering together about things unseen. There were lights on in the house, two upstairs windows illuminated in pale yellow where much of the first floor was dark.

The housekeeper had neglected to turn on the outside lights. I parked in the turnaround and picked my way across the cobblestone courtyard to the shadowy portico that sheltered the entranceway in front. I rang the bell and waited, crossing my arms for warmth. The porch light was finally flipped on and Myrna opened the door a crack.

"Hi, Myrna. Kinsey Millhone. I was here the other day. Donovan invited me for drinks."

Myrna didn't exactly break into song at the news. Apparently, advanced classes in Housekeeper's Training School cautioned the students not to give expression to sudden bursts of joy. In the two days since I'd seen her last, she'd renewed the dye job in her hair and the whole of it was now a white blond that looked like it would be cold to the touch. Her uniform consisted of a gray top worn over matching gray pants. I would have bet money the waistband was unbuttoned underneath the tunic. "This way," she said. Her crepe-soled shoes squeaked slightly on the polished parquet floor.

A woman called down from somewhere above our heads. "Myrna? Was that the front door? We're expecting someone for drinks." I glanced up, following the sound of her voice. A brunette in her late thirties was leaning on the stair rail above our heads. She caught sight of me and brightened. "Oh, hi. You must be Kinsey. You want to come on up?"

Myrna veered off without another word, disappearing into the rear of the house as I climbed the stairs.

Christie held out her hand when I reached the upper landing. "I'm Christie Malek. Nice to meet you," she said as we shook hands. "I take it you've met Myrna."

"More or less," I said. I took her in at a glance, like an instant Polaroid. She was a fine-featured brunette with shiny dark hair, worn shoulder length. She was very slender, wearing jeans and a bulky black-ribbed sweater that came down almost to her knees. She had the sleeves rolled back and her wrists were thin, her fingers long and cool. Her eyes were small, a dark penetrating blue, beneath a lightly feathered brow. Her teeth were as perfect as a mouthwash ad's. The absence of eye makeup gave her a recessive, slightly anxious air, though her manner was friendly and her smile was warm enough. "Donovan called to say he'd be a few minutes late. Jack's on his way home and Bennet's around some place. I'm just going through Bader's papers and I'd love some company."

Still talking to me, she turned and moved toward the master bed-room, which I could see through an open doorway. "We're still looking for the missing will, among other things. Ever hopeful," she added wryly.

"I thought Bennet was going to do that."

"This is how Bennet does things. He loves to delegate."

I hoped there was a touch of irony in her tone. I couldn't be sure so I kept my mouth shut.

The suite we entered was enormous; two substantial rooms separated by a pair of doors that had been pushed into their respective wall pockets. We passed through the outer room, which had been furnished as a bedroom. The walls were padded fabric, covered in rose-colored silk with a watered sheen to the finish. The carpet was off-white, a dense, cut pile. Pale, heavy drapes had been pulled back to reveal the leaded glass windows that looked out onto the cobblestone entrance at the front of the house. There was a marble fireplace on the wall to the left. Two matching sofas were arranged on either side of it, plump, upholstered pieces covered in a subdued floral chintz. The four-poster bed had been flawlessly made, not a ripple or a wrinkle in the snowy-white silk coverlet. The surface of the bed table seemed unnaturally bare, as if once-personal items had now been hidden from sight. It might have been my imagination, but the room seemed to harbor the lingering scent of sickness. I could see that closets were being emptied, the contents—suits and dress shirts—packed into large cardboard boxes supplied by the local Thrift Store Industries downtown.

"This is gorgeous," I said.

"Isn't it?"

Beyond the sliding doors, a home office had been set up, with a large walnut desk and antique wooden file cabinets. The ceilings in both rooms were twelve feet high, but this was by far the cozier of the two. A fire had been laid in a second marble fireplace and Christie paused to add a log to an already snapping blaze. The walls here were paneled in walnut as dark and glossy as fudge. I could see a copier, a fax machine, computer, and a printer arranged on the built-in shelves on either side of the fireplace. A paper shredder stood on one side of the desk, its green On button lighted. I could see printed acknowledgments stacked up waiting to be addressed to those who'd sent flowers to the funeral.

Christie returned to the desk where she'd emptied the contents of two drawers into banker's boxes that she'd labeled with a black marker. There were two big plastic garbage bags bulging with discarded papers. Thick files were stacked on the desktop and a number of empty file folders were strewn across the carpet. This was the kind of task I knew well, classifying the odds and ends left behind by the dead. Below, in the courtyard, we could hear a motorcycle cruise in, the engine being revved once more before it was silenced.

Christie cocked her head. "I hear the Harley. Sounds like Jack's home."

"How's it going so far?"

Her expression was a wry mix of skepticism and despair. "Bader was supremely organized for the most part, but he must have lost his enthusiasm for jobs like this. Look at all this stuff. I swear, if I'm ever diagnosed as terminal, I'm going to clean out my files before I get too sick to care. What if you kept pornographic pictures or something like that? I'd hate to think of someone sorting through my private affairs."

"Nothing in my life is that interesting," I said. "You want help?"

"Not really, but I could use the moral support," she said. "I've been in here for hours. I have to look at every single piece of paper and figure out if it's worth saving, though most aren't as far as I can tell. I mean, what do I know? Anything I'm not sure about, I put in one pile. The really junky stuff, I go ahead and shove in a garbage bag. I don't dare shred a thing and I'm afraid to toss much. I know Bennet. As sure as I pitch something, he tears in here and wants to know where it is. He's done that to me twice and it was just dumb luck the trash hadn't been picked up. I'm out there in the dark, like a bag lady, pulling crumpled papers out of the garbage can. This third pile is everything that looks important. For instance, here's something you might like." She picked up a file from the stack on top of the desk and handed it to me. "Bader must have put this together back in the early sixties."

A quick glance inside revealed a collection of newspaper clippings related to Guy's past misbehavior. I read one at random, an article dating back to 1956 detailing the arrest of two juveniles, boys ages fourteen and thirteen, who were believed to be responsible for a spree of graffiti vandalism. One of the teens was booked into Juvenile Hall, the other released to his parents. There must have been twenty-five such snippets. In some cases, the authorities withheld the names because the boy or boys arrested were still minors. In other articles, Guy Malek was identified by name.

"I wonder why Bader kept clippings. It seems odd," I said.

"Maybe to remind himself why he disinherited the kid. I figure Bennet will want 'em for ammunition if it comes down to that. It's exhausting just trying to make these decisions."

"Quite a job," I said and then shifted the subject matter. "You know, it occurred to me that since the two wills were drawn up only three years apart, the two witnesses for the first might have been witnesses for the second will, too. Especially if they were paralegals or law clerks working in the attorney's office."

She looked at me with interest. "Good point. You'll have to mention that to Donovan. None of us are anxious to see five million bucks flying out the window."

There was a tap at the door and we both turned to see that Myrna had reappeared. "Donovan's home. He asked me to serve the hors d'oeuvres in the living room."

"Tell him we'll be down in a second, as soon as I wash my hands. Oh, and see if you can round up the other two."

Myrna took in the request, murmured something inaudible, and withdrew from the room.

Christie shook her head, lowering her voice a notch. "She may be on the glum side, but she's the only person in the house who doesn't argue with everyone."

8

Lights were on and Donovan was in the living room when Christie and I came downstairs. He'd changed out of his work clothes, pulling on a heavy cream-colored knit sweater over casual pants. He'd exchanged his dress shoes for a pair of sheepskin slippers that made his feet look huge. A fire had been laid and he was poking at the logs, turning a bulky wedge of oak so that its uppermost side would catch. Donovan picked up another piece of wood and thunked it on top. A shower of sparks flew up the chimney. He replaced the fire screen and wiped his hands on his handkerchief, glancing over at me. "I see you've met Christie. We appreciate your coming over. Keeps it simpler all around. Can I make you a drink? We've got just about anything you'd want."

"A glass of Chardonnay would be fine."

"I'll get it," Christie said promptly. She moved over to a sideboard crowded with liquor bottles. A bottle of Chardonnay had been chilling in a cooler beside a clear Lucite ice bucket and an assortment of glasses. She began to peel the foil from the neck of the wine bottle, with a look at Donovan. "You having wine?"

"Probably with dinner. I think I'll have a martini first. Gin is Bennet's winter drink," he added as an aside to me.

Ah, the seasonal alcoholic. What a nice idea. Gin in the winter, maybe vodka in spring. Summer would be tequila and he could round out the autumn with a little bourbon or scotch. While she opened the wine, I took a momentary survey.

Like the bedroom above, this room was immense. The twelve-foot ceiling was rimmed with ten-inch crown molding, the walls papered in a narrow blue-and-cream stripe that had faded with the years. The pale Oriental carpet had to be seventeen feet wide and probably twenty-five feet long. The furniture had been arranged in two groupings. At the far end of the room, four wing chairs faced one another near the front windows. Closer to the center of the room, three large sofas formed a U in front of the fireplace. All of the side pieces—an armoire, an escritoire, and two carved and inlaid wooden tables— were the sort I'd seen in antique stores, heavy, faintly fussy, with price tags that made you squint because you thought you'd read them wrong.

Christie returned with two glasses of wine and handed one to me. She took a seat on one of the sofas and I sat down across from her with a murmured "thanks." The blue floral pattern was faded to a soft white, the fabric threadbare along the arms and the cushion fronts. There was a large brass bowl filled with fresh flowers and several copies of *Architectural Digest* lined up on the square glass coffee table in the crook of the U. There was also an untidy stack of what looked like condolence cards. While I was thinking about it, I took out my typed report and placed it on the table in front of me. I'd leave it for Donovan so he'd have a copy for his files.

I heard footsteps in the hall and the sound of voices. Jack and Bennet came into the living room together. Whatever they'd been discussing, their expressions were now neutral, conveying nothing but benign interest at the sight of me. Bennet wore a running suit of some silky material that rustled when he walked. Jack looked as if he'd just come in off the golf course, his hair still disheveled from the imprint of his visor. He wore a bright orange sweater vest over a pink short-sleeved golf shirt and his gait tended to a lilt as if he were still wearing cleats. Jack poured himself a scotch and water as dark as iced tea while Bennet made a pitcher of martinis that he stirred with a long glass wand. I made note of his vermouth-to-gin ratio—roughly two parts per million. He poured one for himself and one for Donovan, adding olives to both. He brought the martini pitcher over to the coffee table and set it down within range.

While drinks were being poured, various pleasantries were exchanged, none of them heartfelt. As with tobacco, the rituals of alcohol seemed to be a stalling technique until those assembled could get themselves psychologically situated. I had an odd sensation in my chest, the same itch of anxiety I'd felt before a third-grade dance recital in which I played a bunny, not a specialty of mine. My aunt Gin was ill and unable to attend, so I'd been forced to do my hippy-hopping in front of countless alien adults, who didn't seem to find me winsome. My legs were too skinny and my fake ears wouldn't stand up. The brothers Malek watched me with about the same enthusiasm. Donovan took a seat next to Christie on the couch across from me while Jack sat facing the fireplace with Bennet on his left.

It was interesting to see the three brothers in the same room together. Despite the similarities in their coloring, their faces were very different, Bennet's the more so because of his beard and mustache. Donovan and Jack were built along finer lines though neither was as appealing as their errant brother, Guy. Jack leaned forward and began to sift idly through the sympathy cards.

I thought Donovan was on the verge of asking for my report when Myrna came into the room with assorted edibles on a serving tray. The tray itself was the size of a manhole cover, very plain, probably sterling silver, and distinctly tarnished along the edges. The hors d'oeuvres, in addition to what looked like Cheez Whiz on saltines, consisted of a bowl of peanuts and a bowl of unpitted green olives in brine. No one said a word until she'd departed, closing the door behind her.

Jack leaned forward. "What the fuck is this?"

Bennet laughed at the very moment he was swallowing a mouthful of martini. He made a snorting sound as he choked and I saw gin dribble out his nose. He coughed into his handkerchief while Jack shot a smile in his direction. I bet as children they'd paused in the midst of dinner, opening their mouths to one another to exhibit masticated food.

Christie flashed them a look of disapproval. "It's Enid's night off. Would you quit with the criticism? Myrna's a nurse. She was hired to look after Dad, not to wait on the two of you. We're lucky she stayed on and you bloody well know it. Nobody else lifts a finger around here except me."

"Thanks for setting the record straight, Christie. You're a fuckin' peach," Jack said.

"Knock it off," Donovan said. "Could we hold off on this until we hear from her?" He grabbed a handful of peanuts, eating one at a time as his focus returned to me. "You want to fill us in?"

I took a few minutes to detail the means by which I'd managed to locate Guy Malek. Without mentioning Darcy Pascoe or California Fidelity Insurance, I played out the steps that led to the information on his identification card. I'll admit I stretched it out, making it sound more problematic than it had actually been. "As nearly as I can tell, your brother's cleaned up his act. He's working as the custodian for the Jubilee Evangelical Church. I gather he doubles as a handyman for various people in Marcella. He says he's the only one in town doing home maintenance, so he earns decent money, by his standards. His lifestyle is simple, but he's doing okay."

Donovan said, "Is he married?"

"I didn't ask if he was married, but he didn't seem to be. He never mentioned a wife. His housing's provided by the church in exchange for his services. The place is pretty funky, but he seems to manage all right. I grant you these are superficial judgments, but I didn't really stop to investigate."

Bennet shaved an olive with his teeth and placed the pit on a paper napkin. "Why Marcella? That's a dirt bucket of a place."

"The pastor of this fundamentalist church picked him up hitchhiking out on 101 the day he left home. Essentially, he's been in Marcella ever since. The church he joined seems pretty strict. No dancing, card playing, things like that. He did say he had a beer now and then, but no drugs. That's been for the better part of fifteen years."

"If you can believe him," Bennet said. "I don't know how much you could tell from the brief time you spent. You were there for what, an hour?"

"About that," I said. "I'm not exactly an amateur. I've dealt with addicts in the past and believe me, he didn't look like one. I can spot a liar, too."

"No offense," he said. "I'm skeptical by nature when it comes to him. He always put on a good show." He finished his martini, holding the glass by the stem. The last vestiges of the gin formed a distinct scallop along the rim. He reached for the pitcher and poured himself another drink.

"Who else did you talk to?" Donovan asked, reasserting his presence. He was clearly running the show and wanted to make sure Bennet remained aware of it. For his part, Bennet seemed more interested in his martini than the conversation. I could see the lines of tension in his face smooth out. His questions were meant to demonstrate his control of himself.

I shrugged. "I made one stop in town and mentioned Guy in passing to the woman who runs the general store. There couldn't be more than five or six hundred residents and I figure everyone there knows everybody else's business. She didn't bat an eye and had no comment about him one way or the other. The pastor and his wife seemed genuinely fond of him and spoke with some pride of the distance he's come. They could have been lying, putting on a show, but I doubt it. Most people aren't that good at improvising."

Jack picked up a cracker and lifted the dollop of Cheez Whiz off the surface like he was licking the filling from an Oreo. "So what's the deal? Is he born-again? Has he been baptized? Do you think he's accepted our Lord Jesus in his heart?" His sarcasm was offensive.

I turned to stare at him. "You have a problem with that?"

"Why would I have a problem? It's his life," Jack said.

Donovan shifted in his seat. "Anybody else have a question?"

Jack popped the cracker in his mouth and wiped his fingers on a napkin while he munched. "I think it's great. I mean, maybe he won't want the money. If he's such a good Christian, maybe he'll opt for the spiritual over the materialistic."

Bennet snorted with annoyance. "His being a Christian has nothing to do with it. He's penniless. You heard her. He's got nothing. He's flat broke."

"I don't know that he's broke. I never said that," I interjected.

Now it was Bennet's turn to stare. "You seriously think he's going to turn down a great big whack of dough?"

Donovan looked at me. "Good question," he said. "What's your feeling on the subject?"

"He never asked about the money. At the time I think he was more interested in the idea that you'd hired someone to find him. He seemed touched at first and then embarrassed when he realized he'd misunderstood."

"Misunderstood what?" Christie said.

"He thought I'd been asked to locate him because of family interest or concern. It became obvious pretty quickly that the point of the visit was to notify him of his father's death and advise him he was a possible beneficiary under the terms of Bader's will."

"Maybe if he thinks we're all kissy-kissy, he'll give up the money and opt for love instead," Jack suggested.

Donovan ignored him. "Did he say anything about talking to an attorney?"

"Not really. I told him to get in touch with Tasha, but she's the attorney for the estate and she's not going to advise him about that aspect of the situation. If he calls her, she'll refer him to a lawyer unless he already has one."

Donovan said, "In other words, what you're saying is we don't have any idea what he'll do."

Bennet spoke up. "Of course we do. There's no mystery. He wants the *money*. He's not a fool."

"How do you know what Guy wants?" Christie responded with a flash of irritation.

Bennet went right on. "Kinsey should have asked for his signature on a quitclaim. Get him signed off. Make a settlement before he has a chance to think too much."

Donovan said, "I asked Tasha about that. I suggested we draw up a disclaimer, thinking Kinsey could take it with her. Tasha nixed that. She said a disclaimer would be meaningless because he could always maintain later he wasn't properly represented or he was unduly influenced, overcome by the emotions of the moment, shit like that, which would make it useless. I thought her point was well taken. Tell the man his father's dead and then whip out a quitclaim? It's like waving a red flag in front of a bull."

Christie spoke up again, saying, "Kinsey had a good idea. She pointed out that since the two wills were drawn up just three years apart that the witnesses for the second will might have been the same as the ones for the first. If we can track down the witnesses, it's always possible one of them was aware of the provisions."

"Like a secretary or a paralegal?" Donovan asked.

"It's possible. Or maybe the clerk/typist acted as a witness. *Somebody* had to be involved in the preparation of that document," I said.

"If there was one," Jack said.

Donovan's mouth pulled down as he considered the point. "Worth a try."

"To what end?" Jack asked. "I'm not saying we shouldn't make the effort, but it probably won't do any good. You can be a witness to a will without being aware of what's in it. Besides, what if the second will left everything to Guy? Then we'd really be screwed."

Bennet was impatient. "Oh come on, Jack. Whose side are you on? At least the witnesses could testify the second will was signed. I heard Dad say half a dozen times Guy wasn't getting a thing—we all heard him say that—so wouldn't that make a difference?"

"Why should it? Dad had the will. He kept it in a file right upstairs. How do you know he didn't revoke it in the end? Suppose he tore it up before he died? He had notice enough. He knew his days were numbered."

"He would have told us," Bennet said.

"Not necessarily."

"Jesus, Jack. I'm telling you, he said Guy would get nothing. We've been over this a hundred times and he was adamant."

"It doesn't matter what he said. You know how he was when it came to Guy. He never stuck to his guns. *We* might have been forced to toe the mark, but not him."

Donovan cleared his throat and set his glass down with a sharp tap. "All right. Knock it off, you two. This is getting us nowhere. We've been through enough of this. Let's just see what Guy does. We might not have a problem. We don't know at this point. Tasha said she'd contact him if he doesn't get in touch with her first. I might drop him a note myself and we'll take it from there."

Bennet sat up straight. "Wait a minute. Who put you in charge? Why can't we discuss this? It concerns all of us."

"You want to discuss this? Fine. Go ahead," Donovan said. "We all know your opinion. You think Guy's a slimeball. You're completely antagonistic and with *that* attitude, you'll be pushing him right to the wall."

"You don't know any more about him than I do," Bennet said.

"I'm not talking about him. I'm talking about you. What makes you so sure he wants the money?"

"Because he hated us. That's why he left in the first place, isn't it? He'd do anything to get back at us and what better way than this?"

"You don't know that," Donovan said. "You don't know what went on back then. He may not harbor any ill will towards us at all. You go in there punching and he's going to go on the offensive."

"I never did anything to Guy. Why would he hate me?" Jack said blithely. He seemed amused at the fireworks between his two brothers and I wondered if he didn't habitually goad them.

Bennet snorted again and he and Jack locked eyes. Something flashed between them but I wasn't sure what.

Donovan intervened again with a warning look at both. "Could we stick to the subject? Anybody have something new to contribute?"

"Donovan runs the family. He's the king," Bennet said. He looked at me with the slightly liquid eyes of someone who's had too much to drink. I'd seen him suck down two martinis in less than fifteen minutes and who knew what he'd consumed before he entered the room? "The man thinks I'm a dick. He may pretend to be supportive, but he doesn't mean a word of it. He and my father never actually gave me enough money to succeed at anything. And then when I failed— when a business went under—they were quick to point out how I'd mismanaged it. Dad always undercut me and the notion that Guy can come along now and insist on his share is just more of the same as far as I'm concerned. Who's looking out for our interests? It ain't *him*," he said, jerking a thumb at Donovan.

"Wait a minute. Hold it! Where's that coming from?"

"I've never really stood up and asked for what's mine," Bennet said. "I should have insisted a long time ago, but I bought into the program, the story you and Dad cooked up. 'Here, Bennet, you can have this pittance. Do the best you can with this pathetic sum of money. Make something of yourself and there'll be more where that came from. You can't expect us to underwrite the whole venture.' Blah blah blah. That's all I ever heard."

Donovan squinted at him, shaking his head. "I don't believe this. Dad gave you hundreds of thousands of dollars and you pissed it all away. How many chances do you think you get? There isn't a bank in this town that would have given you the first *dime*—"

"Bullshit! That's bullshit. I've worked like a dog and you know it. Hell, Dad had a lot of business failures and so have you. Now suddenly I have to sit here and fuckin' justify every move I make—just to get a little seed money."

Donovan looked at him with disbelief. "Where's all the money your partners put in? You blew that, too. You're so busy playing big shot, you're not tending to business. Half of what you do is outright fraudulent and you know it. Or if you don't, more's the pity because you'll end up in jail."

Bennet pointed a finger, poking the air repeatedly as if it were an elevator button. "Hey, I'm the one taking risks. I'm the one with my ass on the line. You never put yourself out there on the firing line. You played it safe. You were Daddy's little boy, the little piggy who stayed home and did exactly what Daddy said. And now you want credit for being such an all-fired success. Well, fuck that. To hell with you."

"Watch the *f* word. Ladies present," Jack said in a singsong tone.

"Shut up, you little piss. No one's talking to you!"

Christie cast a look in my direction and then raised a hand, saying, "Hey, fellas. Couldn't we postpone this until later? Kinsey doesn't want to sit here and listen to this. We asked her to have a drink, not a ringside seat."

I took my cue from her and used the opportunity to get to my feet. "I think I should leave you alone to discuss this, but I really don't think you need to worry about Guy. He seems like a nice man. That's the bottom line from my perspective. I hope everything works out."

A paragraph of awkward verbiage ensued: apologies for the outburst, hasty explanations of the strain everyone was under in the wake of Bader's death. Personally, I thought they were a bunch of ill-mannered louts and if my bill had been paid I might have told them as much. As it was, they assured me no offense was intended and I assured them, in turn, that none had been taken. I can fib with the best of them when there's money at stake. We shook hands all around. I was thanked for my time. I thanked them for the drink and took my leave of them.

"I'll walk out with you," Christie said.

There was a moment of quiet as we left the living room. I hadn't realized I was holding my breath until the door closed behind us and I could suck in some fresh air.

"Let me grab a jacket," Christie said as we crossed the foyer. She made a detour to the closet, pulling on a dark wool car coat as we passed into the night air.

The temperature had dropped and a dampness seemed to rise up from the cobblestones. The exterior lights were now on, but the illumination was poor. I could see the dim shape of my car, parked on the far side of the courtyard, and we headed in that direction. The lighted front windows threw truncated panels of yellow on the driveway in front of us. In the living room, the three Malek brothers were more than likely engaged in fisticuffs by now.

"Thanks for getting me out of there."

"I'm sorry you had to see that. What a zoo," she said. She shoved her hands in her pockets. "That goes on all the time and it drives me insane. It's like living in the middle of a giant preschool free-for-all. They're all three years old. They're still slugging it out over the same toy truck. The tension in this house is unreal half the time."

"Bennet's drinking doesn't help."

"It's not just that. I came into the marriage thinking I was going to be part of a loving family. I never had any brothers and I thought the idea was keen. They seemed close at first. I mean, they sure fooled me. I guess I should have figured out that three grown men still living together under Daddy's roof didn't exactly speak of mental health, but what did I know? My family's so screwed up, I wouldn't know a

healthy one if it leapt up and bit me. I wanted kids. Looks like I got
'em," she remarked in a wry aside. "I hate sitting around watching
these 'boys' bicker and connive. You ought to see them operate. They
fight over absolutely everything. Anything that comes up, they all
instantly take the most disparate positions possible. Then they all
take sides and form these temporary coalitions. It'll be Donovan and
Jack against Bennet one day. The next day, Bennet and Jack form a
team against Donovan. The allegiances vary according to the subject
matter, but there's never accord. There's never any sense of all for
one and one for all. Everybody wants to be right—morally superior—
and at the same time, everybody feels completely misunderstood."

"Makes me glad to be an orphan."

"I'm with you on *that* one." She paused with a smile. "Or maybe
I'm just annoyed because none of them are ever on my side. I live
with a perpetual stomachache."

"You don't have any kids?"

"Not yet. I keep trying, but of course I can't seem to get pregnant
in this atmosphere. I'm coming up on forty so if something doesn't
happen soon, it's going to be too late."

"I thought women were having babies into their fifties these days."

"Not me. Forget it. Life's hard enough as it is. I mean, what kid
would volunteer to come into a house like *this?* It's disgusting."

"Why do you stay?"

"Who says I'll stay? I told Donovan last fall, I said, 'One more
round, buddy, and I'm outta here.' So what happens next? Bader up
and dies. I don't feel I can walk out when things are such a mess.
Also, I suppose I still harbor the dim hope that things'll work out
somehow."

"I'm sure my finding Guy couldn't be a help," I said.

"I don't know about that. At least now maybe the three of them
will gang up against *him.* In the end, that might be the only issue
they agree on."

I glanced toward the lighted windows of the living room. "You call
that 'agreement'?"

"Oh, they'll get around to it. There's nothing like the common enemy to unify the troops. The truth is, Guy's the one I feel sorry for. They'll take him to the cleaners if they have half a chance and from what you say, he's the best of the lot."

"Donovan seems okay," I said.

"Ha. That's what I thought, too. He puts up a good front, but that's all that is. He's learned how to function in the business world so he's got a little more polish. I'm sure nobody said so, but I know they were impressed with the job you did."

"Well, I appreciate that, but at this point, these people don't need a PI—."

"They need a referee," she laughed. "Tasha didn't do you any favors when she got you involved in this. I'm sorry you had to see 'em at their worst. Then again, at least you can appreciate what I have to live with."

"Don't worry about it. It's finished business," I said.

We said our good-nights and I slid in behind the wheel, taking a few minutes to get my car warmed up. The residual tension had left me feeling icy cold and I drove home with the VW heater level pulled to maximum effect. This consisted of a thin tongue of warm air licking at the bottoms of my shoes. The rest of me was freezing, a cotton turtleneck and wool blazer providing little in the way of insulation. As I turned onto my street, I gave brief consideration to having dinner up at Rosie's. I hadn't managed to eat so much as an unpitted olive at the Maleks' during the cocktail hour. I'd pictured sumptuous canapés that I could chow down instead of dinner, but the uproar had made even the Cheez Whiz seem less than appetizing. At the back of my mind, I knew I was avoiding the idea of going home to an empty apartment. Better now than later. It was only going to get worse.

I parked my car close to the corner and hoofed my way back to Henry's driveway. A dense fog had begun to blow in from the beach and I was heartened by the fact that I'd left a light on in my living room. At least letting myself in wouldn't feel so much like breaking and entering. I passed through the squeaky gate with my house key at the ready, unlocked my door, and tossed my handbag on the kitchen counter. I heard the downstair's toilet flush and a thrill of fear washed over me. Then the bathroom door opened and Robert Dietz walked out, looking as startled as I was. "I didn't hear you come in," he said. "I forgot to give back your key."

"What are you doing here? I thought you left."

"I got as far as Santa Maria and had to come back. I was halfway down the street and I missed you like crazy. I don't want us leaving each other on a bad note."

I felt a pain in my chest, something fragile and sharp that made me take a deep breath. "I don't see a way to resolve our basic differences."

"We can be friends without resolution. I mean, can't we?"

"How do I know?" I tried to shut down, but I couldn't quite manage it. I had an inexplicable urge to weep about something. Usually good-byes do that, tender partings in movies accompanied by music guaranteed to rip your heart out. The silence between us was just as painful to me.

"Have you had dinner?"

"I hadn't decided about that yet. I just had drinks with the Maleks," I said faintly. The words sounded odd and I wanted to pat myself on the chest as a way of consoling myself. I could have handled the situation if only he hadn't come back. The day had been hard, but I'd survived it.

"You want to talk?"

I shook my head, not trusting my voice.

"Then what? You decide. I'll do anything you want."

I looked away from him, thinking about the fearful risks of intimacy, the potential for loss, the tender pain implicit in any bond between two creatures—human or beast, what difference did it make? In me, the instinct for survival and the need for love had been at war for years. My caution was like a wall I'd built to keep me safe. But safety is an illusion and the danger of feeling too much is no worse than the danger of being numb. I looked back at him and saw my pain mirrored in his eyes.

He said, "Come here." He made a gesture with his hand, coaxing me to move closer.

I crossed the room. Dietz leaned into me like a ladder left behind by a thief.

9

Dietz's knee was so swollen and painful he couldn't make it up the stairs, so we unfolded the sofa bed. I brought the duvet down from the loft. We turned off the lamp and crawled naked beneath the comforter's downy weight like polar bears in a cave. We made love in the puffy igloo of the quilt while around us streetlights streamed through the porthole window like moonlight on snow. For a long time, I simply drank in the musky scent of him, hair and skin, feeling my way blindly across all his textured surfaces. The heat from his body thawed my cold limbs. I felt like a snake curling up in a patch of sunlight, warmed to the depths after a long unforgiving winter. I remembered his ways from our three months together—the look on his face, the hapless sounds he made. What I'd forgotten was the smoldering response he awakened in me.

There was a brief time in my youth when my behavior was both reckless and promiscuous. Those were the days when there seemed to be no consequence to sex that wasn't easily cured. In the current marketplace, you'd have to be a fool—or suicidal—to risk the casual encounter without a lot of straight talk and doctors' certificates changing hands. For my purposes, celibacy is my habitual state. I suppose it's a lot like living in times of famine. Without hope of satiation, hunger diminishes and the appetite fades. With Dietz, I could feel all my physical senses quicken, the yearning for contact overcoming my natural reticence. Dietz's injury required patience and ingenuity, but somehow we managed. The process entailed considerable laughter at our contortions and quiet concentration during the moments between.

Finally, at ten, I flung the covers aside, exposing our sweaty bodies to the arctic temperatures surrounding us. "I don't know about you, but I'm starving," I said. "If we don't stop and eat soon, I'll be dead before morning."

Thirty minutes later, showered and dressed, we found ourselves sitting up at Rosie's in my favorite booth. She and William were both working, he behind the bar and Rosie out waiting tables. Ordinarily, the kitchen closed down at ten, and I could see she was just on the verge of saying as much when she noticed the whisker burn that had set my cheeks aflame. I put my chin in my palm, but not before she caught sight of my sex rash. The woman may be close to seventy, but she's not unperceptive. She seemed to take in at a glance both the source of our satisfaction and our avid interest in food. I thought the application of my makeup had successfully disguised my chafed flesh, but she was visibly smirking as she recited the meal she intended to prepare for us. With Rosie, there's no point in even pretending to order. You eat what she decides will be perfect for the occasion. In honor of Dietz's return, I noticed her English was marginally improved.

She parked herself sideways to the table, wiggling slightly in place, refusing to look directly at either of us after that first sly glance. "Now. Here's what you gonna get and don't make with the usual face—like this—while I'm telling you." She pulled her mouth down, eyes rolling, to show Dietz my usual enthusiasm for her choices. "I'm fixing Korhelyleves, is also called Souse's Soup. Is taking couple pounds of sauerkraut, paprika, smoked sausage, and some sour cream. Is guaranteed to perk up tired senses of which you look like you got a lot. Then, I'm roasting you little cheeken that I'm serve with mushroom pudding—is very good—and for efter, is hazel-nut torte, but no coffee. You need sleep. I'm bringing wine in a minute. Don't go way."

We didn't leave until midnight. We didn't sleep until one, wound together on the narrow width of the sofa bed. I'm not accustomed to sleeping with someone else and I can't say it netted me any restful results. Because of his knee, Dietz was forced to lie on his back with a pillow supporting his left leg. This gave me two choices: I could lie pressed against him with my head resting on his chest, or flat on my back with our bodies touching along their lengths.

I tried one and then the other, tossing relentlessly as the hours ticked away. Half the time, I could feel the sofa's metal mechanism cut across my back, but if I switched to the other position with my head on his chest, I suffered from heatstroke, a dead arm, and a canned left ear. Sometimes I could feel the exhalation of his breath on my cheek and the effect drove me mad. I found myself counting as he breathed, in and out, in and out. In moments, the rhythm changed and there'd be a long pause in which I wondered if he were in the process of dropping dead. Dietz slept like a soldier under combat conditions. His snores were gentle snuffles, just loud enough to keep me on sentry duty, but not quite loud enough to draw enemy fire.

I slept finally—amazingly—and woke at seven energized. Dietz had made coffee and he was reading the paper, dressed, his hair damp, a pair of half-glasses sitting low on his nose. I watched him for a few minutes until his gaze came up to mine.

"I didn't know you wore glasses."

"I was too vain before this. The minute you were out the door, I put 'em on," he said with that crooked smile of his.

I turned on my side, folding my right arm under my cheek. "What time will the boys be expecting you?"

"Early afternoon. I have motel reservations at a place close by. If they want to spend the night, I'll have room."

"I'll bet you look forward to seeing them."

"Yes, but I'm nervous about it, too. I haven't seen them for two years—since I left for Germany. I'm never quite sure what to talk about with them."

"What do you talk to anyone about? Mostly bullshit."

"Even bullshit requires a context. It gets awkward for them, too. Sometimes we end up going to the movies just to have something to talk about later. I'm not exactly a fount of paternal advice. Once I quiz them about girlfriends and classes, I'm about out of conversation."

"You'll do fine."

"I hope. What about you? What's your day looking like?"

"I don't know. This is Saturday, so I don't have to work. I'll probably nap. Starting soon."

"You want company?"

"Dietz," I said, outraged, "if you get in this bed again, I won't be able to walk."

"You're an amateur."

"I am. I'm not used to this stuff."

"How about some coffee?"

"Let me brush my teeth first."

After breakfast, we went down to the beach. The day was cloudy, the marine layer holding in the heat like foam insulation. The temperature was close to seventy and the air soft and fruity, with a tropical scent. Santa Teresa winters are filled with such contradictions. One day will feel icy while the next day feels mild. The ocean had a slick sheen, reflecting the uniform white of the sky. We took off our shoes and carried them, scuffling along the water's edge with the frothy play of waves rolling across our bare feet. Seagulls hovered overhead, screeching, while two dogs leaped in unison, snapping at the birds as if they were low-flying Frisbees.

Dietz took off at nine, holding me crushed against him before he got in the car. I leaned on the hood and we kissed for a while. Finally, he pulled back and studied my face. "If I come back in a couple of weeks, will you be here?"

"Where else would I go?"

"I'll see you then," he said.

"Don't worry about me. Any old day will do," I remarked, waving, as his car receded down the block. Dietz hated to be specific about dates because it made him feel trapped. Of course, the effect of his vagueness was to keep me feeling hooked. I shook my head to myself as I returned to my place. How did I end up with a man like him?

I spent the rest of the morning getting my apartment tidied up. It didn't really take much work, but it was satisfying nonetheless. This time I wasn't really feeling depressed. I knew Dietz would be coming back, so my virtuous activity had more to do with reestablishing my boundaries than warding off the blues. Since he'd done the grocery shopping, my cupboard was full and my refrigerator stocked, a state that always contributes to my sense of security. As long as you have sufficient toilet paper, how far wrong can life go?

At lunchtime I spotted Henry sitting in the backyard at a little round picnic table he'd picked up in a garage sale the previous fall. He'd spread out some graph paper, his reference books, and a cross-word key. As a pastime, Henry constructs and sells crossword puzzles for those wee yellow books sold near grocery store checkout lanes. I made a peanut-butter-and-pickle sandwich and joined him in the sunshine.

"You want one?" I asked, holding out my plate.

"Thanks, but I just had lunch," he said. "Where'd Dietz disappear to? I thought he intended to stick around."

I filled him in on the "romance" and we chatted idly while I ate my sandwich. The texture of the peanut butter was a sublime contrast to the crunch of the bread-and-butter pickles. The diagonal cut exposed more filling than a vertical cut would and I savored the ratio of saltiness to tart. This ranked right up there with sex without taking off any clothes. I made a sort of low moan, nearly swooning with pleasure, and Henry glanced up at me. "Give me a bite of that."

I let him have the plump center portion, keeping my fingers positioned so he couldn't take too much.

He chewed for a moment, clearly relishing the intense blend of flavors. "Very weird, but not bad." This is what he always says when he samples this culinary marvel.

I tried another bite myself, pointing to the puzzle he was working on. "How's this one coming? You've never really told me how you go about your business." Henry was a crossword fanatic, subscribing to the *New York Times* so he could do the daily puzzle, which he completed in ink. Sometimes, to amuse himself, he left every other letter blank, or filled in the outer borders first in a spiral moving toward the center. The puzzles he wrote himself seemed very difficult to me, though he claimed they were easy. I'd watched him construct dozens without understanding the strategy.

"I've actually upgraded my technique. My approach used to be haphazard. I'm better organized these days. This is a small one, only fifteen by fifteen. This is the pattern I'm using," he said, indicating a template with the gridwork of black squares already laid in.

"You don't devise the format as well?"

"Usually not. I've used this one several times and it suits my purposes. They're all symmetrical and if you'll notice, no area is closed off. The rules say the black squares can't exceed more than one sixth of the total number. There are a few other rules tossed in. For example, you can't use any words of fewer than three letters, stuff like that. The good ones have a theme around which the answers are organized."

I picked up one of his reference books and turned it over in my hand. "What's this?"

"That book lists words in alphabetical order from three through fifteen letters. And that one's a crossword finisher that lists words in a complicated alphabetical order up through seven letters."

I smiled at the enthusiasm that had crept into his voice. "How'd you get into this?"

He waved dismissively. "Do enough of 'em and you can't help it. You have to have a go at it yourself, just to see what it's like. They even have crossword championships, which started in 1980. You ought to see those puppies go. The puzzles are projected on an overhead screen. A real whiz can answer sixty-four questions in under eight minutes."

"Are you ever tempted to enter?"

He shook his head, penciling in a clue. "I'm too slow and much too easily rattled. Besides, it's a serious business, like bridge tournaments." His head came up. "That's your phone," he said.

"It is? Your hearing must be better than mine." I hopped up from the table and made a beeline for my place, picking up the receiver just as my answering machine did. I reached for the Off button as my voice completed its request for messages. "Hello, hello. It's me. I'm really home," I sang.

"Hey," a man's voice said mildly. "This is Guy. Hope you don't mind my calling on a weekend."

"Not at all. What's up?"

"Nothing much," he said. "Donovan called me at the church. I guess last night the three of them—him and Bennet and Jack—had a meeting. He says they want me to come down for a few days so we can talk about the will."

I felt my whole body go quiet. "Really. That's interesting. You going to do it?"

"I think so. I might, but I'm not really sure. I had a long talk with Peter and Winnie. Peter thinks it's time to open up a dialogue. He's got a prayer meeting in Santa Teresa tomorrow, so it works out pretty good. They can bring me down after church, but he thought it'd be smart to talk to you about it first."

I was silent for a moment. "You want the truth?"

"Well, yeah. That's why I called."

"I wouldn't do it if I were you. I was over there last night and it all seems very tense. It's nothing you'd want to be exposed to."

"How so?"

"Feelings are running high and your showing up at this point is only going to make things worse."

"That was my first reaction, but then I got to thinking. I mean, Donovan called me. I didn't call him," he said. "Seems to me if the three of them are offering a truce, I should at least be willing to meet 'em halfway. It can't hurt."

I suppressed an urge to start shrieking at him. Shrieking, I've discovered, is really not a sound method for persuading other people to your point of view. I'd seen his brothers in action and Guy was no match. I wouldn't trust those three under any circumstances. Given Guy's emotional state, I could see why he'd be tempted, but he'd be a fool to go into that house without counsel. "Maybe it's a truce and maybe not. Bader's death has brought up all kinds of issues," I said. "You go in unprepared and you'll end up taking on a whole raft of shit. You'd be walking into a nightmare."

"I understand."

"I don't think so," I said. "Not to criticize your brothers, but these are not nice fellows, at least where you're concerned. There's a lot of friction between them and your appearance is only going to add fuel to the fire. I mean, honestly. You can't imagine the dynamic." I noticed the pitch and volume of my voice going up.

"I have to try," he said.

"Maybe so, but not *that* way."

"Meaning what?"

"You're going to find yourself in exactly the same position you were in when you left. You'll be the fall guy, the scapegoat for all their hostility."

I could hear him shrug. He said, "Maybe we need to talk about that then. Get it out in the open and deal with it."

"It's out in the open. Those three aren't shy about anything. The conflicts are all right out there in front of God and everyone and believe me, you don't want their venom directed at you."

"Donovan doesn't seem to bear me any ill will and from what he says, Bennet and Jack don't either. The truth is, I've changed and they need to see that. How else can I persuade 'em if it isn't face-to-face?"

I could feel my eyes cross while I tried controlling my impatience. I knew I'd be smarter to keep my mouth shut, but I've never been good at keeping my opinions to myself. "Look, Guy, I don't want to stand here and try to tell you your business, but this isn't about you. This is about their relationship to each other. It's about your father and whatever's been going on in the years since you left. You'll end up being the target for all the anger they've stored up. And why put yourself through that."

"Because I want to be connected again. I screwed up. I admit that and I want to make it up to them. Peter says there can't be any healing unless we sit down together."

"That's all well and good, but there's a lot more at stake. What if the subject of the money comes up?"

"I don't care about the money."

"Bullshit. That's bull. Do you have any idea how much money we're talking about?"

"Doesn't make any difference. The money doesn't matter to me. I don't need money. I'm happy as I am."

"That's what you say now, but how do you know that won't change? Why create problems for yourself later on? Have you talked to Tasha? What's she say about this?"

"I never talked to her. I called the office in Lompoc, but she'd already left for San Francisco and after that, the secretary said she was taking off for Utah on a ten-day ski trip."

"So call her in Utah. They have phones up there."

"I tried that. They wouldn't give me her number. They said if she called in, they'd give her my name and number and she'd call if she could."

"Then try someone else. Call another attorney. I don't want you talking to your brothers without legal advice."

"It's not about legalities. It's about mending the breach."

"Which is exactly what's going to make you a sitting duck. Your agenda has nothing to do with theirs. They don't give a shit about forgiveness, if you'll pardon my French."

"I don't see it that way."

"I know you don't. That's why we're having this argument," I shrieked. "Suppose they try to pressure you into making a decision?"

"About what?"

"About anything! You don't even know what's in your best interest. If your sole aim is to make peace, you're only going to get screwed."

"How can I get screwed if I don't want anything? They can keep the money if that's the only thing standing between us."

"Well, if *you* don't want the money, why not give it to the church?" The minute I said it, I wanted to bite my tongue. His motives were clean. Why introduce the complication?

He was silent for a moment. "I hadn't thought about that. That's a good point."

"Forget it. Just skip that. All I'm saying is don't go in there alone. Get help so you don't do something you'll regret."

"Why don't you go?"

I groaned and he laughed in response. Going with him was the last thing I wanted to do. He needed protection, but I didn't think it was appropriate for me to step in. What did I have to offer in the way of assistance? "Because it's not my place. I'm not objective. I don't know the law and I don't have any idea what your legal position is. You'd be foolish to come down here and have a conversation with them. Just wait for ten days until Tasha gets back. Don't do anything yet. There's no reason you have to hop-to the minute Donovan whistles. You should be doing this on your terms, not his."

I could hear his reluctance to accept what I was saying. Like most of us, he'd made up his mind before he asked. "You know something? This is the truth," he said. "I prayed about this. I asked God for guidance and this was the answer I got."

"Well, try Him again. Maybe you misunderstood the message."

He laughed. "I did that in a way. I opened my Bible and put my finger on the page. Know what the passage was?"

"I can't imagine," I said dryly.

" 'Be it known unto you therefore, men *and* brethren, that through this man is preached unto you the forgiveness of sins: And by him all that believe are justified from all things, from which ye could not be justified by the law of Moses.' " Like many of the faithful, he could recite Bible verses like song lyrics.

This time the silence was mine. "I can't argue that. I don't even know what it means. Look, if you're determined to do this, you'll do it, I'm sure. I'm just urging you to take someone with you."

"I just did. I asked you."

"I'm not talking about me! What about Peter and Winnie? I'm sure they'd be willing to help if you asked and they'd do a much better job. I don't know the first thing about counseling or mediation or anything else. Aside from that, all this family-related stuff gives me the willies."

I could hear Guy smile and his tone was affectionate. "Strange you should say that because somehow it feels like you're part of this. I don't know how, but it sure seems like that to me. Don't you have some kind of issue around family yourself?"

I held the phone away from me and squinted at the handset. "Who, me? Absolutely not. Why would you say that?"

Guy laughed. "I don't know. It just came to me in a flash. Maybe I'm wrong, but it feels like you're connected."

"My only connection is professional. I was hired to do a job.

That's the only link I see." I kept my tone casual to demonstrate my nonchalance, but I was forced to put a hand against the small of my back, where an inexplicable drop of sweat was trickling down into my underpants. "Why don't you have a talk with Peter again. I know you're eager to make amends, but I don't want you walking into the lion's den. We all know how the lions and the Christians came out."

He was silent for a moment and then seemed to change the subject. "Where's your apartment?"

"What makes you ask?" I was unwilling to be specific until I knew where he was headed.

"How about this? Maybe we can do this another way. Donovan says everyone's gone tomorrow until five o'clock. Peter'll give me a lift into town, but his schedule's too tight to do much more than that. If he drops me off at your place, could you give me a ride the rest of the way? You don't have to stay. I understand you don't want to be involved and that's fine with me."

"I don't really see how that addresses the point."

"It doesn't. I'm just asking for a ride. I can handle everything else if you can get me over there."

"You're not going to listen to me, are you," I said.

"I did listen. The problem is I disagree."

I hesitated, but really couldn't see any reason to refuse. I was already feeling churlish because I'd put up such resistance. "That sounds all right. Sure. I can do that," I said. "What time would you get here?"

"Three? Somewhere around then. I don't mean to be a bother. Peter's meeting is downtown, at that church on the corner of State and Michaelson. Is that anywhere close? Because I could walk over to your place and we could go from there."

"Close enough," I said, feeling crabby and resigned. "Look, why don't you give me a call when you get in. I'll swing by the church and pick you up."

"That'd be good. That's great. Are you sure this is okay?"

"No, but don't press your luck. I'm willing to do this much, but don't go asking for reassurance on top of it."

He laughed. "I'm sorry. You're right. I'll see you then," he said. He disconnected on his end.

As I hung up the phone, I was already having doubts. Amazing how quickly someone else's problems become yours. Trouble creates a vacuum into which the rest of us get sucked.

I found myself pacing the living room, inwardly refuting his ridiculous claim about the relevance of his situation to mine. His conflict about family had *nothing* to do with me. I sat down at my desk and made some notes to myself. In case Tasha asked, I thought it might be wise to keep a record of the discussion we'd just had. I hoped he wasn't going to get a bug up his butt about giving all his money to the church. That was really going to cause a problem if he got greedy on behalf of Jubilee Evangelical. I omitted any reference to a charitable donation, thinking if I didn't write it down, the subject wouldn't exist.

I picked up the phone again and put a call through to the Maleks. Myrna picked up and I asked to speak to Christie. I waited, listening as Myrna crossed the foyer and bellowed up the stairs to Christie. When Christie finally picked up the phone on her end, I filled her in briefly on my conversation with Guy. "Will you keep me informed about what's going on?" I asked. "I'll drop him off, but after that he's on his own. I think he needs protection, but I don't want to get into my rescue costume. He's a big boy and this is really none of my business. I'd feel better if I knew there was someone in your camp keeping an eye on him."

"Oh, right. And leave the rescue to me," she said, her tone of voice wry.

I laughed. "Not to get trivial, but he *is* cute," I said.

"Really? Well, that's good. I'm a big fan of cute. In fact, that's how I vote for a presidential candidate," she said. "Personally, I don't think you have anything to worry about. After you left last night, the three of them talked long and hard. Once they got done ripping each other apart, they settled down into some meaningful conversation."

"I'm glad to hear that. I was actually a bit puzzled why Donovan had called him. What's their inclination? Do you mind if I ask?"

"I guess it depends on what he says to them. Ultimately, of course, this is probably something for the lawyers to discuss. I think they want to be honorable. On the other hand, five million dollars might distort anyone's notion of what's fair."

"Ain't that the truth."

10

I pulled over to the curb in front of the Faith Evangelical Church the next afternoon at three. Guy had called me at 2:45 and I'd left the apartment shortly thereafter, taking a few minutes to put gas in my car. The sun was out again and the day felt like summer. I wore the usual jeans and a T-shirt, but I'd traded my Reeboks and sweat socks for a pair of openwork sandals in honor of the sudden heat. The grass on the church lawn had been recently cut and the sidewalk was littered with fine green at the edge. The turf itself featured a pale dun-colored haze where the cut blades had browned in the sun. A number of gullible daffodils had taken these balmy temperatures as an invitation to pop their green shafts into view.

There was no sign of Peter, but Guy was standing on the corner with a backpack at his feet. He spotted my car and pretended to hitchhike, holding his thumb out with a smile on his face. I confess when I saw him I could feel my heart break. He'd had his hair cut and his face was so freshly shaved he still sported a dot of toilet paper where he'd nicked himself. He wore a navy blue suit that didn't fit well. The pants were baggy in the butt and slightly too long, the backs of his trouser cuffs brushing the sidewalk. The jacket was wide across the chest, which made the shoulder pads look as exaggerated as a 1940's zoot suit. The garment had probably been donated to a church rummage sale or maybe he'd bought it from someone weighing forty pounds more. Whatever the explanation, he wore his finery with a self-conscious air, clearly unaccustomed to the dress shirt and tie. I wondered if my own vulnerability had been as apparent during my lunch with Tasha. I'd approached my personal grooming with the same insecurity, perhaps netting myself the same sorry results.

Guy reached for his canvas backpack, clearly happy to see me. He seemed as innocent as a pup. There was a softness about him, something guileless and unformed, as if his association with Jubilee Evangelical had isolated him from worldly influences all these years. The reckless element in his nature was now tamed to a gentleness I'd rarely seen in a man.

He slid into the front seat. "Hey, Kinsey. How are you?" He held his backpack on his lap like a kid on his way to day camp.

I smiled in his direction. "You're all spiffed up."

"I didn't want my brothers to think I'd forgotten how to dress. What do you think of the suit?"

"The color's good on you."

"Thanks," he said, smiling with pleasure. "Oh. By the way, Winnie says hi."

"Hi to her," I said. "What's the deal on your return? When are you planning to go back to Marcella?"

Guy looked away from me out the car window on his side, the casualness of his tone belying its content. "Depends on what happens at the house. Donovan invited me to stay for a couple of days and I wouldn't mind that if everything works out all right. I guess if it doesn't work, it won't make any difference. I got money in my pocket. When I'm ready to leave, someone can give me a ride to the bus."

I was on the verge of volunteering my services and then thought better of it. I glanced over at him, making a covert study of his face in profile. In some lights, he looked every one of his forty-three years. In other moments his boyishness seemed a permanent part of his character. It was as if his development had been arrested at the age of sixteen, maybe twenty at the outside. He was scanning the streets, taking in the sights as if he were in a foreign country.

"I take it you don't get down here that often," I said.

He shook his head. "I don't have much occasion. When you live in Marcella, Santa Teresa seems too big and too far away. We go to Santa Maria or San Luis if we need anything." He looked over at me. "Can we do a quick tour? I'd like to see what's going on."

"I can do that. Why not? We have time."

I circled the block, coming back out onto State Street. I turned left, heading downtown, a short three blocks away. The business district wasn't much more than twenty blocks long and three or four blocks wide, terminating at Cabana Boulevard, which parallels the beach. For many years, the stores along upper State attracted the bulk of the downtown shoppers. Lower State was considered the less-desirable end of town, the street lined with thrift stores, third-rate eateries, a movie theater that smelled of urine, and half a dozen noisy bars and run-down transient hotels. Lately, the area had undergone a resurrection, and the classy businesses had begun to migrate south-ward along the thoroughfare. Now it was upper State that featured deserted storefronts while lower State had captured all the tourist trade. In warm weather, pedestrians drifted up from the beach, a ragtag parade of sight-seers in shorts, licking ice-cream cones.

"It's grown," he remarked.

With a population of eighty-five thousand, Santa Teresa wasn't big, but the town had been flourishing. I tried to see it as he did, catalog-ing in my mind all the changes that had taken place in the last twenty years. Time-lapse photography would have shown tree trunks elongating, branches stretching out like rubber, some buildings erected while others vanished in a puff of smoke. Storefronts would flicker through a hundred variations: awnings, signs, and window displays, the liquidation sales of one business flashing across the plate glass before the next enterprise took its place. New structures would appear like apparitions, filling in the empty spaces until no gaps remained. I could remember when the downtown sidewalks were made wider, State Street narrowing to accommodate the planting of trees imported from Bolivia. Spanish-style benches and telephone booths had been added. Decorative fountains had appeared, looking like they'd been there for years. A fire had taken out two commercial establishments while an earthquake had rendered others unfit for use. Santa Teresa was one of the few towns that looked more elegant as time passed. The strict regulations of the Architectural Board of Review imposed an air of refinement that in other towns was wiped out by gaudy neon, oversized signage, and a hodgepodge of building styles and materials. As much as the local residents complained about the lengthy approval process, the result was a mix of simplicity and grace.

At Cabana, I drove out along the wharf, wheels thumping along the length. I turned at the end until we were headed back toward town. I motored north on State, seeing the same sights again from the reverse perspective. At Olive Grove, I turned right, driving past the Santa Teresa Mission and from there into the foothills where the Malek estate was tucked. I could sense Guy's interest quicken as the road angled upward. Much of the terrain in this area was undeveloped, the landscape littered with enormous sandstone boulders and prickly cactus with leaves as large as fleshy Ping-Pong paddles.

The Malek estate sat close to the borders of the backcountry, an oasis of dark green in a region dense with pale chaparral. At irregular intervals, fires had swept across the foothills in spectacular conflagrations, the blaze advancing from peak to peak, sucking up houses and trees, consuming every shred of vegetation. In the wake of these burns, species of native plants known as fire followers appeared, dainty beauties emerging from the ashes of the charred and the dead. I could still see the occasional black, twisted branches of the manzanitas, though it had been five or six years since the last big fire.

Once again, the iron gates at the entrance stood open, the long driveway disappearing around a shaded curve ahead. Somehow the Maleks' evergreens and palms looked alien set against the backdrop of raw mountains. Entering the estate, I sensed how the years of careful cultivation and the introduction of exotic plants had altered the very air that permeated the grounds.

"You nervous?" I asked.

"Scared to death."

"You can still back out."

"It's too late for that. Feels like a wedding where the invitations have gone out—you know, it's still possible to cancel, but it's easier to go through with it than make a fuss for everyone else."

"Don't turn all noble on me."

"It's not about 'noble.' I guess I'm curious."

I pulled into the courtyard and eased the VW around to the left. The garages at the end of the drive were all closed. The house itself looked deserted. All the windows were dark and most of the draperies were drawn. The visage was scarcely welcoming. The silence was broken only by the idling of my engine. "Well. This is it, I guess. Call if you need me. I wish you luck."

Guy glanced at me uneasily. "You have to leave already?"

"I really should," I said, though the truth was I had nothing else to do that afternoon.

"Don't you want to see the place? Why don't you stay a few minutes and let me show you around."

"I was just here for drinks. It hasn't changed since Friday night."

"I don't want to go inside. I have to work up my nerve. Why don't I show you the place. We could walk around outside. It's really beautiful," he said. He reached out impulsively and touched my bare arm. "Please?"

His fingers were cold and his apprehension was contagious. I didn't have the heart to leave him. "All right," I said reluctantly, "but I can't stay long."

"Great. That's great. I really appreciate this."

I turned off the engine. Guy left his backpack on the front seat and the two of us got out. We slammed the car doors in two quick, overlapping reports, like guns going off. At the last moment, I opened my door again and tossed my handbag in the back before I locked the car. As we crossed the courtyard, Myrna opened the front door and came out on the porch. She was wearing a semblance of uniform; a shapeless white polyester skirt with a matching overblouse, some vague cross between nursiness and household help.

I said, "Hi, Myrna. How are you? I didn't think anyone was here. This is Guy. I'm sorry. I don't remember anyone ever mentioning your last name."

"Sweetzer," she said.

Guy extended his hand, which flustered her to some extent. She allowed him one of those handshakes without cartilage or bone. His good looks probably had the same effect on her that they had on me. "Nice to meet you," he said.

"Nice to meet you, too," she replied by rote. "The family's back around five. You're to have the run of the house. I imagine you remember where your room is if you want to take your things on up."

"Thanks. I'll do that in a bit. I thought I'd show her the grounds first if that's okay with you."

"Suit yourself," she said. "The front door will be open if you want to come in that way. Dinner's at seven." She turned to me. "Will you be staying on as well?"

"I appreciate the invitation, but I don't think I should. The family needs time to get reacquainted. Maybe another time," I said. "I do have a question. Guy was asking about his father and it just occurred to me that you might know as much as anyone else. Weren't you his nurse?"

"One of them," she said. "I was his primary caregiver the last eight months. I stayed on as housekeeper at your brothers' request," she said, looking at Guy. Her delivery was staunch, as if we'd challenged her right to remain on the premises. From what I'd seen of her, she tended to be humorless, but with Guy she'd now added a grace note of resentment, reflecting the family's general attitude.

. Guy's smile was sweet. "I'd like to talk to you about my dad sometime."

"Yes sir. He was a good man and I was fond of him."

There was an awkward moment, none of us knowing how to terminate the conversation. Myrna was the one who finally managed, saying, "Well, now. I'll let you go on about your business. I'll be in the kitchen if you should need anything. The cook's name is Enid, if you can't find me."

"I remember Enid," he said. "Thanks."

As soon as the door closed behind her, Guy touched my elbow and steered me off to the right. We crossed the courtyard together, heat drifting up from the sunbaked cobblestones. "Thanks for staying," he said.

"You're full of thanks," I remarked.

"I am. I feel blessed. I never expected to see the house again. Come on. We'll go this way."

We cut around the south side of the house, moving from hot, patchy sunlight into shade. To me, it felt like another sudden shift in seasons. In the space of fifty feet, we'd left summer behind. In the gloom of heavy shadow, the drop in air temperature was distinct and unwelcome, as if the months were rolling backward into winter again. Vestiges of the hot dry winds blew down the mountainside behind us, tossing restlessly across the treetops above our heads. We rambled beneath a canopy of shaggy-smelling juniper and pine. A carpet of fallen needles dampened our footsteps to a silence.

Near the house, I could see evidence of the gardeners—raked

paths, the trimmed shape of bushes, a profusion of ferns ringed with small perfect stones—but the larger portion of the property was close to wilderness. Many of the plants had been allowed to grow unchecked. A violet-colored lantana tumbled along the terrace wall. A salmon pink bougainvillea climbed across a tangled stretch of brush. To our right, a solid wash of nasturtiums blanketed the banks of an empty creek bed. In the areas of bright sun, where the dry breezes riffled across the blossoms, several scents arose and mingled in an earthy cologne.

Guy seemed to scrutinize every square foot we traversed. "Everything looks so much bigger. I remember when some of these trees were just planted. Saplings were this tall and now look at them."

"Your memories sound happy. That surprises me somehow."

"This was a great spot to grow up. Mom and Dad bought the place when I was three years old. Donovan was five and the two of us thought we'd died and gone to heaven. It was like one great big playground. We could go anywhere we wanted and no one ever had to worry. We made forts and tree houses. We had sword fights with sticks. We played cowboys and Indians and went on jungle expeditions in the wilds of the sticker bushes. When Bennet was a little guy, we used to tie him to a stake and he'd wail like a banshee. We'd tell him we were going to burn him if he didn't shut up. He was younger than us and he was fair game."

"Nice."

"Boy-type fun," he said. "I guess girls don't do that."

"How could your parents afford a place like this? I thought your father made his money later, in the years since you left."

"Mom had some money from a trust fund. The down payment was hers. Actually, it wasn't that much money even for the time. The house was a white elephant. It was on the market for nearly ten years and it was empty all that time. The story we heard was that the previous owner had been murdered. It's not like the house was haunted, but it did seem tainted. Nobody could make a deal work. We were told it fell out of escrow five or six times before my parents came along and bought it. It was big and neglected. The wiring was bad and the plumbing was shot. Daylight was showing through big holes in the roof. Tree rats ran everywhere and there was a family of raccoons living in the attic. It took 'em years to pull it all together. In the meantime, Dad's plan was to buy adjacent properties if they came up for sale."

"What is it now, fifteen acres?"

"Is that right? The original parcel was six. There probably isn't a lot more land available in this area."

"Is this city land or county?"

"We're right at the upper edges of the city limits. Lot of what you're looking at up there is part of the Los Padres National Forest." The term *forest* was a misnomer. The arching mountain range above us was overgrown with nettle, ceanothus, pyracantha, and coastal sage scrub, the soil too poor to support many trees. In the higher elevations, a few pines might remain if the wildfires hadn't reached them.

We passed the tennis court, its surface cracked and weedy along the edges. A tennis racket had been tossed to one side, exposed to the elements long enough to warp, its nylon strings sprung. Beyond the tennis court, there was a glass-enclosed structure I hadn't seen from the drive. The lines of the building were low and straight, with a red-tile roof that had altered with time until its color was the burnt brown of old bricks.

"What's that?"

"The pool house. We have an indoor pool. Want to see it?"

"Might as well," I said. I trailed after him as he approached a covered flagstone patio. He crossed to the building's darkened windows and peered in. He moved to the door and tried the knob. The door was unlocked, but the frame was jammed and required a substantial push before it opened with the kind of scrape that set my teeth on edge.

"You really want to do this?" I asked.

"Hey, it's part of the tour."

To me, it felt like breaking and entering, a sport I prefer to get paid for. The sense of trespass was unmistakable, nearly sexual in tone, despite the fact that we'd been given permission to roam. We entered an anteroom that was used to store an assortment of play equipment: badminton rackets, golf clubs, baseball bats, a rack lined with a full set of croquet mallets and balls, Styrofoam kickboards for the pool, and a line of fiberglass surfboards that looked as if they'd been propped against the wall for years. The gardener was currently keeping his leaf blower and a riding mower in the space to one side. While I didn't see any spiders, the place had a spidery atmosphere. I wanted to brush my clothes hurriedly in case something had dropped down and landed on me unseen.

The pool was half-filled and something about the water looked really nasty. The decking around the pool was paved with a gritty-looking gray slate, not the sort of surface you'd want to feel under your bare feet. At one end of the room was an alcove furnished in rattan, though the cushions were missing from the sofa and matching chairs. The air was gloomy and I could hear the sound of dripping water. Any hint of chlorine had evaporated long ago and several unclassified life-forms had begun to ferment in the depths.

"Looks like it's time to fire the pool guy," I remarked.

"The gardener probably does the pool when he remembers," Guy said. "When we were kids this was great."

"What'd you and Donovan do to Bennet down here? Drown him? Hang him off the diving board? I can just imagine the fun you must have had."

Guy smiled, his thoughts somewhere else. "I broke up with a girl once down here. That's what sticks in my mind. Place was like a country club. Swimming, tennis, softball, croquet. We'd invite dates over for a swim and then we'd end up making out like crazy. Girl in a bathing suit isn't that hard to seduce. Jack was the all-time champ. He was randy as a rabbit and he'd go after anyone."

"Why'd you break up with her?"

"I don't remember exactly. Some rare moment of virtue and self-sacrifice. I liked her too much. I was a bad boy back then and she was too special to screw around with like the other ones. Or maybe odd's the better word. A little nutsy, too needy. I knew she was fragile and I didn't want to take the chance. I preferred the wild ones. No responsibility, no regrets, no holds barred."

"Were your parents aware of what was going on down here?"

"Who knows. I'm not sure. They were proponents of the 'boys will be boys' school of moral instruction. Any girl who gave in to us deserved what she got. They never said so explicitly, but that's the attitude. My mother was more interested in being everybody's pal. Set limits on a kid and you might have to take a stand at some point. She was into unconditional love, which to her meant the absence of prohibitions of any kind. It was easier to be permissive, you know what I mean? This was all part of the sixties' feel-good bullshit. Looking back, I can see how much she must have been affected by her illness. She didn't want to be the stern, disapproving parent. She must have known her days were numbered, even though she survived a lot longer than most. In those days, they did chemo and radiation, but it was all so crudely calibrated they probably killed more people than they cured. They just didn't have the technology or the sophisticated choice of treatments. It's different today where you got a real shot at survival. For her, the last couple of years were pure hell."

"It must have been hard on you."

"Pure agony," he said. "I was the child most identified with her. Don't ask me why, but Donovan and Bennet and Jack were linked to Dad while I was my mother's favorite. It drove me wild to see her fail. She was faltering and in pain, going downhill on what I knew would be her final journey."

"Were you with her when she died?"

"Yes. I was. The rest of 'em were gone. I forget now where they were. I sat in her room with her for hours that day. Most of the time she slept. She was so doped up on morphine, she could hardly stay awake. I was exhausted myself and laid my head on the bed. At one point, she reached out and put her hand on my neck. I touched her fingers and she was gone, just like that. So quiet. I didn't move for an hour.

"I just sat by the bed, leaning forward, with my head turned away from her and my face buried in the sheets. I thought maybe if I didn't look, she might come back again, like she was hovering someplace close and might return to her body as long as no one noticed she'd left. I didn't want to break faith."

"What happened to the girl you broke up with?"

"Patty? I have no idea. I wrote to her once, but never heard back. I've thought of her often, but who knows where she is now or what's happened to her. It might be the best thing I ever did, especially back then. What a bastard I was. I have a hard time connecting. It's like somebody else was doing it."

"But you're a good person now."

He shook his head. "I don't think of myself as good, but sometimes I think I come close to being real."

We left the pool house behind, moving temporarily onto the sunny stretch of lawn where I'd watched Jack hit golf balls. We were on the terrace below the house, shadows slanting toward us as we crossed the grass.

"How do you feel? You seem relaxed," I said.

"I'll be fine once they get here. You know how it is. Your fantasies are always stranger than reality."

"What do you picture?"

He smiled briefly. "I have no idea."

"Well, whatever it is, I hope you get what you need."

"Me, too, but in the long run, what difference does it make? You can't hide from God and that's the point," he said. "For a long time, I was walkin' down the wrong road, but now I've turned myself around and I'm goin' back the other way. At some point, I'll meet up with my past and make peace."

We had, by then, reached the front of the house again. "I better scoot," I said. "Let me know how it goes."

"I'll be fine."

"No doubt, but I'll be curious."

As I got into my car and turned the key in the ignition, I watched him head toward the front door with his backpack. I waved as I passed and then watched him in my rearview mirror as I eased down the drive. I rounded the curve and he was gone from view. It's painful to think of this in retrospect. Guy Malek was doomed and I delivered him into the hands of the enemy. As I pulled through the gates, I could see a car approach. Bennet was driving. My smile was polite and I waved at him. He stared at me briefly and then glanced away.

11

At ten o'clock Monday morning I received a call that should have served as a warning. Looking back, I can see that from that moment on, troubles began to accumulate at an unsettling rate. I'd gotten a late start and I was just closing the front gate behind me when I heard the muffled tone of the telephone ringing in my apartment. I did a quick reverse, trotting down the walkway and around the corner. I unlocked the front door and flung it open in haste, tossing my jacket and bag aside. I snatched up the receiver on the fourth ring, half expecting a wrong number or a market survey now that I'd made the effort. "Hello?"

"Kinsey. This is Donovan."

"Well, hi. How are you? Whew! Excuse the heavy breathing. I was already out the door and had to run for the phone."

Apparently, he wasn't in the mood for cheery chitchat. He got straight to the point. "Did you contact the press?"

It was not a subject I expected the man to broach at this hour or any other. I could feel a fuzzy question mark forming over my head while I pondered what he could possibly be talking about. "Of course not. About what?"

"We got a call from the *Dispatch* about an hour ago. Somebody tipped off a reporter about Guy's return."

"Really? That's odd. What's the point?" I knew the *Santa Teresa Dispatch* occasionally struggled to find noteworthy items for the Local section, but Guy's homecoming hardly seemed like a big-time news event. Aside from the family, who'd give a shit?

"They're playing it for human interest. Rags to riches. You know the tack, I'm sure. A lowly maintenance worker in Marcella, California, suddenly finds out he's a millionaire and comes home to collect. It's better than the lottery given Guy's personal history, as you well know."

"What do you mean, as *I* well know? I never said a word to the press. I wouldn't do that."

"Who else knew about it? No one in the family would leak a story like that. This is a sensitive issue. The last thing we need is *publicity*. Here we are trying to hammer out some kind of understanding between us and the phone hasn't stopped ringing since the first call came through."

"I don't follow. Who's been calling?"

"Who hasn't?" he said, exasperated. "The local paper for starters and then the L.A. *Times.* I guess one of the radio stations got wind of it. It'll go out on the wire services next thing you know and we'll have six friggin' camera crews camped in the driveway."

"Donovan, I swear. If there was a leak, it didn't come from me."

"Well, someone spilled the beans and you're the only one who stands to benefit."

"Me? That makes no sense. How would I benefit from a story about Guy?"

"The reporter who called mentioned you by name. He knew you'd been hired and he was interested in how you'd gone about finding

Guy after all these years. He as good as told me he intended to play that angle: 'Local PI locates heir missing eighteen years.' It's better than an advertisement for all the work you'll get."

"Donovan, stop it. That's ridiculous. I'd never blab client business under any circumstance. I don't need more work. I have plenty." This was not entirely true, but he didn't need to know that. The bottom line was, I'd never give client information to the media. I had a reputation to protect. Aside from ethical considerations, this was not a profession where you wanted to be recognized. Most working investigators keep a very low profile. Anonymity is always preferable, especially when you're inclined, as I am, to use the occasional ruse. If you're posing as a meter reader or a florist delivery person, you don't want the public to be aware of your true identity. "I mean, think about it, Donovan. If I'd actually given him the story, why would he be quizzing you about my methods? He'd know that already so why would he ask you?"

"Well, you might have a point there, unless he was looking for confirmation."

"Oh, knock it off. You're really stretching for that one."

"I just think it's damn suspicious that you got a plug."

"Who's the reporter? Did you ask where he got his information?"

"He never gave me the chance."

"Well, let me put in a call to him. Why don't we just ask him? It might be something simple or obvious once you hear. You remember his name?"

"Katzensomething, but I don't think it's smart for you to talk to him."

"Katzenbach. I know Jeffrey. He's a nice man."

Donovan plowed on, not wanting to yield his ground. "I'm telling you, lay off. I don't want you talking to him about anything. Enough is enough. If I find out you're behind this, I'll sue your ass from here to next Tuesday," he said and banged down the receiver on his end.

The "screw *you*" I offered snappishly came half a second too late, which was just as well.

The minute he'd broken the connection my adrenaline shot up. My mouth was dry and I could feel my heart begin to pound in my ears. I wanted to protest, but I could see how it looked from his perspective. He was right about the fact that I was the only one outside the family who knew what was going on. More or less, I thought, pausing to correct myself. Myrna could have tipped the paper, but it was hard to see why she'd do such a thing. And of course, Peter and Winnie knew what was going on, but again why would either one of them want to make the matter known? I had a strong impulse to pick up the phone and call Katzenbach, but Donovan's admonition was still ringing in my ears. Once in touch, I was worried the reporter would start pumping me for information. Any comment I made might be quoted in a follow-up and then my credibility would be shot for sure.

Dimly, I wondered if Guy could have tipped off the paper himself. It seemed unlikely, but not impossible and I could see a certain canny logic if the move was his. If the issue of his inheritance became public knowledge, his brothers would have a hell of a time trying to screw him out of it. The problem with that notion was that Guy had never demonstrated much interest in the money and he certainly hadn't seemed concerned about protecting his share. Could he be as devious and manipulative as his family claimed?

I snagged my jacket and my handbag and headed out again. I tried to shake off my anxiety as I walked the short distance to my car, which was parked half a block down. There was no way to convince the Maleks of my innocence. Accused of the breach, I found myself feeling apologetic, as if I'd actually been guilty of violating the family's trust. Poor Guy. In the wake of my denial, they'd probably turn on *him*.

By the time I reached the downtown area, I'd managed to distract myself, wondering if I'd find a parking space within a reasonable radius of Lonnie Kingman's building. I tried the spiral approach, like a crime scene investigation, starting at the inner point and working outward. If nothing opened up, I could always use the public parking lot, which was three blocks away.

The second time I circled, I saw a van pull into the stretch of red-painted curb in front of the building. The door on the passenger side slid back and a fellow with a camcorder swung himself out on the walk. The slim blond who anchored the six o'clock news hopped down from the front seat and scanned the numbers on the building, verifying the address from a note on her pad. Coming up from behind, I couldn't see the logo on the side of the van, but it had an aerial on top that looked fierce enough to receive messages from outer space. Oh, shit. As I passed the van, I could see KEST-TV painted on the side. I resisted the urge to speed away as the woman threw a glance in my direction. I peered to my left, turning toward the building across the street. I waved merrily at someone emerging from the Dean Witter office. Maybe the press would mistake me for a cruising mogul with some money to invest. I kept driving, eyes pinned on my rearview mirror as the cameraman and his companion went into the entranceway.

Now what? I didn't like the idea of skulking in the bushes like a renegade. Maybe I was being paranoid and the crew was on its way to cover something else. I drove several blocks before I spotted a pay phone on the corner. I left my car at the curb, dropped a quarter in the slot, and dialed Lonnie's private line. He must have been in court because Ida Ruth picked up, thinking it was him. "Yessir?"

"Ida Ruth, this is Kinsey. Did a TV crew show up looking for me?"

"I don't think so, but I'm back here at my desk. Let me check with Alison up front." She put me on hold for a moment and then clicked back in. "I stand corrected. They're waiting for you in reception. What's going on?"

"It's too complicated to explain. Can you get rid of them?"

"Well, we can get 'em out of here, but there's no way we can keep them from hanging around on the street outside. What did you do, if I may be so bold?"

"Nothing, I swear. I'm completely innocent."

"Right, dear. Good for you. Stick to that," she said.

"Ida Ruth, I'm serious. Here's the deal," I said. I filled her in briefly and heard her cluck in response. "My, oh my. If I were you, I'd lay low. They can't stay long. If you tell me how to reach you, I'll call you when they're gone."

"I'm not sure where I'll be. I'll check back in a bit." I put the receiver down and scanned the street corner opposite. There was a bar on the corner that appeared to be opening. I could see a neon light in the window blink on. As I watched, a fellow in an apron opened the front door and kicked the doorstop into place. I could always hang out in there, drinking beer and sniffing secondhand smoke while I figured out what to do next. On the other hand, come to think of it, I hadn't *done* anything so why was I behaving like a fugitive. I fished around in the bottom of my bag and came up with a second coin. I put a call through to the *Dispatch* and asked for Jeffrey Katzenbach. I didn't know him well, but I'd dealt with him on a couple of occasions in the past. He was a man in his fifties, whose career had been stalled by his appetite for cocaine and Percocet. He'd always been sharp if you caught him early in the day, but as the afternoon progressed, he became harder to deal with. By nightfall, he could still function, but his judgment was sometimes faulty and he didn't always remember the promises he'd made. Two years ago, his wife had left him and the last I'd heard, he'd finally straightened up his act with the help of Narcotics Anonymous. Guy Malek wasn't the only one who'd undergone personal transformation.

When I got through to Katzenbach, I identified myself and we exchanged the usual pleasantries before getting down to business. "Jeffrey, this is strictly off the record. The Maleks are my clients and I can't afford to be quoted."

"Why? What's the problem?"

"There isn't any problem. Donovan's pissed off because he thinks I called you and spoiled the family reunion."

"Sorry to hear that."

"How'd you get wind of it? Or is this a 'confidential source'?"

"Nothing confidential about it. There was a letter on my desk when

I got in last night. We've always encouraged our subscribers to get in touch if they think there's a story we might not've heard about. Sometimes it's just trivia or crank stuff, but this one grabbed my attention."

"Who sent the letter?"

"Some fellow named Max Outhwaite with an address on Connecticut out in Colgate. He thought it was an item worth bringing to our attention."

"How'd he hear about it?"

"Beats me. He talked like he'd known 'em all for years. Basically, the letter says a search was conducted and Bader Malek's son Guy was located after an absence of eighteen years. That's correct, isn't it? I mean, tell me I'm wrong and I'll eat my Jockey shorts."

"You're correct, but so what?"

"So nothing. Like he says, here's this fellow working as a janitor in some backwater town, finds out he's inheriting five million bucks. How often does that happen? He thought the community would be interested. I thought it sounded like a winner so I put a call in to the Maleks. The number's in the book, it didn't require any red-hot detective work. I talked to Mrs. Malek—what's her name, Christie—who confirmed the story before I even got to Donovan. Sure enough, that's the deal unless there's something I missed."

"And I was mentioned by name?"

"You bet. It's one of the reasons I figured it was on the up-and-up. I tried to reach you last night, but all I got was your answering machine. I didn't bother to leave a message. I figured you were on your way over there to help 'em celebrate. How'd you find the guy? Outhwaite's letter says you got a lead on him through the DMV."

"I don't believe this. Who is this man and where's he getting his information?"

"How do I know? He acted like he was maybe a friend of the family. You never talked to him yourself?"

"Jeffrey, knock it off. I didn't call so you could pump me. I'm trying to persuade the Maleks I didn't leak this thing."

"Too bad you didn't. You could have filled in the details. I went back to check with Outhwaite and the guy doesn't exist. There's no Outhwaite in the phone book and no such house number anywhere on Connecticut Avenue. I tried a couple of other possibilities and I came up with blanks. Not that it matters as long as the story's legitimate. I got confirmation from the family."

"What about the L.A. *Times*? How did they get wind of it?"

"Same way we did. Outhwaite dropped 'em a note—almost like a press release. It's been a slow week for news and we're always on the lookout for human-interest stuff. This was better than a little lost kitty-cat trapped in a well. I thought it was worth pursuing, especially when I saw you were involved."

"I wished you'd done some fact checking with me along the way."

"Why? What's the problem?"

"There isn't any *problem*," I said, irritably. "I just think the family might appreciate a little privacy before the whole world rushes in. By the way, Jeffrey, I've heard you tippy-tapping on your keyboard ever since we started this conversation. I told you this is off the record."

"What for? It's a nice story. It's a great fantasy. What's the deal with the Maleks? Why're they so pissed with the coverage? We did front page, second section when Bader Malek died. He was an important figure in the community and they were happy to have the tribute. What's so hush-hush about Guy? Are they trying to cut him out of his inheritance or something?"

I rolled my eyes skyward. The man couldn't help but press for information. "Listen, buddy, I'm as clueless as you. What about the letter? What happened to it?"

"It's sitting right here."

"You mind if I have a copy? It would go a long way toward restoring my credibility. I feel like a fool having to defend myself, but I have a reputation to maintain."

"Sure. I can do that. I don't see why not. We're interested in Guy's perspective if you can talk him into it."

"I'm not trading—but I'll do what I can."

"Terrific. What's your fax number?"

I gave him the number of Lonnie Kingman's machine and he said he'd fax the letter over. If I located Max Outhwaite, Jeffrey wanted to talk to him. Fair enough. I said I'd do what I could. It didn't cost me anything to profess my conditional cooperation. I tried not to be too profuse in my thanks. It's not like I planned to take the letter straight to Donovan, but I was curious about the contents and thought it made sense to have a copy for my files. At some point, Katzenbach would extract something from me in return, but for now, I was fine. I didn't believe Guy would agree to an interview, but maybe he'd surprise me.

I got back in my car and drove over to the public parking lot. From there, I hoofed it to the office on foot. There was no sign of the KEST-TV van out front. I took the stairs two at a time and entered Kingman and Ives through an unmarked door around the corner from the main entrance. In the back of my mind, I was mulling over the possibility that maybe Bennet or Jack had taken the letter to the *Dispatch*. I couldn't see what it would net either of them, but *someone* had an interest in seeing Guy's homecoming splashed across the news and it was someone who knew more than I was comfortable with. Again, I could feel the faint nudge of uneasiness. Darcy Pascoe's computer search had been a bit of a fudge. I hoped she wasn't going to find herself in trouble as a result of my request. I checked the fax machine in Lonnie's office and found the copy of Max Outhwaite's letter sitting in the slot as promised. I went to my office, reading as I went.

Dear Mr. Katzenbach,

Thought you'd be interested in a Modern-Day ''Cinderfella'' story taking place

right here in Santa Teresa! As I recall,
your the reporter, who wrote about Bader
Malek's death last month. Now, word around
town has it that his Probate Attorney hired
a Private Investigater (a ''Female'' no
less) to locate his missing son, Guy. If
you've been around town as long as me,
you'll remember that as a youngster, Guy
Malek was caught in a number of scrapes, and
finally disappeared from the local scene,
nearly twenty years ago. You'd think finding
someone like that after all this time would
prove daunting, but Milhone (the
aforementioned ''Female'' Detective) ran a
DMV check, and turned him up in less than two
days!! Seems he's been up in Marcella ever
since he left, and he's working as a <u>janiter</u>
in a church up there! He's one of those
''Born-Agains,'' who probably didn't have
two nickles to rub together, but his
father's death has turned him into an
instant millionnaire!! I think people would
be heartened to hear how he's managed to
turn his life around, threw his Christian
Faith. Folks might also enjoy hearing what
he's planning to do with his new-found
riches. With all the bad news that besieges
us from day to day, wouldn't this story give
everyone a nice lift? I think it would be a
wonderfull inspiration to the Community!
Let's hope Guy Malek is willing to share the
story of his ''good fortune'' with us. I
look forward to reading such an article and

know you'd do a fine job of writing it! Best
of luck and God Bless!

Sincerely yours,
Max Outhwaite
2905 Connecticut Ave.
Colgate, CA

I noticed I held the letter by the corners, as if to avoid smudging prints, a ridiculous precaution given the fact that it wasn't even the original. The note was neatly typed, with no visible corrections and no words XXX'd out. Granted, there were spelling errors (including my name), an excessive use of commas, a tendency toward the emphatic, and a bit of Unnecessary Capitalization! but otherwise the intentions of the sender seemed benign. Aside from alerting the press to something that was nobody else's business, I couldn't see any particular attempt to meddle in Guy Malek's life. Maximilian (or perhaps Maxine) Outhwaite apparently thought subscribers to the *Santa Teresa Dispatch* would be warmed by this story of a Bad Boy Turned Good and the Resultant Rewards! Outhwaite didn't seem to have an ax to grind and there was no hint of malice to undercut his (or her) enthusiasm for the tale. So what was going on?

I set the letter aside, swiveling in my swivel chair while I studied it covertly out of the corner of my eye. As a "Female" Detective, I found myself vaguely bothered by the damn thing. I didn't like the intimate acquaintance with the details and I couldn't help but wonder at the motivation. The tone was ingenuous, but the maneuver had been effective. Suddenly, Guy Malek's private business had been given a public audience.

I placed the letter in the Malek file, turning it over to my psyche for further consideration.

I spent the rest of the morning at the courthouse, taking care of other business. As a rule, I'm working fifteen to twenty cases concurrently. Not all of them are pressing and not all demand my attention at the same time. I do a number of background checks for a research and development firm out in Colgate. I also do preemployment investigations, as well as skip traces for a couple of small businesses in the area. Periodically, I'm involved in some fairly routine snooping for a divorce attorney down the street. Even in a no-fault state, a spouse might hide assets or conceal the whereabouts of communal items, like cars, boats, planes, and minor children. There's something restful about a morning spent cruising through the marriage licenses and death records in pursuit of genealogical connections, or an afternoon picking through probated wills, property transfers, and tax and mechanics' liens at the county offices. Sometimes I can't believe my good fortune, working in a business where I'm paid to uncover matters people would prefer to keep under wraps. Paper stalking doesn't require a PI to slip into a Kevlar vest, but the results can be just as dangerous as a gun battle or a high-speed chase.

My assignment that Monday morning was to probe the financial claims detailed in a company prospectus. A local businessman had been approached to invest fifty thousand dollars in what looked like a promising merchandising plan. Within an hour, I'd found out that one of the two partners had filed for personal bankruptcy and the other had a total of six lawsuits pending against him. While I was about it, I did a preliminary search for Max Outhwaite, starting with voter registration and working my way through local tax rolls. I crossed the street to the public library and tried the reference department. Under that spelling, there were no Outhwaites listed in the local phone books and none in the city directories going back six years. This meant nothing in particular as far as I could see. It did suggest that "Max Outhwaite" was a nom de plume, but under certain circumstances, I could relate to the maneuver. If I wanted to call an issue to the attention of the local paper, I might conceivably use a fake name and a phony address. I might be a prominent person, reluctant to have myself associated with the subject in question. I might be a family member, eager to get Guy in trouble, but unwilling to take responsibility. Writing such a letter was hardly a crime, but I might feel guilty nonetheless and not want the consequences blowing back on me.

For lunch I bought a sandwich and a soft drink from a vending machine and sat on a stretch of lawn out behind the courthouse. The day was hot, the treetops buffeted by dry winds coming off the desert. The branches of the big evergreens planted close to the street seemed to shimmer in the breeze, giving off the scent of pitch. I leaned back on my elbows and turned my face up to the sun. I can't say I slept, but I gave a good impression of it. At one o'clock, I roused myself and went back to the office where I began to type up my findings for the cases I'd worked. Such is the life of a PI these days. I spend more time practicing my skills with a Smith-Corona than a Smith & Wesson.

12

My run that morning had been unsatisfactory. I'd done what needed
doing, dutifully jogging a mile and a half down the bike path and a
mile and a half back, but I'd never developed any rhythm and the
much-sought-after endorphin rush had failed to materialize. I've noticed on days when the run isn't good, I'm left with an emotional itch
that feels like anxiety, in this case compounded by mild depression.
Short of drink and drugs, sometimes the only remedy is to exercise
again. I swear this is not a compulsion on my part so much as a
craving for relief. I drove over to Harley's Beach and found a parking
spot in the shelter of the hill. The lot was nearly empty, which surprised me somehow. Usually, there's an assortment of tourists and
beachcombers, joggers, lovers, barking dogs, and parents with small
children. Today, all I spotted was a family of feral cats sunning
themselves on the hillside above the beach.

I staggered across an expanse of loose, dry sand until I reached the hard pack at the water's edge. I would have pulled off my shoes and socks, rolling up my pant legs so I could jog in the surf, however someone had recently given me a small book about tide pools. I'd leafed through with interest, imagining myself in the role of inquisitive naturalist, poking among the rocks for tiny crabs and starfish (though their undersides are completely disgusting and gross). Until I read this colorful, informative pamphlet, I'd had no idea what strange, ugly beasties existed close to shore. I'm not the kind of person who sentimentalizes nature. The outdoors, as far as I can see, is made up almost entirely of copulating creatures who eat one another afterward. To this end, almost every known animal has developed a strategy for luring others within range. Among life-forms in the sea—some quite minuscule—the tactic involves thorny parts or pincers or tiny three-jawed mouths or trailing stingers or vicious suckers with which they latch on to one another, causing painful death and dismemberment, all in the name of nourishment. Sometimes the juice is slurped out of the victim long before death occurs. The starfish actually takes out its own stomach, enfolds its live prey, and digests it outside its body. How would you like to put your bare foot down on that?

I ran in my shoes, splashing through the surf when the waves came close. Soon my wet jeans clung to my legs, the heavy fabric cold against my shins. My feet were weighted as though with stones and I could feel the sweat begin to soak through my shirt from the labor of the run. Despite the damp breeze coming off the ocean, the air felt oppressive. For the third day in a row, Santa Ana winds were blasting in from the desert, blowing down the local canyons, pulling moisture from the atmosphere. The mounting heat collected, degree by degree, like a wall of bricks going up. My progress felt slow and I forced myself to focus on the sand shimmering ahead of me. Since I had no way to measure distance, I ran for time, jogging thirty minutes north before I turned and jogged back. By the time I reached Harley's Beach again, my breathing was ragged and the muscles in my thighs were on fire. I slowed to a trot and then geared down to a walk as I returned to my car. For a moment, I leaned panting against the hood. Better. That was better. Pain was better than anxiety any day of the week and sweat was better than depression.

Home again, I left my soggy running shoes on the front steps. I padded upstairs, peeling out of my damp clothes as I ascended. I took a hot shower and then slipped into a pair of sandals, a T-shirt, and a short cotton skirt. It was now close to four and there was no point returning to the office. I brought in the mail and checked for phone messages. There were five: two hang-ups; two reporters who left numbers, asking me to get back to them; and a call from Peter Antle, the pastor of Guy's church. I dialed the number he'd left and he picked up so fast I had to guess he'd been waiting by the phone.

"Peter. I got your message. This is Kinsey in Santa Teresa."

"Kinsey. Thanks for being so prompt. Winnie's been trying to call Guy, but she can't seem to get through. The Maleks have the answering machine on and nobody's picking up. I don't know what Guy's plans are, but we thought we'd better warn him. There are reporters camped out at the gas station across from his place. We have people knocking on the church door and a pile of messages for him."

"Already?"

"That was my reaction. Frankly, I don't understand how this got out in the first place."

"Long story. I'm still in the process of looking into it. I know the family was contacted by the local newspaper first thing this morning. The reporter here had had a letter delivered to him at the paper. I guess something similar was sent to the L.A. *Times*. I haven't seen the news yet, but I have a feeling it's going to get bigger before it goes away."

"It's even worse up here. The town's so small, none of us can manage to avoid the press. Do you have a way to get in touch with Guy? We're here for him if he needs us. We don't want him to lose his footing in the stress of the situation."

"Let me see if I can find a way to get through. I guess this is his fifteen minutes of fame, though frankly, I can't understand why the story's generating so much attention. Why should anyone give a fat rat's . . . aa . . . ah . . . ear? He doesn't even have the money yet and who knows if he'll ever see one red cent."

I could almost see Peter's grin. "Everyone wants to believe in something. For most people, a big windfall would literally be the answer to all their prayers."

"I suppose so," I said. "At any rate, if I reach him, I'll have him give you a call."

"I'd appreciate that."

After we hung up, I flipped on the TV set and tuned in to KEST. The evening news wouldn't air for an hour, but the station often ran quick promos for the show coming up. I suffered through six commercials and caught the clip I'd suspected would be there. The blond anchorwoman smiled at the camera, saying, "Not all news is bad news. Sometimes even the darkest cloud has a silver lining. After nearly twenty years of poverty, a Marcella maintenance man has just learned he'll be inheriting five million dollars. We'll have that story for you at five." Behind her, the camera showed a glimpse of a haggard-looking Guy Malek, staring impassively from the car window as Donovan's BMW swung through the gates of the Malek estate. I felt a pang of guilt, wishing I'd talked him out of coming down. Given his bleak expression, the homecoming wasn't a success. I picked up the phone again and tried the Maleks' number. The line was busy.

I called the number every ten minutes for an hour. The Maleks had probably taken the phone off the hook, or maybe their message tape was full. In either event, who knew when I'd get through to him.

I debated with myself briefly and then drove over to the house. The gate was now closed and there were six vehicles parked along the berm. Reporters loitered, some leaning against their car fenders, two chatting together in the middle of the road. Both men were smoking and held big Styrofoam coffee cups. Three camera units had been set up on tripods and it looked as if the troops were prepared to stay. The late-afternoon sun slanted between the eucalyptus trees across from the Malek property, dividing the pavement into alternating sections of light and shadow.

I parked behind the last car and went on foot as far as the call box near the front gate. All activity behind me ceased and I could feel the attention focus on my back. No one answered my ring. Like the others, I was going to have to hang around out here, hoping to catch sight of one of the Maleks exiting or entering the grounds. I tried one more time, but my ringing was greeted with dead silence from inside the house.

I returned to my car and turned the key in the ignition. Already, a dark-haired woman reporter was ambling in my direction. She was probably in her forties, with oversized sunglasses and bright red lips. As I watched, she fumbled in her shoulder bag and pulled out a cigarette. She was tall and slender, decked out in slacks and a short-cropped cotton sweater. I marveled she could bear it with the heat sitting where it was. Gold earrings. Gold bracelets. A daunting pair of four-inch heels. For my taste, walking in high heels is like trying to learn to ice-skate. The human ankle does not take readily to such requirements. I admired her balance, though I realized when she reached me that in bare feet she'd probably be shorter than I. She made a circling motion, asking me to roll down my car window.

"Hi. How are you?" she said. She held up the cigarette. "You have a light for this?"

"Sorry. I don't smoke. Why don't you ask one of them?"

She turned, her gaze sliding back to the two men standing in the road. Her voice was husky and her tone was dismissive. "Oh, them. That's the boys' club," she remarked. "Those two won't even give you the time of day unless you have something to trade." Her eyes flicked back to me. "What about you? You don't look like a reporter. What are you, family friend? An old sweetheart?"

I had to admire the placid way she eased right into it, casual, unconcerned. She was probably wetting her pants, hoping I'd provide a little tidbit so she could scoop her competition. I started rolling up my window. Quickly, she raised her handbag and turned it sideways, inserting it into the space so the window wouldn't close all the way. There was now a seven-inch gap where her leather bag was wedged.

"No offense," she said, "but I'm curious. Aren't you that private investigator we've heard so much about?"

I turned the key in the ignition. "Please remove your bag." I cranked the window down about an inch, hoping she'd pull the bag free so I could be on my way.

"Don't be in such a hurry. What's the rush? The public has a right to know these things. I'm going to get the information anyway so why not make sure it's accurate? I heard the kid spent a lot of time in jail. Was that here or up north?"

I cranked the window up a notch and put the car in gear. I pushed my foot down lightly on the gas pedal and eased away from the berm. She held on to the bag by its strap, walking beside the car, continuing the conversation. I guess she was accustomed to having the driver at her mercy once she used the old handbag trick. I increased my speed sufficiently to force her into a trot. She yanked the strap, yelling "Hey!" as I began to accelerate. I couldn't have been driving more than two miles an hour, but that's a tough pace to maintain when you're wearing heels that high. I inched my foot down on the gas. She released the bag and stopped where she was, watching with consternation as I pulled away. I passed the two guys in the road who seemed to enjoy the rude comment she was yelling after me. I couldn't hear the words, but I got the drift. In the rearview mirror, I saw her flip me the bird.

She removed a high heel and flung it at my rear window. I heard a mild thump on impact and saw the shoe bounce off behind me as I picked up speed. The long strap of the handbag dangled and flapped against the car door. About a hundred yards down the road, I paused long enough to roll down my window and give the bag a shove. I left it there in the road, curled like a possum, and drove to my apartment.

There were two newspapers on the sidewalk when I got home. I picked up both and left one on Henry's back doorstep before I let myself in. I turned on some lights and poured myself a glass of wine, then sat at the kitchen counter and spread the paper out in front of me. The story was in the second section and the tone was odd. I'd expected a fairy-tale version of Guy's life to date, his estrangement from the family and his subsequent spiritual transformation. Instead, Jeff Katzenbach had patched together, in excruciating detail, an inventory of all the sins from Guy's youth: countless episodes of reckless driving, vandalism, drunk and disorderly conduct, assault and battery. Some charges dated back to his juvenile record and should have been purged or remained sealed by the courts. Where had Katzenbach gotten his information? Some of it, of course, was a matter of public record, but I wondered how he'd known to look. He'd obviously been tipped off by Max Outhwaite's reference to Guy's earlier scrapes. I thought back uneasily to the file of news clippings Bader Malek had kept. Was there any way he could have seen that? This would have been a second leak of sorts. The first was the fact of Guy's return; the second, this detailed criminal history. I noticed Katzenbach had couched his revelations in typical journalistic fudgings. The word *alleged* appeared about six times, along with *confidential sources, informants close to the family, former associates,* and *friends of the Maleks who asked to remain anonymous.* Far from celebrating Guy's good fortune, the public was going to end up resenting his sudden wealth. Reading between the lines, you could tell Katzenbach considered Guy Malek an undeserving scoundrel. Somehow his current church affiliation looked self-serving and insincere, the convenient refuge of a culprit hoping to make himself look good in the eyes of the parole board.

For supper, I made myself a hot hard-boiled egg sandwich with lots of mayonnaise and salt and perched at the counter eating while I scanned the rest of the paper. I must have been more absorbed than I thought because when the telephone shrilled, I flung my sandwich sideways in response. I snatched up the receiver, heart thumping as though a gun had just been fired in my ear. If this turned out to be a reporter, I was going to hang up. "Yes."

"Hey."

"Oh shit. Guy, is that you? You scared the hell out of me." I leaned down and gathered up the remains of my sandwich, popping the crust in my mouth while I licked at my fingers. There was mayonnaise on the floor, but I could tend to that later.

"Yeah, it's me. How are you?" he said. "I tried calling a while ago, but you were out, I guess."

"Thank God you called. I was just over at the house, but I couldn't get anyone to answer my ring. What's happening?"

"We just finished dinner. Have you seen the news?"

"I have the paper in front of me."

"Not so good, huh."

"It's not that bad," I said, hoping to cheer him up. "It does look like somebody's really got it in for you."

"That's my assumption," he said lightly.

"Are you all right? Peter called earlier. He's been trying to get in touch, but all he's managed so far is the answering machine. Did you get his message?"

"No, but why would I? Everybody here is pissed at me. They think I notified the paper, trying to get attention. There's a powwow on for later, after Donovan gets home. He's got a meeting until nine. The delay's making me sick. Reminds me of that old business, 'You wait until your father gets home and he'll give you the what for.' "

I found myself smiling. "You want me to come get you? I can be there in fifteen minutes."

"Yes—no—I don't know what I want. I'd like to get out of here, but I don't dare take off with things as they are."

"Why not? The damage is done. Whoever spilled the beans, made it look as bad as they could. If *you'd* leaked the news, you'd have put a different spin on it."

"How would I manage that? You can't put a different spin on the truth."

"Of course you can. It's called politics."

"Yeah, but I did all those things. This is just payback time. I told you I was bad. At least, now you know the worst."

"Oh stop that. I don't care about that stuff. All I care about is getting you out of there."

"You want to come for a visit? I could sneak out for a few minutes. Jack and Bennet are downstairs and Christie's in the office, going through some of Dad's old papers."

"Sure. I can pop back over there. What do you want me to do? Shall I ring from the gate?"

"No, don't do that. I'll meet you out on Wolf Run Road," he said. "If the side gate's locked, I can scale the wall. I'm an expert at getting out. When I was a kid I used to do it all the time. That's how I managed to get in so much trouble back then."

"Why don't you bring your backpack and let me spirit you away," I said. "I'll drive you to Marcella and you can hire an attorney to handle your interests from here on."

"Don't tempt me. Right now, all I need is civilized conversation. Park in that little grove of trees just across from the gate. I'll be out there in fifteen minutes."

I took a few minutes to tidy up the kitchen and then I changed into jeans, a dark shirt, and my Reeboks. The evening air felt uncharacteristically warm, but I wanted to be prepared for night maneuvers if need be. Once at the Maleks', I took a quick swing by the front gate. There were now two more news crews and the gathering had taken on the feel of a vigil outside a prison. Portable lights had been turned on and a man with a microphone spoke directly to a camera, making gestures toward the house. I saw the dark-haired reporter, but she didn't see me. She seemed to be bumming a light for her cigarette from a poor unsuspecting "source."

I followed the wall, circling the property as I turned left on Wolf Run. I spotted the gate, a dark blot in an otherwise unbroken expanse of wall. I pulled off onto the berm across the road, gravel crackling under my wheels. I shut down the engine and sat there, listening to the tick of hot metal and the murmur of the wind. There weren't any street lamps along this section of the road. The high night sky was clear, but the moon had been reduced to the merest sliver, a frail curve of silver in a sky pale with stars. The dust in the air was as fine as mist. In the ambient light, the pavement was a dull, luminous gray. The stucco wall enclosing the Malek property had been robbed of its pink luster and stretched now like a ghostly band of drab white. June and July were traditionally dry and I associated the Santa Ana winds with the end of summer—late August, early September, when the fire danger was extreme. For years, January had been the rainy season, two weeks of rain that we hoped would fill our annual quota. Yet here we were with the dry wind tossing in the treetops. The bend and sway of tree boughs set up a hushed night music, accompanied by the rustling percussion of dry palm fronds, the occasional snap of tree limbs. By morning, the streets would be littered with dead leaves and the small withered skeletons of broken branches.

The gate opened without a sound and Guy emerged, head down. He wore a dark-colored jacket, his fists shoved into his pockets as though he were cold. I leaned over and unlocked the door on the passenger side. He slid into the seat and then pulled the door shut without slamming it. He said, "Hey. Thanks for coming. I thought I'd go crazy without a friendly face. I'd have called you before, but they were watching me like a hawk."

"No problem. I don't know why you don't break and run while you can."

"I will. Tomorrow. Or maybe the day after that. I told you we're supposed to have another meeting tonight just to talk about some things."

"I thought you already talked."

"Well, we did. We do. Every time I turn around, we have another chat."

"That's because you haven't knuckled under yet," I interjected.

"I guess that's it." He smiled in spite of himself. His tension was contagious and I could have sworn I smelled alcohol on his breath. I found myself with my arms crossed, one leg wound around the other as if to protect myself.

"I feel like we're having an affair," I said.

"Me, too. I used to meet girls out here in the old days when I was grounded. I'd slip over the wall and we'd screw in the backseat of a car. There was something about the danger set me on fire, and them, too. Made most of 'em seem more interesting than they were."

"I know this is none of my business, but have you been drinking?" I asked.

He turned and looked out the passenger window, shrugging. "I had a couple of drinks last night before all this shit came down. I don't know what got into me. Don't get me wrong—they were being nice at that point, but you could tell they were nervous and so was I. I'm ashamed to say this, but the alcohol did help. It mellowed us out and smoothed the conversation. Tonight was pretty much the same except everybody's mood was different. Cocktail hour comes along and those guys really hit it."

"Bennet and his martinis."

"You bet. I figure that's the only way I'll get through. Peter wouldn't be too happy with me, but I can't help it. I can feel myself sliding back to my old ways."

"What'd you think of Christie?"

"She was nice. I liked her. I was surprised at Bennet—at the weight he'd put on, but Jack seemed the same, still nuts about golf. And Donovan hasn't changed."

"What've they said to you so far?"

"Well, we talked some about the money, what else? I mean, the subject does come up. It's like Donovan says, we can't just ignore the issue. It's like this big dark cloud hanging over us. I think we were all uncomfortable at first."

"Have you resolved anything?"

"Well, no. Nothing much. At first, I think they were wondering, you know, generally, about my attitude. Now, anything I say and everybody jumps right on in. Tell you the truth, I'd forgotten what they're like."

"How do they seem to you?"

"Angry. Underneath it all, they're pissed. I keep feeling the anger coming up inside me, too. It's all I can do to keep a lid on it."

"Why bother? Why not blow? The three of them certainly don't hesitate."

"I know, but if I flip my lid that's only going to make matters worse. I'm trying to show 'em I've changed and then I find myself feeling like I always did. Like I want to smash lamps, throw a chair through a window, get stoned or drunk or something bad like that."

"That must be a trial."

"I'll say. I mean, literally. All I can think about is maybe this is some kind of test of my faith."

"Oh, it is *not*," I said. "It may be a test of your patience, but not your faith in God."

He shook his head, pressing his hands down between his knees. "Let's talk about something else. This is making me so tense I could fart."

I laughed and changed the subject. For a while we chatted about inconsequential matters. Hunched there in the front seat, I was reminded of the occasional dates I had in high school where the only hope of privacy was remaining closed away in some kid's car. On chilly evenings, the front windshield would fog up even if all we did was talk. On warm nights like this, we'd sit with the windows rolled down, radio tuned to some rock and roll station. It was Elvis or the Beatles, clumsy moves and sexual tension. I don't even remember now what we talked about, those lads and I. Probably nothing. Probably we drank purloined beer, smoked dope, and thought about the incredible majesty of life.

"So what else's going on? Aside from interminable meetings?" I asked. Like a rough place on a fingernail, I couldn't resist going back to it. Apparently, Guy couldn't resist it either because we fell right into the subject again.

This time he smiled and his tone seemed lighter. "It's nice to see the house. I found some letters of my mother's and I read those today. She's the only one I ever missed. The rest of 'em are a waste."

"I don't want to say I told you so, but I did predict this."

"I know, I know. I thought we could just sit down like grown-ups and clean up some old business, but it doesn't really happen like that. I mean, I keep wondering if there isn't some kind of defect in me because everything I do just seems to come out wrong. Whatever I say seems 'off,' you know? They look at me like I'm speaking in tongues and then I see them exchange these looks."

"Oh, I know that one. Jack and Bennet are big on flicking looks back and forth."

"That's the easy part, but there's worse."

"Like what?"

"I don't even know how to describe it. Something under the surface. Something slides right by and no one owns up to it, so then I start questioning my own thought process. Maybe I'm nuts and it's not them after all."

"Give me an example."

"Like when I told 'em I'd like to give something to the church? I honestly don't want the money for me. I mean that. But Jubilee Evangelical saved my life and I want to give something back. To me, that doesn't seem so wrong. Does it seem wrong to you?"

"No, not at all."

"So, I say that and all of a sudden we're in the middle of a power play. Bennet's saying how it really doesn't seem fair. You know how he talks with that slightly pompous air of his. 'Our family's never been religious. Dad worked for the good of us all, not for the benefit of some church he never heard of.' He says it all in this completely rational tone and pretty soon I wonder if what I want to do is right after all. Maybe they have a point and *my* values are screwed up."

"Sure they have a point. They want you to relinquish all claim so they can divide up your portion among themselves. They know perfectly well you're entitled to a quarter of his estate. What you do with your share is none of their business."

"But how come I end up the magnet for all that rage?"

"Guy, stop. Don't do that. That's the third time you've said that. Don't get into self-blame. The gamesmanship has obviously been going on for years. That's got to be why you left in the first place, to get away from that stuff. I swear they were behaving the same way before you showed up."

"You think I should leave?"

"Well, of course I do! I've said it all along. You shouldn't take their abuse. I think you should get the hell out while you have the chance."

"I wouldn't call it 'abuse.' "

"Because you're used to it," I said. "And don't get sidetracked. Your brothers aren't going to change. If anybody goes down for the count, it's going to be you."

"Maybe so," he said. "I don't know. I just feel like I have to stay since I've come this far. If I cut and run, we're never going to find a way to work this through."

"I can tell you're not listening, but please, *please,* don't agree to anything without talking to an attorney first."

"Okay."

"Promise me."

"I will. I swear. Well, I gotta go before somebody figures out I've escaped."

"Guy, you're not sixteen. You're forty-three years old. Sit here if you want. You can stay out all night. Big whoop-dee-do. You're an adult."

He laughed. "I *feel* like I'm sixteen. And you're cute."

He leaned over quickly and brushed my cheek with his lips. I could feel the soft scratch of his whiskers against my face and I caught a whiff of his aftershave.

He said, "Bye-bye and thanks." Before I could respond, he was out of the car, shoulders hunched up against the wind as he moved to the gate. He turned and waved and then he was swallowed up by the dark.

I never saw him again.

13

Guy Malek was killed sometime Tuesday night, though I didn't actually hear about it until Wednesday afternoon. I'd spent most of the day over at the courthouse sitting in on the trial of a man accused of embezzlement. I hadn't been associated with the case—undercover cops had nailed him after seven months of hard work—but some years before, I'd done surveillance on him briefly at the request of his wife. She suspected he was cheating, but she wasn't sure with whom. Turned out he was having an affair with her sister and she broke off relations with both. The man was dishonest to the core and I confess I found it entertaining to watch the legal system grind away at him. As often as I complain about the shortage of justice in this world, I find it infinitely satisfying when the process finally works as it should.

When I got back to the office after court adjourned, there was a message from Tasha waiting on my machine. I noticed, in passing, it was the Maleks' number she'd left. I called, expecting to have Myrna pick up. Instead Tasha answered as if she'd been manning the phones. The minute I heard her, I realized how irritated I was that she'd gone out of town just as Guy arrived. If she'd been doing her job, she might have steered the family off their campaign of pressure and harassment.

Smart mouth that I am, I launched right in. "At long last," I said, "it's about time you got back. All hell's broken loose. Have you heard what's going on? Well, obviously you have or you wouldn't be there. Honestly, I adore Guy, but I can't stand the rest of 'em—"

Tasha cut in, her voice flat. "Kinsey, that's why I called. I cut my trip short and flew back from Utah this afternoon. Guy is dead."

I was silent for a beat, trying to parse the sentence. I knew the subject . . . *Guy* . . . but the predicate . . . *is dead* . . . made no immediate sense. "You're kidding. What happened? He can't be *dead*. When I saw him on Monday he was fine."

"He was murdered last night. Somebody smashed his skull with a blunt instrument. Christie found him in bed this morning when he didn't come down for breakfast. The police took one look at the crime scene and got a warrant to search the premises. The house has been swarming with cops ever since. They haven't found the murder weapon, but they suspect it's here. They're still combing the property."

I kept getting hung up about two sentences back. "Somebody killed him in bed? While he *slept?*"

"It looks that way."

"That's disgusting. That's awful. You can't be serious."

"I'm sorry to spring it on you, but there isn't any nice way to put it. It *is* disgusting. It's terrible. We're all numb."

"Has anybody been arrested?"

"Not at this point," she said. "The family's doing what they can to cooperate, but it doesn't look good."

"Tasha, I don't believe this. I'm sick."

"I am, too. A colleague called me in Utah this morning after

Donovan called him. I left everything behind and got myself on a plane."

"Who do they suspect?"

"I have no idea. From what I've heard, Jack and Bennet were both out last night. Christie went to bed early and Donovan was watching TV upstairs in their sitting room. Myrna's apartment is off the kitchen in back, but she says she was dead to the world and didn't hear anything. She's currently down at the station being interviewed. Christie came in a little while ago. She says the detectives are still talking to Donovan. Hang on."

She put a hand across the mouthpiece and I heard her in a muffled discussion with someone in the background. She came back on the line, saying, "Great. I just talked to the homicide detective in charge of things here. He wants to keep the phone line open, but says if you want to come over. he'll tell the guys at the gate to let you in. I told him he ought to talk to you since you were the one who found Guy in the first place. I told him you might have something to contribute."

"I doubt that, but who knows? I'll be there in fifteen minutes. Do you need anything?"

"We're fine for the moment. If no one's at the gate, the code is 1-9-2-4. Just punch the number in at the call box beside the drive. See you shortly," she said.

I grabbed my blazer and my handbag and went out to my car. The day had been mild. The high winds had moved on, taking with them the unseasonable heat. The light was waning and as soon as the sun set, the temperatures would drop. I was already chilled and I shrugged into my blazer before I slid beneath the wheel. Earlier in the day, I'd tried to use my wipers and washer fluid to clean the dust off my windshield and now it was streaked in a series of rising half moons. The hood of my car was covered with the same fine layer of dust, as pale as powder, and just as soft by the look of it. Even the seat upholstery had a gritty feel to it.

I put my hands together on the steering wheel and leaned my forehead against them. I had absolutely no feeling. My interior process was held in suspended animation, as if the Pause button had been pushed on some remote control. How was it possible Guy Malek was gone? For the past week, he'd been such a presence in my life. He'd been both lost and found. He'd occupied my thoughts, triggering reactions of sympathy and exasperation. Now I couldn't quite remember his face—only a flash here and there, the sound of his "Hey," the whiskery brush of his chin on my cheek. He was already as insubstantial as a ghost, all form without content, a series of fragmented images without permanence.

What seemed so odd was that life just went *on*. I could see traffic passing along Cabana Boulevard. Two doors away, my neighbor raked brittle leaves into a pile on his lawn. If I turned on the car radio, there'd be intervals of music, public service announcements, commercials, and news broadcasts. Guy Malek might not even be mentioned on some stations. I'd lived my entire day without any intuition that Guy had been murdered, no tremor whatsoever in my subterranean landscape. So what's life about? Are people not really dead until we've been irrefutably informed? It felt that way to me, as though Guy had, just this moment, been jettisoned out of this world and into the next.

I turned the key in the ignition. Every ordinary act seemed fraught with novelty. My perceptions had changed, and with them many of my assumptions about my personal safety. If Guy could be murdered, why not Henry, or me? I drove on automatic pilot while the street scenes slid past. Familiar neighborhoods looked odd and there was a moment when I couldn't recall with any certainty what town I was in.

Approaching the Maleks', I could see that traffic had increased. Cars filled with the curious cruised by the estate. Heads were turned almost comically in the same direction. There were cars parked on both sides of the road out front. Tires had chewed into the grass, plowing down bushes and crushing the stray saplings. As each new car appeared, the assembled crowd would turn, craning and peering to see if it was someone of note.

My car didn't seem to generate a lot of interest at first. I guess nobody could believe the Maleks would drive a VW bug, especially one like mine, with its dust and assorted dings. It was only when I pulled up at the gate and gave my name to the guard that the reporters surged forward, trying to catch a glimpse of me. They seemed to be fresh troops. I didn't recognize anyone from my earlier trip over.

Somehow the national media had already managed to get camera crews assembled, and I knew that by seven the next morning, someone closely associated with the Maleks would be seen in a three-minute interview. I don't know how the major networks make arrangements so quickly. It was one of the miracles of technology that less than twenty-four hours after Guy Malek's death, somebody would do a close-up of a tear-stained face, maybe Christie's or Myrna's or even Enid's, the cook I'd yet to meet.

There was a black-and-white patrol car parked to one side, along with a vehicle from a private firm. I spotted the security guard pacing along the road, trying to keep the crowd from moving in too close. A uniformed police officer checked my name on his clipboard and waved me in. The gate swung inward by degrees and I idled the engine until the gap was sufficient to ease through. In that brief interval, there were strangers knocking on my car window, yelling questions in my direction. With their various handheld mikes extended, they might have been offering gimcracks for sale. I kept my eyes straight ahead. When I pulled forward through the gate, two male reporters continued to trot alongside me like cut-rate Secret Service agents. The security guard and the cop both converged, cutting off their progress. In my rearview mirror, I could see them begin to argue with the officer, probably reciting their moral, legal, and Constitutional rights.

My heart rate picked up as I eased up the driveway toward the house. I could see five or six uniformed officers prowling across the property, eyes on the ground as if hunting for four-leaved clovers. Light tended to fade rapidly at this hour of the day. Shadows were already collecting beneath the trees. Soon they'd need flashlights to continue the search. There was a second uniformed officer posted at the front door, his face impassive. He walked out to meet my car and I rolled down my window. I gave him my name and watched him scan both his list and my face. Apparently satisfied, he stepped away from the car. In the courtyard to my left, there were already numerous cars jammed into the cobblestone turnaround. "Any place in here all right?"

"You can park in the rear. Then come around and use the front door to go in," he said, and motioned me on.

"Thanks."

I pulled around to the left and parked my car at the far end of the three-car garage. In the diminishing light, a cluster of three floods, activated by motion sensors, flashed on to signal my presence. Except for the kitchen on this end of the house and the library on the other, most of the windows along the front of the house were dark. Around the front, the exterior lighting seemed purely decorative, too pale to provide a welcome in the accumulating gloom.

The uniformed police officer opened the door for me and I passed into the foyer. The library door was ajar and a shaft of light defined one pie-shaped wedge of the wood parquet floor. Given the quiet in the house, I was guessing the technicians were gone—fingerprint experts, the photographer, the crime scene artist, coroner, and paramedics. Tasha appeared in the doorway. "I saw you pull in. How're you doing?"

I said "Fine" in a tone that encouraged her to keep her distance from me. I noticed I was feeling churlish, as much as with her as with circumstance. Homicide makes me angry with its sly tricks and disguises. I wanted Guy Malek back and with some convoluted emotional logic, I blamed her for what had happened. If she hadn't been my cousin, she wouldn't have hired me in the first place. If I hadn't been hired, I wouldn't have found him, wouldn't even have known who he was, wouldn't have cared, and would have felt no loss. She knew this as well as I did and the flicker of guilt that crossed her face was a mirror to mine.

For someone who'd flown back from her vacation in haste, Tasha was flawlessly turned out. She wore a black gabardine pantsuit with a jacket cropped at the waist. The slim, uncuffed trousers had a wide waistband and inverted pleats in front. The jacket had brass buttons and the sleeves were trimmed with a thin gold braid. Somehow the outfit suggested something more than fashion. She looked crisp, authoritative, and diminutive, the dainty MP of lawyers here to keep matters straight.

I followed her into the library with its clusters of dark red cracked leather chairs. The red Oriental carpets looked drab at this hour. The tall leaded glass windows were tinted with the gray cast of twilight, as chilly as frost. Tasha paused to turn on table lamps as she crossed the room. Even the luster of the dark wood paneling failed to lend coziness to the cold stone hearth. The room was shabby and smelled as musty as I remembered it. I'd first met Bennet here just a week ago.

I left my handbag beside a club chair and circled the room restlessly. "Who's the chief investigator? You said there was someone here."

"Lieutenant Robb."

"Jonah? Oh, terrific. How perfect."

"You know him?"

"I know Jonah," I said. When I'd met him, he was working Missing Persons, but the Santa Teresa Police Department has a mandatory rotation system and detectives get moved around. With Lieutenant Dolan's retirement, there was an opening for a homicide investigator. I'd had a short-lived affair with Jonah once when he was separated from his wife, a frequent occurrence in the course of their stormy relationship. They'd been sweethearts since seventh grade and were no doubt destined to be together for life, like owls, except for the intervals of virulent estrangement coming every ten months. I suppose the pattern should have been evident, but I was smitten with him. Later, not surprisingly, she crooked her little finger and he went back to her. Occasionally now, the three of us crossed paths out in public and I'd become an expert at pretending I'd never dallied with him between my Wonder Woman sheets. This probably accounted for his willingness to have me on the scene. He knew he could trust me to keep my mouth shut.

"What's the story?" she asked.

"Nothing. Just skip it. I feel bitchy, I guess, but I shouldn't take it out on you."

I heard footsteps on the stairs and looked up as Christie came in. She wore bulky running shoes and a warm-up suit in some silky material, the blue of the fabric setting off the blue in her eyes. She wore scarcely any makeup and I wondered if this was the outfit she was wearing when Guy's body was discovered. The library, like the living room, was equipped with a wet bar: a small brass sink, a minirefrigerator, an ice bucket, and a tray of assorted liquor bottles. She moved over to the fridge and removed a chilled bottle of white wine. "Anybody want a glass of wine? What about you, Kinsey?"

I said, "Alcohol won't help."

"Don't be absurd. Of course it will. So does Valium. It doesn't change reality, but it improves your attitude. Tasha? Can I interest you in a glass of Chardonnay? This is top of the line." She turned the bottle so she could peer at the price tag on the side. "Nice. This is $36.95."

"I'll have some in a bit. Not just yet," Tasha said.

Mutely, the two of us watched while Christie cut the foil cap from a wine bottle and used a corkscrew. "If I smoked, I'd have a ciggie, but I don't," she said. She poured herself some wine, the bottle clinking clumsily on the rim of the Waterford crystal. "Shit!" she said, pausing to inspect the damage. A jagged crack ran down the side. She dumped the contents in the sink and tossed the glass in the trash. She picked up a second glass and poured again. "We need a fire in here. I wish Donovan were home."

"I can do that," I said. I moved over to the hearth and removed the fire screen. There were six or seven hefty pieces of firewood in a brass carrier. I picked up one and chunked it onto the grate.

"Make sure you don't destroy any evidence," she said.

I looked up at her blankly.

"Ted Bundy killed one of his victims with a hunk of wood," she said, and then shrugged with embarrassment. "Never mind. Not funny. What a day," she said. "I can't figure out how to handle it. I've felt drunk since this morning, completely out of control."

I stacked two more logs on the grate while she and Tasha talked. It was a relief to be involved in a task that was basic and inconsequential. The wood was beautifully seasoned oak. Most of the heat would go straight up the chimney, but it would be a comfort nonetheless. I flicked on the electric match, turned the key in the gas starter, and listened to the comforting *whunk* as the jets ignited. I replaced the fire screen, pausing to adjust the height of the flame. Belatedly, I tuned into their conversation.

Tasha was saying, "Did you ask to have an attorney present?"

"Of course I didn't ask for an attorney. I didn't *do* anything. This was just routine," Christie said irritably. She remained standing behind the bar, leaning against its leather surface. "Sorry. What's the matter with me? I'm completely frazzled."

"Don't worry about it. Who's still down there?"

"Jack and Bennet, I think. They kept everybody separated like they did here. So absurd. What do they think, Donovan and I aren't going to discuss it in detail the minute we can put our heads together?"

"They don't want to risk your influencing one another," I said. "Memory's fragile. It's easily contaminated."

"None of us have anything much to report," she said. "I drank too much at dinner and fell asleep by nine. Donovan was watching TV in the sitting room off our bedroom."

"What about Guy?"

"He went up to bed about the same time I did. He was drunk as all get-out thanks to Bennet's martinis." She caught sight of her fingertips and frowned to herself. She turned away from us and ran water in the sink. "They took prints for comparison."

Tasha directed a brief comment to me. "After the body was removed and the fingerprint techs were finished, the homicide investigator had one of the Maleks' housecleaning crew come over and walk through Guy's room with him describing the usual position of furniture, lamps, ashtrays, that sort of thing."

"Did they find anything?"

"I have no idea. I'm sure she was cautioned to keep her mouth shut. I know they tagged and bagged a bunch of items, but I don't know exactly what or why they were significant. Now they've brought in additional officers and started a grid search of the grounds. Apparently, they spent a lot of time down in the pool house earlier."

Christie broke in. "I could see them from up in my room checking perimeter gates, any point of entrance or exit."

"They're still out there on the property. I noticed that when I came in. But why check the exterior? It almost had to be someone in the house."

Christie bristled. "Not necessarily. What makes you say that? We have people all over. Maybe fifteen a week, with the gardeners and the car washers, housecleaners, and the woman who takes care of the plants. We have no idea where those people come from. For all we know, they're convicted felons or escapees from a mental institution."

I wasn't going to speak to her flight of fancy. If the notion gave her comfort, let her hang on to it. "It's always possible," I said, "but I'm assuming none of them have access to the house at night. I thought you had an alarm system."

"Well, we do. The police were interested in the system as well, but that's the problem," she said. "With all the high winds we've had here the past couple of days, windows were blowing open and the alarm kept going off. It happened twice Monday night after we'd all gone to bed. Scared the shit out of me. We finally turned it off so it wouldn't happen again. Last night, the system wasn't on at all."

"When do they think Guy was killed?" I asked.

"Around ten, I gather. Between ten and eleven. The detective

didn't actually say that, but I noticed that was the period that seemed
to interest him. Bennet and Jack were both out until late."

A woman in a housekeeper's uniform, with an apron tied over it,
peered in at the door. She was short and round, and looked like
someone whose eating habits had long ago outstripped any fat-
burning activities. She was probably in her mid-forties, with dark
hair pulled back neatly under a red-and-white bandanna she'd
wrapped around her head. I wasn't sure if the purpose was ornamental or meant to keep falling hair from seasoning the food. "Excuse
me. I'm sorry to interrupt, but I'm wondering what time you want
dinner served."

Christie made a face. "My fault, Enid. I should have talked to you.
Donovan's not back yet and I'm not really sure about Jack and Bennet. What are we having? Will it hold?"

"Baked chicken breasts. I stopped off at the market on my way in
to work. I went ahead and changed the menu, so there's plenty if
you're having extra people. I did up some oven-roasted potatoes and
a casserole of sweet-and-sour cabbage. I can wait and serve if you
like." Somehow she managed to indicate without a word that waiting
around to serve dinner was the last choice on her list.

"No, no, no. I don't want you to do that. Just leave things in the
oven and we can help ourselves. As soon as you're ready, go ahead
and take off. I know you were in early."

"Yes, ma'am. Myrna called me. I came as soon as I heard."

"Have the police talked to you? I'm assuming they have. They
talked to everyone else."

Enid picked at her apron uncomfortably. "I talked to Lieutenant
Bower shortly before you did, I believe. Do you want me tomorrow at
the usual time?"

"I don't know yet. Call me in the morning and we'll see what's
going on. I may want you here early if that's all right with you."

"Of course."

As soon as she withdrew, Christie said, "Sorry for the interruption.

That's Enid Pressman. She's the cook. I guess I could have introduced you. I didn't mean to be rude. Tasha's met her before."

"That's perfectly all right," I said. I made a quick mental note to have a chat with Enid at some point. She'd neatly avoided relating much in the way of information.

Tasha said, "Maybe I will have that drink. Here, let me get it. You look exhausted. We need to sit."

Christie had put the wine bottle in a cooler and now grabbed two more glasses. Tasha moved over to the bar and took the cooler from her, setting it down on a table between two chairs. Christie quizzed me with a gesture, asking if I was ready to have wine.

"I'm fine for now, but go ahead," I said.

Christie curled up in one of the leather chairs. She tucked her legs under her and crossed her arms.

I took the chair closest to the fireplace while Tasha perched on the arm of the chair next to Christie's. Tasha said, "What about Bennet? Where was he last night?"

"I'm not really sure. You'd have to ask him about that."

"And Jack?"

"Over at the country club with a hundred other fellows. There's a pro-am tournament coming up this weekend. Practice rounds start on Thursday. He went to the pairings' party with a friend of his."

"That should be easy enough to verify," Tasha said.

"Would you quit talking like that? He didn't kill Guy and neither did I."

"Christie, I'm not accusing you. I'm trying to analyze your position here. Given the situation, suspicion's bound to fall on one of you. I don't mean you specifically, so don't take offense. Other people may have access to the property, but who'd have a better motive than the family? There's a lot of money at stake."

"But Tasha, that's ridiculous. If one of us were going to kill him, why do it here? Why not somewhere else? Make it look like an accident or random violence."

I raised my hand like a student. "Think of the convenience. If you kill a man in his sleep, you don't have to worry about him putting up a fight."

Jonah Robb appeared in the doorway, his gaze fixed on Christie. "We'll be taking off shortly. The bedroom's still sealed pending the coroner's report. It's strictly off-limits until you hear from us. We'll be here early tomorrow morning to finish things up."

"Of course. Will there be anything else?"

"I understand your brother-in-law received some mail . . ."

"We gave that to the other detective, Lieutenant Bower."

Jonah nodded. "Fine. I'll check with her."

"Do you have any idea what time we can expect my husband? When I left the station, he was still being interviewed."

"I'll have him call if he's there when I get back to the station. With luck, he'll be done and on his way home."

"Thanks."

Jonah's gaze came to rest on mine and he tilted his head. "Can I see you out here?"

I got up and crossed the room. He held the door open and we went into the hall.

He said, "Donovan tells us you were the one who located Guy on behalf of the estate."

"That's right."

"We're going to want to talk to you in the morning, picking up background information."

"Of course. Glad to help. I can stop by at nine on my way into work," I said. "What's this business about the mail?"

"I haven't seen it yet," he said obliquely, meaning *none-of-your-beeswax*. We looked at each other for perhaps half a moment longer than was absolutely essential. I'd always thought Jonah was good looking. Black Irish, I think they call them. Blue eyes, coal black hair. He looked worn-out and tense, his eyes surrounded by a lacework of fine lines, his skin looking coarser than I remembered. Perhaps as a side effect of my renewed sexuality, I found myself sizing up the men in my life. With Jonah, there was a dark radiance in the air. I felt like a fruit fly, wondering if the pheromones were mine or his.

"How's Camilla?"

"She's pregnant."

"Congratulations."

"It's not mine."

"Ah."

"What about you? You involved with anyone these days?"

"Could be. It's hard to know."

His smile was brief. "See you in the morning."

That you will, I thought.

14

Once Jonah was gone, I found myself reluctant to return to the library. I could hear Christie and Tasha talking together companionably, their voices light, the conversation interspersed with nervous laughter. The subject had obviously changed. The ego is ill-prepared to deal with death for long. Even at a wake or a funeral, the topic tends to drift to safer ground whenever possible. I scanned the empty foyer, trying to get my bearings. Across from the library was the living room. I'd been in there, but I'd never seen the rest of the ground floor.

I passed under the stairs to an intersecting corridor that branched off in both directions. I caught a glimpse of a powder room across the hall. I saw two doors on the right, but both were closed. Under the circumstances, I thought it unwise to snoop indiscriminantly. In the unlikely event I encountered a cop, I was roaming in the guise of someone looking for the kitchen so I could offer my help.

Before, the house had felt comfortable despite the touches of shabbiness that appeared throughout. Now I was acutely aware of the imprint of Guy's murder. The very air seemed heavy, the gloom as languorous as a dense fog drifting through the rooms.

I took a left, moving toward the unhappy scent of cooked cabbage at the end of the hall. In a sudden glimpse of the future, I could envision the day when this house would be sold to a private boys' school and the smell of cruciform vegetables would overpower all else. Young lads in hard shoes would clatter through the halls between classes. The room where Guy had been bludgeoned to death would be turned into a dormitory where adolescent boys would abuse themselves surreptitiously after lights out. Always, there would be rumors about the pale apparition gliding down the corridor, hovering on the landing at the turn of the stairs. I found myself walking quickly, anxious for human company.

Beyond the dining room and butler's pantry, the swinging door to the kitchen stood open. The room looked vast to me, but then my entire culinary kingdom would fit in the rear of a moderately priced station wagon. The floors were pale, glossy pegged oak planks stretching out in all directions. The custom cupboards were dark cherry and the counters were topped with mottled green marble. There were sufficient cookbooks, utensils, and small appliances in view to furnish one small section of a Williams-Sonoma retail outlet. The stove top looked bigger than the double bed in my loft and the refrigerator had clear doors with all the contents on view. To the right, there was the equivalent of a little sitting area; and beyond, there was a glassed-in porch that extended the entire length of the room. Here the lush scent of roast chicken and garlic overrode the odor of cooked cabbage. Why does someone else's cooking always smell so much better than your own?

Myrna had come back from the police station. She and Enid were standing together near one of the two kitchen sinks. Myrna's face looked puffy and the prickle of red around her eyes suggested she'd been crying, not within the last few minutes, but perhaps earlier in the day. Enid had pulled on a poplin raincoat and the yards of tan fabric gave her the hapless form and shape of a baked potato. She'd removed her bandanna. Bareheaded, she had a wiry bird's nest of hair that was dark strands streaked with gray. Tea mugs in hand, they must have been having a few last words about the murder because both looked up guiltily as I came in. Given their proximity to events, the two of them must have been privy to just about everything. Certainly, the family wasn't shy about airing their conflicts. God knows they'd squabbled in front of me. Enid and Myrna must have picked up on plenty and probably compared notes.

Enid said, "Can I help you?" She was using the same tone museum guards take when they think you're about to reach out and touch something on the far side of the rope.

"That's what I came to ask," I said. "Can I do anything to help?" Little Miss Goody Two-shoes working on a Girl Scout merit badge.

"Thanks, but everything's under control," she said. She emptied her mug in the sink, opened the dishwasher, and set it in the top rack. "I better go while I can," she murmured.

Myrna said, "I can walk you out if you want."

"I'll be fine," Enid replied. "I can turn on the lights in back." And then with a look at me, "Can I fix you a cup of tea? The water's hot. I'm just on my way out, but it won't take but a minute."

"I'd like that," I said. I'm not that fond of tea, but I had hoped to prolong the contact.

"I can do it," Myrna said. "You go on."

"Are you sure?"

"Absolutely. We'll see you tomorrow."

Enid reached out and patted Myrna on the arm. "Well. Bye-bye. I want you to talk to my chiropractor about that bursitis and you call if you need me. I'll be home all evening." Enid took up a wide canvas tote and disappeared through the utility room, moving toward the backdoor.

I watched Myrna plug in the electric tea kettle. She opened a cabinet nearby and took down a mug. Wincing, she reached for a canister and removed a tea bag that she placed in the mug. Meanwhile, outside, I could hear a car door slam shut and moments later, the sound of Enid starting her car.

I moved over to the counter and perched on a wooden stool. "How're you doing, Myrna? You look tired," I said.

"That's my bursitis flaring up. It's been bothering me for days," she said.

"The stress probably contributes."

Myrna pursed her lips. "That's what my doctor says. I thought I'd seen everything. I'm used to death. In my job, I see a lot of it, but this . . ." She paused to shake her head.

"It must have been hellish around here today. I could hardly believe it when Tasha told me," I said. "You've worked for the Maleks, what . . . eight months?"

"About that. Since last April. The family asked me to stay on after Mr. Malek died. Somebody had to take responsibility for running the house. Enid was tired of doing it and I didn't mind. I've managed many a household, some of 'em a lot bigger than this."

"Couldn't you be making a lot more money as a private-duty nurse?"

She took down a sugar bowl and found a creamer that she filled from a carton of half-and-half in the refrigerator. "Well, yes, but I needed some relief from all the terminal illness. I become attached to my patients and where does that leave me when they pass? I was living like a Gypsy, moving from job to job. Here I have a small apartment of my own and the duties are largely supervisory. I do light cooking occasionally on Enid's nights off, but that's about it. Of course, they complain. They're hard to please sometimes, but I don't let it bother me. In some ways, I'm used to it. The sick are often difficult and it doesn't mean anything. I let it roll right off me."

"I take it you were here last night."

The tea kettle began a hoarse whisper that rapidly turned into a shriek. She paused to unplug it and the shrill sound subsided as though with relief. I waited while she filled the mug and brought it over to me. "Thanks."

I could see her hesitate, apparently debating with herself about her next comment. "Is something bothering you?" I asked.

"I'm not sure what I'm allowed to say," she hesitated. "The lieutenant asked us not to talk to the press . . ."

"Not surprising," I said. "Have you seen 'em out there?"

"Like vultures," she remarked. "When I came back from the station, they were all yelling and vying for my attention, pushing microphones in my direction. Made me want to pull my jacket right up over my face. I felt like one of those criminals you see on the television."

"It's probably only going to get worse. This started out as a minor human-interest story. Now it's big news."

"I'm afraid so," she said. "But to answer your question, yes, I was here, but I didn't hear anything. I've had trouble sleeping lately with this arm of mine. Ordinary analgesics don't begin to touch the pain, so I'd taken a Tylenol with codeine and a prescription sleeping pill. I don't do that often because I dislike the effect. Leaves me feeling logy the next morning, like I never quite wake up. Also, I find the sleep so deep it's almost not restful. I went to bed about eight-thirty and didn't stir until nearly nine this morning."

"Who discovered the body?"

"I believe it was Christie."

"What time was this?"

"Shortly after ten. I'd made myself a cup of coffee and I was back here in the kitchen, watching the morning news on that little TV set. I heard all the commotion. They were supposed to meet for breakfast to talk about the will, and when Guy didn't come down, I guess Bennet got furious. He thought Guy was playing games, at least that's what Christie told me later. Bennet sent her upstairs to fetch him.

Next thing I knew they'd dialed 9-1-1, but I still wasn't sure what was going on. I was just on my way out there when Donovan came in. He looked awful. He'd lost all his color and was white as a sheet."

"Did you see the body?"

"I did, yes. He asked if I'd go up. He thought there might be something I could do, but of course there wasn't. Guy must have been dead several hours by then."

"There's no doubt?"

"Oh, none. Absolutely. He was cold to the touch and his skin was waxen. His skull had been crushed and there was blood everywhere, most of it dried or congealed. Given his injuries, I'd say death must have been quick, if not instantaneous. Also, messy. I know the police have been puzzled by that aspect of the murder."

"Which aspect?"

"What the killer did with his own clothes. Not to be gross about it, but there would have been quite an area of splatter. Blood and brain material. There's no way you could leave the premises without attracting attention. The detectives were interested in a number of articles of clothing. They asked for my help since I take items to the cleaners."

"Did they find anything significant?"

"I don't know. I gave them everything that was going out today. They talked to Enid at length, but I'm not sure what they wanted with her."

"You have any idea what the weapon was?"

"I wouldn't hazard a guess. That's not an area where I feel qualified to comment. There was nothing in the room, at least as far as I could see. I did hear one of the detectives say the autopsy was scheduled first thing tomorrow morning. I imagine the medical examiner will have an opinion," she said. "Have you been hired by the family to investigate?"

I could feel the lie form, but then thought better of it. I said, "Not yet. Let's hope it doesn't come to that. I can't believe anybody in the family is going to turn out to be responsible."

I expected her to pipe up with protests and reassurances, but the quiet that followed was significant. I could sense a desire to confide, but I couldn't imagine what. I let my gaze rest on hers with an expression I hoped appeared trustworthy and encouraging. I could almost feel my head tilt like a dog trying to decipher the direction of a high-pitched whistle.

She'd become aware of a dried speck on the counter and she worked at it with her fingernail, not looking at me. "This is really none of my business. I had only respect for Mr. Malek . . ."

"Absolutely."

"I wouldn't want anyone to think badly of me, but I can't help but hear things while I'm going about my business. I'm paid well and God knows, I enjoy the work. Or at least I did."

"I'm sure you're only trying to help," I said, wondering where she was going with this.

"You know, Bennet never agreed to share the money. He wasn't convinced that was Bader's intention and neither was Jack. Of course, Jack sided with Bennet in just about everything."

"Well, maybe they weren't convinced, but given the missing will, I don't know what choice they had, short of court action. I gather nothing was settled."

"Not at all. If they'd settled their business, Guy would have gone home. He was miserable here. I could see it in his face."

"Well, that's true. When I talked to him on Monday, he admitted he'd been drinking."

"Oh, especially last night. They started with cocktails and went through four or five bottles of wine with dinner. And then, port and liqueurs. It was still going on when I went off to bed. I helped Enid with the dishes and she could see how exhausted I was. Both of us heard them quarreling."

"Bennet and Guy quarreled?"

She shook her head, lips moving.

I cupped a hand to my ear. "Excuse me. I didn't hear that."

She cleared her throat and raised her voice half a notch. "Jack.

Guy and Jack quarreled before Jack went off to his country club. I told the lieutenant about it and now I'm wondering if I should have kept my mouth shut."

"The truth is the truth. If that's what you heard, you had to tell the police."

"You don't think he'll be mad?" Her tone was anxious, her expression almost childlike in its apprehension.

I suspected the entire family would have fits when they heard, but we all had an obligation to cooperate with the police investigation. "Maybe so, but you can't worry about that. Guy was *murdered* last night. It's not up to you to protect anyone."

She nodded mutely, but I could see she remained unconvinced.

"Myrna, I mean this. Whatever happens, I don't think you should feel responsible."

"But I didn't have to volunteer the information. I like Jack. I can't believe he'd hurt anyone."

"Listen, you think I'm not going to end up in the same position? The cops are going to talk to me, too. I have to go down there tomorrow and I'm going to end up doing exactly what you did."

"You are?"

"Of course. I heard them quarrel the night I came here for drinks. Bennet and Donovan were going at it hammer and tongs. Christie was the one who told me they did it all the time. That doesn't make 'em killers, but it's not up to us to interpret the facts. You have to tell the cops what you heard. I'm sure Enid will back you up. Nobody's going to be arrested on that basis anyway. It's not like you saw Jack coming out of Guy's room with a bloody two-by-four."

"Not at all. Of course not." I could see some of the tension begin to leave her face. "I hope you're right. I mean, I can see what you're saying. The truth is the truth. All I heard was a quarrel. I never heard Jack threaten him."

"Exactly," I said, with a glance at my watch. It was nearly six by then. "If you're through for the night, I better let you go. I probably ought to get on out of here myself, but first I want to have a little chat with Christie."

Anxiety flickered in her eyes. "You won't mention our conversation?"

"Would you quit *worrying?* I won't say a word and I don't want you saying anything either."

"I appreciate that. I believe I would like to go wash my face."

I waited until Myrna had disappeared through the utility room, moving toward her apartment. My tea was untouched. I emptied my cup and left it in the sink. Despite Enid's good example, I've never owned a dishwasher and don't know the first thing about loading one. I pictured one false move and every dish would go flying, crashing in a heap of rubble. I returned to the library. Christie and Tasha had turned on the television set. Christie held the remote and she was switching from channel to channel to see if she could catch the news. She pressed the Mute button when I came in, turning to look at me. "Oh, there you are. Come in and join us. Tasha thought you were gone."

"I'm on my way," I said. "I went out to the kitchen to see if I could help out there. Could I ask you a question before I take off? I heard you mention the mail when you were talking to Lieutenant Robb. Can I ask what that was?"

"Sure. Uhm, let's see. I guess late Monday afternoon someone put an unsigned letter in the mailbox. The envelope had Guy's name on it, but there was no return address. He left it on the hall table when he went to bed last night. I thought the police might want to take a look."

"Was it typed or handwritten."

"The envelope was typed."

"Did you read the letter?"

"Of course not, but I know it bothered Guy. He didn't say what it was, but I gather it was something unpleasant."

"Did he ever mention a Max Outhwaite? Does the name mean anything to you?"

SUE GRAFTON

"Not that I remember." She turned to Tasha. "Does it ring a bell with you?"

Tasha shook her head. "What's the connection?"

"That's how the reporter first heard Guy was back. Someone named Max Outhwaite dropped off a letter at the *Dispatch*, but when Katzenbach checked it out, there was no one by that name and no such address. I double-checked as well and came up blank."

"Never heard of him," Christie said. "Is there any chance he's connected to one of Guy's old sprees? Maybe Outhwaite was somebody Guy mistreated back then."

"Possible," I said. "Do you mind if I check Bader's file upstairs?"

"What file?" Tasha asked.

Christie answered before I did. "Bader kept a folder of newspaper clippings about Guy's various arrests and his scrapes with the law. It goes back quite a way."

"I'll tell you something else crossed my mind," I said. "This Outhwaite, whoever he is, certainly put Jeff Katzenbach on the trail of Guy's criminal history. I'm not sure Jeff would have known about it otherwise. The minute I saw the letter, I remember wondering if it was really Bennet or Jack who tipped him off somehow."

"Using Outhwaite's name?"

"It seems possible," I said.

"But why would either of them do that? What's the point?"

"That's the problem. I don't know. Anyway, I could be off base on this one," I said. "I do like the idea that Outhwaite's someone Guy sinned against in the old days."

"Take the file if you want. It was still on the desk in Bader's office last I saw."

"Let me pop upstairs and grab it. I'll be right back."

I moved out of the library and crossed the foyer. Maybe when I talked to Jonah, he'd level with me about the letter. I went up the steps two at a time, studiously avoiding a look down the hall. I had no idea which room Guy had been in, but I didn't want to go near it. I took a hard left at the head of the stairs and went straight to Bader's

188

room, where I opened the door and flipped on the overhead light. Everything seemed to be in order. The room was cold and smelled slightly musty from disuse. The overhead illumination was dim and the pale colors in the room looked flat. I passed through to the office beyond, hitting switches as I went. Bader's life force was being systematically erased. Closets had been emptied, all the personal items removed from his desktop.

I surveyed the surrounding area. I spotted the folder with all the newspaper articles about Guy's past behavior, relieved that the cops hadn't swept through and taken it. On the other hand, the search warrant probably wasn't that broad. The list of property to be seized might have been directed only toward the murder weapon itself. I leafed through the clippings, speed-reading for content, looking for the name *Outhwaite* or anything close. There was nothing. I checked through some of the stray folders on the desk, but found nothing else that seemed relevant. One more dead end, though the idea was sound—someone with a grudge making Guy's life difficult. I pressed the file under my arm and left the room, turning off the lights as I went.

I pulled the door shut behind me, pausing in the hallway outside the master suite. Something felt wrong. My first urge was to scurry down the stairs toward the lighted rooms below, but I found myself slowing. I could hear a crackling sound and I peered to my left. The far end of the corridor was enveloped in shadow, except for an X of crime scene tape across three doorways. As I watched, the tape seemed to become nearly luminous, vibrating audibly as if rattled by wind. I thought for a moment the tape would break free, clicking and snapping as though a current were moving through it. The air on the landing was chilly and there was the faint scent of something animal—wet dog or old fur. For the first time, I allowed myself to experience the horror of Guy's death.

I began to descend, one hand on the railing, the other clutching the file. I pivoted, reluctant to turn my back on the darkness behind me. For a moment, I scrutinized the stretch of corridor I could see.

Something hovered in my peripheral vision. I turned my head slowly, nearly moaning with fear. I could see sparkles of light, almost like dust motes materializing in the stillness. I felt a sudden flush of heat and I could hear ringing in my ears, a sound I associated with childhood fainting spells. My phobia about needles had often inspired such episodes. When I was young, I was often subjected to a typhoid inoculation, a tine test for tuberculosis, or a periodic tetanus injection. While the nurse took the time to pooh-pooh my fears, assuring me "big girls" didn't put up the fuss I did, the ringing would begin, building to a high pitch and then silence. My vision would shrink, the light spiraling inward to a tiny point. The cold would rush up and the next thing I'd know, there'd be anxious faces bending over me and the sharp scent of smelling salts held under my nose.

I leaned back against the wall. My mouth flooded with something that tasted like blood. I closed my eyes tightly, conscious of the thudding of my heart and the clamminess in my palms. While Guy Malek slept, someone had crept along this hallway in the darkness last night, toting a blunt object of sufficient brute matter to extinguish his life. Less than a day ago. Less than a night. Perhaps it had taken one blow, perhaps several. What troubled me was the notion of that first bone-crushing crack as his skull shattered and collapsed. Poor Guy. I hoped he hadn't wakened before the first blow fell. Better he slept on before the last sleep became final.

The ringing in my ears went on, mounting in intensity like the howling of wind. I was weighted with dread. Occasionally in nightmares, I suffer from this effect—an overpowering urge to run without the ability to move. I struggled to make a sound. I would have sworn there was a presence, someone or something, that hovered and then passed. I tried to open my eyes, almost convinced I'd see Guy Malek's killer passing down the stairs. My heartbeat accelerated to a life-threatening pitch, thrumming in my ears like the sound of running feet. I opened my eyes. The sound ceased abruptly. Nothing. No one. The ordinary noises of the house reasserted themselves. The scene before me was blank. Polished floor. Empty hall. Incandescent light from the chandelier. Glancing back down the corridor, I could see that the X's of crime scene tape was simply tape again. I sank down on the stairs. The whole of the experience had surely taken less than a minute, but the rush of adrenaline had left my hands shaking.

Finally, I roused myself from the step where I'd been sitting for God knows how long. From somewhere downstairs, I could hear a mix of male and female voices, and I knew without question that Donovan, Bennet, and Jack had returned from the police station, arriving while I was still in Bader's office. Below me, the library door stood open. Tasha and Christie must have gone to join them. Faintly, from the direction of the kitchen, I could hear the clatter of ice cubes and the clink of bottles. Drink time again. Everybody in the house seemed to need alcohol along with extended psychiatric care.

I completed my descent, anxious to avoid encountering the family. I returned to the library, peering in with caution, relieved to see the room empty. I grabbed up my handbag and shoved the file down in the outside pocket, then headed for the front door, heart still pounding. I pulled the door shut behind me, careful to soften the sound of the latch clicking into place. Somehow it seemed important to slip away undetected. After my experience on the stairs—whatever it was—I was incapable of making superficial conversation. It didn't seem unreasonable to suppose that someone in this household had murdered Guy Malek and I'd be damned if I'd make nice until I knew who it was.

15

Back in my neighborhood, parking spaces were at a premium and I was forced to leave my VW almost a block away. I locked the car and trotted to my apartment. It was fully dark by then and a chill shivered in the trees like wind. I crossed my arms for warmth, clutching the strap of my handbag as it bumped against my side. I used to carry a handgun as a matter of course, but I've given up that practice. I moved through the gate, which gave its usual welcoming squeak. My place was dark, but I could see the lights on in Henry's kitchen. I didn't want to be alone. I headed for his backdoor and rapped on the glass.

He emerged moments later from the living room. He gave a half wave when he saw me and crossed to let me in. "I was just watching the news. The murder's on all channels. Sounds bad."

"Awful. It's vile."

"Have a seat and get warmed up. It's gotten nippy out there."

I said, "Don't let me interrupt. I'll be fine sitting here."

"Don't be silly. You look cold."

"I'm freezing."

"Well, wrap up."

I put my bag down and grabbed his afghan, folding its weight around me like a shawl as I slid into his rocking chair. "Thanks. This is great. I'll be warmer in a minute. It's mostly tension."

"I'm not surprised. Have you eaten supper yet?"

"I think I had lunch, but I can't remember what I ate."

"I've got beef stew if you want. I was just about to have a bowl myself."

"Please." I watched as Henry adjusted the flame under the stew. He took out a loaf of homemade bread, sliced it thickly, and placed it in a basket with a napkin folded over it. He assembled bowls and spoons, napkins, and wine glasses, moving around the kitchen with his usual ease and efficiency. Moments later, he set bowls of stew on the table. I left his rocking chair and shuffled over to the kitchen table still wrapped in his afghan. He pushed the butter in my direction as he settled in his chair. "So tell me the story. I know the basic details. They've been blasting that across the TV screen all afternoon."

I began to eat as I talked, realizing how hungry I was. "You may know more than I do. I'm too smart to stick my nose in the middle of a homicide investigation. These days it's hard enough to put a case together without an outsider interfering."

"You're not exactly an amateur."

"I'm not an expert either. Let the techs and forensic specialists give it their best shot. I'll keep my distance unless I'm told otherwise. My stake's personal, but it's really not my business. I liked Guy. He was nice. His brothers piss me off. This is great stew."

"You have a theory about the murder?"

"Let's put it this way. This is not a case where some stranger broke in and killed Guy in the middle of a robbery. The poor man was asleep. From what I heard, everybody'd been drinking, so he more than likely passed out. He wasn't used to hard liquor, especially in massive quantities, which is how the Maleks go at it. Somebody knew where his room was and probably knew he was in no condition to defend himself. I tell you, with the possible exception of Christie, I've developed such an aversion to that family I can hardly bear to be under the same roof with them. I feel guilty about Guy. I feel guilty about finding him and guilty he came back. I don't know what else I could have done, but I wish I'd left him in Marcella where he was safe."

"You didn't encourage him to return."

"No, but I didn't argue that strenuously either. I should have been more explicit. I should have detailed their attitude. I thought the danger was emotional. I didn't think anyone would go after him and bludgeon him to death."

"You think it was one of his brothers?"

"I'm tempted by the idea," I said reluctantly. "It's a dangerous assumption and I know I shouldn't jump to conclusions, but it's always easier to pin suspicion on someone you dislike."

By eight-thirty that night, I was back in my apartment with the door locked. I sat at the kitchen counter for what felt like an hour before I worked up the courage to call Peter and Winnie Antle, who'd been following the story on the Santa Maria news station. The entire church congregation had come together earlier that evening, shocked and saddened by the murder. I hoped to cushion their loss, though in reality their faith provided them more comfort than I was able to offer. I told them I'd do what I could to keep in touch, and I broke the connection feeling little or no solace. Once the lights were turned out, I lay in my bed with a stack of quilts piled over me, trying to get warm, trying to make sense of what had happened that day. I was weighted with dread. Guy's death had generated something far worse than grief. What I experienced was not sorrow, but a heavy regret that was wedged in my chest like an undigested lump of hot meat. I didn't sleep well. My eyes seemed to come open every twenty min-

utes or so. I changed positions and adjusted the covers. First I was
too hot, then too cold. I kept thinking the next arrangement of limbs
would offer sufficient comfort to lure me to sleep. I lay on my stomach with my arms shoved under my pillow, turned on my back with
my shoulders uncovered. I tried my left side, knees pulled up, arms
tucked under, switched to my right side with one foot sticking out. I
must have set the alarm without thinking about it because the next
thing I knew, the damn thing was going off in my ear, bringing me
straight up out of the only decent sleep I'd managed all night. I
turned off the alarm. I refused to run. There was no way I was
budging from the chrysalis of heat-generating quilts. Next thing I
knew, it was nine-fifteen and I felt compelled to drag myself out of
bed. I had a date with Jonah Robb down at the police station. I
checked my reflection in the bathroom mirror. Nice. My color was
bad and I had bags under my eyes.

As it turned out, it wasn't Jonah I spoke to but Lieutenant Bower.
She kept me waiting for fifteen minutes, sitting on a little two-person
bench in what I suppose would be referred to as the lobby at the
police station. Under the watchful gaze of the officer at the desk, I
shifted in my seat and stared at the rack of crime prevention pam-
phlets. I also eavesdropped shamelessly while six whining drivers
came to complain about their traffic tickets. Finally, Lieutenant
Bower peered around the door from the Investigative Division. "Miss
Millhone?"

I'd never met Betsy Bower, but I'd been curious about her. The
name suggested someone perky and blond, a former varsity cheer-
leader with terrific thighs and no brains. To my dismay, Lieutenant
Bower was the least perky woman I'd had the pleasure to meet. She
was the police equivalent of an Amazon: statuesque, eight inches
taller than I, and probably fifty pounds heavier. She had dark hair
that she wore skinned straight back, and little round, gold-rimmed
glasses. She had a flawless complexion. If she wore makeup at all, it
was artfully done. When she spoke, I caught sight of endearingly
crooked teeth, which I realized later might have explained her reluc-

tance to smile. It was also possible she didn't like me and longed to squash me like a bug.

I followed her into a small cubicle with two wooden chairs and a scratched wooden table that had a tendency to wobble if you tried to rest your arm on it, pretending to be relaxed. She had nothing with her—no pen, no legal pad, no file, no notes. She looked directly at me, offering a few brisk sentences after which it was my turn. Somehow I had the feeling she'd remember every word I said. More likely our conversation was being recorded surreptitiously. I would have done a furtive feel-check for wiring along the underside of the table, but I was worried about the wads of old chewing gum and dried boogers parked there.

She said, "We appreciate your coming in. I understand you were hired by the estate to locate Guy Malek. Can you tell me how you went about that?" Her gaze was watchful, her manner subdued.

The question caught me by surprise. I felt a sudden flash of fear, color rising in my cheeks as if I'd just emerged from a tanning booth. I stalled like a little airplane with a tank full of bad fuel. Too late, I realized I should have prepared for this. Ordinarily, I don't lie to police officers because that would be very naughty, wouldn't it? At heart, I'm a law-and-order type. I believe in my country, the flag, paying taxes and parking tickets, returning library books on time, and crossing the street with the light. Also, I'm inclined to get tears in my eyes every time I hear the National Anthem sung by somebody who really knows how to belt it out. Right then, however, I knew I was going to have to do a little verbal tap dance because how I "went about" finding Guy Malek wasn't exactly legitimate. Neither Darcy Pascoe nor I had any business dipping into CFI's computer system to do a DMV check on a matter completely unrelated to an insurance claim. I'd probably violated some kind of civil ordinance or penal code number something-something. At the very least, the two of us were in serious breach of company policy, department regulations, common decency, and proper etiquette. This might well go down on my permanent record, something my elementary school principal had threatened me with every time I fled school with Jimmy Tait in the fifth and sixth grades. I didn't think what I'd done was a jailable offense, but I was, after all, sitting at the police station and I did have my private investigator's license to protect. Since I'd now hesitated a conspicuous five seconds, I thought it was wise to launch in on *something*.

I said, "Ah. Well. I met with Donovan, Bennet, and Jack Malek last Wednesday. In the course of those conversations, I was given Guy Malek's date of birth and his Social Security number. So late in the day on Thursday, I went over to the DMV offices and asked the clerk if there was any record of a driver's license in Guy Malek's name. The information that came back was that his license had been surrendered in 1968, but that he'd been issued a California identification card. His mailing address was listed in Marcella, California. I reported that to Tasha Howard, the attorney for the estate, and to Donovan Malek, who authorized me to drive up to Marcella to verify the address. Marcella's a small town. I wasn't there ten minutes before I got a line on Guy. Frankly, I didn't think he should come down here."

"Why is that?"

Hey, as long as my butt wasn't on the line, I didn't care who I ratted out here. "His brothers were upset at having to give him a share of their father's estate. They felt he'd been paid all the monies he was entitled to. There was the issue of a second will, which came up missing when the old man died. Bennet was convinced his father had disinherited Guy, but since that will was never found, the prior will was the one being entered into probate." I did a little detour at that point, giving Lieutenant Bower the gist of the business about Max Outhwaite, whose letter to the *Dispatch* had set all the adverse publicity in motion. She didn't leap up with excitement, but it did serve to distract her (I hoped) from the issue of my illegal computer access.

She took me through a series of questions related to the Maleks' attitude toward Guy, which I characterized as hostile. I told her about the outburst I'd witnessed between Donovan and Bennet. She asked me a number of pointed questions about Jack's statements regarding Guy, but I honestly couldn't think of anything he'd said that suggested a homicidal bent. In our initial conversation, he'd expressed bitterness at Guy's defection, but that had been almost eighteen years ago, so I wasn't convinced it was relevant. Though I didn't say so to her, I'd pegged Jack as the family mascot, someone harmless and doglike, trained to distract others with his antics. I didn't feature him as a prime player in any ongoing domestic drama.

"When did you last talk to Guy?" she asked.

"He called Monday night. He needed a break so I drove over to the house and met him near the side gate. I was glad to hear from him. I'd been worried because I knew the media had picked up the story. Peter Antle, the pastor of his church up north, had been trying to get in touch with him. The house was literally under siege and it wasn't possible to get a call through. I'd driven over there once before, hoping to make contact, and I'd just about given up."

"Why were you so interested in talking to him?"

"Largely, because Peter and his wife, Winnie, were concerned."

"Aside from that."

I stared at her, wondering what she had in mind. Did she think I was *romantically* involved? "You never met Guy," I said, stating it as fact and not a question.

"No." Her face was without animation. Her curiosity was professional and had an analytic cast to it. That was her job, of course, but I found myself struggling to articulate his appeal.

"Guy Malek was a beautiful man," I said in a voice suddenly fragile. Inexplicably, I found myself pricked by grief. My eyes stung with tears. I could feel my face get puffy and my nose turn hot. It seemed odd that in Henry's company I'd felt nothing while there, but in the face of Betsy Bowers's cold authority, all my unprocessed sorrow was surfacing. I took a deep breath, trying to cover my emotions. I was avoiding her eyes, but she must have picked up on my distress because she produced a tissue from somewhere that suddenly appeared in my field of vision. I took it with gratitude, feeling vulnerable and exposed.

Within moments, I was fine. I have strong self-control and managed to get my emotions back in the box again. "Sorry. I'm not sure where that came from. I really haven't felt much sorrow since I heard about his death. I should have guessed it was down there. He was a good person and I'm really sorry he's gone."

"I can understand that," she said. "Would you care for some water?"

"I'll be fine," I said. "It's funny—I really only saw him three times. We talked on the phone, but we weren't exactly best friends. He seemed boyish, a young soul. I must have a weakness for guys who never quite manage to grow up. I'd already given Donovan an invoice and I figured my job was done. Then Guy called on Saturday. Donovan had called him, urging him to come down so they could talk about the will. Personally, I didn't think the visit was such a hot idea, but Guy was determined."

"Did he say why?"

"He had emotional accounts to pay. At the time he left home, he was messed up on drugs. He'd been in a lot of trouble and alienated just about everyone. Once he was settled in Marcella, he cleaned up his act, but he'd left a lot of unfinished business. He said he wanted to make his peace."

"When you last spoke to him, did he mention contact with other people from his past?"

"No. I know a letter was delivered—Christie mentioned it last night—but that came on Monday and Guy never said a word about it when I saw him. As far as I know, there was nothing else. Was it significant?"

"We'd rather not discuss the content until we check it out."

"Who wrote it? Or would you rather not discuss that either?"

"Right."

"Was it typed?"

"Why do you ask?"

"Because of the letter to the *Dispatch* that generated all the hype. If the papers hadn't been tipped off, no one would have known he was back in town."

"I see what you're saying. We'll follow up."

"Can I ask about the autopsy?"

"Dr. Yee hasn't finished yet. Lieutenant Robb is there now. We'll know more when he gets back."

"What about the murder weapon?"

Her face went blank again. I was wasting my breath, but I couldn't seem to let go. "You have a suspect?" I asked.

"We're pursuing some possibilities. We're doing backgrounds on a number of people associated with the family. We're also checking everybody's whereabouts to see if all the stories add up."

"In other words, you won't say."

Chilly smile. "That's correct."

"Well. I'll do what I can to help."

"We'd appreciate that."

She made no move to close, which was puzzling. From my perspective, we'd pretty much wound up our chat. She'd asked all her questions and I'd told her what I knew. In the unspoken structure of a police interview, Detective Bower was in charge and I'd have to dance to her tune. In the unexpected pause, I could see that it was suddenly her turn to stall.

She said, "Rumor has it you're involved with Lieutenant Robb."

I squinted at her in disbelief. "*He* told you that?"

"Someone else. I'm afraid this is a small town, even smaller when it comes to law enforcement. So it's not true?"

"Well, I *was* involved, but I'm not now," I said. "What makes you ask?"

The look on her face underwent a remarkable alteration. The careful neutrality fell away and in one split second, she went from blank to blushing.

I sat back in my chair, taking a new look at her. "Are you *smitten* with him?"

"I've been out with him twice," she said cautiously.

"Ohhh, I see. Now I get it," I said. "Listen, I'm fond of Jonah, but it's strictly over between us. I'm the least of your worries. It's the dread Camilla you'd better be concerned about."

Detective Betsy Bower had abandoned any pose of professionalism. "But she's living with some guy and she's *pregnant.*"

I raised a hand. "Trust me. In the continuing saga of Jonah and Camilla, the mere fact of this infant has no bearing on their relationship. He may act like he's cured, but he isn't, believe me. Camilla and Jonah are so enmeshed with each other I don't know what it would take to split up their act. Actually, now that I think about it, you probably have as good a shot at it as any."

"You really think so?"

"Why not? I was always too caught up in my own abandonment issues. I hated being a minor player in their little theater production. We're talking seventh-grade bonding. Junior high school romance. I couldn't compete. I lack the emotional strength. You look like you could tackle it. You have self-esteem issues? Are you a nail biter? Bed wetter? Jealous or insecure?"

She shook her head. "Not a bit."

"What about confrontation?"

"I like a good fight," she said.

"Well, you better get ready then because in my experience, she's indifferent to him until someone else comes along. And for God's sake, don't play fair. Camilla goes for broke."

"Thanks. I'll remember. We'll be in touch."

"I can't wait."

On the street again, I felt as if I was emerging from a darkened tunnel. The sunlight was harsh and all the colors seemed too bright. Nine black-and-white patrol cars were lined up along the curb. Across the street, a row of small California bungalows were painted in discordant pastel shades. Flowering annuals in fuchsia, orange, and magenta stood out in bold relief against the vibrant green of new foliage. I left my car in the public parking lot and walked the remaining blocks to work.

I entered Kingman and Ives by the unmarked side door. I unlocked my office and let myself in, glancing down at the floor. On the carpet, there was a plain white business-size envelope with my name and address typed across the front. The postmark was Santa Teresa, dated Monday P.M. Distracted, I set my bag on the desk, took out Bader's file, and set it on top of the file cabinet. I went back to the letter and picked it up with care. I centered it on my desk, touching only the corners while I lifted the handset and dialed Alison in reception.

"Hi, Alison. This is Kinsey. You know anything about this letter that was slipped under my door?"

"It was delivered yesterday afternoon. I held on to it up here, thinking you'd be back and finally decided it was better to go ahead and stick it under your door. Why, did I do something wrong?"

"You did fine. I was just curious."

I put the phone down and stared at the envelope. I'd picked up a fingerprint kit at a trade show recently and for a moment I debated about dusting for latents. Seemed pointless to tell the truth. Alison had clearly handled it and even if I brought up a set of prints, what was I to do with them? I couldn't picture the cops running them on the basis of my say-so. Still, I decided to be cautious. I took out a letter opener and slit the flap of the envelope, using the tip to slide the note onto my desk. The paper was cheap bond, folded twice, with no date and no signature. I used a pencil eraser to open the paper, anchoring opposite corners with the letter opener and the edge of my appointment book.

Dear Miss Milhone,

I thought I should take a moment to
inlighten you on the subject of Guy Malek. I

wonder if you rilly know who your dealing
with. He is a liar and a theif. I find it
sickning that he could get a second chance
in life threw the acquisition of Sudden
Riches. Why should he get the benefitt of five
million dollars when he never urned one red
cent? I don't think we can count on him
making amens for his passed crimes. You
better be carefull your not tared with the
same brush.

I found a transparent plastic sleeve and slid the letter inside, then opened my desk drawer and took out the copy of the letter Max Outhwaite had written to Jeffrey Katzenbach, placing the two side by side for comparison. On superficial examination, the typefont looked the same. As before, my name was misspelled. Thanks, it's two *l*'s, please. The sender seemed to have a problem distinguishing *your* from *you're* and consistently reversed the two. The use of *threw* for *through* was the same, but there were other oddities of note. My letter was less than half the length of the one to Katzenbach, yet it had more spelling mistakes. To my untutored eye, the two sets of errors were curiously inconsistent. If the writer were relying strictly on phonetics, why would words like *acquisition, aforementioned,* and *besieges* be spelled right? Certainly in my letter, there were far fewer commas, exclamation points, and Capitalizations! It was possible there was a certain level of carelessness at work, but I also had to wonder if the writer weren't simply *pretending* to use language badly. There was something vaguely amusing about the use of the word *amens* instead of *amends,* especially in the context of a born-again.

From another angle, why affix the name *Max Outhwaite* to the first letter, tacking on the embellishment of a phony address, and leave mine unsigned? I had to guess that *Outhwaite* imagined (quite correctly, as it turned out) that an unsigned letter to the *Dispatch* would get thrown in the trash. It was also likely the sender had no idea I'd end up with both. While I understood the reasoning behind the letter to the *Dispatch,* why this one to me? What was Outhwaite's intent?

I took out my magnifying glass and cranked up my three-way bulb to maximum illumination. Under magnification, other similarities became apparent. In both documents, the letter *a* was twisted on its axis, leaning slightly to the left, and on the lowercase *i* a portion of the serif was broken off along the bottom. Additionally, the lowercase *e, o, a,* and *d* were dirty and tended to print as filled dots instead of circles, suggestive of an old-fashioned fabric ribbon. On my portable Smith-Corona, I'd been known to use a straight pin to clean the clogged typewriter keys.

I left the letters on my desk and took a walk around the room. Then I sat down in my swivel chair, opened my pencil drawer, and pulled out a pack of index cards. It took me fifteen minutes to jot down the facts as I remembered them, one piece of information per card until I'd exhausted my store. I laid them out on my desk, rearranging the order, shuffling them into columns, looking for connections I hadn't seen before. It didn't amount to much from my perspective, but there'd soon be more information available. The autopsy was done by now and the medical examiner would have a concrete opinion about the manner and cause of death. We were all assuming Guy died from blunt-force trauma to the head, but there might be some underlying pathology. Maybe he'd died of a heart attack, maybe he'd been poisoned, expiring in his sleep before the first blow was struck. I couldn't help but wonder what difference any of it made. Guy would be laid to rest, his body probably taken back to Marcella for burial up there. The various forensic experts would go on sifting through the evidence until the case was resolved. Eventually, the story would be told in its entirety and maybe I'd understand then how everything fit. In the meantime, I was left with all the unrelated fragments and a sick feeling in my stomach.

I took the letters down the hall, the one still encased in its plastic sleeve. At the Xerox machine, I made a copy of each so that I now had two sets. The copies I placed in my briefcase, along with the

notes I'd made on my index cards. The originals I locked away carefully in my bottom drawer. When the phone rang, I let the answering
machine pick up. "Kinsey, this is Christie Malek. Listen, the police
were just here with a warrant for Jack's arrest—"

I snatched up the receiver. "Christie? It's me. What's going on?"

"Oh, Kinsey. Thank God. I'm sorry to bother you, but I didn't
know what else to do. I put a call through to Donovan, but he's out in
the field. I don't know where Bennet's gone. He left about nine,
without a word to anyone. Do you know the name of a good bail
bondsman? Jack told me to get him one, but I've looked in the Yellow
Pages and can't tell one from the other."

"Are you sure he's in custody? They didn't just take him to the
station for another interview?"

"Kinsey, they put him in *handcuffs*. They read him his rights and
took him off in the back of an unmarked car. We were both in shock.
I don't have any money—less than a hundred bucks in cash—but if I
knew who to call . . ."

"Forget about the bondsman. If Jack's being charged with murder,
it's a no-bail warrant. What he needs is a good criminal attorney and
the sooner the better."

"I don't know any attorneys, except Tasha!" she shrieked. "What
am I supposed to do, pick a name out of a *hat?*"

"Wait a minute, Christie. Just calm down."

"I don't want to calm down. I'm scared. I want help."

"I know that. I know. Just wait a minute," I said. "I have a suggestion. Lonnie Kingman's office is right next door to mine. You want me
to go see if he's in? You can't do better than Lonnie. He's a champ."

She was silent for an instant. "All right, yes. I've heard of him.
That sounds good."

"Give me a few minutes and we'll see what we can do."

16

I caught Lonnie's secretary, Ida Ruth, on her way back from the kitchen with a coffeepot in hand. I hooked a thumb in the direction of Lonnie's door. "Is he in there?"

"He's eating breakfast. Help yourself."

I tapped on the door and then opened it, peering in. Lonnie was sitting at his desk with an oversized plastic container of some kind of chalky-looking protein drink. I could see bubbles of dried powder floating on the surface and the barest suggestion of a milky mustache on Lonnie's upper lip. From assorted bottles, he'd emptied out a pile of vitamins and nutritional supplements, and he was popping down pills between sips of a shake so thick it might have been melted ice cream. One of the gel caps was the size and the color of a stone in a topaz dinner ring. He swallowed it as though he were doing a magic trick.

Lonnie more nearly resembles a bouncer than an attorney. He's

short and stocky—five feet four, two hundred four pounds—bulging
with muscles from his twenty years of power lifting. He's got one of
those revved-up metabolisms that burns calories like crazy and he
radiates high energy along with body heat. His speech is staccato and
he's generally amped up on coffee, anxiety, or lack of sleep. I've
heard people claim he's on the sauce—shooting anabolic steroids in
concert with all the iron he pumps. Personally, I doubt it. He's been
manic for the whole nine years of our acquaintance and I've never
seen him exhibit any of the rage or aggression allegedly generated by
extended steroid use. He's married to a woman with a black belt in
karate and she's never once complained about testicles shriveled to
the size of raisins, another unhappy side effect of steroid abuse.

His usually shaggy hair had been trimmed and subdued. His dress
shirt was pulled tightly across his shoulders and biceps. I don't know
his neck size, but he claims a tie makes him feel he's on the brink of
being hanged. The one he was wearing was pulled askew, his collar
unbuttoned, and his suit jacket off. He'd hung it neatly from a hanger
hooked through the handle of a file drawer. His shirt was spanking
white, but badly wrinkled, and he had rolled up the sleeves. Sometimes he wears a vest to conceal his rumpled state, but not today. He
swallowed the last of a palmful of pills, holding up a hand to indicate
that he was aware of me. He chugged off the balance of his protein
drink and shook his head with satisfaction. "Whew, that's good."

"Are you tied up at the moment?"

"Not at all. Come on in."

I entered the office and closed the door behind me. "I just gotta
call from Christie Malek. Have you been following that story?"

"The murder? Who hasn't? Sit, sit, sit. I'm not due in court until
two P.M. What's up?"

"Jack Malek's been arrested and needs to talk to an attorney. I
told Christie I'd see if you were interested." I took a seat in one of
two black leather client chairs.

"When was he picked up?"

"Fifteen or twenty minutes ago, I'd guess."

Lonnie began to screw the lids back on the motley collection of bottles sitting on his desk. "What's the deal? Fill me in."

I brought him up to speed on the case as succinctly as possible. This was our first conversation about the murder and I wanted him to have as thorough an understanding as I could muster on short notice. As I spoke, I could see Lonnie's gears engage and the wheels start to turn. I was saying, "Last I heard—this was from the housekeeper— Guy and Jack quarreled after hours of heavy drinking and Jack went off to a pairings' party at the country club."

"I wonder how the cops are gonna bust that one. You'd think at least half a dozen people would have seen him there." Lonnie shot a glance at his watch and began to roll his sleeves down. "I'll pop on over to the station house and see what's going on. I hope Jack has sense enough to keep his mouth shut until I get there."

He pushed away from his desk and took his suit jacket from the hanger. He shrugged himself into it, secured his collar button, and slid his tie into place. Now he looked more like a lawyer, albeit a short, beefy one. "By the way, where does Jack fit? He the oldest or the youngest?"

"The youngest. Donovan's the oldest. He runs the company. Bennet's in the middle. I wouldn't rule him out if you're looking to divert suspicion. He was the most vocal in his opposition to Guy's claim on the estate. You want me to do anything before you get back?"

"Tell Christie I'll be in touch as soon as I've talked to him. In the meantime, go on over to the house. Let's put together a list of witnesses who can confirm Tuesday night. The cops find the murder weapon?"

"They must have. I know they did a grid search of the property because I saw 'em doing it. And Christie says they carted off all kinds of things."

"Once I finish with Jack, I'll have a chat with the cops and find out why they think he's good for this. It'd be nice to have some idea what we're up against."

"Am I officially on the clock?"

He looked at his watch. "Go."

"The usual rates?"

"Sure. Unless you want to work for free. Of course, it's always possible Jack won't hire me."

"Don't be silly. The man's desperate," I said. I caught Lonnie's look and amended my claim. "Well, you know what I mean. He's not hiring you because he's desperate—"

"Get out of here," Lonnie said, smiling.

Briefcase in hand, I hiked back over to the public parking lot, where I retrieved my car. My attitude toward Jack Malek had already undergone a shift. Whether Jack was guilty or innocent, Lonnie would hustle up every shred of exculpatory evidence and plot, plan, maneuver, and strategize to establish his defense. I was no particular fan of Jack's, but working for Lonnie Kingman I'd be kept in the loop.

As I approached the Maleks', I was relieved to see that the roadway on either side of the estate was virtually deserted. The shoulder was churned with tire prints, the ground strewn with cigarette stubs, empty cups, crumpled paper napkins, and fast-food containers. The area outside the gate had the look of abandonment, as if a traveling circus had packed up and crept away at first light. The press had all but disappeared, following the patrol car taking Jack to County Jail. For Jack, it was the beginning of a process in which he'd be photographed, frisked, booked, fingerprinted, and placed in a holding cell. I'd been through the process myself about a year ago and the sense of contamination was still vivid. The facility itself is clean and freshly painted, but institutional nonetheless; no-frills linoleum and government-issue furniture built to endure hard wear. In my brush with them, the jail officers were civil, pleasant, and businesslike, but I'd felt diminished by every aspect of the procedure, from the surrender of my personal possessions to the subsequent confinement in the drunk tank. I can still remember the musky smell in the air, mixing with the odors of stale mattresses, dirty armpits, and bourbon fumes being exhaled. As far as I knew, Jack had never been arrested and I suspected he'd feel as demoralized as I had.

As I drove the VW up to the gate, a hired security guard stepped forward, blocking my progress until I identified myself. He waved me on and I eased up the driveway into the cobblestone courtyard. The house was bathed in sunlight, the grounds dappled with shade. The old, sprawling oak trees stretched away on all sides, creating a hazy landscape as if done in watercolors. Tones of green and gray seemed to bleed into one another with the occasional spare sapling providing sharp contrast. I could see two gardeners at work; one with a leaf blower, one with a rake. The sounds of machinery suggested that branches were being trimmed somewhere out of sight. The air smelled of mulch and eucalyptus. There was no sign of the search team and no uniformed officer posted at the front door. To all intents and purposes, life had reverted to normal.

Christie must have been watching, perhaps hoping for Donovan. Before I was even out of the car, she'd come onto the porch and down the steps, walking in my direction. She wore a white T-shirt and dark blue wraparound skirt, her arms folded in front of her as though for comfort. The sheen in her dark hair had faded to a dull patina, like cheap floor wax on hardwood. Her face showed little of her emotions except for a thin crease, like a hairline crack, that had appeared between her eyes. "I heard the car on the drive and thought it might be Bennet or Donovan. Lord, I'm glad to see you. I've been going crazy here by myself."

"You still haven't gotten through to Donovan?"

"I left word at the office, saying it was urgent. I didn't want to blab all our business to his secretary. I've been waiting by the phone, but so far I haven't heard a word from him. Who knows where Bennet is. What about Lonnie Kingman? Did you talk to him?"

I filled her in on Lonnie's intentions. "Have the police unsealed the bedroom?"

"Not yet. I meant to ask about that when they showed up this morning. I thought they came to *do* something up there. Take photographs or measure or move the furniture. I never imagined they were here to arrest anyone. I wish you could have seen Jack. He was scared to death."

"I'm not surprised. What about you? How are you holding up?"

"I'm antsy. And feel my fingers. They're as cold as ice. I catch myself pacing, half the time jabbering away. This is all so unreal. We may have problems, but we don't kill one another. It's ridiculous. I don't understand what's going on. Everything was fine and now this." She seemed to shudder, not from cold, but from tension and anxiety. In the wake of Jack's arrest, she'd clearly erased all her earlier complaints.

I followed her around the front and into the house. The foyer felt chilly and again I was struck by the shabbiness. A wall sconce hung awry. In the hanging chandelier, several flame-shaped bulbs were missing and some were tilted like crooked teeth. The tapestries along the wall were genuine, faded and worn, depicting acts of debauchery and cruelty picked out in thread. I felt my gaze pulled irresistibly toward the stairs, but the landing above was empty and there was no unusual sound to set my teeth on edge. The house was curiously quiet, given events of the past few days. These people didn't seem to have friends rushing in with offers of help. I wasn't aware of anyone bringing food or calling to ask if there was anything to be done. Maybe the Maleks were the sort who didn't invite such familiarities. Whatever the reason, it looked like they were coping without the comfort of friends.

Christie was still chatting, processing Jack's arrest. I've noticed that people tend to drone on and on when they're unnerved. "When I saw Detective Robb on the doorstep, I honestly thought they were coming with information and then they asked if Jack was in and I still didn't think anything about it. I don't even know what's supposed to happen next."

We moved into the library, where I sank into a club chair and Christie paced the floor. I said, "I guess it depends on what he's charged with and if bail's been set. Once he's booked in, the DA has twenty-four hours to file his case. Jack has to be arraigned within forty-eight hours, excluding Sundays and holidays, of course. So this is what, Thursday? They'll probably take him before a magistrate today or tomorrow."

"What's arraignment? What does that mean? I don't know the first thing. I've never known anyone who's been arrested, let alone charged with *murder*."

"Arraignment's the process by which he's formally charged. They'll take him into court and identify him as the person named in the warrant. He'll be told the nature of the charges against him and he'll be asked to plead guilty, not guilty, or no contest."

"And then what?"

"That's up to Lonnie. If he thinks the evidence is weak, he'll demand a preliminary hearing without waiving time. That means within ten court days—two weeks—they'll have to have him in there for a prelim. For that, the prosecuting attorney's present, the defendant and his counsel, the clerk, and the investigating officer, blah, blah, blah. Witnesses are sworn in and testimony's taken. At the end of it, if it appears either that no public offense has been committed or that there's not sufficient cause to believe the defendant's guilty, then he's discharged. On the other hand, if there's sufficient evidence to show the offense has been committed and sufficient cause to believe the defendant's guilty, then he's held to answer. An information's filed—that's a formal, written accusation—in Superior Court, he enters a plea, and the matter's set for trial. There's usually a lot of bullshit thrown in, but that's essentially what happens."

She paused in her pacing and turned to stare at me, aghast. "And Jack's in *jail* all this time?"

"He's not allowed to post bail on a homicide."

"Oh my God."

"Christie, I've been in jail myself. It's not the end of the world. The company's not that great and the food's off the charts when it comes to fat content—hey, no wonder I liked it," I added in an aside.

"It isn't funny."

"Who's being funny? It's the truth," I said. "There are worse things in life. Jack might not like it, but he'll survive."

She reached out and placed a hand on the mantelpiece to steady herself. "Sorry. I'm really sorry. I didn't mean to snap at you."

"You better have a seat."

She did as I suggested, perching on the edge of the chair next to mine. "You must have come for some reason. I never even asked what it was."

"Lonnie was hoping you'd know who was at the club that night. We need someone who can verify Jack's presence at the pairings' party."

"That shouldn't be too hard. I guess the police are already talking to people at the country club. I'm not sure what the deal is on that. I've gotten two calls this morning, one from Paul Trasatti, who says he needs to talk to Jack, like pronto."

"Were they together Tuesday night?"

"Yes. Jack picked him up and took him to the club. I'm sure they sat at the same table. Paul can give you the names of the other eight sitting with them. This is all so crazy. How can they possibly think Jack's guilty of anything? There must have been tons of people there that night."

"What's Paul's number?"

"I don't know. It's got to be in the book. I'll go look it up."

"Don't worry about it. I can check that out in a bit. Once he confirms Jack's alibi, it should go a long way."

Christie made a face. " 'Alibi.' God, I can't stand the word. Alibi implies you're guilty and you've cooked up some story to cover your ass."

"Can I use your phone?"

"I'd prefer it if you'd wait until Donovan or Bennet check in. I want to keep the line free until I hear from them. I hope you don't mind."

"Not at all," I said. "You mentioned the police picking up some items. Do you have any idea what they took?"

She leaned her elbows on her knees and put her hands across her eyes. "They left a copy of the warrant and a list of items seized. I know it's around here somewhere, but I haven't seen it yet. Donovan went down to the pool house as soon as they left. He says they took a lot of sports equipment—golf clubs and baseball bats."

I winced, thinking of the impact of such items on the human skull. Switching the subject, I asked, "What about Bennet? Where was he that night?"

"He went back to the restaurant he's remodeling, to see what the workers had done that day. Construction's been a nightmare and he spends a lot of time down there."

"Did anybody see him?"

"You'd have to ask him," she said. "Donovan and I were here. We'd had quite a lot to drink at dinner and I went straight to bed." There was a marked tremor in the hand Christie was running through her hair.

"Have you had anything to eat?"

"I couldn't touch a bite. I'm too anxious."

"Well, you ought to have *something*. Is Enid here yet?"

"I think so."

"Let me check in the kitchen and have her make you a cup of tea. You should have a cookie or a piece of fruit. You look awful."

"I feel awful," she said.

I left her in the library and headed down the hall. I couldn't believe I'd put myself on tea detail again, but simply being in the house made me tense. Any activity helped. Besides, I didn't want to pass up the chance to talk to Enid if she was on the premises.

"Me again," I said when I entered the kitchen.

She was standing at the island with a cutting board in front of her, smashing garlic with the blade of a Chinese cleaver. She was wrapped in a white apron with a white cotton scarf around her head, looking as round and as squeezable as a roll of toilet paper. While I watched, she laid down assorted sizes of unpeeled cloves, placed the wide blade on top of them, and pounded once with her fist. I could feel myself flinch. If the blade were angled incorrectly, she was going to end up whacking down on it with the outer aspect of her own hand, hacking straight to the bone. I stopped in my tracks. With her eyes pinned on me politely, she repeated the process, fist smashing down. She lifted the blade. Under it, the hapless garlic had been crushed like albino cockroaches, the peel sliding off with the flick of a knife tip.

"I thought I'd fix Christie a cup of tea," I said. "She needs something in her system—do you have a piece of fruit?"

Enid pointed at the refrigerator. "There are grapes in there. Tea bags up in the cabinet. I'd do it myself, but I'm trying to get this sauce under way. If you set up a tray, I'll take it in to her."

"No problem. You go right ahead."

She leaned to her left and slid open a compartment in which the trays were stored, pulling out a teak server with a rim around the edge. She placed it on the marble counter next to six big cans of crushed tomatoes, two cans of tomato paste, a basket of yellow onions, and a can of olive oil. On the stove top, I noticed a stainless steel stockpot.

I moved over to the cabinet and removed a mug, pausing to fill the electric kettle as I'd seen Myrna do. I glanced at Enid casually. "You have paper napkins somewhere?"

"Third drawer on the right."

I found the napkins and placed one, along with a teaspoon, on the tray. "I take it you heard about Jack's arrest."

She nodded assent. "I was coming in the gate just as they were taking him away. I wish you could have seen the look on his face."

I shook my head regretfully, as if I gave a shit. "Poor thing," I said. "It seems so unfair." I hoped I hadn't laid it on too thick, but I needn't have worried.

"The police were asking about his running shoes," she said. "Something about a pattern on the soles—so there must have been bloody footprints in the bedroom where Guy was killed."

"Really," I replied, trying to disguise my startlement. Apparently, she felt no reluctance about discussing the family's business. I'd thought I'd have to be cunning, but she didn't seem to share Myrna's reservations about tattling. "They picked up the shoes yesterday?"

"No. They called me this morning at home. Before I left for work."

"Lieutenant Robb?"

"The other one. The woman. She's a cold fish, I must say. I hope she's not a friend of yours."

"I only met her this morning when I went in to be interviewed."

She flicked me a look as if taking my measure. "Myrna tells me you're a detective. I've seen 'em on the TV, of course, but I never met one in real life."

"Now you have," I said. "In fact, I work in the same firm as Jack's attorney, Lonnie Kingman. He's on his way over to the station house to talk to Jack." I was anxious to press her on the matter of the shoes, but worried she would clam up if I seemed too intent.

She dropped her eyes to her work. She was tapping the Chinese cleaver in a rapid little dance that reduced all the garlic to the size of rice grains. "They searched for the shoes all day yesterday. You've never seen anything like it. Going through all the closets and trash cans, digging in the flowerbeds."

I made a little mouth noise of interest. It was clear Enid had an avid interest in all the trappings of police work.

She said, "They told me I was actually the one who put 'em on the right track. Of course, I had no idea the shoes would turn out to be Jack's. I feel terrible about that. Myrna's beside herself. She feels so guilty about mentioning the quarrel."

"It must have been a shock about the shoes," I prodded.

"Jack's my favorite among the boys. I came to work here twenty-five years ago. This was my first job and I didn't expect to stay long."

"You were hired as a nanny?"

"The boys were too old for that. I was more like a companion for Mrs. Malek," she said. "I never trained as a cook. I simply learned as

216

I went along. Mrs. Malek—Rona—was beginning to fail and she was in and out of the hospital all the time back then. Mr. Malek needed someone to run the house in her absence. Jack was in junior high school and he was pretty much at loose ends. He used to sit out in the kitchen with me, hardly saying a word. I'd bake a batch of cookies and he'd eat a whole plate just as fast as he could. He was really like a little kid. I knew what he was hungry for was his mother's praise and attention, but she was much too sick. I did what I could, but it nearly broke my heart."

"And Guy was how old?"

She shrugged. "Eighteen, nineteen. He'd already given them years of aggravation and grief. I never saw anything like him for the trouble he made. It was one scrape after another."

"How did he and Jack get along?"

"I think Jack admired and romanticized him. They didn't pal around together, but there was always a certain amount of hero worship. Jack thought Guy was like James Dean, rebellious and tragic, you know, misunderstood. They never had all that much to do with one another, but I can remember how Jack used to look at him. Now, Bennet and Jack, they were close. The two younger boys tended to gravitate to one another. I never had much use for Bennet. Something sneaky about him."

"What about Donovan?"

"He was the smartest of the four. Even then he had a good head for business, always calculating the odds. When I first came to work, he'd already been off to college and was planning to come back and work for his dad full-time. Donovan loves that company more than any man alive. As for Guy, he was the troublemaker. That seemed to be his role."

"You really think Jack might have been involved in Guy's death?"

"I hate to believe it, but I know he felt Guy broke faith with him. Jack's a fanatic about loyalty. He always was."

"Well, that's interesting," I said. "Because the first time I was here, he said much the same thing. He was off at college when Guy left, wasn't he?"

Enid was shaking her head. "That wouldn't have mattered. Not to him. Somehow, in Jack's mind, when Guy went off on his great adventure, he should have taken him along."

"So he saw Guy's departure as betrayal."

"Well, of course he did. Jack's terribly dependent. He's never had a job. He's never even had a girl. He has no self-esteem to speak of and for that, I blame his dad. Bader never took the time to teach them they were worth anything. I mean, look at the reality. None of them has ever left home."

"It couldn't be healthy."

"It's disgraceful. Grown men?" She opened the can of olive oil and poured a short stream in the stockpot while she turned up the flame. She moved the cutting board from the counter and balanced the edge of it on the pot, sliding garlic across the surface. The sound of sizzling arose, followed moments later by a cloud of garlic-scented steam.

"What's the story on the shoes? Where did they turn up?"

She paused to adjust the flame and then returned the board to the counter, where she picked up an onion. The peeling was as fragile as paper, crackling slightly as she worked. "At the bottom of a box. You remember the cartons of Bader's clothing Christie packed away? They were sitting on the front porch. The Thrift Store Industries truck stopped by for an early-morning pickup first thing yesterday."

"Before the body was discovered?"

"Before anyone was even up. I don't know how I connected it. I saw the receipt lying on the counter and didn't think much about it. Later, it occurred to me—if the shoes weren't on the premises, they must be somewhere else."

"How'd you figure out where they were?"

"Well, that's just it. I was loading the dishwasher, you know, humming a little tune, and boom, I just knew."

"I've done the same thing. It's almost like the mind makes an independent leap."

Enid flashed me a look. "Exactly. He must have realized he left a shoe print on the carpeting upstairs."

"Did you see it yourself?"

"No, but Myrna says she saw it when she went in Guy's room." She paused, shaking her head. "I don't want to think he did it."

"It *is* hard to believe," I said. "I mean, in essence, he must have killed Guy, seen the footprint, slipped off his shoes, and shoved them in the box on his way out of the house. He was lucky—or thought he was."

"You don't sound convinced."

"I just have trouble with the notion. Jack doesn't strike me as that decisive or quick. Doesn't that bother you?"

She thought about that briefly and then gave a shrug of dismissal. "A killer would have to depend on luck, I guess. You can't plan for everything. You'd have to ad-lib."

"Well, it backfired in this case."

"If he did it," she said. She picked up a can and tilted it into the electric opener. She pressed a lever and watched as the can went round and round, rotating blades neatly separating the lid from the can. Kitchens are dangerous, I thought idly as I looked on. What an arsenal—knives and fire and all that kitchen twine, skewers, meat pounders, and rolling pins. The average woman must spend a fair portion of her time happily contemplating the tools of her trade: devices that crush, pulverize, grind, and puree; utensils that pierce, slice, dissect, and debone; not to mention the household products that, once ingested, are capable of eradicating human life along with germs.

Her eyes came up to mine. "Do you believe in ghosts?"

"No, of course not. What makes you ask?"

She glanced toward the corner of the kitchen where I noticed, for the first time, a staircase. "Yesterday I went upstairs to put some linens away. There was a Presence in the hall. I wondered if you believed in them."

I shook my head in the negative, remembering the chill in the air and the roaring in my ears.

"This one smells of animal, something damp and unclean. It's very strange," she said.

17

I left the Maleks' shortly after one o'clock. Driving home, I spotted a pay phone at a corner gas station. I pulled in and parked. Outside the service bay, a group of kids from the local alternative high school had organized a car wash. According to the hand-lettered sign, the price was $5.00 and proceeds were being used to pay for a trip to San Francisco. There was not a customer in sight. Buckets of soapy water waited at the ready and the kids milled around in a manner that suggested they were about to spray one another down with hoses. With luck, I wouldn't end up in the line of fire.

I looked up Paul Trasatti in the telephone book. There were two numbers listed; one a residence on Hopper Road, the other—with no address—simply said Paul Trasatti, Rare Books. I found a handful of loose change at the bottom of my handbag and fed coins into the slots. I dialed the business number first, thinking it more likely I'd catch him at his desk. Trasatti answered before the phone on his end had finished ringing the first time.

"Trasatti," he said, tersely. He sounded like a man who'd been waiting for a call regarding drop-off instructions for the ransom money.

"Mr. Trasatti, my name is Kinsey Millhone. I'm a private investigator, working with Jack Malek's attorney. You knew he'd been arrested?"

"I heard about that this morning. I called to talk to Jack and his sister-in-law told me they'd just taken him away. Did she tell you to call?"

"Well, no. Not really. I—"

"How'd you get my number?"

"I looked you up in the telephone book. I need information and I thought maybe you could help."

"What kind of information?"

"I'll be talking to Lonnie Kingman and I know he'll want to hear about Jack's activities that night."

"Why can't he ask Jack?"

"I'm sure he will," I said, "but we're going to need someone who can verify Jack's claims. Christie says he drove you over to the country club Tuesday evening. Is that true?"

There was a fractional hesitation. "That's right. He picked me up after dinner. Truth is, I ended up trading places with him, so I was the one driving. He was too tipsy. This is strictly off the record, right?"

"I'm not a journalist, but sure. We can keep it off the record, at least for now," I said. "Tipsy, meaning drunk?"

"Let's just say I was the designated driver in this case."

I closed my eyes, listening for the subtext, while cars passed back and forth on the street behind me. "Were you seated at the same table?"

"Tables were reserved. We had assigned seats," he said. He was being as cagey as a politician. What was going on here?

"That's not what I asked. I'm wondering if you can verify his presence at the pairings' party."

A brief, most curious silence ensued. "Can I ask you a question?" he said.

"What's that?"

"If you're working for this attorney . . . what'd you say his name was?"

"Lonnie Kingman."

"Okay, this Kingman fellow. I know he can't repeat anything said between him and Jack, but what about you? Does the same thing apply to you?"

"Our conversation isn't privileged, if that's what you want to know. Anything relevant to Jack's defense, I'll be reporting to Lonnie. That's my job. I *can* be trusted with information. Otherwise, I'd be out of business by now," I said. "Were you sitting with Jack?"

"See, that's what the police have been asking me," he said. His mouth must have been dry because I could practically hear him lick his lips before he spoke. "Jack's a good friend and I don't want to get him in any more trouble than he's in. I've done everything I could short of telling lies."

"You don't want to lie to the cops," I said. Maybe the line was tapped and they were checking my attitude.

"Well, no, I wouldn't. And that's just it," he said. "I didn't come right out and say so, but there was a stretch when Jack was, you know, uhm, off somewhere. What I mean is, I couldn't say he was right there in my line of sight."

"Uhn-hun. How long a stretch?"

"Might have been as much as an hour and a half. I didn't think anything of it at the time, but you know, later—like when this other business came up—I did wonder about the time frame. I wouldn't want to be quoted, but just between us."

"Do you know where he was?"

"I know where he *said* he was. Out walking the tenth hole."

"In the *dark?*"

"That's not as odd as it sounds. I've done the same thing myself. Smokers go outside to have a cigarette sometimes. Most club members know the course by heart so it's not as if you're likely to get lost or fall down a hole."

"But why would he do that in the middle of a pairings' party?"

"He was upset—I'd say real upset—when he came to pick me up. That's another reason I insisted on driving. Jack tends to be careless about things like that."

"Did he say what upset him?" I waited. "I can keep it to myself," I said.

"He said him and Guy got into an argument."

"About what?"

"Probably the money. I'd say the money."

"You're talking about the money Guy was due to inherit."

"That's right."

"So Jack was drunk and upset and when the two of you arrived at the club, he disappeared."

"Uhn-hun."

"Did you believe him?"

"About taking a walk? More or less. I mean, it makes sense—you know, if he was trying to sober up and cool off."

"And *did* he seem cooler when he got back?"

For a moment, I thought the line went dead. "Mr. Trasatti?"

"I'm here. See, the thing is, he didn't actually get back in time to give me a ride. I had to find someone else."

"And that's what you told the police?"

"Well, I had to. I felt bad, but they were real persistent and it's like you said, I couldn't *lie*."

"Was his car still there?"

"I think so. I couldn't swear to it. I thought I saw it in the parking lot when I was set to go, but I might have been mistaken."

"But you're sure there was no sign of Jack?"

"That's right. A friend of mine said he saw him take off across the fairway at the first hole. Then this other fellow ended up giving me a ride home."

"Can I have both those names?" I cocked one shoulder, anchoring the handset against my ear while I fumbled in my bag for a pen and a scrap of paper. I made a note of the names, neither of which rang a bell. "And how did you find out where Jack had been?"

"He called first thing the next morning to apologize and that's when he explained."

"He called Wednesday morning?"

"I just said that."

"I wanted to make sure I understood you correctly. Do you remember what time he called?"

"About eight, I guess."

"So this was before anyone knew Guy Malek was dead."

"Must've been. I know Jack never mentioned it. You'd think if he knew he'd have spoken up."

"Is there anything else you remember from your conversation with him?"

"Not that I can think of. I probably got him in enough trouble as it is. I hope you won't tell him I told you all this."

"I doubt I'll have occasion to talk to Jack," I said. "I appreciate your help. You may hear from Lonnie Kingman or me again on this." You're certainly going to end up on the witness stand, I thought.

"I guess it can't be helped," he said glumly, as if reading my mind. He disconnected before I could press him for anything else.

I checked the pile of change I'd laid on the shelf near the coin box. I dropped more coins in the slot and dialed Lonnie's private line. He picked up on his end without identifying himself.

"This is Kinsey," I said. "How'd it go?"

"Don't let me handle any sharps. I might open a vein."

"You heard about the shoes?"

"Did I ever," he said. "Lieutenant Robb delivered the happy news with glee."

"I take it the pattern on the sole matched the print at the scene."

"Oh, sure. And to make things even better, he says the lab found bits and pieces of Guy Malek's brain spattered on the instep. I mean, Jesus, how's Jack going to explain a fleck of brain matter buried in the eyelet of his shoes? This is not like 'Oh gee fellas, Guy-accidentally-cut-himself-and-must-have-bled-on-me.' "

"What'd Jack have to say?"

"I haven't had a chance to ask. Once he invoked, the cops hustled him out to County Jail for booking. I'm going out there later and have a long chat with him. He'll probably tell me the shoes were stolen. Oh yeah, right."

"What about the murder weapon?"

"They found a baseball bat shoved in with a bunch of sports equipment down at the pool house. Somebody'd made a clumsy attempt to wipe it clean, but traces of blood were still on the hitting area. At least there were no prints, so we can thank God for small favors. What about his alibi? I hope you're going to tell me a hundred club members had an eye on him at all times."

"No such luck," I said. I laid out the sequence of events as Paul Trasati had reported them.

I could hear Lonnie sigh. "Too bad Jack wasn't out there screwing somebody's wife. You have a theory, I'm sure."

"He could have left the club on foot. There are half a dozen places near the road where he could've climbed the fence."

"And then what?" Lonnie said. "The country club is miles from the Malek estate. How's he going to get from there to the house again without somebody seeing him?"

"Lonnie, I hate to tell you this, but the man has a Harley-Davidson. He could have hidden his motorcycle earlier. The house might be an hour away on foot, but it's only ten minutes by car."

"But so what? Where was Bennet that night? And what about Donovan. He was right there on the premises when the murder occurred."

"I can talk to Bennet this afternoon."

"Did anybody see Jack climb the fence? I doubt it. Anybody see the Harley during the period we're discussing?"

"I can check it out," I said.

"I know the line the cops are taking. They're saying Jack's room adjoined Guy's. All he had to do was slip from one room to the other, bash his brains out, and slip back again."

"Not that simple," I said. "Don't forget he's got to hide the shoes at the bottom of the thrift box, wipe the blood off the bat, and return it to the pool house before he hightails it back to the country club."

"Good point. Is there a guardhouse at the club? Someone might have noted what time he left."

"I'll pop over there and check. I can also clock the time it takes to get from there to the house and back."

"Hold off on that. We'll get to that eventually. For now, let's focus on finding someone else to blame."

"That shouldn't be too hard. I mean, Jack's not the only one with access to Guy's room. Anybody in the house could have entered the same way. The cops have the murder weapon, but from what you've said, they don't have Jack's fingerprints."

"Yeah, they can't find anybody else's either."

"So how are they going to prove Jack was wielding the damn thing? Maybe he was framed."

Lonnie snorted in my ear. "Somebody'd have to take a pair of forceps and fuckin' *tweeze* up brain material, then tiptoe into Jack's room, find the shoes in the closet, and deposit all the little brainy bits."

"It's always possible, though, isn't it?"

"It's possible Santa Claus came down the chimney and did the deed himself. Stinks. The whole thing stinks."

"I like the idea about eyewitnesses. So far it doesn't sound like there's anyone who can place him at the murder scene."

"Not so far, no, but I'm sure the cops are out scouring the neighborhood."

"Well, then we'll scour some, too."

"You're such an optimist," he said.

I laughed. "Actually, I can't believe I'm standing here defending him. I don't even like Jack."

"We're not paid to like him. We're being paid to get him out of this," Lonnie said.

"I'll do what I can."

"I know you will."

Before I left the service station, I paused long enough to pull up to the pump so I could fill my gas tank. On the hood of my car, the early-morning dew had now combined with the dust from Monday's Santa Ana winds. My former VW was dingy beige and never showed dirt. With this snappy 1974 model, the streaks were more conspicuous, rivulets of pale blue cutting through a speckled patina of soot. A bird had passed its judgment on the hood as well. I paid for the gas and then turned the key in the ignition, peered over my right shoulder, and backed up into the area where the car wash was being held. The kids began to whistle and clap, and I found myself smiling at their enthusiasm.

I stood to one side while one of them crawled inside with a bottle of window cleaner. Another fired up the Shop-Vac and began to suck grit off the floor mats. A crew of three were sudsing down the outside, all of them towering over the vehicle. The kid with the Shop-Vac finished cleaning the interior and I watched him approach from the far side of the car with an envelope in hand. He held it out to me. "Have you been looking for this?"

"Where did that come from?"

"I found it beside the passenger seat in front. Looks like it slipped down in the crevice."

"Thanks." I took the envelope, half expecting to see the now-familiar typeface. Instead, my name was scrawled across the front in ballpoint pen. I waited until the kid had moved away and then I opened the envelope and removed the single sheet of paper. The message was handwritten in black ink; the penmanship distinct, a peculiar blend of cursive and printing. I flicked a glance at the signature. *Guy Malek.* I could feel ice crystals forming between my shoulder blades.

Monday night. Waiting for you to show.

Hey K . . .

Sure hope I have the nerve to pass you this note. I guess I must have if you're reading it. I haven't asked a girl on a date since I was fifteen years old and that didn't work out so hot. I got a big zit on my chin and spent the whole evening trying to think up excuses to keep my face turned the other way.

Anyway, here goes.

Once this family mess is settled, would you like to take off for a day and go to Disneyland with me? We could eat snowcones and do Pirates of the Caribbean and then take the boat ride through Small World singing that song you can't get out of your head for six months afterward. I could use some silliness in my life and so could you.

Think on't and let me know so I can stock up on Clearasil.

Guy Malek

P.S. Just for the record, if anything should happen to me, make sure my share of Dad's estate goes to Jubilee Evangelical Church. I really love those folk.

By the time I finished reading, my eyes had filled with tears. This was like a message from the dead. I stared off across the street, blinking rapidly. I could feel pain in my chest and my facial features were instantly defined by heat as my nasal passages seized up. I wondered if grief had the capacity to suffocate. In conjunction with the sorrow came a rush of pure rage. I sent Guy my thoughts across the Ether. I'm going to find out who killed you and I'm going to find out why. I swear I will do this. I swear it.

"Miss? Your car's ready."

I took a deep breath. "Thanks. It looks great." I gave the kid ten bucks and took off with the radio cranked up full blast.

When I got home, I spotted Robert Dietz's little red Porsche parked out in front of my apartment. I set my briefcase on the pavement while I stood at the curb and studied it, afraid to believe. He'd told me he was going to be gone two weeks. This was just coming up on one. I circled the car and checked the license plate, which read DIETZ. I picked up my briefcase and let myself in the gate. I rounded the corner and unlocked my door. Dietz's suitcase was sitting beside the couch. His garment bag was hooked across the top of the bathroom door.

I said, "Dietz?"

No response.

I left my handbag and the briefcase on the counter and crossed the patio to Henry's, where I peered in the kitchen window. Dietz was sitting in Henry's rocking chair, his pant leg pulled up to expose his injured knee. The swelling had visibly diminished and from various gestures he was making, it seemed safe to guess he'd had the fluid drained out of it. Even his pantomime of a hypodermic needle being stuck into his flesh made my palms start to sweat. At first he didn't see me. It was like watching a silent movie, the two men earnestly engrossed in medical matters. Henry, at eighty-five, was so familiar to me—handsome, good-hearted, lean, intelligent. Dietz was constructed along sturdier lines—solid, tough, stubborn, impulsive, just as smart as Henry, but more streetwise than intellectual. I found myself smiling at the two of them. Where Henry was mild, Dietz was restless and rough, without artifice. I valued his honesty, distrusted his concern, resented his wanderlust, and yearned for definition in our relationship. In the midst of all the heaviness I felt, Dietz was leavening.

He glanced up, spotting me. He raised a hand in greeting without rising from the chair.

Henry crossed to the door and let me in. Dietz lowered his pant leg with a brief aside to me about a walk-in medical clinic up in Santa Cruz. Henry offered coffee, but Dietz declined. I don't even remember now what the three of us talked about. In the course of idle chitchat, Dietz put his hand on my elbow, setting off a surge of heat. Out of the corner of my eye, I caught his quizzical look. Whatever I was feeling must have been transmitted through the wires to him. I must have been buzzing like a power line because even Henry's easy flow of conversation seemed to falter and fade. Dietz glanced at his watch, making a startled sound as if late for an appointment. We made our hasty excuses, moving out of Henry's backdoor and across to my place without exchanging a word.

The door closed behind us. The apartment felt cool. Pale sunlight filtered through the shuttered windows in a series of horizontal lines. The interior had the look and the feel of a sailboat: compact, simple, with royal blue canvas chairs, walls of polished teak and oak. Dietz undid the bed in the window bay, easing out of his shoes. I slipped my clothes off, aware of flickering desire as each garment was removed. Dietz's clothes joined mine in a heap on the floor. We sank together, in a rolling motion. The sheets were chill at first, as blue as the sea, warming at contact with our bare limbs. His skin was luminous, as polished as the surface of an abalone shell. Something about the play of shadows infused the air with a watery element, bathing us both in its transparent glow. It felt as if we were swimming in the shallows, as smooth and graceful as a pair of sea otters tumbling through the surf. Our lovemaking played out in silence, except for a humming in his throat now and then. I don't often think of sex as an antidote to pain, but that's what this was and I fully confess—I used intimacy with the one man to offset the loss of the other. It was the only means I could think of to console myself. Even in the moment, what seemed odd to me was the flicker of confusion about which man I betrayed.

Later, I said to Dietz, "Are you hungry? I'm starving."

"I am, too," he said. Gentleman that he was, he'd padded over to the refrigerator where he stood buck naked in a shaft of hot light, contemplating the interior. "How could we be out of food? Don't you eat when I'm gone?"

"There's food," I said defensively.

"A jar of bread-and-butter pickles."

"I can make sandwiches. There's bread in the freezer and half a jar of peanut butter in the cupboard up there."

He gave me a look like I'd suggested cooking up a mess of garden slugs. He closed the refrigerator door and opened the freezer compartment, poking through some cellophane-wrapped packages of meat products covered in ice crystals and suffering from freezer burn. He closed the freezer, returned to the sofa bed, and got under the sheets. "I'm not going to last long. We have to eat," he said.

"I couldn't believe you came back. I thought you were taking the boys off on a trip."

"Turns out they had plans to go camping with friends in Yosemite and didn't know how to tell me. When I read about the murder in the Santa Cruz papers, I told them I needed to drive back. I felt guilty as hell, but they were thrilled to death. Given the perversity of human nature, it pissed me off somehow. They could hardly get me in the car fast enough. I pull away and I'm looking in the rearview mirror. They don't even stop to wave. They're galloping up the outside stairs to grab their sleeping bags."

"You had a few days together."

"And that was good. I enjoyed them," he said. "So tell me about you and what's been happening down here."

Having been through the drill with Lonnie, I laid out events with remarkable efficiency, faltering only slightly in my account of Guy. Even the sound of his name touched a well of sorrow in me.

"You need a game plan," he said, briskly.

I waggled my hand, maybe-so-maybe-not. "Jack will probably be arraigned tomorrow if he hasn't been already."

"Will Lonnie waive time?"

"I have no idea. Probably not."

"Which means he'll insist on a prelim within ten court days. That doesn't give us much time. What about this business of Max Outhwaite? We could try chasing that down."

I noted the "we," but let it sit there unacknowledged. Was he seriously proposing help? "What's to chase?" I asked. "I tried the hall of records and voter registration. Also the city directories. The name's as phony as the address."

"What about the crisscross?"

"I did that."

"Old telephone books?"

"Yeah, I did that, too."

"How far back?"

"Six years."

"Why six? Why not take it all the way back to the year Guy Malek left? Even before that. Max Outhwaite could be the victim of a rip-off during his teen crime years."

"If the name's a fake, it's not going to matter how far back I go."

"In other words, you were too lazy," he said, mildly.

"Right," I said, without taking offense.

"What about the letters themselves?"

"One's a fax. The other's typed on ordinary white bond. No distinguishing marks. I could have dusted for prints, but there didn't seem to be much point. We've got no way to run them and nothing for comparison even if a latent turned up. I did put the one letter in a plastic sleeve to protect it to some extent. Then I made copies of both letters. I left one set at the office, locked away in my desk. I get paranoid about these things."

"You have the other set here?"

"In my briefcase."

"Let's take a look."

I pushed the sheet back and got up. I retrieved my briefcase from the kitchen counter and sorted through the contents, returning to the

sofa bed with my pack of index cards and the two letters. I slid
between the sheets again and handed him the paperwork, turning
over on my side so I could watch him work. He put his glasses on.
"This is really romantic, you know that Dietz?"

"We can't screw around all day. I'm fifty. I'm old. I have to save
my strength."

"Yeah, right."

We propped up the pillows and settled in side by side while Dietz
read the two letters and thumbed through my index cards. "What do
you think?" I asked.

"I think Outhwaite's a good bet. Seems like the object of the
exercise is to find another candidate, divert attention from Jack if
nothing else."

"Lonnie said the same thing. The evidence looks damning, but it's
all circumstantial. Lonnie's hoping we can find someone else to point
a finger at. I think he favors Donovan or Bennet."

"The more the merrier. If the cops think Jack's motivation was
Guy's share of the inheritance, then the same case could be made for
the other two. It would have been just as easy for one of them to slip
into Guy's room." He was thumbing through the index cards. He
held a card up. "What's this mean? What kind of scam are you
referring to?"

I took the card and studied it. The note said: *widow cheated out of
nest egg.* "Oh. I'm not sure. I wrote down everything I could remember from my first interview with Donovan. He was talking about the
scrapes Guy'd been in over the years. Most sounded petty—acts of
vandalism, joyriding, stuff like that—but he was also involved in a
swindle of some kind. I didn't ask at the time because I was just
starting my search and I was focusing on ways to track him down. I
didn't care what he'd done unless it somehow pertained."

"Might be worth it to take a good hard look at his past. People
knew he was back. Maybe somebody had a score to settle."

"That crossed my mind, too. I mean, why else would Max Outhwaite notify the paper?" I said. "I've also toyed with the idea that one of Guy's brothers might have written the letters."

"Why?"

"To make it look like he had enemies, someone outside the family who might have wanted him dead. By the way, Bader kept a file of newspaper clippings, detailing Guy's escapades."

Dietz turned and looked at me. "Anything of interest?"

"Well, nothing jumps right out. I've got it at the office, if you want to see for yourself. Christie offered to let me take it when I was at the house."

"Let's do that. It sounds good. It might help us develop another lead." He went back to the two letters, analyzing them closely. "What about the third one? What did Guy's letter say?"

"I have no idea. Lieutenant Bower wouldn't tell me and I couldn't get much out of her. But I'd bet money it's the same person in all three cases."

"Cops probably have their forensic experts doing comparisons."

"Maybe. They may not care about Max Outhwaite now that Jack's in custody. If they're convinced he's good for it, why worry about someone else?"

"You want some help with the grunt work?"

"I'd love it."

18

I dropped Dietz at the public library while I drove out the freeway to Malek Construction. I hadn't expected to be gone long, but as I turned into the parking lot, I spotted Donovan getting into a company truck. I called his name and gave a quick wave, pulling into a visitor's space two spots away from his. He waited while I approached and then leaned over and rolled down the window on the passenger side.

Donovan's face creased with a smile, his dark eyes all but invisible behind dark sunglasses. "How are you?" he asked. He slid his glasses up on top of his head.

"Fine. I can see I caught you on your way out. Will you be gone long? I have some questions."

"I've got some business at the quarry. I'll only be gone about an hour if you want to come along with me."

I thought about it briefly. "Might as well," I said.

He moved his hard hat from the passenger seat to the floor, then opened the truck door for me. I hopped in. He wore blue jeans and a jean vest over a blue plaid sportshirt with the sleeves rolled up. His feet were shod in heavy-duty work boots with soles as waffled as tire treads.

"Where's the quarry?"

"Up the pass." He fired up the pickup and pulled out of the parking lot. "What's the latest word from Jack?"

"I haven't talked to him, but Lonnie Kingman had a meeting with him before they took him off to jail. You talked to Christie?"

"I took a late lunch," he said. "I must have gotten home about ten minutes after you left. I had no idea this stuff was going on. How's it looking at this point?"

"Hard to say. Lonnie's in the process of working out his strategy. I'll probably take a run over to the country club later to start canvassing members who were there on Tuesday. We'd love to find someone who could place Jack at the club between nine-thirty and eleven-thirty."

"Shouldn't be too hard."

"You'd be surprised," I said.

I'm about as perky as an infant when it comes to riding in trucks. Before we'd even reached the narrow highway that snaked up the pass, I could feel the tension seeping out of me. There's something lulling being a passenger in a moving vehicle. In Donovan's pickup, the combination of low grinding sound and gentle bumping nearly put me to sleep. I was tired of thinking about murder, though I'd have to bring the subject around to it eventually. In the meantime, I asked him about the business and took inordinate pleasure in the length of his reply. Donovan steered with one hand, talking over the rattle of the truck.

"We've gotten into recycle crushing where we take broken concrete and asphalt. We have a yard in Colgate where we collect it and we have a portable plant—well, we have two portable plants now—one in Monterey and one in Stockton. I think we were one of the first in this area to do that. We're able to crush the materials into road base that meets the specifications. It costs more to haul the materials here than it does the material itself, so you have a cost advantage in the haul."

He went on in this vein while I wondered idly if it might be worthwhile to verify his claims about the company's solvency. When I tuned back in, he was saying, "Right now, we produce about the same quantity out at the rock quarry as we do out at the sand and gravel mine. By far the majority of the sand and gravel operation goes into the production of asphalt concrete. We're the closest asphalt concrete plant to Santa Teresa. We used to have one in Santa Teresa where we hauled in the sand and the gravel and the liquid asphalt and we made it there, but again, it was more economical to make the product here and haul it into Santa Teresa. I'm probably the only man alive who rhapsodizes about road base and Portland Cement. You want to talk about Jack."

"I'd rather talk about Guy."

"Well, I can tell you Jack didn't kill him because it makes no sense. The first thing the cops are going to look at is the three of us. I'm surprised Bennet and I aren't under scrutiny."

"You probably are, though at the moment, all the evidence seems to point to Jack." I told him about the running shoes and the baseball bat. "You have any idea where the Harley-Davidson was that night?"

"Home in the garage, I'd guess. The Harley's Jack's baby, not mine. I really didn't have occasion to see it that night. I was upstairs watching TV."

We headed up the pass on a winding road bordered by chaparral. The air was still, lying across the mountains in a hush of hot sun. The woody shrubs were as dry as tinder. Farther up the rocky slopes, weeds and ornamental grasses—ripgut and woodland brome, foxtail fescue and ryegrass—had spread across the landscape in a golden haze that softened the stony ridges. Scarcely a breeze stirred outside, but late in the day, the warm descending air would begin to blow down the mountainside. Relative humidity would drop. The wind, squeezing through the canyons, would start picking up speed. Any tiny flame from a campfire, burning cigarette, or the inadvertent spark from weed abatement equipment, might be whipped up in minutes to a major burn. The big fires usually struck in August and September after months under high-pressure areas. However, lately the weather had been moody and unpredictable and there was no way to calculate the course it might take. Below us and at a distance, the Pacific Ocean stretched away to the horizon in a haze of blue. I could see the irregularities of the coastline as it curved to the north.

Donovan was saying, "I didn't see Jack that night once he left for the club so I can't help you there. Aside from his whereabouts, I guess I'm not really sure what you're looking for."

"We can either prove Jack didn't do it or suggest someone else who did. Where was Bennet that night? Can he account for his time?"

"You'd have to ask him. He wasn't home, I know that much. He didn't come in until late."

"The first time we met you told me about some of Guy's bouts with the law. Couldn't someone have a grudge?"

"You want to go back as far as his days in Juvenile Hall?"

"Maybe. And later, too. You mentioned a 'widder' woman he cheated out of money."

Donovan shook his head. "Forget it. That's a dead end."

"How so?"

"Because the whole family's gone."

"They left town?"

"They're all dead."

"Tell me anyway."

"The widow was a Mrs. Maddison. Guy was gone by then and when the old man heard what Guy'd done, he refused to make good. It was one of the few times he got tough. I guess he'd finally gotten sick of cleaning up after him. He told the woman to file charges, but I'm sure she never got around to it. Some people are like that. They don't take action even when they should."

"So what's the story?"

We reached the summit and the road opened out to a view I love, a caramel-colored valley dotted with dark green mounds of live oak. Ranches and campgrounds were woven into the land, but most were invisible from up here. The two-lane highway widened into four and we sped across the span of the Cold Spring Bridge. "Guy got involved with a girl named Patty Maddison. That's two *d*'s in Maddison. She had an older sister named Claire."

I heard a dim clang of recognition, but couldn't place the name. I must have made some kind of sound because Donovan turned and gave me a quick look. "You know her?" he asked.

"The name's familiar. Go on with the story. It'll come to me."

"Their old man never had a dime, but he'd somehow acquired some rare documents—letters of some kind—worth a big chunk of change. He'd been sick and the deal was, when he died the mother was supposed to sell 'em to pay for the girls' educations. The older sister had graduated from a college back East and she was waiting around to go to medical school. Some of the money was earmarked for her and some for Patty's college.

"The Christmas before he took off, Guy knocks on this woman's door. He says he's a friend of Patty's and presents himself as an appraiser of rare documents. He tells her there's some question about the authenticity of the letters. Rumor has it, says he, these are fakes and he's been hired by the father to take a look at them."

"This was while the father was still alive?"

He shook his head. "He'd been dead a month by then. He died at Thanksgiving time. Mom's feeling very nervous because the letters are really all she has. She doesn't know beans about an appraiser being hired, but it all sounds legitimate—like something her husband would have done toward the end—so she hands the letter over to Guy and he takes them away."

"Just like that?" I asked. "She didn't ask for ID or credentials?"

"Apparently not. He had some business cards done up and he handed her one, which she took at face value. You have to under-

stand, this was all pieced together months afterward. What the hell
did she know? She needs an appraisal done anyway in preparation
for selling."

"I can't believe people are so trusting."

"That's what keeps con artists in business," he said.

"Go on."

"Well, Guy keeps the letters for two weeks. He claims he's sub-
jecting them to a number of scientific tests, but what he's really doing
is making copies, elaborate forgeries. Or, not so elaborate as it turns
out. At any rate, he's putting together a set of fakes good enough to
pass superficial inspection. After two weeks, he takes the copies
back and gives her the bad news. 'Golly, gee, Mrs. Maddison, these
really *are* fakes,' he says, 'and they're not worth a *dime.*' He tells her
to ask any expert and they'll tell her the same. She nearly drops dead
from shock. She takes 'em straight to another expert and he confirms
what Guy's said. Sure enough, the letters are completely worthless.
So here's this lady whose husband's dead and she suddenly has
nothing. Next thing you know, she's knocking on Dad's door demand-
ing restitution."

"How'd she figure out it was Guy?"

"He'd been seeing Patty Maddison . . ."

I said, "Ohhh. That Patty. I get it. Guy told me about her the day
we walked the property. He said he'd broken up with her. Sorry to
interrupt, but I just remembered where I'd heard the name. So how'd
they know it was him? Did Patty point a finger?"

Donovan shook his head. "Far from it. Patty tried to protect him,
but Guy had just taken off and Mrs. Maddison put two and two
together."

"Mrs. Maddison hadn't met him?"

"Only the one time when he showed up for the appraisal. Obviously, he didn't use his own name."

Donovan slowed and turned left off the main highway. We followed
a two-lane paved road for a mile until it turned to gravel, small rocks
popping as the truck bounced upward. Ahead, I could see white dust,

like smoke, drifting across the road as it curved around to the left where it widened to reveal the quarry site. Massive benches of raw soil and rock had been cut into the hillside. There were no trees and no vegetation in the area. The din of heavy machinery filled the still mountain air. Much of the area was a flat, chalky gray contrasting sharply with the surrounding gray-green hills and a sky of pale blue. The mountains beyond were cloaked in dark green vegetation interspersed with the gold of short dry grassy patches. Tiers had been cut into the side of the hill. Everywhere there were steep piles of earth and gravel, shale and sandstone, eroding raw earth and rock. Conveyor belts trundled rock upward toward the crusher, where rocks as big as my head were being shaken down into vibrating jaws that reduced them to rubble. Rugged horizontal and inclined screens and feeders sorted the crushed rock into various sizes.

Donovan pulled up close to a trailer, turned off the ignition, and set the hand brake. "Let me take care of business and I can finish the story on the way back. There's a hard hat in the back if you want to take a walk around."

"You go ahead. I'll be fine."

Donovan left me in the pickup while he conferred with a man in coveralls and a hard hat. The two disappeared into the trailer while I waited. From a distance, the machinery was the size of Matchbox toys. I watched as a conveyor belt moved loose rock in a steady stream that poured off the end into a cascading pile. I lifted my chin, shifting my sights to the countryside stretched out in a pristine canvas of hazy mountain and low-growing dark green. I let my gaze drift across the site, trying to make sense out of what Donovan had said. As nearly as I remembered Guy's passing reference to Patty, he saw his discretion with her as his one decent act. He'd described her as unstable, emotionally fragile, something along those lines. It was hard to believe he'd try to convince me of his honor when he'd gone to such lengths to rip her mother off. In truth, he'd ripped Patty off too since the money from the letters was supposed to go to her.

The sun was beating down on the cab of the pickup. Donovan had left the windows open so I wouldn't cook to death. White dust clouded the air and the growling of heavy equipment battled the quiet. I could hear the clank of metal, the high whine of shifting gears as a wheel loader grumbled across flat ground as barren as a moonscape. I unsnapped my seat belt and slouched down on my spine with my knees propped on the dashboard. I didn't want Guy to be guilty of a crime of this magnitude. What was done was done, but this was bad, bad, bad. I was prepared for pranks, willing to accept minor acts of mischief, but grand larceny was tough to overlook, even at this remove.

I didn't realize I'd been dozing until I heard the crunch of work boots and Donovan opened the truck door on the driver's side. I awoke with a start. He kicked the sides of his boots against the floor frame, knocking gravel loose before he slid in beneath the steering wheel. I sat up and refastened my seat belt.

"Sorry it took so long," he said.

"Don't worry about it. I was just resting my eyes," I said dryly.

He slammed the door, clicked his seat belt into place, and turned the key in the ignition. Within moments, we were bouncing down the road toward the highway again. "Where was I?" he asked.

"Guy switched a set of forged letters for the real ones and then disappeared. You were saying your father refused to make good."

"I'll say. The letters were worth something close to fifty thousand dollars. In those days, Dad didn't have that kind of money and wouldn't have paid anyway."

"What happened to the letters? Did Guy sell them?"

"He must have, because as far as I know, they were never seen again. Paul Trasatti could tell you more. His father was the appraiser brought in once the switch was made."

"So he was the one who confirmed the bad news to Mrs. Maddison?"

"Right."

"What happened to her?"

"She was a lush to begin with and she'd been popping pills for years. She didn't last long. Between the alcohol and cigarettes, she was dead in five years."

"And Patty?"

"That was unfortunate. In May of that year—this was two months after Guy left—Patty turned up pregnant. She was seventeen years old and didn't want anyone to know. She'd had a lot of mental problems and I think she was worried they'd put her away, which they probably would have. At any rate, she had an illegal abortion and died of septicemia."

"What?"

"You heard me right. She had what they referred to as a 'backroom' abortion, which was more common than you'd think. Procedure wasn't sterile—just some hack down in San Diego. She developed blood poisoning and she died."

"You're kidding."

"It's the truth," he said. "We weren't down on Guy for nothing. I know you think we're nothing but a bunch of hostile jerks, but this is what we've had to live with and it hasn't been easy."

"Why wasn't something said before now?"

"In what context? The subject never came up. We all knew what happened. We discussed it among ourselves, but we don't run around airing our dirty laundry in front of other people. You think we like owning up to his part in it?"

I brooded about it, staring out at the passing roadside. "I'm really having trouble believing this."

"I'm not surprised. You don't want to think Guy would do a thing like that."

"No, I don't," I said. "Guy told me Patty was hung up on him. He considered it his one decent act that he didn't seduce her when he had the chance. Now why would he say that?"

"He was hoping to impress you. Stands to reason," he said.

"But there wasn't any context. This was passing conversation, something he brought up. He didn't go into any detail. What's to be impressed about?"

"Guy was a liar. He couldn't help himself."

"He might have been a liar back then, but why lie about the girl all these years later? I didn't know her. I wasn't pressing for information. Why bother to lie when he had nothing to gain?"

"Look, I know you liked him. Most women did. You start feeling sorry for him. You feel protective. You don't want to accept the fact he was twisted as they come. This is the kind of shit he pulled."

"It isn't that," I said, offended. "He'd undergone a lot of soul-searching. He'd committed his life to God. There wasn't any point fabricating some tall tale about Patty Maddison."

"He was busy revising history. It's something we all do. You repent your sins and then in memory, you start cleaning up your past. Pretty soon, you're convinced you weren't nearly as bad as everyone said. The other guy was a jerk, but you had good reason for anything you did. It's all bunk, of course, but which of us can stand to take a look at ourselves? We whitewash. It's human nature."

"You're talking about the Guy Malek of the old days. Not the one I met. All I know is, I have a hard time picturing Guy doing this."

"You knew him less than a week and believed everything he said. He was a bad egg."

"But Donovan, look at the nature of his crimes. None of them were like this," I said. "As a kid, he was into vandalism. Later, he stole cars and stereos to pay for drugs. Forgery's too sophisticated a scheme for someone who spent his days getting high. Trust me. I've been high. You think you're profound but you're barely functional."

"Guy was a bright boy. He learned fast."

"I better talk to Paul," I said, unwilling to concede.

"He'll tell you the same thing. In fact, that's probably what put the idea in Guy's head in the first place. You have a good friend whose dad deals in rare documents, it doesn't take any great leap to figure it out when you've got access to something valuable."

"I hear what you're saying, but it isn't sitting right."

"You know anything about liars?" Donovan asked.

"Sure, I think I can say so. What about 'em?"

"A liar—a truly dedicated liar—lies because he can, because he's good at it. He lies for the pure pleasure, because he loves getting away with it. That's how Guy was. If he could tell you some lie—even if it meant nothing, even if there was nothing to be gained—he couldn't resist."

"You're telling me he was a pathological liar," I said, restating his claim in a tone of skepticism.

"I'm saying he enjoyed lying. He couldn't help himself."

"I don't believe that," I said. "I happen to think I'm a pretty good judge of liars."

"You know when some people lie, but not all."

"What makes you such an expert," I said, beginning to take offense. Donovan was just as annoyed with me.

He made a dismissive gesture. I suspected he wasn't used to having women argue with him. "Forget it. Have it your way," he said. "I can tell I'm not going to persuade you of anything."

"Nor I you," I said tartly. "What happened to the older sister?"

Donovan grimaced with exasperation. "Are you going to take my word for it or is this an excuse for another round of arguments?"

"I'm arguing about Guy, not the Maddisons, okay?"

"Okay. Claire—the older one—abandoned her plans for med school. She had no money and her mom was sinking like a stone. For a while she came back to take care of her. That was maybe six months or so. Once mom was gone, she went back to the East Coast—Rhode Island or some place. Might have been Connecticut. She got married to some fellow, but it didn't work out. Then about a year ago, she offed herself. Or so I heard."

"She committed suicide?"

"Why not? Her whole family was gone. She had no one. The family was a bit dicey to begin with—bunch of manic-depressives. I guess something must have finally pushed her over the edge."

"What'd she do, jump off a building?"

"I don't know how she did it. I wasn't being literal. There was a notice in the local paper. It happened back east somewhere."

I was silent again. "So maybe one of the Maddisons killed Guy. Wouldn't that make sense?"

"You're fishing. I just told you, they're all gone."

"But how do you know there isn't someone left? Cousins, for instance? Aunts and uncles? Patty's best friend?"

"Come on. Would you really murder someone who wronged a relative of yours? A sibling, maybe. But a cousin or a niece?"

"Well, no, but I'm not close to my relatives. Suppose something like that happened to your family."

"Something did happen to my family. Guy was killed," he said.

"Don't you want revenge?"

"Enough to kill someone? Absolutely not. Besides, if I cared enough to kill, I wouldn't wait this long. You're talking eighteen years."

"But Guy was missing all that time. You notice, once he came home, he was dead within days."

"True enough," he said.

"Does the name Max or Maximilian Outhwaite figure into this in any way? It could even be Maxine. I can't swear to gender."

Donovan turned and looked at me with surprise. "Where'd you come up with that one?"

"You know the name?"

"Well, sure. Maxwell Outhwaite's the name Guy used on the business cards he made to cheat Mrs. Maddison."

I squinted at him. "Are you sure?"

"That isn't something I'd forget," he said. "How'd you come across it?"

" 'Max Outhwaite' was the one who wrote the letters to the *Dispatch* and the L.A. *Times*. That's how the press knew Guy was home."

19

Once back at Malek Construction, I left Donovan in the parking lot and picked up my car. I was feeling anxious and confused. This Max Outhwaite business made no sense at all. Maybe Dietz had come up with a line on him. Throw the Maddisons into the mix and what did it add up to? I glanced at my watch, wincing when I saw how late it was. The trip up the pass had taken more than an hour and a half.

Dietz was waiting in front of the public library. I pulled over to the curb and he slid into the passenger seat. "Sorry I'm late," I said.

"Don't worry about it. I got news for you. Outhwaite's a myth. I checked the city directories for the last twenty-five years and then went across the street and checked the County Clerk's office. No one by that name was ever listed in the phone book or anywhere else. No marriages, no deaths, no real property, building permits, lawsuits, you name it. Everybody alive leaves a trail of some kind. The name has to be phony unless we're missing a bet."

"There *is* a connection, but it's not what you'd expect," I said. I filled him in on my conversation with Donovan while we headed for home. I'd forgotten how nice it was to have someone to consult. I told him about the Maddisons and Guy's alleged involvement in the family's downfall. "Maxwell Outhwaite was the name used by the fictitious appraiser who stole fifty thousand dollars worth of rare documents. I'm not convinced it was Guy, but Donovan seems to take it for granted. Now, honestly," I said. "If you'd known about the Maddisons, wouldn't you have told someone?"

"Namely you?"

"Well, yes, me," I said. "Donovan could have *mentioned* it. Same with Max Outhwaite. The name pops up again years later—why didn't he tell someone?"

"Maybe Katzenbach never told him there was a letter and that Outhwaite was the name of the sender."

"Oh. I see what you're saying. I guess it's possible," I said. "It still annoys me no end. I wish we could find the typewriter. That would be a coup."

"Forget it. There's no way."

"What makes you say that? It has to be around here somewhere. Someone typed both those letters on the same machine."

"So what? If I were writing poison-pen notes, I'd hardly sit at my desk and use my own IBM. I'm too paranoid for that. I'd use one of the rental typewriters at the public library. Or maybe find a place selling typewriters and use one of theirs."

"This machine isn't new. The typeface has an old-fashioned look to it and a lot of the letters are clogged. It's probably got a fabric ribbon instead of carbon film."

"Those typewriters at the library aren't exactly hot off the assembly line."

"Pick me up some samples and we'll do a comparison. There are a couple of typeface defects that should help us pin it down. I'm sure a document expert could find others. I've only eyeballed it."

"The clogged letters don't mean much. Go after 'em with cleaning fluid and poof, those are gone."

"Sure, but don't you think the majority of people who write anonymous letters assume they're safe from discovery?"

"They might assume they're safe, but they're not," Dietz said. "The FBI maintains extensive files of anonymous letters. Plus, they have samples of type from most known machines. Post Office does, too, and so does the Treasury Department. They can determine the make and model of almost any machine. That's how they nail cranks, especially people who send threatening letters to public officials. The only way to play it safe is to dismantle the machine."

"Yeah, but who's going to trash a typewriter? If you thought you were safe enough to use your own machine, you wouldn't turn around and toss it in the garbage afterward. And in this case, why bother? Those letters were a nuisance, but hardly actionable."

Dietz smiled. "What, you picture it sitting out on someone's desk?"

"Maybe. It's possible."

"Keep an eye out."

"I know you're just saying that to humor me," I said.

"What else did Donovan have to say about the Maddisons?"

"Not much. He claims they're all gone, but I don't think we should take his word for it."

"It's worth pursuing," Dietz said. "As stories go, it's not bad."

"What do you mean, 'it's not bad'? I think it's fabulous. I mean, talk about a motive for murder. It's the best lead we've had—"

"The only lead," he pointed out.

I ignored the obvious. "On top of that, we have Outhwaite, who seems to tie right back to them."

"Shouldn't be too hard to track down the name Maddison with two *d*'s. Even if they're not local, they had to come from somewhere."

"Donovan says the father died around Thanksgiving of 1967 and

Patty followed, probably in May or June of 1968. The mother died five years later, but that's as much as I know. You may not find Claire at all. He says she moved back to the East Coast and married. He does remember reading about her death in the local paper, so there must have been a notice in the *Dispatch*. Maybe she kept her maiden name?"

"I'll get on it first thing."

"You will? I can't believe you're volunteering. I thought you hated doing this stuff."

"Good practice. It's nice to keep a hand in. This way I know I haven't lost my touch," he said. "We might try the newspaper morgue if we can get Katzenbach's cooperation. They might have old clips on the Maddisons along with the obits."

"That's a sexy suggestion."

"I'm a sexy guy," he said.

When we got home, I changed into my sweats in preparation for jogging. I had slept through my usual six A.M. run and I was feeling the effects. I left Dietz in the living room with his leg propped up, icing his bum knee while he flipped from channel to channel, alternately watching CNN, talk shows, and obscure sporting events. I headed out the front door, thankful for the opportunity to spend time alone.

There was scarcely any breeze coming off the ocean. The late-afternoon sun had begun to fade, but the daylong baked beach was still throwing off heat saturated by the smell of kelp and brine. The fronds of the palm trees looked like construction paper cutouts, flat dark shapes against the flat blue sky. I lengthened my stride, running at a pace that felt good. The stiffness and fatigue gradually gave way to ease. My muscles became liquid and sweat trickled down my face. Even the burning in my chest felt good as my body was flooded with oxygen. At the end of the run, I flung myself down on the grass, where I lay panting. My mind was a blank and my bones were washed clean. Finally, my breathing slowed and the run-generated heat in my body seeped out. I did a series of stretches and then roused myself. As I headed for home, I could feel the return of the Santa Ana winds lufting down the mountainside. I showered and changed clothes, throwing on a T-shirt and jeans.

Dietz and I had dinner up at Rosie's. William was working behind the bar again. At the age of eighty-seven, this was like a whole new career for him. Since their marriage, the two of them had settled into a comfortable routine. More and more, Rosie seemed to be turning management over to him. She'd always maintained tight control of the day-to-day operation, but William had persuaded her to pay decent wages and as a consequence, she'd been able to hire better employees. And she'd begun to delegate responsibility, which gave her more time to spend with him. William had given up some of his imaginary illnesses and she'd surrendered some of her authoritarianism. Their affection for each other was obvious and their occasional spats seemed to blow over without incident. Dietz was talking to William about Germany, but I was only half attentive, wondering if the two of us would ever reach an accommodation. I pictured Dietz at eighty-seven, me a comparatively youthful seventy-two; retired from the stresses of private-eye work, riddled with arthritis, bereft of our teeth. What would we do, open a private-detective school?

"What are you thinking? You look odd," he said.

"Nothing. Retirement."

"I'd rather eat my gun."

At bedtime, Dietz offered to hobble up the spiral stairs. "My knee's killing me again so I'm probably not much good except for company," he said.

"You're better off downstairs. My bed's not big enough, especially with that knee of yours. I'd just lie there worrying I'd bump you wrong."

I left him below opening up the sofa bed while I ambled up the stairs, talking to him over the rail.

"Last chance," he said, smiling up at me.

"I'm not sure it's smart getting used to you."

"You should take advantage while you can."

I paused, looking down. "That's the difference between us in a nutshell, Dietz."

"Because I live in the moment?"

"Because for you that's enough."

First thing Friday morning, Dietz took his car and headed over to the *Santa Teresa Dispatch* offices while I drove to Paul Trasatti's house. Hopper Road was located midway between the Maleks' and the country club. The neighborhood was small, the street lined with elm trees and dappled with shade. The house was built in the style of an English country cottage, the sort you'd see pictured on a deck of playing cards; gray stone with a thatched roof that undulated like an ocean wave where the gables appeared. The windows were small-paned, leaded glass, the wood trim and the shutters painted white. Two narrow stone chimneys bracketed the house like a pair of matching bookends. The yard was enclosed with a white picket fence, pink and red hollyhocks planted along the front. The small yard was immaculate, thick grass bordered in dark ivy with small flowerbeds along the brick walk leading to the door. Birds twittered in the young oak growing at the corner of the property.

I'd called the night before, of course, wanting to be certain Trasatti would be home. Even on the porch, I could smell bacon and eggs and the scent of maple syrup. My whimper probably wasn't audible above the sound of the mower two doors down. In response to my ring, Trasatti came to the door with his napkin in hand. He was tall and thin, as bald as a lightbulb. He had a large nose, thick glasses, and a jutting chin. His chest was narrow, slightly sunken, swelling to a thickened waistline. He wore a white dress shirt and a pair of stovepipe pants. He frowned at me, looking at his watch with surprise. "You said nine."

"It is nine."

"This says eight." He held his watch to his ear. "Shit. Come on in.

You caught me at breakfast. Have a seat in here. I'll be back in a second. You want coffee?"

"I'm fine. Take your time," I said.

The living room was small and perfectly appointed, more like a doctor's office than a place to put your feet up. The furniture had a vaguely Victorian air, though to my untutored eye, it didn't appear to be the real thing. The chairs were small and fussy, rimmed with carved wooden fruit. There were three dark wood tables topped with pink-veined marble slabs, an array of Sotheby's catalogs neatly lined up on one. The carpeting was a short-cut wool pile, pale blue with a border of Chinese dragons and chrysanthemums. Two cloisonné vases were filled with artificial pink and blue flowers of some generic sort. A clock on the mantel had a second hand that clicked distinctly as it inched its way around. I leafed through a Sotheby's catalog, but didn't see much of interest except a letter from the Marquis de Sade, which was being offered at two thousand dollars. The passage quoted was in French and seemed petulant. There was also a pretty little greeting from Erik Satie to Mme Ravel with "decorated borders and raised blind relief heading showing in colour two hands held in front of a rose . . ." Lots of talk about *"jolies fleurs"* and *"respecteuse-ments."* My thoughts exactly. I've often said as much.

I strolled the perimeter, taking in numerous framed letters and autographs. Laurence Sterne, Franz Liszt, William Henry Harrison, Jacob Broom (whoever he was), Juan José Flores (ditto). There was a long, incomprehensible letter bearing the signature S. T. Coleridge, and some kind of receipt or order blank signed by George Washington. There was another letter written in a crabbed hand, dated August 1710, fraught with brown ink and cross-outs and looking crumpled and stained. Who'd had the presence of mind to save all this litter? Were there people with foresight going through the dust-bins back then?

Across the hall, I could see what must have been a dining room done up as an office. There were bookshelves on every wall, some extending across the windows, which greatly diminished the incoming light. Every surface was stacked ten deep, including tables, chairs, and floors. No typewriter on the premises as far as I could see. I had no reason to think Trasatti was involved, but it would have been nice to have a piece of the puzzle fall into place. The air smelled of old dust and book mold, glue, aging paper, and dust mites. A large tortoiseshell cat picked its way daintily across a desk piled with books. This creature had only a stump for a tail and looked like it might be searching out a place to pee.

"Making yourself at home?" came the voice behind me.

I started, making ever so slight a leap.

"I was admiring this enormous cat," I said casually.

"Sorry if I startled you. That's Lady Chatterley."

"What happened to her tail?"

"She's a Manx."

"She looks like a character," I said. Animal people seem to love it when you say things like this. Trasatti didn't seem to warm to it. He gestured me into the office, where he took a seat at his desk, pushing aside an irregular stack of hardback books.

"No secretary?" I asked.

"Business isn't big enough for clerical help. Anything I need done, I use the Mac upstairs. Go ahead and make a space for yourself," he said, indicating the only chair in the room.

"Thanks." I placed some books, a briefcase, and a pile of newspapers on the floor, and sat down.

"Now what can I help you with? I really can't add to what I've already given you in regard to Jack," he said.

"This was in regard to something else," I said while the fifteen-pound cat hopped onto my lap and settled between my knees. Up close, Lady Chatterley smelled like a pair of damp two-week-old socks. I scratched that little spot just above the base of its tail which made the back end of the cat rise up until its rosebud was staring me in the face. I pushed the back end down. I peppered my preface with lots of reassuring phrases—"off the record," "just between us," and other felicitous expressions of confidentiality—before getting down to business. "I'm wondering what you can tell me about the Maddisons—Patty and her sister, Claire."

He seemed to take the question in stride. "What would you like to know?"

"Anything you care to tell," I said.

Paul straightened the stack of books in front of him, making sure all the edges were aligned and the top right-hand corners matched. "I didn't know the sister. She was older than we were. She was off at college by the time the family moved into the area and Patty started hanging out with Guy."

"The Maddisons were new in town?"

"Well no, not really. They'd been living out in Colgate and bought a house closer in. They never had the kind of money we did, the rest of us—not that we were wealthy," he added. "Bader Malek did well back in those days, but he wasn't what you'd call rich."

"Tell me about Patty."

"She was pretty. Dark." He put his hand at eye level, indicating bangs. "Hair down to here," he said. "She'd kind of peer out like this. She was strange, lots of phobias and nervous mannerisms. Bad posture, big tits. She chewed her nails to the quick and liked to stick herself with things." Trasatti put his hands in his lap, trying not to touch the items on his desk.

"She stuck herself? With what?"

"Needles. Pencils. Safety pins. I saw her burn herself one time. She put a lighted cigarette on her hand—casually, like it was happening to someone else. She never even flinched, but I could smell cooked flesh."

"Was Guy serious about her?" I pushed the cat's hind end down again and it began to work its claws into the knees of my jeans.

"She was serious about him. I have no idea what he thought of her."

"What about the others? Donovan and Bennet."

"What about them?"

"I just wondered what they were up to during this period."

"Donovan was working for his dad, as I remember. He was always working for his dad, so that's a safe bet. Jack was back at school by then, so he was only home on occasion. Christmas and spring break."

"And his mother's funeral," I said. I extracted the cat's claws from my knee and held its right paw between my fingers. I could feel its claws protrude and retract, but the cat seemed content, probably thinking about mice. "What about Bennet? Where was he?"

"Here in town. He and I were both finishing at UCST."

"Majoring in what?"

"My major was art history. His was economics or business, maybe public finance. He switched around some. I forget."

"Did it surprise you when Patty turned up pregnant?"

Trasatti snorted, shaking his head. "Patty would screw anyone. She was desperate for attention and we were happy to oblige."

"Really," I said. "Donovan never said she was promiscuous."

"She wasn't the only one. There was lots of screwing in those days. Free love, we called it. We were all smoking dope. Bunch of small-town hippies, or as close as we could get. We were always horny and hungry. Half the girls we hung out with were as fat as pigs. Except for Patty, of course, who was gorgeous, but whacked out."

"Nice of you boys to help yourselves to a minor," I said. "Given her loose ways, how'd you know the baby was Guy's?"

"Because she said it was."

"She could have lied. If she was crazy and stoned, she might have made things up. How do you know the baby wasn't yours?"

Trasatti shifted uncomfortably. "I had no money to speak of. Where's the benefit in claiming it's mine. The Maleks had class. She might have been crazy, but she wasn't stupid. It's like the old joke—"

"I know the old joke," I said. "Was there ever any proof? Did anybody run blood tests to establish paternity?"

"I hardly think so. I'm sure they didn't. This was sixty-eight."

"How do you know Guy wasn't blamed because it was convenient? He was gone by then. Who better to accuse than a chronic screwup like him?"

Trasatti picked up a pencil and then put it down. His expression had gone blank. "What does this have to do with Jack? I thought you were working to try to get him off."

"That's what I'm doing."

"Doesn't sound like that to me."

"Donovan told me about Patty yesterday. I thought the story might pertain, so I'm following up. Did you ever see the letters Guy allegedly forged?"

"Why put it that way? It's what he did."

"Did you actually see him do it."

"No, of course not."

"Then it's all supposition. Did you ever see the letters?"

"Why would I?"

"Your father did the appraisal when the forgeries were discovered. I thought he might have showed you the copies, if he was training you to follow in his footsteps."

"Who told you that?"

"He handed the business over to you, didn't he?"

Trasatti smiled at me, blinking. "I don't understand where you intend to go with this. Are you accusing me of something?"

"Not at all," I said.

"Because if you are, you're out of line."

"That wasn't an accusation. I never said you did anything. I'm saying Guy Malek didn't. I'm saying someone else did it all and blamed him. What about 'Max Outhwaite'? How does he fit in?"

"Outhwaite?"

"Come on, Trasatti. That's the name Guy supposedly used on his fake business cards."

"Right, right, right. I remember now. Sure thing. I knew it sounded familiar. What's the link?"

"That's why I'm asking you. I don't know," I said. "I think the story of Patty Maddison ties in somehow. Her death, the forged letters. I'm just fishing around."

"You better try something else. The family's gone."

"What makes you so sure?"

Paul Trasatti was silent. He began to arrange a row of paper clips on the side of a magnetized holder on his desk. Each one had to be exactly the same distance from the one above it and the one below.

"Come on. Just between us," I said.

"I tried to find them once."

"When was this?"

"About ten years ago."

"Really," I said, trying not to seem interested. "What was that about?"

"I was curious. I thought there might be other rare documents. You know, passed down to other members of the family."

"How'd you go about it?"

"I hired a genealogist. I said I was trying to find some long-lost relatives. This gal did a search. She took months. She traced the name back to England, but on this end—the California branch—there weren't any male heirs and the line died out."

"What about aunts, uncles, cousins . . . ?"

"The parents were both the only children of only children. There was no one left."

"What happened to the copies of the documents?"

"The forgeries were destroyed."

"And the originals?"

"No one's ever seen them again. Well, I haven't in any case. They've never come up for sale in all the years I've done business."

"Do you know what they were?"

"I have the itemized list. My dad kept meticulous records. You want to see it?"

"I'd love to."

Trasatti got up and crossed to a closet. I caught a glimpse of a wall safe and four gray metal file cabinets. Above them, on shelves, there was a series of old-fashioned card files. "I'm going to get all this on computer one of these days." He seemed to know right where he was going and I wondered if this was something he'd done recently. He extracted a card, glanced at it briefly, and then closed the drawer again. He left the closet door ajar and returned to his desk, handing me the card as he passed my chair. The cat had gone to sleep, lying across my knees like a fifteen-pound bag of hot sand.

The list detailed six documents: a framed Society of Boston Membership Certificate and a personal letter, both signed by George Washington and valued at $11,500 and $9,500, respectively; a judicial writ signed by Abraham Lincoln, dated December 1847, valued at $6,500; a wartime document signed by John Hancock, valued at $5,500; a ten-page fragment from an original manuscript by Arthur Conan Doyle valued at $7,500; and a letter signed by John Adams, valued at $9,000.

"I'm impressed," I said. "I don't know beans about rare documents, but these seem fabulous."

"They are. Those prices you're looking at are twenty years out of date. They'd be worth more today."

"How did Patty Maddison's father get his hands on items like these?"

"Nobody really knows. He was an amateur collector. He picked some up at auction and the rest, who knows? He might have stolen them for all I know. My father'd heard about 'em, but Francis—Mr. Maddison—would never let him examine them."

"His widow must have been an idiot to hand 'em over the way she did."

Trasatti made no comment.

"How did Guy hear about the letters?" I asked.

"Patty probably told him."

"Why would she do that?"

"How do I know? Showing off. She was nuts. She did all kinds of weird things."

I saw him glance at his watch. "You have an appointment?" I asked.

"As a matter of fact, I'm hoping we can wrap this up. I have work to do."

"Five minutes more and I'll be on my way."

Trasatti shifted restlessly, but motioned me on.

"Let me try out a little theory. None of this came to light until after Guy took off, right?"

Trasatti stared at me, without offering encouragement.

I was forced to go on, feeling like Perry Mason in a courtroom confrontation, only this wasn't going as well as his always did. "So maybe Jack was the one who got Patty knocked up. I heard Jack was the randy one. According to Guy, he screwed anything that moved."

"I told you he was off at college. He wasn't even here," Trasatti said.

"He came back for his mother's funeral and again for spring break. That was March, wasn't it?"

"I really don't remember."

"As I understand it, Guy had hit the road by then. Jack felt betrayed. He was crushed that Guy'd left without him so maybe he turned to Patty for consolation. At that point, she must have needed comfort as much as he did."

Trasatti kept his face expressionless, his fingers laced together on the desk. "You're never going to get me to say anything about this."

"Jack could have forged the letters. You two were buddies. Your father was an appraiser. You could have cooked up the scheme yourself and showed Jack how to do it."

"I'm finding this offensive. It's pure speculation. It doesn't mean a thing."

I let that one slide, though what he said was true. "Everything was cool until Guy came home again."

"What difference would that make?"

"In the old days, Guy took the blame for everybody's sins, so it just stands to reason everyone felt safe until he showed up again."

"I'm not following."

"Maybe the motive for Guy's murder was never money," I said. "Maybe Jack was just trying to protect himself."

"From what? I don't get it. There's really nothing at stake. The theft was eighteen years ago. The statute of limitations has run out. There's no crime on the books. Even if your guess is correct, Jack's the one who ends up with his ass in a sling. You said you were here to help, but it's blowing right back on him."

"You know what? Here's the truth. I don't really give a shit what blows back on him. If he's guilty, so be it. That isn't my concern."

"Well, that's nice. You want me to pick up the phone and call Lonnie Kingman? He's going to love your attitude and so will Jack. As far as I know, he's the one paying your bills."

"You go right ahead. Lonnie can always fire me if he doesn't like what I'm doing."

20

I stopped at a pay phone and put a call through to Lonnie, who had the good grace to laugh when he heard my account of the conversation with Paul Trasatti. "Forget it. The guy's a prick. He was just on the phone to me, whining and complaining about harassment. What a jerk."

"Why's he so worried about Jack?"

"Forget Jack for now. I'll take care of him. You better go talk to Bennet; I couldn't get to him. According to the grapevine, he's talking to an attorney in case the hairy eyeball of the law falls on him next. He's still got no alibi, as far as I've heard."

"Well, that's interesting."

"Yeah, people are getting nervous. That's a good sign," he said. He gave me the address of Bennet's restaurant, which was located downtown on a side street off State. The neighborhood itself was marked by a tire store, a minimart, a video rental shop, and a billiard parlor where fights erupted without much provocation beyond excess beer. Parking didn't seem to be readily available and it was hard to picture where the restaurant trade would be coming from.

Apparently, the place had once been a retail store, part of a chain that had filed for bankruptcy. The old sign was still out, but the interior had been gutted. The space was cavernous and shadowy, the floor bare concrete, the ceiling high. Heating ducts and steel girders were exposed to view, along with all of the electrical conduit. Toward the rear, an office had been roughed in: a desk, file cabinets, and office equipment arranged in a bare-framed cubicle. The back wall was solid and through a narrow doorway, I could see a toilet and a small sink with a medicine cabinet above it. It was going to take a lot of money to complete construction and get the business on its feet. No wonder Bennet had been so eager to get his hands on the second will. If Guy's share was divided among his brothers, each would be richer by more than a million, which he could clearly use.

To the right, a huge rolling metal door had been opened onto a weedy vacant lot. Outside, the sun was harsh, sparkling on the broken bottles while its heat baked a variety of doggy turds. There was not a soul in sight, but the building was wide open and I kept thinking Bennet, or a construction worker, would show up before long. While I waited, I wandered into the office area and took a seat at Bennet's desk. The secretarial chair was rickety and I imagined he made his phone calls upright with his hip resting on the desk, which seemed sturdier. Everything in the office had an air of having been borrowed or picked up on the cheap. The calculator tape showed a long series of numbers that didn't add up to anything. I could have checked in the drawers, but I was too polite. Besides, my recent clash with Paul Trasatti had chastened me some. I didn't want Lonnie getting two complaints in a single day.

There was a manual typewriter sitting on a rolling cart. My gaze slid across it idly and then came back. It was an ancient black Underwood with round yellowed keys that looked like they'd be hard to press. The ribbon was so worn it was thin in the middle. I looked over at the rolling door and then surveyed the whole of the empty restaurant space. Still no one. My bad angel was hovering to my left. It was she who pointed out the open packet of typing paper sitting right there in plain sight.

I pulled out a sheet and rolled it into the machine, settling myself on the wobbly typing chair. I typed my name. I typed that old standby: *The quick brown fox jumps over the lazy dog.* I typed the name *Max Outhwaite.* I typed *Dear Miss Milhone.* I peered closely. The vowels didn't appear to be clogged, which (as Dietz had pointed out) didn't mean that much. This could still be the typewriter used for the notes. Maybe Bennet had simply made a point of cleaning his keys. I pulled the paper out and folded it, then stood up and slipped it in the pocket of my jeans. When I got back to the office, I'd see if the defective *a* and *i* were visible under magnification. I still hadn't seen the anonymous letter Guy had received the Monday before he died, but maybe Betsy Bower would relent and let me pirate a copy.

The telephone rang.

I stared at it briefly and then lifted my head, listening for footsteps heading in my direction. Nothing. The phone rang again. I was tempted to answer, but I really didn't need to because the answering machine kicked in. Bennet's voice message was brief and very businesslike. So was the caller.

"Bennet. Paul here. Give me a call as soon as possible."

The machine clicked off. The message light blinked off and on. My bad angel tapped me on the shoulder and pointed. I reached out and pressed DELETE. A disembodied male voice told me the message had been erased. I headed for the front door, breaking into a trot when I reached the street. Trasatti was a busy boy, calling everyone.

A Harley-Davidson rumbled into view. Shit. Bennet was back just when I thought I'd escaped. I slowed my pace, as if I had all the time in the world. Bennet rolled Jack's motorcycle up to the curb less than ten feet away. He killed the engine and popped the kickstand into place. He peeled off his helmet and cradled it under his arm. I noticed his hair was tightly frizzed and matted with sweat. Despite the heat, he was wearing a black leather jacket, probably protection in case he flipped the bike and skidded. "Working again?"

"I'm always working," I said.

"Did you want to talk to me?" His jacket creaked when he walked. He headed into the restaurant.

I followed. "How goes construction? It's looking pretty good," I said. It looked like a bomb crater, but I was kissing butt. Our footsteps echoed as we crossed the raw concrete floor.

"Construction's slow."

I said, "Ah. What's your target for opening?"

"April, if we're lucky. We have a lot of work to do."

"What kind of restaurant?"

"Cajun and Caribbean. We'll have salads and burgers, too, very reasonably priced. Maybe jazz two nights a week. We're really aiming for the singles' market."

"Like a pickup bar?"

"With class," he said. "This town doesn't have a lot going on at night. Get some dance music in here weekends, I think we're filling a niche. A chef from New Orleans and all the hot local bands. We should pull crowds from as far away as San Luis Obispo."

"That sounds rowdy," I said. We'd reached the office by then and I saw him flick a glance at his answering machine. I was only half listening, trying to think how to keep the conversation afloat. "Any problem with parking?"

"Not at all," he said. "We'll pave the lot next door. We're in negotiations at the moment. There's room for thirty cars there and another ten on the street."

"Sounds good," I said. He had an answer for everything. Mr. Slick, I thought.

"I'll comp you some tickets for the grand opening. You like to dance?"

"No, not really."

"Don't worry about it. We'll get you in and you can cut loose.

Forget your inhibitions and get down," he said. He snapped his fingers, dipping his knees in a move meant to be oh so hip.

My least favorite thing in life is some guy encouraging me to "cut loose" and "get down." The smile I offered him was paper thin. "I hope this business with Jack has been resolved by then."

"Absolutely," he said smoothly, his expression sobering appropriately. "How's it looking so far?"

"He can't account for his time, which doesn't help," I said. "The cops are claiming they found a bloody print from his shoe on the carpet up in Guy's room. I won't bore you with details. Lonnie wanted me to ask where you were."

"The night of the murder? I was club-hopping down in L.A."

"You drove to Los Angeles and back?"

"I do it all the time. It's nothing. Ninety minutes each way," he said. "That night, some of the time I was on the road."

"Did you have a date?"

"This was strictly business. I'm trying to get a feel for what works and what doesn't, sampling menus. You know, listening to some of the L.A. bands."

"I'm assuming you have credit card receipts to back you up."

A fleeting change of expression suggested I'd caught him out on that one. "I might have a few. I'll have to look and see what I've got. I paid cash in the main. It's easier that way."

"What time did you get in?"

"Close to three," he said. "You want to come in the back? I've got some beer in a cooler. We could have a drink."

"Thanks. It's a bit early."

"Where you going?"

"Back to the office. I have a meeting," I said.

On the way back to the office, I stopped off at a deli and picked up some soft drinks and sandwiches. Dietz had said he'd be joining me as soon as he'd finished his research. I stashed the soft drinks in the little refrigerator in my office and dumped my handbag on the floor beside my chair. I put the sack of sandwiches on the file cabinet and grabbed the folder full of clippings, which I tossed on my desk. I sat down in my swivel chair and assembled my index cards, the typewritten letters, and the sample I'd just taken from Bennet's machine, lining everything up in an orderly fashion. In the absence of definitive answers, it's good to look organized.

I turned on the desk lamp and pulled out my magnifying glass. The type was no match. I was disappointed, but I wasn't surprised. I took Guy's last letter from my handbag and read the contents again. Aside from his invitation to Disneyland, which I'd have accepted in a flash, I realized that what I was looking at, in essence, was a holographic will. The letter was written entirely by hand and he'd specified in the postscript what he'd wanted done with his share of his father's estate. I didn't know all the technicalities associated with a holographic will, but I thought this might qualify. The handwriting would have to be verified, but Peter Antle could do that when I saw him next. I knew Guy had received a disturbing letter late that Monday afternoon, and whatever its contents, he must have been sufficiently alarmed to want to make his wishes clear. I got up and left the office, taking his letter with me to the copy room. I ran a Xerox and then locked the originals with the others in my bottom drawer. The copy I slid in the outer pocket of my handbag.

I tried to picture Guy, but his face had already faded in my mind's eye. What remained was his sweetness, the sound of his "Hey," the feeling of his whiskers when he'd brushed my cheek with his lips. If he'd lived, I'm not sure we would have had a very strong relationship. Kinsey Millhone and a born-again was probably not a combination that would have gone anywhere. But we might have been friends. We might have gone to Disneyland once a year to experience some silliness.

I went back to my index cards and began to make notes. Every investigation has a nature of its own, but there are certain shared characteristics, namely the painstaking accumulation of information and the patience required. Here's what you hope for: a chance remark from the former neighbor on a skip-trace, a penciled notation on the corner of a document, an ex-spouse with a grudge, the number on an account, an item overlooked at the scene of a crime. Here's what you expect: the dead ends, bureaucratic bullheadedness, the cul-de-sacs, trails that go nowhere or simply fade into thin air, denials, prevarications, the blank-eyed stares from all the hostile witnesses. Here's what you know: that you've done it before and you have the toughness and determination to pull it off again. Here's what you want: justice. Here's what you'll settle for: something equivalent, the quid pro quo.

I glanced down at my desk, catching sight of the label on the file of clippings. The label had been neatly typed: *Guy Malek, Dispatch Clippings*. The two letters from Outhwaite were lined up with the label itself, which is what made me notice for the first time that the lowercase *a* and the lower case *i* were both defective on all three documents. Was that true? I peered closely, picking up my magnifying glass again and scrutinizing the relevant characters. It would take a document expert to prove it, but to me it looked like the letters had been typed on the same machine.

I reached for the phone and called the Maleks. In the tiny interval between punching in the number and waiting for it to ring, I was scrambling around in my imagination, trying to conjure up a reason for the call I was making. Shit, shit, shit. Christie picked up on her end, greeting me coolly when I identified myself. I figured she'd talked to Paul Trasatti, but I didn't dare ask.

I said, "I was just looking for Bennet. Is he home, by any chance? I stopped by the restaurant, but he was out somewhere."

"He should be here in a bit. I think he said he was coming home for lunch. You want him to call you?"

"I'm not sure he'll be able to reach me. I'm down at the office, but I've got some errands to run. I'll call back later."

"I'll pass the message along." She was using her good-bye tone.

I had to launch in with something to keep the conversation afloat.

269

"I talked to Paul this morning. What an odd duck he is. Is he still on medication?"

I could hear her focus her attention. "Paul's on medication? Who told you that? I never heard that," she said.

I let a beat pass. "Uhh, sorry. I didn't mean to breach anybody's confidence. Forget I said anything. I just assumed you knew."

"Why bring it up at all? Is there a problem?"

"Well, nothing *huge*. He's just so paranoid about Jack. He actually sat there and accused me of undermining Jack's credibility, which couldn't be further from the truth. Lonnie and I are working our butts off for him."

"Really."

"Then he turned around and called Lonnie. I think he's probably on another phone rampage, hounding everyone he knows with those wild stories of his. Ah, well. It doesn't matter. I'm sure he means well, but he's not doing anybody any favors."

"Is that what you wanted to talk to Bennet about?"

"No, that was something different. Lonnie wanted me to verify Bennet's whereabouts Tuesday night."

"I'm sure he'll be happy to talk to you. I know he's told the police and they seem satisfied. I can leave him a note."

"Perfect. I'd appreciate that. Can I ask you about something? You remember the file I borrowed?"

"With all the clippings?"

"Exactly. I wondered about the label. Did you type that yourself?"

"Not me. I never took typing. My mother warned me about that. Bader probably typed the label or he gave it to his secretary. He thought typing was restful. Shows how much he knew."

"That must have been a while ago. I don't remember seeing a typewriter in his office when I was there."

"He got himself a personal computer a couple of years ago."

"What happened to the typewriter?"

"He passed it on to Bennet, I think."

I closed my eyes and stilled my breathing. Christie's attitude had changed and she was sounding friendly again. I didn't want to alert her to the importance of the information. "What'd Bennet do with it? That's not the one he's using at the restaurant, is it?"

"Nuhn-uhn. I doubt it. It's probably in his room. What's this about?"

"Nothing much. No big deal. Just a little theory of mine, but I'd love to see it sometime. Would it be all right with you if I stopped by to take a look?"

"Well, it's all right with me, but Bennet might object unless he's here, of course. His room is like the inner sanctum. Nobody goes in there except him. We're just on our way out. We have an appointment at eleven. Why don't you ask Bennet when you talk to him?"

"I can do that. No problem. That's a good idea," I said. "And one more quick question. The night of the murder, could you really see Donovan? Or did you just assume he was watching television because the set was turned on in the other room?"

Christie put the phone down without another word.

The minute I hung up, I wrote a hasty note to Dietz, put a couple of pieces of blank paper in the file, and shoved it in my handbag. I headed out the side door and took the stairs down to the street, skipping two at a time. I wasn't sure which "we" had an appointment at eleven, but I was hoping it was Christie and Donovan. If I could get to the Maleks' before Bennet came home, I could probably bullshit my way upstairs and take a look at the machine. It had occurred to me more than once that Jack or Bennet might be behind the letters and the leak to the press. I couldn't pinpoint the motivation, but getting a lock on the typewriter would go a long way toward shoring up the connection. I was also thinking tee-hee on you, Dietz, because I'd told him whoever wrote the letters wouldn't trash the machine. It's the same way with guns. Someone will use a handgun in the commission of a crime and instead of disposing of the weapon, he'll keep it in his closet at home or shove it under the bed. Better to pitch it in the ocean.

I reached the Maleks' in record time, burning up the route I'd driven so many times before. As I approached the estate, I could see the front gates swing open and the nose of a car just appearing around the curve in the drive. I slammed on my brakes and slid into the nearest driveway, fishtailing slightly, my eyes pinned on my rearview mirror for a moment until the BMW sped past. Donovan was driving, his gaze fixed on the road ahead. I thought I caught sight of Christie, but I couldn't be sure. I heard a car horn toot and looked out through my windshield. The Maleks' neighbor, in a dark blue station wagon, was waiting patiently for me to get out of his driveway. I made lots of sheepish gestures as I put my car in reverse. I backed out of the driveway and pulled over to let him pass. I mouthed the word *Sorry* as he turned to look at me. He smiled and waved, and I waved back at him. Once he was out of sight, I pulled out, crossing the road to the Maleks' entrance gates.

The security guard had been relieved of his duties. I leaned out toward the call box and punched in the gate code Tasha had given me. There was a happy peeping signal. The gates gave a little wiggle and then swung open to admit me. I eased up the driveway and around the curve. Vaguely, it occurred to me that Christie might have stayed home. I'd have to think of a whopper to account for my arrival. Oh, well. Often the best lies are the ones you think up in a pinch.

There were no cars in the courtyard, a good sign I thought. Two of the three garages were standing open and both were empty. I had to leave my vehicle out front, but there didn't seem to be any way around that. If my purpose was legitimate, why would I bother to conceal my car? If the Maleks returned, I'd find a way to fake it. I bypassed the front door and hiked around to the kitchen, pulling the file from my handbag as I rounded the house. Enid was visible through the bay window, standing at the sink. She spotted me and waved, moving toward the backdoor to let me in. She was still drying her hands on a towel when she stepped back, allowing me to precede her into the room.

I said, "Hi, Enid. How are you?"

"Fine," she said. "What are you doing coming to the backdoor?

You just missed Christie and Donovan going out the front." She was wearing a big white apron over jeans and a T-shirt and her hair was neatly tucked under a crocheted cap.

"Really? I didn't see them. I rang the front doorbell twice. I guess you couldn't hear me so I thought I'd come around. I can't believe I missed them. My timing's off," I said.

I could see the ingredients for a baking project laid out on the counter: two sticks of butter with the paper removed, a sixteen-ounce measuring cup filled with granulated sugar, a tin of baking powder, and a quart container of whole milk. The oven was preheating and a large springform pan had already been buttered and floured.

She returned to the counter where she picked up her sifter and began sifting cake flour into a mountain that had a perfect point on top. While I watched, she used a spatula to scoop more flour. I seldom bake anything and when I do, I tend to assemble the items as needed, not realizing I'm missing some essential ingredient until I get to the critical moment in the recipe. "Quickly fold in whipped egg whites and finely minced fresh ginger . . ." Enid was methodical, washing up as she went along. I knew she wouldn't bake anything from mixes and her cakes would never fall.

"Where'd everybody go? I didn't see any cars in the garages," I said.

"Myrna's lying down. I imagine she'll be up in a bit."

"What's wrong with her? Is she ill?"

"I don't know. She seems worried and I don't think she's been sleeping that well."

"Maybe I should talk to her. Where's everyone else?"

"Christie says Bennet's coming home at lunchtime. She and Donovan went over to the funeral home. The coroner's office called. The body's being released this afternoon and they've gone to pick out a casket."

"When's the funeral? Has anybody said?"

"They're talking about Monday, just for family and close friends. It won't be open to the public."

"I should think not. I'm sure they've had their fill of media attention."

"Can I help you with anything?"

"Not really. I talked to Christie a while ago and told her I'd be returning this file. She said to stick it in Bader's office. I can let myself out the front door when I'm done."

"Help yourself," she said. "Take the back stairs if you want. You know how to find the office?"

"Sure. I've been up there before. What are you making?"

"Lemon pound cake."

"Sounds good," I said.

I trotted up the back stairs, folder in hand, slowing my pace when I reached the top landing. The back hall was utilitarian, floors uncarpeted, windows bare. This mansion was built in an era when the wealthy had live-in servants who occupied nooks and crannies squeezed into wings at the rear of the house, or wedged into attic spaces that were broken up into many small rooms. Cautiously, I opened a door on my left. A narrow stairway ascended into the shadows above. I eased the door shut and moved on, checking into a large linen closet and a cubicle with an ancient commode. The corridor took a ninety-degree turn to the right, opening into the main hall through an archway concealed by heavy damask drapes on a wrought-iron rod.

I could see the polished rail of the main stair at the midpoint in the hall. Beyond the stair landing, there was another wing of the house that mirrored the one I was now in. A wide Oriental runner stretched the length of the gloomy hall. At the far end, damask drapes suggested an archway and yet another set of stairs. The wallpaper was subdued, a soft floral pattern repeated endlessly. At intervals, tulip-shaped crystal fixtures were mounted on the walls. They'd probably been installed when the house was built and converted at some point from gas to electricity.

There were three doors on my left, each sealed with an enormous X of crime scene tape. I had to guess that one door led to Guy's bedroom, one to Jack's, and one to the bathroom that connected the two. On the right, there were two more doors. I knew the second was Bader's suite: bedroom, bath, and home office. The door closest to me was closed. I flicked a look behind me, making sure Enid hadn't followed. The whole house was silent. I put my hand on the knob and turned it with care. Locked.

Well, now what? The lock was the simple old-fashioned type requiring a skeleton key that probably fit every door up here. I scanned the hall in both directions. I didn't have time to waste. Bader's suite was closest. I did a racewalk to his bedroom and tried the knob. This room was unlocked. I peered around the door. There was a key protruding neatly from the keyhole on the other side. I extracted it and hurried back to Bennet's room. I jammed the key in the lock and tried turning it. I could feel the key hang, but there was some tolerance to the lock. I applied steady pressure while I jiggled the door gently. It took close to thirty seconds, but the key gave way suddenly and I was in.

21

I scanned the room quickly, taking in as much as I could. Two table lamps had been left on. This had to be Bennet's bedroom. He was still in possession of all the paraphernalia from his boyhood hobbies. Model airplanes, model cars, stacks of vintage comic books, early issues of *MAD* magazine, Little League trophies. He'd framed a paint-by-numbers likeness of Jimmy Durante and a color snapshot of himself at the age of thirteen wearing spiffy black dress pants, a pink dress shirt, and a black bolo tie. His bulletin board was still hanging on the back of his closet door. Tacked to the cork were various newspaper headlines about the assassinations of Martin Luther King, Jr., and Bobby Kennedy. There were photographs of the *Apollo 8* spacecraft the day it was launched from Cape Kennedy. A framed movie poster from *The Odd Couple* still hung above his unmade bed. It wasn't hard to pinpoint the peak year in his life. There was no memorabilia beyond 1968.

I flicked on the overhead light and crossed the room, placing my handbag on the floor near my feet. His desk was built-in and ran along the front wall from one side of the room to the other, punctuated by two windows. Bookshelves had been hung on the wall above the desk. Most of the books looked dated, the titles suggestive of textbooks accumulated over the years. I let my gaze skip across the spines. *Ring of Bright Water*, Maxwell; *No Room in the Ark*, Moorehead; *Stalking the Edible Life*, Gibbons; *The Sea Around Us*, Carson. Little or no fiction. Not surprising somehow. Bennet didn't strike me as intellectual or imaginative. A personal computer occupied his desk at center stage, complete with an oversized printer. The machine had been shut down and the glassy gray screen of the monitor reflected distorted slices of the light from the hall door. Everything was a jumble; bills, loose papers, invoices, and stacks of unopened mail everywhere. I spotted the typewriter to the left, covered with a black plastic typewriter "cozy" complete with dust. A stack of books had been placed on top.

I backed up and stuck my head out into the hallway. I did a quick survey, seeing no one, and then closed myself into Bennet's room. If I were caught, there was no way I was going to explain my presence. I went back to the desk, lifted the stack of books from the typewriter, and removed the cover. The machine was an old black high-shouldered Remington with a manual return. Bader must have hung on to the damn thing for forty years. I reached into my bag and removed a piece of blank paper from the folder. I rolled it into the machine, typing precisely the phrases and sentences I'd typed before. *The quick brown fox jumps over the lazy dog.* The typewriter made a racket that seemed remarkably noisy, but it couldn't be helped. With the door to the hall closed, I thought I was safe. *Dear Miss Milhone. Max Outhwaite.* Even at a glance, I knew I was in business. The *a* and the *i* were both askew. This was the machine I'd been looking for. I rolled the paper from the machine, folded it, and slipped it in my pocket. Out of the corner of my eye, the name Outhwaite suddenly popped into view. Was I seeing things? I checked the line of textbooks again, squinting as I pulled out the two books that caught my attention. *Ring of Bright Water*, Gavin Maxwell, was the first in that row. In the middle, about six books down, was *Atlantic: History of an Ocean.* The author was Leonard Outhwaite. I stared, feeling rooted in place. Gavin Maxwell and Leonard Outhwaite. *Maxwell Outhwaite.*

I slipped the cover over the typewriter and put the stack of books back in place. I heard a low rumble, like thunder. I paused. Empty coat hangers began to ring, tinkling together in the closet like wind chimes. All the joints in the house began to squeak quietly and the window glass gave a sharp rattle where the putty had shrunk away from the panes. Nails and wood screws chirped. I put a hand on the bookshelf to steady myself. Under me, the whole house shifted back and forth, perhaps no more than an inch, but with a movement that felt like a sudden gust of strong wind or a train rocking on a track. I didn't feel any fear, but I was alert, wondering if I'd have time to clear the premises. An old house like this must have survived many a temblor, but you never quite knew what was coming with these things. So far, I pegged it in the three- or four-point range. As long as it didn't go on and on, it shouldn't do much damage. Lights flickered faintly as if wires were loose and touching one another intermittently. The strobe effect sparked a series of jerky pale blue images, in the midst of which a dark shape appeared across the room. I peered, blinking, trying to see clearly as the shadow moved toward one corner and then blended into the wall.

I made a small sound in my throat, paralyzed. The trembling gradually ceased and the lights stabilized. I clung to the bookshelf and leaned my head weakly on my arm, trying to shake off the frosty feeling that was creeping down my spine. Any minute, I expected to hear Enid calling from the kitchen stairs. I pictured Myrna on her feet, the three of us comparing notes about the earthquake. I didn't want either one of them coming up to search for me. I snagged my handbag and crossed the room. I moved out into the hall, looking quickly in both directions. I locked the door behind me, cranking the key in the lock so hard it nearly bent under my hand.

I ran down the hall on tiptoe, making a hasty detour into Bader's room. I put the key back in the door where I'd found it, then crossed swiftly into his home office. I opened a file cabinet and shoved the folder between two unrelated files where I could find it later. I crossed the room again and went out into the corridor. I walked quickly toward the heavy drapes at the end of the hall, pushed my way through the arch, and hurried along the back corridor. I clattered down the stairs and into the kitchen. There was no sign of Myrna. Enid was calmly pouring a thick yellow batter into the springform pan.

I put my hand on my chest to still my breathing. "Jesus. That was something. I thought for a minute there we were really in for it."

She looked up at me blankly. I could tell she didn't have the faintest idea what I was talking about.

I stopped in my tracks. "The temblor," I said.

"I wasn't aware of any temblor. When was this?"

"Enid, you're kidding. Don't do this to me. It must have been at least four points on the Richter scale. Didn't the lights flicker down here?"

"Not that I noticed." I watched her use a rubber spatula to sweep the last of the batter from the bowl into the pan.

"The whole house was shifting. Didn't you feel *anything*?"

She was silent for a moment, her gaze dropping to her bowl. "You hang on to people, don't you?"

"What?"

"You have trouble letting go."

"I do not. That's not a bit true. People tell me I'm too independent for my own good."

She was shaking her head before I reached the end of the sentence. "Independence has nothing to do with hanging on," she said.

"What are you talking about?"

"Ghosts don't haunt us. That's not how it works. They're present among us because we won't let go of *them*."

"I don't believe in ghosts," I said, faintly.

"Some people can't see the color red. That doesn't mean it isn't there," she replied.

When I reached the office, Dietz was sitting in my swivel chair with his feet up on the desk. One of the sandwich packets had been opened and he was munching on a BLT. I still hadn't eaten lunch so I reached for the other sandwich. I removed a soft drink from the refrigerator and sat down across from him.

"How'd you do at the *Dispatch*?"

He laid the four Maddison obituaries on the desk so I could study them. "I had Jeff Katzenbach dig through the files. Mother's maiden name was Bangham, so I went over to the library and checked the city directory for other Banghams in the area. None. Three of those obits I've verified at the Hall of Records, checking death certificates. Claire's still a question mark."

"How so?" I popped the top on my soda can and began to pick at the cellophane and plastic packet in which my sandwich was sealed.

Dietz was saying, "There's no suggestion how she died. I'd be interested in seeing if we can get the suicide confirmed just to put that one to bed. I got the name of a PI in Bridgeport, Connecticut, and left a lengthy message with her service. I'm hoping someone will return my call."

"What difference does it make how she died?" I tried biting the seal on the cellophane. Was this kiddie-proof, like poison? Dietz held his hand out for the wrapped sandwich and I passed it across the desk to him.

"Suppose she was murdered? Suppose she was the victim of a hit-and-run accident?" He freed the sandwich and gave it back to me.

"You've got a point," I said. I paused to eat while I reread the information. The obits were in date order, starting with the father's death in late November 1967. Dietz had had all four of them copied onto one page.

MADDISON, Francis M., 53,
departed suddenly on Tuesday, November 21. Loving, adored husband of 25 years to Caroline B. Maddison; beloved father to daughters, Claire and Patricia. He was a service manager at Colgate Automotive Center and a member of the Community Christian Church. He was much loved and will be missed by family and friends. Funeral: 11:30 A.M. Friday. In lieu of flowers, donations to the American Heart Association would be appreciated.

I glanced up at him and said, "Fifty-three. That's young."
"They were all young," Dietz said.

MADDISON, Patricia Anne, 17,
died Thursday, May 9, at Santa Teresa Hospital. She is survived by her loving mother, Caroline B. Maddison, and a devoted sister, Claire Maddison. At the family's request, services will be private.

MADDISON, Caroline B., 58,
died Tuesday, August 29, at her home after a lengthy illness. She was born on January 22 to Helen and John Bangham, in Indianapolis, Indiana, graduating from Indiana University with a degree in home economics. Caroline was a devoted wife, mother, a homemaker, and a Christian. Preceded in death by her husband, Francis M. Maddison, and her daughter Patricia Anne Maddison. Survived by loving daughter Claire Maddison of Bridgeport, Connecticut. No services are planned. Contributions may be made to Hospice of Santa Teresa.

SUE GRAFTON

MADDISON, Claire, 39,
formerly of Santa Teresa, died Saturday, March 2, in
Bridgeport, Connecticut. Daughter of the late Francis M.
and Caroline B. Maddison, Claire was preceded in death
by her only sister, Patricia. Claire graduated from Santa
Teresa High School in 1963 and the University of Connecticut in 1967. She pursued her secondary teaching cre-
dential and M.A. in Romance Languages at Boston
College. She taught French and Italian at a private girls'
academy in Bridgeport, Connecticut. Service, Tuesday in
the Memorial Park Chapel.

I read Claire's death notice twice. "This was just last year."

"Thank goodness she'd gone back to her maiden name," he said.
"I don't know how we'd have found her if she'd been using her ex-
hubby's moniker."

"Whoever he was," I said. "She'd probably been divorced for
ages. There wasn't much family to speak of. You watch the names
of the survivors diminish until there's no one left. It's depressing,
isn't it?"

"I thought the mother might have surviving family members in
Indiana, but I can't seem to get a line on them," Dietz said. "I tried
directory assistance in Indianapolis. There weren't any Banghams
listed, so at least on the face of it, we're not talking about a large
close-knit clan. Just to be on the safe side, I checked the CALI
Directory and put a call through to an Indianapolis private investigator. I asked him to check Caroline Bangham's birth records to see if
that nets us anything. We might not glean much, but he said he'd get
back to us."

I made a face. "You know what? I think we're spinning our wheels
on this one. I just don't buy the idea that some distraught family
member would seek revenge eighteen years later."

"Maybe not," he said. "If it weren't for Bader's death, there

282

wouldn't have been a reason to look for Guy at all. He might have gone on living in Marcella for the rest of his days."

"It wasn't strictly Bader's death. It was the will," I said.

"Which brings us back to the five million."

"I guess it does," I said. "I'll tell you what hurts. I feel like I was part of what happened to Guy."

"Because you found him."

"Exactly. I didn't cause his death, in any strict sense of the word, but if it hadn't been for me, he'd be safe the way I see it."

"Hey, come on. That's not true. Tasha would have hired herself some other detective. Maybe not as good as you . . ."

"Don't suck up."

"Look, someone would have found him. It just happened to be you."

"I suppose," I said. "It still feels like shit."

"I'm sure it does."

The phone rang. Dietz answered and then handed me the handset, mouthing the name *Enid*.

I nodded and took the phone. "Hi, Enid. This is Kinsey. How are you?"

"Not so good," she said, fretfully. "Did Myrna call you?"

"Not as far as I know. Let me check my messages." I put a hand across the mouthpiece. "Did the Maleks' housekeeper call or leave a message for me?"

Dietz shook his head and I went back to Enid. "No, there's nothing here."

"Well, that's odd. She swore she was going to call you. I made her promise she would. I went to the supermarket and I was only gone fifteen or twenty minutes. She said she'd be here when I got back, but she's gone and there's no sign of her. I thought you might have asked her to come in."

"Sorry. I never heard from her. What'd she want to talk to me about?"

"I'm not sure. I know something's been bothering her, but she wouldn't be specific. Her car's still out back. That's what's so strange," she said.

"Could she have gone to the doctor's? If she really wasn't feeling well, she might have called a cab."

"It's always possible, but you'd think she would have waited to have me take her. This is just so unlike her. She told me she'd help me with dinner. I have a meeting at seven and I have to be out of here early. We discussed it in detail."

"Maybe she's out walking somewhere on the property."

"I thought of that," she said. "I went out there myself, calling, but she's disappeared."

"Enid, let's be realistic. I don't think being gone less than an hour constitutes a disappearance."

"I'm worried something's happened."

"Like what?"

"I don't know. That's why I called you. Because I'm scared."

"What's the rest?"

"That's it."

"No, it's not. You're leaving something out. I mean, so far this doesn't make sense. Do you think she's been abducted by aliens, or what?"

I could hear her hesitation. "I got the impression she knew something about the murder."

"Really. She said that?"

"She hinted as much. She was too nervous to say more. I think she saw something she wasn't supposed to see that night."

"She told me she was sleeping."

"Well, she was. She'd taken some pain medication and a sleeping pill. She slept like the dead, but then she remembered later that she woke up at one point to find someone standing at the foot of her bed."

"Wait a minute, Enid. You're not talking about this woo-woo stuff . . ."

"Not at all. I promise. This is what she said. She said she thought she'd been dreaming, but the more she thought about it, the more convinced she was that it was real."

"What was?"

"The person she saw."

"I gathered that, Enid. Who?"

"She wouldn't tell me. She felt guilty she hadn't said anything before now."

"Myrna feels guilty about everything," I said.

"I know," Enid said. "But I think she was also worried about the consequences. She thought she'd be in danger if she opened her mouth. I told her to tell the police, in that case, but she was afraid to do that. She said she'd rather talk to you first and then she'd talk to them. It's not like her to go off without a word."

"You did check her room?"

"That's the first thing I did. And that's the other thing that bothers me. Something doesn't seem right. Myrna's very fussy. Everything has to be just so with her. I don't mean to criticize, but it's the truth."

"Her room is messed up?"

"It's not exactly messed up, but it doesn't look right."

"Who else is there? Is anybody home besides you?"

"Bennet was here, but I think he's gone. He came in for lunch. I fixed him a sandwich and he took it up to his room. He must have left again while I was at the market. Christie and Donovan are due back any minute. I don't mean to be a bother, but I don't feel right about this."

Dietz was giving me an inquisitive look. Having eavesdropped on my end of the conversation with her, he was suitably mystified. "Hang on a second." I put a palm across the mouthpiece. "How long will you be here?"

"At least an hour," he said. "If you'd ever get off the phone, I might get this call from the East Coast that I've been waiting for. What's the problem?"

"It's Myrna. I'll tell you in a minute." I went back to Enid. "Why don't I come over there," I said. "She might have mentioned something to Christie before they left for the funeral home. You're sure she didn't leave a note?"

"Positive."

"I'll be there in fifteen minutes."

"I don't want you to go to any trouble."

"It's no trouble."

I took my sandwich and soda with me, driving with one hand while I finished my lunch. I kept the chilled soda can between my thighs. Shifting gears is a pain in the ass when you're trying to dine in style. At least I knew the route. I could have done it with my eyes shut.

Enid had left the gate open for me. I pulled into the courtyard and left my car in a spot I was beginning to think should be reserved for me. Donovan's pickup truck was parked to one side of the garage. At first, I thought he was back, but then I remembered that he'd been driving the BMW when he left. Both the open garages were still empty. The driveway angled up along the house on the left. For the first time, I noticed a separate parking pad nearby with spaces for three vehicles. Currently, I could see a bright yellow VW convertible and what looked like a Toyota, a pale metallic blue, maybe three or four years old.

Enid had the backdoor ajar and was standing in the opening. She'd taken off her apron to do the marketing and she now wore a jacket as though chilled by circumstance.

I moved into the utility room. "Still no sign of her?" I asked, following Enid through a door that opened into a rear hall.

"Not a peep," she said. "I'm sorry to be a bother. I'm probably being silly."

"Don't worry about it. You've had a murder in the house. Everybody's nerves are on edge. Is one of those cars out there hers?"

"The Toyota," she said. She paused in front of a door at the end of the hall. "This is hers."

"Have you tried knocking on her door since we talked?"

Enid shook her head. "I think I scared myself. I didn't want to do anything until you arrived."

"Geez, Enid. You're scaring me," I said. I knocked on the door, my head tilted against the panel, listening for sounds that might indicate Myrna was back. I was reluctant to barge right in. She might be napping or naked, just out of the shower. I didn't want to catch her with her dentures out or her wooden leg unstrapped. I tapped again with one knuckle. "Myrna?"

Dead silence.

I tried the knob, which turned easily. I opened the door a crack and peered around the frame. The sitting room was empty. Across from me, the door to the bedroom was standing open and the room appeared to be empty. "Myrna, you in here? It's Kinsey Millhone," I said. I waited a moment and then crossed the room. In passing, I put my hand on the television set, but the housing was cold.

"I told you she wasn't here," Enid said.

I looked into the bedroom. I could see why Enid felt something was wrong. On the surface, both rooms seemed tidy and untouched, but there was something amiss. It was the little things, the minutiae. The bed was made, but the coverlet was not quite smooth. A picture on the wall was ever so slightly tilted.

"When was the last time you actually saw her?" I leaned down and peeked under the bed, feeling like an idiot. There was nothing under there except an old pair of bedroom slippers.

"Must have been noon."

"Was Bennet here at that point?"

"I don't remember. He was gone when I got back from the market. That's all I know."

In the sitting room, the shade on the floor lamp was askew and it was clear from the dents in the carpet the base had been moved from its usual place. Had there been a struggle of some kind? I looked in the closet. Enid followed me like a kid, about three steps back, possibly feeling the same eerie sense of intrusion that I felt.

"Can you tell if all her clothes are here? Anything missing? Shoes? Coat?"

Enid studied the rack. "I think everything's here," she said and then pointed. "That's her suitcase and her garment bag."

"What about her handbag?"

"It's in the kitchen. I knew you'd ask so I opened it. Her wallet's in there, driver's license, cash, all that stuff."

I moved into the bathroom. I heard a little pop under my shoe, followed by the kind of scratching sound that makes you think of broken glass on ceramic floor tile. I looked down. There was a touch of dry soil, as from the bottom of a shoe, and two tiny pieces of gravel. "Be careful. I don't want us to disturb that," I said to Enid, who was crowding into the room on my heels.

"Was someone in here?"

"I don't know yet. It could be."

"It looks like someone tried to straighten up and didn't do a very good job of it," she said. "Myrna always left notes if she was going somewhere. She wouldn't just walk out."

"Don't start babbling. I'm trying to concentrate."

I checked the medicine cabinet. All the obvious toiletries were still sitting on the shelf: toothbrush, toothpaste, deodorant, odds and ends of makeup, prescription bottles. The shower curtain was bone-dry, but a dark blue washcloth had been draped over the rim of the basin and it had been recently used. I peered closely at the basin. There was a trace of water around the small brass ring fixture for the outflow valve. Unless my eyes were deceiving me, the water was ever so faintly pink. I lifted the washcloth and squeezed out some of the excess water. There was a splash of bright red against the white of the basin. "You better call 9-1-1. This is blood," I said.

While Enid went off to call the police, I closed the door to Myrna's apartment and I retraced my steps through the utility room to the backdoor. In the kitchen, I could hear Enid on the phone, sounding shaken and slightly shrill. Someone must have been waiting to catch Myrna alone. Outside, I crossed the small back patio and took a right at the driveway. Myrna's car was locked, but I circled the exterior, peering in at the front seats and backseats. Both were empty. Nothing on the dashboard. I was curious if the trunk was locked, but I didn't want to touch it. Let the cops do that. To the right, the driveway formed a dead end with space for three more cars. Beyond that, I saw a long line of drab pink stucco wall and a tangle of woods. Suppose she'd been killed in haste? What would you do with the body?

I headed back toward the garages. Donovan's pickup was parked much closer to the front of the house than the back. There was something about the traces of gravel and dried soil that bothered me. I put a hand out. The hood of the pickup was warm. I walked around the truck, hands behind my back as I scrutinized the exterior. The bed liner was littered with gravel and dead leaves. I peered over the tailgate, looking closely at the liner. There was what looked like a dark smear on one edge. I left that alone. Whatever had happened, they couldn't blame Jack this time.

In the distance, I heard the rumble of a motorcycle and moments later, I looked up to see Bennet roaring down the drive on Jack's Harley-Davidson. I moved away from the truck, watching as he went through his parking ritual. His black leather gloves looked as clumsy as oven mitts. He pulled them off and laid them on the seat, placing his helmet on top. He didn't seem that thrilled to see me. "What are you doing here?"

"Enid called about Myrna. When did you last see her?"

"I saw her at breakfast. I didn't see her at lunch. Enid told me she wasn't feeling well. What's going on?"

"I have no idea. Apparently, she's disappeared. Enid called the police. They'll be here shortly, I'd imagine."

"The police? What for?"

"Why don't you save the bullshit for the cops." I said.

"Wait a minute. 'Bullshit'? What's the matter with you? I'm tired of being treated like a creep," he said.

I started walking away.

"Where are you going?"

"What difference does it make? If I stand here another minute, I'll just end up insulting you."

Bennet walked alongside me. "That wouldn't be a first. I heard about your meeting with Paul. He was pissed as hell."

"So what?" I said.

"I know you think we did something."

"Of course I do!"

He touched my arm. "Look. Hang on a minute and let's talk about this."

"Go ahead and talk, Bennet. I'd love to hear what you have to say."

"All right. Okay. I might as well level with you because the truth isn't nearly as bad as you think."

"How do you know what I think? I think you cheated the Maddisons out of fifty thousand dollars' worth of rare documents."

"Now wait a minute. Now wait. We didn't mean any harm. It was just a prank. We wanted to go to Vegas, but we were broke. We didn't have a dime between us. All we wanted was a few bucks. We were only kids," he said.

"Kids? You weren't kids. You were twenty-three years old. You committed a felony. Is that your rationalization, calling it a prank? You should have gone to prison."

"I know. I'm sorry. It got out of hand. We never thought we could pull it off and by the time we realized how serious it was, we didn't have the courage to admit what we'd done."

"It didn't seem to bother you to blame Guy," I said.

"Listen, he was gone. And he'd done all that other stuff. The family was down on him and Dad just assumed. We were assholes. I know that. We were wrong. I've never felt right about it since."

"Well, that absolves you," I said. "What happened to the letters? Where are they?"

"Paul has them at his place. I told him to destroy them, but he couldn't bear to do it. He's been afraid to put them in circulation."

I could feel my mouth pull down with disgust. "So you didn't even get the money? You are a creep," I said. "Let's talk about Patty."

"The baby wasn't mine. I swear. I never screwed her."

"Paul did, didn't he? And so did Jack."

"A lot of fellas screwed her. She didn't care."

"Not Guy. He never laid a hand on her," I said.

"Not Guy," he repeated. "I guess that's true."

"So whose baby was it?"

"Probably Jack's," Bennet said. "But that doesn't mean he killed Guy. I didn't either. I wouldn't do that," he said.

"Oh, come on. Grow up. You never accepted any responsibility for what happened, the whole lot of you. You let Guy take the blame for everything you did. Even when he came back, you never let him off the hook."

"What was I supposed to say? It was too late by then."

"Not for him, Bennet. Guy was still alive at that point. *Now*, it's too late."

I looked up to see Enid standing by the hedge. I had no idea how much she'd overheard. She said, "Your partner's on the phone. The police are on the way."

I moved past Enid and walked down the short flight of stairs, crossing the patio to the kitchen door. I found the handset on the counter and I picked it up. "It's me. What's going on?"

"Are you all right? You sound bad."

"I can't stop to tell you. It would take too long. I should have fallen on Bennet and beat the man to death."

"Catch this. I just had a chat with the private investigator in Bridgeport, Connecticut. This gal was at the courthouse when she called in to pick up messages. She went right to the clerk and filled out a request for Claire Maddison's death certificate."

"What was the cause of death?"

"There wasn't one," he said. "As long as she was at it, she made a couple more phone calls and got her last known address. According to the utility company, Claire was living in Bridgeport until last March."

"How did the *Dispatch* end up printing her obituary?"

"Because she sent them one. No one ever asked for proof. I called the *Dispatch* myself and verified the whole procedure. They take down the information and they print it as given."

"She made the whole thing up?"

"I'm sure she did," he said.

"So where did she go?"

"I'm just getting to that. This PI in Bridgeport picked up one more little item. Claire never worked as a teacher. She was a private-duty nurse."

"Shit."

"That's what I said. I'm coming over. Don't do anything until I get there," he said.

"What's to do? I can't move."

How long did I stand at the kitchen counter with the phone in my hand? In a flash, I could see how all the pieces fit. I was missing a few answers, but the rest of them finally fell into place. Somehow Claire Maddison heard about Bader's terminal illness. She shipped the *Dispatch* an obituary just to close that door. She turned herself into Myrna Sweetzer, packed her personal belongings, and headed back to Santa Teresa. Bader was difficult. As a patient, he was probably close to impossible. He must have gone through a number of private-duty nurses, so it was only a matter of Myrna's biding her time. Once she was in the house, the family was hers. She had waited a long time, but the chance to wreak havoc must have been something she savored.

I tried to put myself in her place. Where was she now? She'd accomplished much of her mission, so it was time to fade. She'd left her car, her handbag, and all her clothes. What would I do if I were Claire Maddison? The whole psychodrama of the missing Myrna was just a cover for her escape. She must have pictured the cops digging up the property, looking for a body that was never there. To have the disappearance play out properly, she had to make an exit without being seen, which ruled out a taxicab. She might steal a car, but that was risky on the face of it. And how would she leave town? Would she hitchhike? A motorist passing through might never be aware that anyone was missing or presumed dead. Plane, train, or bus?

She might have a confederate, but much of what she'd done to date required a solitary cunning. She'd been gone more than an hour— plenty of time to walk through the back of the property to the road. I lifted my head. I could hear voices in the foyer. The cops had probably arrived. I didn't want to go through this whole rigmarole. Enid was saying, "It was just so unlike her so I called . . ."

I slipped out the backdoor, racewalking across the patio and out to the driveway. I got in my car and turned the key in the ignition. My brain was clicking along, trying to make sense of circumstances. Claire Maddison was alive and had been living in Santa Teresa since last spring. I wasn't really sure how she'd managed the setup, but I was relatively certain she was responsible for Guy's death. She'd also gone to some lengths to implicate the others, setting it up so that Jack looked guilty, with Bennet as the backup in case the evidence of Jack's culpability failed to persuade police.

The gate swung open in front of me. I reached the road and turned left, trying to picture the way the property was laid out in relation to the surrounding terrain. I didn't imagine she'd head into the Los Padres National Forest. The mountain was too steep and too inhospitable. It was possible, of course, that in the last eighteen years, Claire Maddison had become an expert at living in the wild. Maybe she planned to make a new home for herself among the scrub oaks and chaparral, feasting on wild berries, sucking moisture from cactus pads. More likely, she'd simply crossed the few acres of undeveloped land that lay between the Maleks' and the road. Bader had purchased everything within range, so it was possible she was still trudging across acreage he owned.

I tried to think what she'd do once she hit the main artery. She could choose left or right, setting out in either direction on foot. She could have hidden a bicycle somewhere in the brush. She might depend on her ability to thumb a ride. Maybe she'd called a taxicab and had it waiting when she emerged on the road. Again, I dismissed that option because I didn't really think she'd take the risk. She wouldn't want to have anyone who could identify or describe her later. She might have purchased another vehicle and parked on a side street, gassed up and ready to be driven away. I tried to remember what I knew of her and realized just how little it was. She was approaching forty. She was overweight. She made no effort to enhance her personal appearance. Given cultural standards, she'd made herself invisible. Ours is a society in which slimness and beauty are equated with status, where youth and charm are rewarded and remembered with admiration. Let a woman be drab or slightly overweight and the collective eye slides right by, forgetting afterward. Claire Maddison had achieved the ultimate disguise because, aside from the physical, she'd adopted the persona of the servant class. Who knows what conversations she'd been privy to straightening the bed pillows, changing the sheets. She'd run the household, served canapés, and freshened the drinks while the lords and ladies of the house had talked on and on, oblivious to her presence because she wasn't one of them. For Claire, it had been perfect. Their dismissal of her would have fueled her bitterness and hardened her determination to take revenge. Why should this family, largely made up of fakes, enjoy the privileges of money while she had nothing? Because of them, she'd been cheated of her family, her medical career. She'd been robbed, violated, and abused, and for this she blamed Guy.

I was now on the two-lane road that I was guessing defined the Malek property along its southernmost boundary. I found a city map in my glove compartment and flapped it open as I drove. I made a clumsy fold and propped it up against the steering wheel, searching for routes while I tried not to ram into telephone poles. I started with the obvious, turning off at the first street, driving in a grid. I should have waited for Dietz. One of us could have been watching for pedestrians while the other drove. How far could she get?

I returned to the main road and drove on for maybe half a mile. I spotted her tramping along a hundred yards ahead of me. She was wearing jeans and good walking shoes, toting a backpack, no hat. I rolled down the window on the passenger side. As soon as she heard the rattle of my VW, she glanced once in my direction and then stared doggedly at the pavement in front of her.

"Myrna, I want to talk to you."

"Well, I don't want to talk to you."

I idled alongside her while cars coming up behind me honked impatiently. I motioned them around, keeping an eye fixed on Myrna who trudged on, tears running down her face. I gunned the engine, speeding off, pulling into the berm well ahead of her. I turned the engine off and got out, walking back to meet her.

"Come on, Myrna. Slow down. It's finally over," I said.

"No, it's not. It's never over until they pay up."

"Yeah, but how much? Listen, I understand how you feel. They took everything you had."

"The bastards," she said.

"Myrna . . ."

"My name is Claire."

"All right, Claire then. Here's the truth. You killed the wrong man. Guy never did anything to you or to your family. He's the only one who ever treated Patty well."

"Liar. You're lying. You made that up."

I shook my head. "Patty slept around. You know she had problems. Those were wild times. Dope and free love. We were all goofy with goodwill, with the notion of world peace. Remember? She was a flower child, an innocent—"

"She was schizophrenic," Claire spat.

"Okay. I'll take your word for it. She probably did LSD. She ate mushrooms. She stuck herself with things. And all the fellows took advantage of her, except Guy. I promise. He really cared about her. He told me about her and he was wistful and loving. He'd tried to get in touch. He wrote to her once, but she was dead by then. He had no idea. All he knew was he never heard from her and he felt bad about that."

"He was a turd."

"All right. He was a turd. He did a lot of shitty things back then, but at heart, he was a good man. Better than his brothers. They took advantage of him. Patty probably wished the baby was his, but it wasn't."

"Whose then?"

"Jack's. Paul Trasatti's. I'm not really sure how many men she slept with. Guy didn't forge the letters, either. That was Bennet and Paul, a little scheme they cooked up to earn some money that spring."

"They took everything away from me. Everything."

"I know. And now you've taken something away from them."

"What?" she said, her eyes blazing with disdain.

"You took the only decent man who ever bore the Malek name."

"Bader was decent."

"But he never made good. Your mother asked him for the money and he refused to pay."

"I didn't blame him for that."

"Too bad. You blamed Guy instead and he was innocent."

"Fuck off," she said.

"What else? What's the rest? I know there's more to this," I said. "You wrote the anonymous letter to Guy, the one the cops have, right?"

"Of course. Don't be dumb. I wrote all the letters up on Bennet's machine. For Guy's letter, I used the Bible. I thought he'd like that . . . a message from Deuteronomy . . . 'And thy life shall hang in doubt before thee; and thou shalt fear day and night, and shalt have none assurance of thy life.' You like that?"

"Very apt. A good choice," I said.

"That's not all, doll. You missed the best part . . . the obvious
. . . you and that fancy-pants probate attorney. I found both wills
months ago when I first started working here. I searched through
Bader's files every chance I had. I tore up the second will so someone
would have to go out looking for Guy. You did all the work for me. I
appreciate that."

"What about the blood in your bathroom? Where did that come
from?"

She held her thumb up. "I used a lancet. I left a couple drops on
the patio and another in the truck. There's a shovel behind the tool-
shed. That's got blood on it, too."

"What about the dirt and gravel on the bathroom floor?"

"I thought Donovan should have a turn in the barrel. Didn't you
think of him when you saw it?"

"Actually he did cross my mind. I'd have gone after him if I hadn't
figured out what was going on. But what now? None of this is going to
work. The whole plan's caving in. Trying to hike out was dumb. You
weren't that hard to find."

"So what? I'm out of here. I'm tired. Get away from me," she said.

"Myrna . . ." I said, patiently.

"It's Claire," she snapped. "What do you *want?*"

"I want the killing to stop. I want the dying to end. I want Guy
Malek to rest easy wherever he is."

"I don't care about Guy," she said. Her voice quaked with emotion
and her face looked drawn and tense.

"What about Patty? Don't you think she'd care?"

"I don't know. I've lost track. I thought I'd feel better, but I don't."
She walked on down the road with me trotting after her. "There aren't
any happy endings. You have to take what you get."

"There may not be a happy ending, but there are some that sat-
isfy."

"Name one."

"Come back. Own up to what you did. Turn and face your demons
before they eat you alive."

She was weeping freely, and in some curious way, she seemed very beautiful, touched with grace. She turned and started walking backward, her arm out, hand turned up, as though thumbing a ride. I was walking at the same pace, the two of us face-to-face. She caught my eye and smiled, shot a look over her shoulder to check for traffic coming the other way.

We had reached an intersection. There was a wide curve in the road ahead. The stoplight had changed and cars had surged forward, picking up speed. Even now, I'm not certain what she meant to do. For a moment, she looked at me fully and then she made a dash for it, flinging herself into the line of traffic like a diver plunging off a board. I thought she might escape destruction because the first vehicle missed her and a second car seemed to bump her without injury or harm. The drivers in both lanes were slamming on their brakes, swerving to avoid her. She ran on, stumbling as she entered the far lane. An oncoming car caught her and she sailed overhead, as limp as a rag doll, as joyous as a bird.

Epilogue

Peter and Winnie Antle came down for Guy's funeral service, which Peter conducted Monday afternoon. I thought the Maleks might object, but they seemed to think better of it. Tasha agreed to submit Guy's holographic will for probate and eventually his portion of the estate will be passed on to Jubilee Evangelical Church. I said nothing of Claire's destruction of the second will. Guy deserved his fair share and I don't think the family will make a fuss about his final wishes.

Last night, Guy Malek came to me in a dream. I don't remember now what the dream was about. It was a dream like any other, set in a landscape only half familiar, filled with events that didn't quite make sense. I remember feeling such relief. He was alive and whole and so very like himself. Somehow in the dream, I knew he'd come to say good-bye. I'd never had a chance to tell him how much he'd meant to me. I hadn't known him long, but some people simply affect us that way. Their sojourn is brief, but their influence is profound.

I clung to him. He didn't speak. He never said a word, but I knew he wanted me to let him go. He was far too polite to chide me for my reluctance. He didn't hurry me along, but he let me know what he needed. In the dream, I remember weeping. I thought if I refused, he would be mine to keep. I thought he could be with me forever, but it doesn't work that way. His time on earth was done. He had other places to go.

In the end, I set him free, not in sorrow, but in love. It wasn't for me. It was something I did for him. When I woke, I knew that he was truly gone. The tears I wept for him then were the same tears I'd wept for everyone I'd ever loved. My parents, my aunt. I had never said good-bye to them, either, but it was time to take care of it. I said a prayer for the dead, opening the door so all the ghosts could move on. I gathered them up like the petals of a flower and released them to the wind. What's done is done. What is written is written. Their work is finished. Ours is yet to do.